MW01234576

The Marshal and the Fatal Foreclosure

A NELSON LANE FRONTIER MYSTERY

The Marshal and the Fatal Foreclosure

C. M. Wendelboe

FIVE STAR
A part of Gale, a Cengage Company

LIBRARY OF CONGRESS CATALOGING-IN-PUBLICATION DATA

Names: Wendelboe, C. M., author.
Title: The marshal and the fatal foreclosure / C.M. Wendelboe.
Description: First edition. | Waterville, Maine : Five Star, [2022] | Series: A Nelson Lane frontier mystery |
Identifiers: LCCN 2022004299 | ISBN 9781432895426 (hardcover)
Subjects: LCGFT: Detective and mystery fiction. | Novels.
Classification: LCC PS3623.E53 M366 2022 | DDC 813/.6—dc23/eng/20220203
LC record available at https://lccn.loc.gov/2022004299

First Edition. First Printing: September 2022
Find us on Facebook—https://www.facebook.com/FiveStarCengage
Visit our website—http://www.gale.cengage.com/fivestar
Contact Five Star Publishing at FiveStar@cengage.com

Printed in Mexico
Print Number : 1 Print Year : 2022

ACKNOWLEDGEMENTS

I wish to thank Campbell County (Wyoming) Rockpile Museum Director Robert A. Henning and local attorney Deb Michaels for their assistance in period research, as well as the Campbell County Library for research maps and material from the Depression era. I thank Campbell County rancher James Hall for his ranching advice, and also editors Diane Piron-Gelman and Erin Bealmear for their work on this project.

This novel is dedicated to all law enforcement, firefighters, and first responders in Campbell County, Wyoming, who have worked through the rigors of this pandemic and face the dangers of that disease every day on the job.

Chapter 1

"You made another enemy, you know that?" Maris Red Hat said between spits of Virgin Leaf Tobacco juice out the window of Nelson's panel truck.

Nelson chuckled. *Wonder when was the last time she could say she was a virgin?*

Maris wiped her mouth with her heavy denim coat sleeve. "DeMyron's not going to like the insult. That young deputy's full of piss and vinegar—and himself. He's not going to cotton to this."

Nelson slowed to allow four doe antelope to cross the county road. The small spike buck lay back watching, protecting his ladies before prancing after them across the dirt road and into the ditch. "I didn't intend offending Deputy Duggar, but Sheriff Jarvis insisted we take the lead on this investigation. He thinks his deputy's not quite experienced enough to handle a death call."

When Sheriff Jarvis had called Nelson from a funeral he was attending in Phoenix, he'd asked Nelson if he would *assist* Deputy Duggar with the investigation. "DeMyron's hell on wheels when it comes to busting illegal stills and breaking up fights between cowboys," Jarvis had said, "but this will be a first for him. Even though it's just a hunting accident, I want to make sure DeMyron gets it right. This will be the first unattended death the kid's been on since I hired him."

"U.S. marshals don't handle hunting accidents," Nelson had

argued. "Hell, most places they don't even handle dead men except to evict them from their ranches under foreclosure."

"Hold up your right hand."

"What?"

"Your hand," Jarvis repeated. "Hold up your hand so I can swear you in as a special deputy for Campbell County. Just so you'll have jurisdiction to examine this dead hunter and make a determination. Or at least steer DeMyron into a determination."

Nelson felt silly as he raised his hand and held the phone in the other. Jarvis said, "Do you—"

"I do."

"There," Jarvis said. "You is now deputized."

"I really have other things to do—"

"Tell me, Nels, what would you be doing in my county if I didn't ask you to help DeMyron out?" Jarvis had asked, then answered his own question. "You'd be here trying to evict poor ol' Graber off his ranch."

"How'd you know about that?"

Jarvis laughed. "I know *everything* that happens in Campbell County. *When* I'm in my county. But I'm stuck here with my sister and a brother for another two or three weeks while we get Dad's estate settled. Until then, humor me and teach DeMyron a little about investigating." Then he added, "You and your deputy Red Hat go easy on Graber."

"How'd you know about Maris . . ." But Jarvis had already hung up.

"How much farther?" Nelson asked his deputy.

Maris rolled down the side window that had frosted over and stuck her head out, swatting at snow pelting her eyes as she looked around. "This is only my second trip to the eastern part of the state . . . DeMyron said it was a half-mile past the Graber

Ranch. Ought to be just over that hill."

"You sure?"

Maris rolled up the window and dried her face with her bandana. "I ought to know the Graber Ranch after that SOB put the run on me yesterday."

Yesterday, Nelson had sent Maris over to the place, a small spread a few miles north of Gillette, to serve eviction notices on Ulysses S. Graber. Routine, like so many others he and Maris had to evict during this damned Depression. It seemed that most of his days were spent foreclosing on hapless ranchers and farmers who had gotten caught up in hard times like everyone else.

"This Graber character pulled a rifle on me," Maris sputtered when she'd called Nelson at his office in Buffalo. "That old bastard stuck his Winchester in my face and told me never to come back. Ever. I thought about sticking *my* rifle under *his* nose, but figured I'd better call you first." Nelson had managed to talk her down, but the calming didn't come easy. Maris Red Hat, called *Maseha'e*—Crazy Woman by her Southern Cheyenne people in Oklahoma—would have bulled her way back to the Graber ranch, and the shooting would have started shortly thereafter.

Right now, all Nelson wanted was to sit over a frozen pond somewhere watching a hole in the ice for some unlucky trout to grab his bait. But he didn't need a shootout to attract the attention of his Washington bosses with an election looming. And he sure didn't want anything to happen to Maris over some rancher being foreclosed by the bank in Billings, so he'd made the four-hour drive over to Gillette.

After they had gone nearly ten miles, Maris jabbed her finger at the windshield. "That's the sheriff's truck parked next to that barbed wire fence, a hundred yards down the fence line." Nelson turned down the two-track where Maris motioned, the ruts made by the sheriff's truck already filling in with snow. He stopped a few yards behind the Chevy just as its driver stepped out of the cab. The man stood to his full height and arched his back, stretching, before slamming the truck door closed.

Nelson guesstimated Deputy Duggar was nearly as tall as he—a few inches over six feet—and he carried his two-hundred-and-twenty-some pounds like an athlete. Which he had been before being thrown off a bull and gored, ending his rodeo career last year at age twenty-six. He settled his Stetson down over his eyes and bent against the wind as he glared at Nelson through the windshield of Nelson's panel truck.

"I'd take it easy on this one," Maris advised as she slipped her gloves on. "You get in this hot-headed feller's face and he might be more than you'd want to tangle with."

Nelson sat for a moment after shutting the engine off. "I don't want to get into an argument with *anybody* over some hunter's dumb luck. Let's see what mood this young deputy is in."

Nelson pulled his sheepskin collar up as he stepped out of his truck. He walked toward Deputy Duggar and offered his hand. Duggar ignored it. "My hands are too cold to take out of my pocket for a . . . handshake." He spat a string of tobacco juice, which carried on the stiff wind and slapped the hood of Nelson's panel truck. "Sheriff Jarvis *ordered* me to work with you, Marshal, is why I'm still here waiting. Let's get this over with so's I can go indoors somewhere with a mug of hot coffee."

Nelson looked around the barren prairie but saw only cactus and rocks and Russian thistles blown into the fence. "Where's this hunter who had the accident?"

DeMyron shook his head. "I'm not that dumb that I contaminated the scene, even though it *is* just an accidental death." He chin-pointed toward where the body presumably was. "He's down in a draw along this fence line. You and"—he winked at Maris—"sweet cheeks follow me."

DeMyron started down a gradual embankment just deep enough to conceal where the victim lay. Nelson and Maris followed. As they approached the corpse, Nelson stopped DeMyron. "Hold up a minute."

DeMyron scowled at him. "Hold up for what? It's colder'n a well digger's ass out here."

"Humor me," Nelson said, "and the poor well diggers you're cussing while I look things over before we get any closer."

DeMyron threw up his hands. "Only because Sheriff Jarvis said you're in charge." He blew on his fingers. "The sooner we get this croaker back to town, the better my frigid bones will feel."

No more frigid than the victim's, Nelson thought as he walked a loose circle around the body, staying five yards away as he studied the scene.

"Let's just get him hauled up and into the funeral home," DeMyron said, his teeth clattering. "Whatcha' waiting for?"

Nelson stopped and said over his shoulder, "I'm waiting for the victim to speak to me."

DeMyron tilted his head back and laughed. "That's a good one. And what do you expect the . . . victim to say to you? Or maybe he'll sing 'Zippity Do Dah' out his ass."

Nelson ignored DeMyron as he bent over the hunter for a better look, cursing Harper Jarvis under his breath. *Why the hell did you want me to try to teach this knot-head anything?* He turned back to the corpse. The man lay frozen halfway over a fence where he had fallen. Red-tinted snow showed faintly, covered by fresh powder, which meant the victim hadn't moved after his gun accidentally discharged into his head.

Nelson squatted close to the body and looked at the man's gunshot-distorted face, partially covered by the cruel snow. The hunter was a little older than DeMyron, Nelson guessed, and his blood-matted black hair fluttered every time a gust of wind assaulted the body. One stiff hand jutted up from the snow as if pointing an accusing finger skyward.

And the gun. It lay next to the victim where he had apparently just stepped over the fence into the adjacent pasture before catching the trigger on a piece of clothing, or perhaps a stalk of blowing Russian thistle. Whatever it was had discharged the rifle, a Remington Model 8 just like the one Yancy Stands Close carried as a tribal policeman on the Wind River Reservation.

"There must be some compelling reason you're just standing there." DeMyron was flapping his arms to keep warm like a big, blond gooney bird trying to take flight.

"He's waiting for me to bless the body," Maris volunteered. "You know us Indians—we need a ceremony for everything. This one ought to take no more than an hour."

"You're shittin' me!" DeMyron said.

Maris laughed. "Of course. The best thing about this job is shittin' naïve white boys."

"I ain't naïve—"

"Children," Nelson said. "Can we just see what the victim has to say?"

Now it was DeMyron's turn to chuckle. "Like this frozen piece of meat's gonna tell us anything."

"He will if you look and listen," said Nelson. "And if you ask the right questions. Victims tell you things. They whisper in your ear—"

"You drink some nasty bathtub gin lately, talking out of your head—"

"By the position of the body, they tell you how they died. By the extent and location of their injuries, they tell you even more. By what you find around them, they speak to you. If you'd keep that pneumonia hole under your nose shut for a moment and let me concentrate, *this* man just might tell me what happened."

Nelson stood and arched his back. He was getting too old for this. He walked a tight circle around the corpse, which lay with one leg resting on the top strand of barbed wire. Seeing nothing that stood out, he squatted beside the man and brushed the fresh layer of powder away with his glove. Frozen snow encrusted the hunter's face, with no ice formations around the mouth or nose. "This feller didn't breathe after his gun discharged into his head," Nelson said. *That's one small blessing.*

He pulled at the man's coat. A fashionable lightweight garment more suited to summers than the dead of winter here in Wyoming. It was frozen and stiff, and Nelson had to yank on it to unzip it.

"Guy must have been new to the area, dressed like a city boy," DeMyron noted.

"See," Nelson said, "he told us something already." A moment later, his guess was confirmed when Nelson found a thin leather wallet inside the victim's shirt pocket. It contained no money, and only a simple identification card from a company. "Gene Bone," Nelson said, and handed the card to DeMyron. "Know him?"

DeMyron glanced at it briefly before handing it to Maris. "Says here this man's from someplace in Nevada. How the hell should I know him?"

"Maybe the marshal figured you got around a little," Maris said, and Nelson recognized the big, taunting grin on her face. "Like maybe you keep your ears to the ground like your sheriff does when he's back in Campbell County."

"I get around, sweet cheeks. But I don't know *this* feller."

Nelson stood between them. The last thing he needed was to break up a fight when DeMyron called Maris *sweet cheeks* one more time. "DeMyron, what do you see here?" Nelson asked and held up his hand so Maris wouldn't answer. He knew Maris could read the scene as Nelson had; he just didn't know if De-

Myron could. Examining where the victim lay would force the deputy to learn how to look at a death scene—accidental or otherwise—objectively. "What do you think happened?"

"Think?" DeMyron blurted out. "I *know* what happened."

"Then by all means," Maris said, with a wave of her arm at the corpse, "give us your best assessment."

DeMyron turned his coat collar up and nodded toward the victim. "Man obviously was climbing over the fence to go after a deer. Maybe an antelope. Saw none in this field and decided to look in the next pasture." He pointed to the field on the other side of the fence from where the victim lay.

"Go on," Nelson prodded.

DeMyron smiled as if he had scored a big victory against Maris. "He had a round in the chamber like a dummy—and something tripped the trigger. Maybe the fence. Maybe his finger or loose piece of clothing. Maybe he dropped the gun climbing over the fence and that's when it discharged. Who knows. We have hunters do themselves in most every deer season from what Sheriff Jarvis says." He dug into his coat pocket and came away with a plug of tobacco. "Hell, I had a pard when I was a rodeo rider, kilt hisself much the same way in the Big Horns. He was stepping over a log, looking for elk. Damn rifle fell. And he was DRT."

"DRT?"

"Sure," DeMyron said. "Just like Sheriff Jarvis says—Dead Right There."

"That's your final assessment?" Nelson pressed. He had come to the same conclusion DeMyron had . . . before Nelson looked more closely at the scene. "That he had an unfortunate accident?"

"It is."

"And not that someone shot him and left him?"

DeMyron scoffed. "Of course not. The man's rifle discharged—"

"Then where's the shell casing? An autoloader like this would have expelled the cartridge casing."

"Must be under the snow somewhere."

"Find it."

"You find it," DeMyron said, sticking his hands in his jacket pockets.

"No," Nelson said, "*you* find it. I've found enough spent casings in my lifetime. Besides, Sheriff Jarvis wanted us to *assist* you in this investigation."

"*What* investigation!" DeMyron said. "This guy's a hunter . . ." He pulled his hands back out of his jacket and held them up in resignation. "Okay. I'll find the damned cartridge case."

DeMyron got down on all fours and began brushing snow away from the body. A few seconds later, a bright copper case glinted in the sun. He picked the case up from where it lay inches away from victim and blew snow off it before handing it to Nelson. "It's a .30 caliber Remington case, just like his gun. Satisfied?"

"Don't give it to me," Nelson said, "or to Maris. It's *your* evidence."

"Evidence of what? This is getting a little old—"

"Evidence of an accidental death, if that's what plays out."

DeMyron shrugged and was about to shove the casing into his jeans when Maris stopped him. "I'd be careful with the *evidence.*"

DeMyron sighed and tucked the shell casing into his jeans with exaggerated care. "Can we get this croaker to the coroner now?"

"Not until we talk to the landowner. Maris said he found the victim."

DeMyron pulled his collar up tighter and turned his back to the wind. "Rick Jones. Owns this fence"—he tapped the barbed wire—"between his place and the Graber Ranch. Only because Lucky's not ambitious enough to put up a fence and maintain it."

"Lucky?"

DeMyron tipped his head southward. "Sure, the rancher—if you can call him that—who owns that little spot of heaven he calls his ranch a half-mile thataway. We know him by *Lucky* 'cause he's anything but."

Nelson cupped his hand over a match and lit a Chesterfield. "What did Rick Jones say when he called your office?"

DeMyron shrugged. "Just that some damn dumb hunter got hisself kilt crossing Rick's fence. Rick found him when he was out checking cows this morning. Said he'd be at home warming by the fire if we had any questions."

"And he didn't mention anything about the way Gene Bone's dressed?"

"Dressed? Like how?"

Nelson glanced at Maris. "Want to take this?"

"Be happy to," she said and stepped closer to DeMyron. "You must have hunted these parts before, right?"

"All my life. Got my nicest five-by-five mulie not a mile from here."

"And when you hunt"—she turned her head and winked at Nelson—"do you dress as light as this guy? In this weather?"

"I never, but maybe this guy's used to the cold?"

"From the Nevada desert, according to his ID card?" Maris said. "Deputy, this guy should have been dressed like an Eskimo."

"A what?"

"An Indian that lives up north. Like me."

DeMyron stepped away. "You don't look Indian."

"I'm not from the Wind River," Maris said. "But my point still holds—this guy probably wouldn't be out hunting dressed like *this.*"

"He might be if he just stepped out of his truck to follow a deer," DeMyron blurted out.

"Then where's his vehicle?" Nelson asked.

"Vehicle?" DeMyron said, reaching for a pouch of tobacco in his shirt pocket.

Maris reached over, pinched some loose leaf from DeMyron's pouch, and stuffed it inside her cheek. "Yes. A vehicle. Like you drove up here in. Like me and the marshal drove up here in. Where's Gene Bone's outfit?"

"How should I know?" DeMyron said, quickly pocketing his tobacco before Maris grabbed more. "Listen, all I know is, Rick Jones called and said a hunter died crossing his fence. I didn't have time to look for no vehicle."

"Well, you sure will have time to look for it after the coroner picks him up." Nelson started for his panel truck, then stopped and turned to Maris, who was following close behind him. "Whyn't you stay and help Deputy Duggar when the coroner gets here."

"Help *him*?"

"Sure," Nelson said. "You know Sheriff Jarvis wants us to *assist* his deputy in this."

Maris motioned for Nelson to step further from DeMyron and covered her mouth with her hand. "You're not going to saddle me with some wet nose deputy."

"One of us has to help him."

"What are *you* going to be doing while me and DeMyron help load the body into the meat wagon?"

"I'll be stopping at the Graber ranch to serve the foreclosure notice that you weren't able to. After that, I'm going to drop by and talk with Rick Jones." Nelson nodded in DeMyron's direction. "Which is preferable to listening to all his rodeo exploits while waiting for the coroner."

Chapter 2

Nelson drove back the way he and Maris had come and stopped at the mailbox. It was in the shape of a rooster with a faded *Graber* painted on the side. The door had blown off sometime in the past, and the tired post holding it against the stiff Wyoming wind listed heavily to starboard. But that was all right, Nelson thought. *There's no mail in it anyhow.*

He drove down the long drive, keeping the panel truck atop the deep-frozen mud ruts as he fought to avoid slipping off and getting stuck. A foot of snow had blown over the road, and the last thing he needed was to have to borrow Graber's team of horses to pull him out of a drift.

Nelson saw the ranch house smokestack poking up over the top of the road even before he dipped down the drive. He tapped the brakes as his panel truck started sliding off the ruts and he managed to stop the truck in the yard. A sorrel mare showing more ribs than a critter ought to slowly walked to the edge of the corral and hung her sad head over the top rail that threatened to break down. She swung her slack jaw towards Nelson, eying him suspiciously. He noted that—like him—the horse only saw through one eye, the other clouded over and graying. The old swayback gave a snort before returning to the barnyard and the safety of her three-sided enclosure.

A chicken coop occupied one outside wall of the weathered barn. Four anemic chickens, looking like the wind had taken off half their feathers, stood next to a rooster too cold and tired to strut. The old boy limped—if roosters can limp—and didn't look like he could get the job done even if he could catch his brood. Nelson concluded they were all safe from marauding predators—no fox or coyote in his right mind would risk a load of buckshot from Lucky for *those* chickens.

Nelson slipped his Springfield rifle out of the worn leather scabbard resting in front of the passenger seat and flicked off the safety. Maris had given him grief about the old bolt-action ever since she'd come up from Oklahoma to take the job as one of Nelson's deputies. Before the Great War, he had carried a lever gun, a Winchester or Marlin like most other folks in Wyoming. But serving with the Marines in France, he'd developed a lasting love for the rifle. It had more range and accuracy than lever guns and didn't jam, as did autoloaders like the one Gene Bone had carted out into the field. And from what Maris told him about her earlier encounter with rancher Graber and his rifle, Nelson might need the Springfield today.

As he stood behind the safety of the truck door fifteen yards from the ranch house, he looked things over, half expecting rounds to come winging his way. The house—what was left of it—leaned like the barn and corral did, from the wind and lack of maintenance over years, Nelson guessed. A porch swing swayed in the stiff breeze, held to the top of the dilapidated porch by one rusty chain, the other broken and dangling.

He looked away as if he could envision his Helen swinging with him on the porch of their cabin at the foothills of the Big Horns. When she died six years ago, Nelson took their porch swing down. He would never use it again. *They* would never use it again, and it was one more thing he had to do following her death to keep his sanity. And keep from falling off the wagon into the stupor of drunken self-pity, as he had done too many times when she was alive.

He clutched the rifle in his hand and approached the rotting, caved-in porch, keeping a tractor with the motor torn apart between himself and the door and windows of the house. He paused and crouched behind the tractor, the engine looking like it had a cracked block, old oil having seeped out of the crack and onto the frame splotched with red somewhere under the rust and grime. *Are you in the house, Lucky Graber? Last thing I want is for either one of us to get hurt over your crappy piece of ranchland here.*

After several minutes where Nelson saw no movement, nothing to indicate Lucky was inside and waiting to open fire, he stood slowly and left the safety of the tractor to approach the house. He kept the rifle close beside his leg and breathed deeply, calming himself as he walked the last ten yards and stepped onto the porch. The bottom step gave way under his weight, and he jerked his foot free of the boards before taking the last two onto the porch proper, careful not to fall through other weather-worn boards.

He rapped lightly on the door, afraid it would break inward if he knocked more forcefully. When he got no response, he rapped harder, and still harder when Lucky failed to answer.

Nelson bent to a window on one side of the door and rubbed the grime away, then cupped his hand over his eyes and peeked inside. He saw no movement, the kitchen empty, a table propped up by a tree stump to replace a broken leg. Food of some sort had run over a pan on the cookstove and caked down the side, while a dark-brown jug hung by the sink with a ladle sticking in the water.

"I hope to hell you're not dead," Nelson said, startling himself. He had gone to another ranch house this summer and, finding no one at *that* house, had looked in the barn. The rancher was there, hanging by his neck from a rafter. As nasty as Maris said Lucky had been to her, Nelson still preferred to talk to a *live* Lucky Graber.

He turned and looked the place over. A wagon with side racks stood beside a water well, the bucket swinging with the wind. Recent marks showed where a car or truck had driven away from the yard. Lucky's? Nelson hoped so. Hoped he wouldn't find the rancher swinging like he did the last one.

He checked the two-holer as he passed it on his way to the barn. No Lucky inside reading a Monkey Ward catalogue. When he reached the barn, he stood to one side of the tall doors and slowly opened one. He called Lucky's name but received no answer.

Nelson swung the door all the way open to let in light before entering. He waited until his eyes adjusted to the dimness, then stepped inside. The barn—four stalls on each side—contained no hay. No straw. No animals. Most importantly, no Lucky Graber.

"You horse's patoot," Nelson said. "I'll bet you've made yourself scarce just so you can't be served papers." But he had to admit he would have done the same if a U.S. marshal was about to kick him off *his* property.

He left the barn and glanced at the corral. The old mare left the safety of the barnyard and stared at Nelson as she approached a dwindling mound of hay.

Nelson set his rifle down and picked up a three-tine pitchfork, the fourth one having busted off, leaving the tool with a rusted stub in the middle. He slung a forkful of what looked like second-cut hay into a feed trough. "That's about the best I can do for now, old girl," he said as he stuck the pitchfork in the hay. "If your owner had any cake, I'd let you have it. Lord knows you need some minerals by the looks of you."

The sorrel *snorted* at Nelson. She limped toward the feed trough and began devouring the hay.

He squatted and looked at the mare's hooves, long and split and chipped. "Damn you, Lucky Graber. You let the poor girl's hooves grow so long she can't hardly walk. But we'll fix that," he said to the mare, as he headed for the panel truck and the hoof nippers and file stashed in his toolbox.

Nelson fought the same frozen mud ruts on his way out of the treacherous long drive while he inched towards the county road. A newer Dodge Brothers stake truck neared, the driver stopping beside Nelson and climbing out. A man of average height, he had a floppy hat tied over his ears and a knitted scarf tied tight around his neck. He stuffed his hands in his coat pockets while he stood shivering outside Nelson's window. "You looking to buy ol' Lucky's ranch out from under me?"

"How's that?"

"Lucky's ranch. I live right over the fence." He nodded to the north.

"You're Rick Jones, then?"

Rick nodded. "I've been trying to buy it off that deadbeat for a couple years, but he won't sell to *me*."

Nelson pulled back his coat to reveal his marshal's badge.

Rick's eyebrows rose as Nelson killed the panel truck's engine and joined him out on the road. "I heerd there was a marshal come to nudge ol' Lucky off his place. But I heerd it was some good-lookin' filly."

"As you can see," Nelson said, "I am neither a filly nor good looking. But I am here to evict Ulysses Graber. Know where I can find him?"

Rick tilted his head back and laughed. "Ain't heerd Lucky been called his Christian name for donkey's years. Not that he's a Christian or anything."

"You know where he is?" Nelson pressed.

"Say, you got a smoke?"

Nelson took a pack of Chesterfields from his shirt pocket and shook one out for each of them. Rick accepted the cigarette with a nod of thanks and patted his pocket for a match.

"More 'n likely Lucky's in town," he said, "like he is most Mondays instead of where he oughta be, tending to what's left of his ranch. You can find him at the R&R Café there by the railroad depot in Gillette. He'll be playing cards with that no-account hired hand of mine." Rick cupped his hand around the burning match Nelson offered and blew it out once his cigarette caught fire. "Tell Mac to get his ass back to the ranch if you go there."

"Mac?"

"Mac McKeen. He'll be the easy one to spot—he ain't got no calluses on his hands like he earns his pay or anything. He'll be sitting with that lug of a boy of his, Toby, drooling over his old man's shoulder. Probably losing their shirts to Natty Barnes there at the R&R."

The rancher climbed back into his truck. Nelson motioned for him to roll down his window. "Mr. Jones—"

"Rick."

"Rick—you never asked if I had any papers for *you.* Seems like every other time I'm in the country serving eviction notices, everyone else gets as nervous as a cat in a room full of rocking chairs. Folks want to know if I have papers for *them.*"

Rick laughed. "I was born under a lucky star, I suppose. I could have been run off last year when I couldn't make my payments. But Stockman's Bank there in Billings gave me an extension on my note. Helped me get on my feet. Hell, I even hired Mac off the bread line in Billings just to help out, not that he's much good."

"Just what this country needs—more benevolent bankers," Nelson said, but he knew if some banker overlooked Rick's bad loan, there was another motive besides being kindhearted. Few bankers nowadays had a heart. "You deal with this Stockman's Bank much, do you?"

Rick flicked his ash out the window. "For nearly ten years I have. Stockman's bought out the Bank of Gillette when that fiasco happened in '29. I heerd they bought the notes for a nickel on the dollar, but they've been good to work with. It's only been this last year that they've started kicking folks off their ranches."

Nelson recalled that scandal. Nine years ago, the president of the Bank of Gillette—owner of the Peerless Coal Mine—had invested heavily to promote the mine only to have it shut down. Defunct. And with it, the bank's funds. The man had taken the only way out that he knew—he ate the barrel of his pistol rather than face the humiliation of what he'd done to his family and the town.

Nelson dug the foreclosure paper out of his pocket. Stockman's Bank in Billings was the mortgage holder for the Graber ranch. "Same bank that holds your note wants Lucky removed."

"That's what I can't figure out—why they would even want him off his place. You've seen it—would you want the bother of taking the place back?"

"Can't say as I would," Nelson said. "But there's got to be some reason."

"It's sure as hell not to resell for grazing. Lucky's only got a section of land, and the bank wouldn't be able to recuperate even a fraction selling it. You'd think if the bank wanted to make money, they damn sure wouldn't grab Lucky's property. Be more trouble than the place is worth just getting it ready to sell. Hell, they even foreclosed on the Bates place just down the road—that's the spread with another big ol' barn that looks like it'll topple over with the next wind."

Nelson suppressed a grin at Rick's use of *recuperate* for *recoup.* "But Lucky's place isn't so worthless that you don't want to buy it?"

Rick waved a hand in the air as if brushing the argument

aside. "It'd just be easier for me if I owned his place—it'd beat getting on Lucky every time the fence went down when my bull got into his heifers."

"What heifers?" Nelson asked. "I didn't see any."

"Exactly. Lucky pissed his small herd away, and now every time my bull wanders off, he winds up at Lucky's. And every time, I worry that bastard will fill me full o' holes soon's I step onto his land to fetch my bull."

"Speaking of fences," Nelson said, "what can you tell me about that dead man you found half sprawled across yours?"

"Wonder when you'd get to that." Rick flicked his cigarette butt into the snow. "All's I know is just what I told DeMyron. I come on to that hunter when I was out checking cows. I was going to just haul him on into the funeral home, but I was a-horseback and didn't want to cart a bloody body across my saddle back to my place. Besides, I was afeared my buckskin would spook smelling the blood. He's a two-year-old I bought on the Crow Reservation last summer, and he's a bit randy. Buggers said he was broke, but I got a sore behind to prove he weren't broke to a saddle *at all.* Barely halter broke, he was. But being a U.S. marshal, you wouldn't know a hell of a lot about riding rough stock."

Nelson still felt pain in his own backside from the many times he'd been thrown from saddle broncs and bulls back in his younger days. Back in his rodeo days. Back before the Great War in France and the *kriegsmortar* that would take his sight in one eye and lead him on the road to alcohol before Helen rescued him. Back before Nelson drove her to an early death with his drinking. "I can't say as I've ridden a horse lately," he told Rick, leaving out that the only reason he hadn't was that he preferred mules and hadn't sat a horse in years. "I'm glad you left the man just where he was until we could investigate properly."

"What's to investigate? I'm no federal marshal, but even I could see the damn fool tried crossing the fence onto my land without securing his gun. Killing himself when something tripped the trigger. Not the first time that's happened, nor will it be the last. Ain't no deer worth the price he paid for his stupidity."

"Man's name was Gene Bone. Know him?"

Rick shook a cigarette out of his own pack without offering Nelson one. After he lit it and watched the smoke rings filter out his truck window, he said, "Didn't know the feller, but if I'd have caught him hunting on my land without my permission, *I* might have been the one that drilled him."

"Thanks," Nelson said and turned to get back in his truck.

Rick stuck his head out his own vehicle's window. "You see that no-good hired hand of mine, you tell him to come back to the ranch with that feed I told him to pick up. I have work for him. That's if he wants to eat again. You tell him that for me."

Chapter 3

By the time Nelson parked his panel truck in the Chicago, Burlington, and Quincy Railroad depot the sun was nearly down, but he could clearly see a freight train roll to a stop beside the café twenty yards away. 'Bos riding the rails jumped off before the railroad bulls could catch and thump them, men as weary of this damned Depression as everyone else but with no place to go. No place to call home, their turkeys slung over their shoulders their only possession. They would scatter among the town, watching warily for any law dogs. They'd seek out houses with an *X* chalked on the side, made by other hobos telling their compatriots the owners of those houses were easy marks for a free meal.

Nelson ignored them as he walked to the R&R Café next to the tracks, built so that railroaders coming off their shift could sit for a hot meal. When he entered to the tinkling of a cowbell above the door, men seated in a corner booth glanced his way. The men, dressed in dirty bib overalls and short-brimmed railroader hats, went back to eating their lunch.

A table in another corner of the café hosted a young couple, probably off the bus that ran through town going west. Their heads were together, and laughter filled their conversation as they split a piece of pie between them.

Nelson glanced around and spotted Lucky—he was wearing striped bib overalls, just like Rick Jones had said. But, unlike the railroaders, with the shop-worn overalls of honest working men, Lucky's had more holes than a cheese grater and not in the areas you'd expect a working man's clothes to wear—elbows and knees. His thin arms jutted from his tattered red union suit, and cardboard stuck out of the bottom of his boots where he'd stuffed it to plug the holes in his soles. He sat at a table, looking over the top of a pair of reading glasses taped together with a dirty Band-Aid while he stared at cards clutched tightly in his hand. "Call. With three kings."

"Shit," the man next to him said and threw down his cards. "All's I got is a pair of eights."

Lucky swept up his pot. "Mac, you're just not lucky against ol' Lucky today."

The third man at the table had folded his cards right before the drama and leaned closer to Mac. "Maybe your boy Toby's been giving you bad luck, slobbering over your shoulder like he always does."

A kid of seventeen-going-on-twenty-seven, by his size and three o'clock shadow at ten in the morning, stood in back of Mac McKeen. He stared down at the card game, yet appeared not to see it, a blank expression pasted across his pockmarked face. His bib overalls looked like they'd been handed down from his father, who would just come up to Toby's chest by the looks of him. They showed dried manure on the bottoms, stains on the elbows and knees where he'd knelt. *Somebody in the family has to work or Rick would put the run on them,* Nelson figured.

"Natty, you leave Toby alone," Lucky said. "He's a good boy."

Natty slapped Toby on the back. "I know that. Just giving him a little crap," he said as he exaggerated holding his nose. "Lord knows he's gotten into enough of that lately."

"Kid's been helping me and Rick out," Mac said. "Just earning his keep."

Natty sipped his cup of coffee and looked up at Nelson filling the doorway to the café. "Hey big 'un—you want to try your hand at a little five card draw?"

Nelson walked toward the table, the foreclosure notice sticking out of his shirt pocket. "I have my vices, but gambling's not one of them."

"Then what will you have this morning?" Natty waved his hand to get the waitress's attention. A girl in her early twenties, looking more like she ought to be a flapper in a big city, glanced warily toward the table. Her coiffured hair and the painted-on lines at the backs of her legs where silk stockings should have been if she could afford it made her look *cheap.* "Marley, girl, get your pretty little butt on over here. We got us a new friend, and I'll buy his coffee today."

She grabbed a coffee pot and a cup and walked—no, sashayed—over to the table. She flashed a broad smile and stuck the stub of a pencil behind her ear while she craned her neck up to look at Nelson. "Coffee all you want, sugar?"

He felt himself blush and knew she'd seen it, too. His own daughter, Polly, was only younger than Marley by a year or two. "That's all I'll have."

Marley winked and set the full cup on the table in front of the empty chair before swinging her hips as she returned to the counter.

Natty said, "What brings you here to Gillette, friend? And have a seat before I get a stiff neck looking up at you."

Nelson pulled his sheepskin coat aside to show his badge. "Here on business."

Lucky stood abruptly, knocking his chair over. He moved away from Nelson, his eyes darting to the door and back to Nelson, veins throbbing in his pencil neck. "I reckon you're here to kick me off my land."

"I ought to toss you behind bars the way you threatened my deputy," Nelson said.

"She wasn't nice," Toby blurted out. He walked away from

Mac and stood beside Lucky. "She would have . . ." He sputtered but could not find the right word. "She would have. . ."

"Evicted," Mac said. "The word's *evicted.*"

Toby nodded. "That's just what she would have done. Evicted Lucky from his ranch, and she wasn't nice about it."

"Were you there?"

Mac stood and draped an arm around his son. "Marshal, Toby don't mean nothin'. He's just a little"—he cupped his hand to his mouth and lowered his voice—"slow. The boy's just a mite slow. But he's a good kid. He's just sticking up for his friend. Lucky's the only friend Toby has, really."

"I can stick up for my ownself, Toby," Lucky said, jabbing the air as if he wanted to jab Nelson in the chest. But he was wise enough not to. "I ain't accepting papers. I've worked that ranch for nigh on twenty years, and no bank's gonna kick me off it."

Nelson took the coffee and sipped lightly, sizing Lucky up. The man looked as if he hadn't eaten a decent meal in weeks by the way his bib overalls hung on his gaunt frame. One frayed strap of his bibs falling off his shoulder. Nelson found it hard to feel sorry for him if he was here playing poker instead of minding his ranch. Still, Lucky had won a sizable pot, more than twenty dollars, and maybe this was the only way he could make money if he was as crappy a rancher as Rick Jones claimed.

Nelson took out the eviction paper from his pocket. "I have no choice. It's my job, even though I hate doing it. I want you off within five days." He tapped the foreclosure notice folded in his hand. "That ought to give you enough time to move."

"By Gawd, I'll not move off," Lucky blurted, spittle flying, dribbling down onto his chin whiskers that were caked with tobacco juice. "And if you and that lady deputy of your'n come around the place to kick me off, I'll have my gun handy."

He turned and started for the door. "Don't leave. There's another matter we need to discuss," Nelson yelled after him, but Lucky had already busted through and gone running down the street. Through the café's front window, Nelson saw him hop into a Model T missing one fender and drive off, kicking up snow and dirt behind him.

Mac shook his head as he watched Lucky's retreat. "He's more bark than bite, Marshal. Don't hurt him when you kick him off his ranch." He turned to Toby. "Let's go pick up that chicken feed and cake for the cows." He stood and walked toward the door, then stopped and turned around. "I'd still watch my backside around Lucky," he told Nelson. "I've seen him shoot antelope two city blocks away with that old rifle of his."

Toby brushed past Nelson, glaring, keeping the marshal in his line of sight as he followed his father out of the café.

"Sit, Marshal," Natty said when they'd left. "And have a refill." He whistled for Marley. "Need a refill here, honey."

The waitress came over with the coffee pot and refilled their cups, narrowly avoiding Natty's swat at her rump before fleeing to safety behind the counter. Natty looked after her for a moment before telling Nelson, "I know you have a job to do, Marshal. But when you kick Lucky off, be gentle. Seems like bad fortune just comes and sleeps with him every night. The poor bastard can't catch a break."

"He a jinx, is he?"

"Lord, throw me to the hogs if I'm lying—Lucky exemplifies *un*lucky. His only boy got himself killed in France during the war. Then his wife died of diphtheria not a month before the crash of '29, and he had to sell most of his cattle when the market fell out. He even raised some pigs to be sold to make cholera serum, but the market fell out of that, too, and he lost every one of them. Hell, the last bred heifer he had come down with dystocia, and he lost the calf *and* the cow."

Growing up on a ranch, Nelson had seen many times where

the calf breached backwards in the heifer, the umbilical cord breaking, the unborn calf injecting amniotic fluid and being stillborn. And, like Lucky's cow, its mother sometimes died as well. "Looks like he was pretty lucky this morning."

"He has his good days at the cards," Natty said. "And he's been selling a few eggs to get by."

"At a dime for a dozen, he can't be making much money."

"He also takes in hunters wanting to bag a deer or pronghorn now and again. Makes a few bucks thataway."

"And comes in here every Monday to play cards, if Rick Jones has it right."

"That blowhard!" Natty stood and began pacing the floor. The coffee cup clutched in his hand sloshed over, but he paid it no mind. "Rick needs to keep his nose out of other people's business. Fact is, Lucky does what he can to survive." He lowered his voice. "Poaching a deer now and again for something to eat. Can't hardly fault him for that."

Nelson couldn't fault Lucky. There were more times in his life than he liked to recall where he'd had to take a deer or an elk just for camp meat.

He finished his coffee and looked at Marley, who was eying him painfully. He shook his head—she needn't come over to refill his cup and run the gauntlet of Natty's wandering hands. "Where does Lucky get the money to play poker if he's sucking the hind tit?"

"Like I said, he sells a few eggs. Guides a few hunters—"

"And has one of his friends help him win a pot or two?"

Natty stopped his coffee cup midway to his mouth. "What're you talking about? What friend's been helping him—"

"You, Natty." Nelson nodded to Marley. "I'll have that refill now."

When she came to the table, Nelson stepped between her and Natty until she finished pouring. She made her escape back to the counter without incident.

"What friend's been helping Lucky?" Natty repeated.

"You," Nelson answered. "I saw the way you dealt that last hand, dealing from the bottom to give Lucky that king he needed."

"I did not—"

"And the way you put an oh-so-tiny crimp in that king to mark the card." Nelson shook his head. "I've seen sharks, and you're one of the best . . . I'll hand that to you." He leaned over the table. "Thing I want to know is, why give Lucky a winning hand and lose your own money?"

Natty set his empty cup down and hung his head. "You caught me, Marshal. I admit I dealt Lucky a winning hand today—"

"And cheated Mac McKeen."

Natty shrugged. "Mac's not rolling in dough, but he's doing a lot better than Lucky nowadays. Rick gives Mac a half beef every year and an old house to live in on the ranch." He held up his hand as if in surrender. "You're not going to arrest me, are you?"

Nelson laughed. "I have other things to do than bust card sharks. Besides, it almost sounds like you're doing a good thing by helping Lucky win sometimes."

Natty sat back and patted his belly. "That's me—the Robin Hood of Gillette, Wyoming."

"I wouldn't go that far," Nelson said and turned to leave.

"No need to hightail it out of here. The cook makes a mean bowl of antelope chili."

"Like I said, I have other things to do."

Natty snapped his fingers. "That's right, that hunter who got himself killed. What did you find out about him?"

"Very little yet. What do you know about the man—Gene Bone, by his identification card?"

"Young feller? Stocky? Kind of swarthy complexion like some of those Mideasterners have?"

Nelson nodded.

"He came into the café now and again, though he kept to himself. Never said as much as 'good morning.' Standoffish is how he came across until one morning, if I recall . . ."

Nelson waited for the rest, Natty holding his explanation like a trained actor waiting for the right delivery. "Until a couple mornings ago. The guy finished his breakfast and sauntered on over to us. Asked if he could sit in on the game. I'm telling you, Marshal—only 'cause you don't arrest card sharks—that man was hell on wheels with a deck of cards. I'd no sooner double deal myself into a straight than he'd somehow come up a flush and beat hell out of me. I'd deal myself a full house, and damned if he wouldn't show four of a kind. Plumb cleaned me out, and Mac, too. Pert' near a hundred dollars that feller walked away with." Natty got a faraway look. "I sure wish to hell he hadn't killed himself hunting so's I could win my money back."

Chapter 4

Maris let Nelson into the courthouse through the back entrance and looked both ways before closing the door. "Didn't figure you wanted to deal with her right now."

"I don't understand—"

"The newspaper. That nosy reporter from the *Gillette Daily Journal* ambushed me last night when I pulled into the motor lodge. Wanted to know all the details about the dead man."

"What reporter?"

"Some drifty dame that's annoying as hell," Maris said, leading the way upstairs. "She wants to scoop the *News Record* reporter. I'm sure I saw her slinking around the courthouse when I pulled in."

"You're right," Nelson said. "I don't want to talk with her or any reporter. I can't say as the local papers have been supportive of us marshals. Every time we serve notice on some poor rancher or farmer, we're portrayed as the bad guy."

"Then we'd best figure out how to leave the courthouse without her spotting us." Maris spit the last of her chaw into a trash can and nibbled on the tip of her bandana, a wry smile spreading across her face. "What did that peckerwood Lucky Graber have to say when you finally slapped papers on him? I'd have loved to have been there."

"I found him at the R&R having breakfast with Natty Barnes and Mac and his boy—"

"How did he take being evicted?" Maris pressed, almost giddy with anticipation.

"I finally heard why he's called *Lucky.*" Nelson told Maris about the many bad things that had befallen Ulysses S. Graber. "Poor bastard can't catch a break. I feel sorry for him."

"Hell, even *I* feel sorry for him," Maris said, "but when you served the eviction notice—"

"I didn't serve the papers."

"What!"

"I just . . . couldn't right then," Nelson said. "Lucky is one obnoxious feller, I'll admit, but I just had a *feeling* there was more to his foreclosure than simply him being lazy. And after Natty gave me the skinny about Lucky's string of bad luck, well"—he kicked a stone on the floor with the toe of his boot—"I just couldn't right then."

"But you *have* to. You always told me to leave your emotions at the front gate when dealing with folks."

Nelson shrugged. "I know I have to kick him off his place. But as soon as I slap paper on him, he *has* to be moved out in five days. I'll hunt him up at the end of the week and serve him. But waiting to *officially* serve him notice will give the poor slob a little more time to get his things in order and move. Not that it appears as if he has much to drag away." Nelson followed Maris into the sheriff's office. "What have you found out about our dead hunter?"

"Besides him being a *dumb* dead hunter?" Maris said. "DeMyron just got off the phone with the sheriff in New Jersey, who gave some interesting information about our victim." She closed the door. "Let's jaw over coffee. You can regale me with *your* exploits. I could use some time listening to all the wild and wonderful things *you've* done. I'm sure it'll beat DeMyron's heroics in his twenty-six years that I can about recite from memory by now."

"I detect a hint of sarcasm."

Maris shook her head. "No hint about it. The man's head is so swelled, it can barely fit through the door. Got to calling himself Dick Tracy on a horse."

Nelson smiled. "Maybe you could be DeMyron's Tess Trueheart. You could sidle up close and take the rough edges off the kid."

"It'd take a hell of a bastard file to take the rough edges off Deputy DeMyron. But I bow to my boss being the first to talk with Mister Detective about our hunter."

The secretary, Bonnie Matchuk, perched over her typewriter, her fingers dancing across the worn black keys of the Underwood, the current edition of *True Confessions* propped open in front of her. Just in case she got a free moment to catch up on her drama. She never looked up as she said, "God's gift is in his office if that's who you're looking for."

"Thanks, Bonnie." Maris led Nelson down a dim hallway. They passed a door with *Harper L. Jarvis–Sheriff* stenciled on it and continued to DeMyron's office, unmistakable with its two-inch-high letters proclaiming its occupant Campbell County's only deputy.

DeMyron leaned back in his chair, his boots propped on an open desk drawer, sipping coffee out of a tin cup when they entered. He looked up at Nelson and said, "I bet you want to know what this . . . *hick* . . . found out about our dead hunter. Pour yourself a cup and have a seat."

Nelson poured coffee and offered Maris some, but she waved it away. "I've had about enough of DeMyron's free Campbell County coffee."

Nelson sniffed the brew. A faint bean aroma with a tint of what . . . paint thinner? He couldn't put his finger on it, but he was committed to drinking it now that DeMyron had offered it.

Nelson took off his Stetson and draped it over a pronghorn hat rack that hung on the wall plastered with *Wanted* posters.

"Let's have it. What's the skinny on our Gene Bone?"

DeMyron swung his booted feet around and thudded them on the floor with a flourish as he grabbed a file folder. "Our Gene Bone works—worked—as a mining engineer in Tonopah, Nevada. He's been with the company pictured on that business card for the last couple years, ever since he moved out of New Jersey."

"Where did you get that pearl of information?"

"I have my contacts," DeMyron said proudly.

Maris caught Nelson's eye. "He made a cold call to the Newark police right after I found an old bank card wadded up in the bottom of Gene's wallet."

"I *would* have found that bank card if you'd have given me a chance."

"Enough," Nelson said. "Will *somebody* tell me *something* about Gene Bone?"

"We found very little about our victim," DeMyron admitted. "When I called the bank in New Jersey, the teller was reticent, to say the least. He confirmed that someone had used this bank card, but the account was closed two years ago, and he didn't know where the owner had moved to."

"The teller said 'someone,' and not Gene specifically?"

"She didn't know who closed the account, as there was no notation as to who handled it."

"But she knew Gene?" Nelson drank some coffee and made a face.

"She danced around that," DeMyron said, "and suggested I contact the police department."

"Why the mystery?" Nelson asked. "It sounds as if she knew this Gene Bone but just didn't want to talk about him?"

"That's about the long and short of it," DeMyron said.

Nelson took one more assault-to-his-taste-buds sip of coffee and tossed the rest in the water basin atop a wooden pedestal.

"Are you going to leave me in suspense as to what the Newark police said?"

DeMyron nodded at Maris. "I passed the ball to her," he blurted out, "while I told Bonnie what to type for my report."

"In other words," Maris said, "DeMyron found out his phone interview skills were a bit lacking and wanted me to step in."

DeMyron glared at Maris and shook his head. "I gotta get some fresh air." He stood and snatched his jacket from the coat rack. "It'll give me a chance to have a smoke," he muttered before walking out the door.

Maris looked after him. "Kind of testy, isn't he?"

Nelson shrugged. "He'll have to get used to working with someone more experienced than he is. Especially a woman. Since he's Sheriff Jarvis's only deputy, he's used to being the cock of the walk. Used to being *in charge.* He'll get over it."

"He'd better, or that temper of his will get him in trouble. And as big as that boy is, he could do a lot of damage if he goes off. The way folks said he tossed steers around in the rodeo, he's stout as all get out."

Nelson agreed. "But neither of us has time to nursemaid him. If Jarvis hired him, Nelson figured he could damn well keep DeMyron in his place until the sheriff returns from that funeral. "Now what did the Newark police tell you—did they know Gene?"

"They did, but under the name Bonelli. Gino Bonelli. He apparently changed his name after he moved from Jersey."

"Why?"

Maris shrugged. "The lieutenant I spoke with didn't know but claimed they had little contact with Gino. He said the campus police at New York University had some dealings with Gene when he was enrolled there and suggested I should start with them. I got the impression the police commander"—she ruffled through her notes—"Lieutenant Quinn, wanted to tell me more. That he held back. All he'd say is that they'll notify us if they come cross anything in their files. I haven't gotten a chance to call the university police yet."

"We need to find Gene's—Giono's—next of kin to do the death notification."

"The lieutenant said he would handle it."

"To Gino's father?"

"To his only living relative—his brother, Bruno Bonelli."

Nelson frowned in thought. "That name ring a bell?"

"Like Quasimodo it does, but I can't place it right this moment, either," Maris answered. "Hell, I couldn't place it ever since I heard it, and I know there's *something* there. I'll probably connect the dots about the time I'm falling asleep."

"So, we really know little more about our victim that we did before," Nelson said, "because if the Newark police knew more, the information would roll off your tongue."

"It would. But you'll find out more from Gino himself."

"How's that?"

"Gino's death was unattended. *Somebody's* gotta go with the body to Billings, and I don't think you want to trust DeMyron to take it there and muck things up. And me"—Maris exaggerated a coughing fit—"I better take a day of rest under the covers with chicken soup. Try to get rid of my cold."

"So, you've found your own *chicken soup* already . . . your own *victim* here in Gillette?"

Maris's answer was her best Betty Page grin, and Nelson knew some hapless rancher would soon be helping Maris. Under the covers.

"It'd better be a quick romance," Nelson said.

"How's that, boss?"

"While I take the dearly departed up to Billings for his autopsy, DeMyron and you will both have to hit the pavement. Find out just where Gino was staying while he was here in town. You might start with the car we can't find—"

"Got that covered." Maris took her notebook back out of her jeans pocket. "I talked with Marley down at the café. The morning Natty and Mac were getting fleeced in that poker game by Gino, Mac gave Toby a nickel to buy a soda down at the general store. Marley said the kid never made it. She saw him standing outside gawking at something. Just standing and staring, so Marley went out. Toby was gaping at a Cadillac roadster. It was muddy and snow-caked under the wheel well like any ranch car, but it was new. And fancy. Marley said the only other one in town is owned by the president of the First State Bank."

"It was Gino's Cadillac?"

"Who else?" Maris said and pocketed her notebook. "When was the last time you saw a new Caddy in these parts? Had to be Gino's."

"What color was it?"

Maris shrugged. "Marley couldn't recall precisely. She was like Toby—just in awe of it. All she knew was that it was a lighter color—cream, maybe beige." Maris lowered her voice as if the waitress were in the room with them. "I'm thinking Marley is a bit . . . dense."

Chapter 5

The fence posts droned on as he passed them mile after mile, and Nelson thought how he hadn't wanted to spend an entire day driving to Billings. The autopsy on Gino Bonelli would take *some* time, but at least it would be interesting. Unlike this boring drive. Then the eight-hour drive back to Gillette tomorrow, and he'd be about drove-out for a while.

The week had all started so well with him planning to do some ice fishing until Maris had called about Lucky Graber threatening her and running her off his ranch. Now, Lucky had skipped out. Nelson had driven back out to Lucky's, but the man was not at his ranch, and no one in town admitted they had seen him. "Keep trying to locate him," Nelson had told her as they loaded Gino into the back of Nelson's truck this morning that he had—appropriately—bought from the funeral home in Sheridan last year. "I want to know if Gino had permission to hunt on Lucky's property."

"You're thinking Lucky caught him and confronted him? Maybe things got out of hand, and he drilled Gino?" Maris asked as she closed the back doors of the panel truck. "I'm still holding out for an accidental death, with Gino's rifle discharged, the spent round right beside him. Only way it could have happened."

"Unless they tussled with the rifle," Nelson said. "Gun went off, and the bullet hit Gino in the head. Lucky got scared and lit out."

"Didn't light out very far," Maris said as she shook snow off her gloves. "You spoke with him at the R&R yesterday morning. If he was going to flee after a killing, he'd have done so yesterday."

"He might have figured the only one that was investigating Gino's apparent hunting accident was a rookie deputy. Like Sheriff Jarvis said, DeMyron's hell in a bar fight, but he's never investigated a dead body before. With you and me thrown into the investigation, Lucky might've thought he'd be found out and fled." Nelson opened the truck door and climbed behind the wheel. "We'll see what magic the medical examiner can conjure up at autopsy that might help us."

A cow elk grazed beside the road, and Nelson slowed in case she darted out as he kicked around the scenarios in his mind. While he continued west out of Gillette, he'd begun thinking more about the possibility that Gino and Lucky *had* tussled with the rifle and it went off. After much deliberation and counting of fence posts as he went on this monotonous drive, he admitted to himself that Maris might be right. Even if Lucky was a scrapper, he would take about half a second to size Gino up and see he didn't want anything to do with him. Not that Gino was such a large man, but that Lucky was so . . . anemic. Almost frail. But if they did argue, Lucky's only option was shooting the bigger man.

Nelson turned onto a snow-packed gravel road that would skirt the river and cut twenty miles off his trip, the smooth V-8 pulling effortlessly up a steep hillside as he downshifted. "What were you doing here in Gillette, because you sure as hell weren't hunting, dressed as light as you were. No hat. No gloves," Nelson asked, as if the corpse could answer. "If you were hunting, you'd at least have asked permission from Lucky and Rick Jones. Bought maps of the area. People would have noticed you." Except for that one morning where he'd cleaned out Natty and Mac at poker, no one had noticed Gino around town.

Nelson thought back to the many times he had hunted, preferring to go with a pard or two. Not that Nelson particularly liked people—which he had grown not to—but that a hunting partner would stop you from doing something stupid like crossing a fence with a loaded gun. It would be so easy for Nelson to rule it accidental—a hunter crossing the fence with gun in hand. A semiautomatic rifle with a light trigger touching *something* that caused the gun to discharge. The spent rifle casing landing right at Gino's feet.

But gnawing at Nelson was the question of Gino's vehicle, for he surely wouldn't have borrowed a horse to ride, not the way he was dressed, risking his pointy-toed fancy shoes hanging up in the stirrups if he had to bail out of the saddle for any reason. Gino had to have driven and parked close to where he was found. But where was his Caddy? Or did someone drop him off by Lucky and Rick's fence, intending to pick Gino up later? A date he would never keep.

Nelson was missing something, he was certain, something that would keep him here investigating, something preventing him from knocking that hole in the ice and dropping his fishing line in. Something that would keep him in Campbell County far longer than he wanted.

Baggy's Diner sat at the outskirts of Sheridan. Nelson parked beside a Buick roadster and an Autocar and got out just as the owner emerged with a toothpick stuck between his lips. The fellow glanced at the panel truck, then stopped and looked closer before saying, "Didn't this belong to Happy's Funeral Home?"

"Why?"

"I think my uncle was transported to his grave in it." The portly man laughed while he buttoned up his coat and donned another pair of gloves. "Now all you need is a dead body to haul around, and you'd be complete."

"If you only knew," Nelson said. He started for the diner, then stopped the man before he climbed into his own truck. "You from these parts?"

"I haul gravel on the side." The man nodded toward the truck. "Got a small operation couple miles east of Buffalo. Why?"

"You ever see a new Cadillac driving these roads?"

"Can't say as I have."

"Beige or cream colored?"

"It could be most any color and—if it's a Caddy—it'd stick out."

"Thanks, bud," Nelson said, thinking the man was a hell of a lot tougher than him, driving in these freezing temperatures in a truck with an open cab. But then, folks did what they could during this Depression just to get by.

Nelson entered the diner and sat at the counter beside two old men nursing their morning coffee over a game of dominoes. "I darn'd near didn't make it out a couple weeks ago," one of the men said, and dabbed egg out of his scraggly beard that reached to his chest. "He would have had me dead to rights, and I wouldn't be here talking with you. I'd be in the pokey."

Nelson felt guilty eavesdropping until the smaller man said, "He nearly nabbed me last year, too. Onliest thing that saved me was an early snow squall. By the time he made it down to the draw, I'd dismantled my still and was long gone."

"Someone out to get you fellers?" Nelson asked.

Long Beard looked around the diner. No one paid them any mind, yet he lowered his voice and said, "Sheriff Jarvis, over there in Gillette. I had me a nice setup down by the Powder River—put out ten gallons of mash a day. 'Till him and that deputy found it. Lucky to have gotten outta there with just my old gray pony."

"Don't blame you," the other man said, scratching the

dominoes' core on a piece of paper. "I moved west out of Campbell County and set up my operation again, but Jarvis has offered to help Sheriff Lord in bustin' up stills here in Sheridan County." The thin man looked over at Nelson. "What's your stand on this Prohibition thing?"

"Unofficially, I figure a man ought to get his drink someplace besides folks cooking bathtub gin or coffin varnish in old, rusty barrels. That's preferable to men dying of alcohol poisoning."

"Now wait a minute," Long Beard said. "Most of us hereabouts pride ourselves in turning out a safe product—"

"Do you drink it yourself?"

The man paused for a long moment before saying, "You couldn't pay me enough to drink that tarantula juice. But dammit, it's a way to make *some* kinda living nowadays." He looked Nelson up and down. "What do you do for a living?"

Nelson pulled his jacket aside. The man grabbed the edge of the counter as if his heart were failing him, his gaze fixed on the marshal's star. "You almost sounded like you approve of moonshine a moment ago."

"That was my *unofficial* opinion. Officially, I'd have to smash any still I found. Just like Sheriff Jarvis and Sheriff Lord here in Sheridan. You fellers set up new stills hereabouts, did you?"

Without another word, both men turned toward the door and disappeared, leaving their breakfast and their dominoes at the table.

"Good for those two old farts to get a little spooked." Baggy Adams set a cup of coffee in front of Nelson. "They was talkin' like they was fixin' to set up another still in this county. They think it'll be safe here." He laughed. "But ol' Sheriff Lord's damn near as lethal as Jarvis sniffing out them moonshiners. And we damn sure have enough men here making panther piss as it is. But what brings you over here, Nels, surely not to spook a couple old roosters?"

"Been a death over in Campbell County." Nelson lowered his voice. "Some young feller from Nevada."

"By way of New Jersey."

"How'd you hear—"

"I hear things," Baggy said. "All sorts of things. Sounds like it was that guy's first—and last—time in the field hunting deer if the rumors are true."

"It appears that way."

"Since when does a U.S. marshal get roped into investigating hunting accidents?"

"Since Sheriff Jarvis went out of town. His pappy passed, and he asked me to help his deputy out."

"With an accidental death?" Baggy repeated.

"If it *was* accidental," Nelson said and tapped his finger on the picture of an omelet on the front of the menu. "We have to treat it like it's a homicide for now. But the way I figure it, as soon as the autopsy's done and this case is closed, I'll be back home dropping my pole through the ice."

Baggy left Nelson looking at the noon customers, the usual gathering of men working this Depression. Three oil drillers in a booth talked low together as if their hole might be discovered and they'd be cheated out of their money. At the booth across from them, a man burst into a coughing fit like Nelson had seen with other men wearing the same perpetually coal-dirty clothes. The Peerless Mine, and later the WyoDak mine east of Gillette, employed men from all around the area who ignored the possibility of getting black lung from the constant coal dust. This man probably lived here but drove to the mine in Gillette every day. He might have been a career miner, working copper until the Anaconda Mine by Butte had to lay off most of their crew after the '29 crash. *That man will be dead before he turns fifty.* But at least he went to work every day, even if it was a two-hour drive to the mine. He would stay in a wall tent with other miners at the man camp and be home with his family in a couple days. Wherever home was. *If* he didn't have some lethal accident and *if* the dust didn't kill him first.

Baggy set the omelet in front of Nelson and he made short work of it. He finished his coffee and sopped up the last of the egg with his toast. As he stood to pay Baggy, Nelson asked, "By the way, have you seen anyone driving a beige or cream-colored Cadillac roadster who might have stopped here this last week?"

Baggy set the coffee pot on the counter beside the register and blew his nose in his apron. "There was some guy pulled into the lot a few days ago driving one."

"What'd he look like?"

Baggy shrugged. "He never came in. But Mel—that's the guy you was jawing with in the parking lot—came in the diner that morning and went to a couple fellers he knew in that booth." He pointed to the booth where the oil men sat.

"The man I spoke with in the lot denied having seen a Cadillac hereabouts."

"Don't blame him," Baggy said. "I figured the guy musta been selling opium out of his car. Maybe hooch. After Mel come in and whispered something to them, they were digging their wallets out even before they got to the door." He held up his hands as if in surrender. "But I'm telling you, Nels, I'm not into drugs or moonshine in my place. Ever."

"I know," Nelson said. "Where can I find this Mel with the Autocar, and what's his last name?"

"Can't help much there. All's I know is, he has some part-time gravel hauling business, but he's a full-time railroader. Might catch up with him at the Gillette terminal." He snapped his fingers. "This Caddy you're looking for have anything to do with the dead hunter?"

"It could," Nelson answered. "Or not. I'd like to talk with

Mel, though. If he comes in, tell him to call the sheriff's office in Campbell County."

Chapter 6

At the morgue in Billings, Nelson helped Dr. Barr load the body onto a rolling cart. “You didn’t say much about this one when you called,” she said as she wheeled Gino Bonelli into her examination room.

“Let’s say I didn’t want to taint your findings with my gut feelings.”

The medical examiner exaggerated looking at Nelson’s belly and laughed. “Must be some kind of gut feeling. But you’re right—wait until I’m done before you tell me how you and our victim met.” She threw the sheet off the corpse. “Grab his legs, and we’ll scoot him over.”

They moved Gino to the examination table, the wooden laminate top showing scars and stains from a hundred bodies. “You’re willing to stick around and observe the festivities?” Dr. Barr said.

“I’ve seen enough dead people in my lifetime. I’m content to wait in your dismal office and drink your week-old coffee until you’re done.”

“Suit yourself.” She grabbed a scalpel and turned to the victim. “The fun begins without you.”

“Are you trying to get in touch with your feminine side?” Dr. Barr asked as she entered her small office and eyed the magazine in Nelson’s hand. The autopsy had taken two hours, and she dropped into the captain’s chair at her desk. “ ’Cause it wouldn't hurt you none to look at us women's side, you being a widower and all."

Nelson closed the cover and put the current edition of *I Confess* on the stand in front of the small divan. "I read just about *all* the fine recipes in *Woman's Home Companion,* and thought I'd crack that other magazine and read their true confessions. You ladies don't actually believe that dribble?"

"What dribble?" Dr. Barr said as she opened her desk drawer. "It's gotta be real or else a woman wouldn't be allowed to put her name on the article."

"Doctor," Nelson said, leaning closer, "the article I just scanned was written by *Anne Nynomous.* Probably penned by a man anyway, like most of the articles."

"Well, I don't care," the pathologist said. "Confession magazines are . . . good for the soul." She blew dust out of a coffee cup and grabbed a bottle from the drawer, then poured three fingers of whisky into the cup. "For medicinal purposes," she said.

"Like confession magazines are therapeutic?"

"You got it." She held up her cup for a toast. "To that poor sucker you brought in, just waiting to tell us things." She lifted the drink to her lips, then paused and said, "You're not going to arrest me for this little nip, I hope."

"And actually have someone to talk to on my drive back to the pokey in Wyoming? I'm tempted. But go ahead and get knee-walking drunk. All I want to know is what you found out."

Dr. Barr sipped lightly while she glanced at her notes.

"You going to leave me in suspense?" Nelson asked.

"I ought to," she said, "unless you tell me something of the circumstances surrounding the victim's death."

Nelson explained how Gino was found, one leg resting on a fence he'd been crossing, his discharged semiautomatic Remington rifle beside him. "Dressed more like he was going to the theater than out hunting in the cold. That's about all we have to go on so far."

"Is the victim's rifle a .30 caliber?"

"It is."

She handed Nelson a blunted bullet. Deformed soft lead, it was still easy to tell what it was. "It's a .30 caliber, all right. Apart from that, I don't have the resources to determine anything more. I hear the Bureau of Investigations is making good progress in determining all sorts of things from bullets and guns. That'll be up to you to send it off to them. But don't hold your breath. They're backlogged about a year."

"I heard Hoover set up what he calls the Scientific Crime Detection Laboratory this year," Nelson said. "A three-dollar title that only means it ought to be fully operational ten years from now."

"You sure you don't want a drink?" Dr. Barr said. "You sound like you're getting frustrated."

Doctor Janice Barr was one of the few people who knew Nelson had been a raging alcoholic who had driven his wife into an early grave. Even after so many years of sobriety, Nelson still didn't trust himself enough to let his daughter, Polly, live with him, fearing the stress of raising a teenage girl might just push him off the ledge of sobriety. For now, her being raised by Helen's sister was working out just fine. "I'll pass."

"I wouldn't have it any other way," Dr. Barr said and set her glass aside. "But if this tempts you too much—"

Nelson waved a hand. "Not anymore. A couple years ago I'd have reached for a tiny sip, that would lead to a bigger sip, that would lead to a full-out drunken bender. But I can handle watching someone else get stinko now." He held up his coffee mug. "My real drink of choice now is . . . whatever the hell you call that *stuff* in the pot."

She laughed. "Well, if that won't knock you off the wagon,

nothing would." She scooted her chair closer, and the smile left her face. "I don't think your victim was killed with his own gun crossing a fence."

"I suspected as much. Go on."

"A.30 caliber rifle round is powerful. All .30 calibers are. If the gun had discharged mere inches from his head—such as when he was crossing the fence—the bullet would have exited his skull. I found *that*"—she nodded toward the slug—"just under the scalp. And I could find no powder stippling on the face where it should have been. No burning of the hair like there'd be if the gun went off that close. I thought at first it was because the wind and the snow blew away any—"

"There still would have been some evidence of powder stippling," Nelson said, thinking it through. "There would be some tattooing of the skin if the gun was discharged up to maybe . . . twenty feet away . . . there should have been some. I would have found minute particles of unburnt gunpowder if the gun *were* close when it went off."

"Also," Dr. Barr said, "there was an odd trajectory." She stood and positioned herself looking away from Nelson as she closed her eyes. "I see the victim walking, maybe running away, when he heard something behind him." She turned her face partially towards Nelson and indicated with her finger. "The bullet went in and slightly up the victim's open mouth. Between his lips and teeth, coming to rest in his cranial cavity." She sat back down and finished her whisky. "Your man in there was shot quite a ways from where he lay and I would wager he was looking back at his killer. Screaming."

"But the spent cartridge . . ." Nelson began, then quieted, suddenly realizing why the cartridge lay at the victim's feet, when the Remington autoloader should have thrown it farther away. *That* was what had nagged at him before. The scene was a staged accident.

Now all he had to do was figure out who staged it.

A piece of cake.

CHAPTER 7

While Dr. Barr sewed up Gino Bonelli's body in preparation for transport back to Gillette tomorrow morning, Nelson drove through downtown Billings toward Stockman's Bank. He'd had hours to think about Lucky Graber and his plight on the drive up to the pathologist's office. Lucky had been a victim like many other ranchers and farmers in Wyoming with the coming of the Depression. He had lost crops. He had lost livestock, though Nelson had to admit much of it was Lucky's own doing. Most ranchers in his boots would have been hitting the fields, salvaging what crops they could, tending to what livestock remained. Not gallivanting into town once or twice a week to have coffee and play cards hoping to hit that one big pot, that pot being twenty dollars on a good day. And only when Natty cheated to allow Lucky to win.

Nelson passed the newly built Fox Theater on North Broadway. He had not been inside, but Yancy had when he dated a widow in Billings. He had gone off the rails describing the opulent interior with the velvet curtains, the plush seats. But Yancy now and again drove to Montana on theater and dance nights, too. A regular gad-about-town.

Nelson turned the corner onto Third Avenue. Stockman's Bank loomed large in the foreground—five stories that shouted success. Nelson parked the panel truck in the spacious parking lot.

He passed two men on the sidewalk in stylish tweed suits

who looked at the big shabby man in the sheepskin coat walking into the bank building. They dipped their heads together and whispered while one pointed to Nelson. *Might as well tell me I'm too poor to go in here,* he thought.

He stopped just inside the door and read the legend beside the elevator. Businesses took up the first four floors, while the bank occupied the entire fifth level. When the elevator door opened, Nelson stepped inside and stood across from the operator. "You're headed to the fifth floor?" the man asked.

"I am," Nelson answered. "How'd you know?"

The man—Nelson's age, but with hands as smooth as any Palmolive commercial—grinned through chipped teeth. "I've been in this building most of my life. And I seen when a man is wanting a loan from the fifth floor."

"Long time to be hauling folks up and down."

The man's smile waned. "I used to be the office manager for Montana Wheat Company. We had near the entire fourth floor for our offices. That was before this Depression hit. Before we all lost our jobs."

"How'd you fall into this one?" Nelson asked.

"Mr. Olssen at the bank," the man said. "He saw I was struggling, so he gave me this job. It's nothing like I had, but it puts food on the table for me and the missus. One of these days"—he winked—"one of these days I'll be back in my old office." He got a faraway look in his eyes, and Nelson knew the man didn't believe himself. "One of these days."

The elevator door opened at the fifth floor, and Nelson stepped out into a common area. Light-brown carpeting blended into the beige-colored walls, the pleated window drapes open to allow sunlight in. Occasional chairs sat around a central coffee table with various magazines and newspapers laid out on its lacquered cherrywood surface for patrons to browse. The area was spotless. Efficient.

He walked to the receptionist's desk. She was typing, her fingers a blur. She looked up at Nelson, mouthed *just a moment,* and finished her work before she stood. "May I help you?" She looked at Nelson's patched jeans, the hole in the elbow of his jacket that he'd sewn shut, his hair sticking out of his Stetson and badly needing a cut.

"I'm looking for Andvari Olssen," Nelson said.

She paused, then said, "It's been a long time since I heard Andy called by his birth name. What is the nature of your visit . . . a loan, perhaps? Referral for a job?"

"Professional visit." Nelson pulled back his jacket to show the receptionist his badge.

"You're here to talk about the foreclosures," she said, "like many other sheriffs?"

"Marshal," he corrected. "And it's about a particular foreclosure across the border in Wyoming."

"Then I'm certain that Andy will see you. Wait here a moment, please."

She turned on her heels and disappeared down a blind corridor. When she returned, she followed a large man several inches taller than Nelson, six foot four or maybe five. He likely weighed as much as Nelson, too, but it was hard to tell, as his bulk was concealed under a well-fitting sharkskin and wool suit. His pearl-colored ascot seemed to blend with his blond, wispy hair parted in the middle and held in place by lavender-scented brilliantine. His sky-blue eyes met Nelson's, and he smiled wide, thrusting out his hand. "Pamela said a U.S. marshal wanted me. Andy Olssen. Hope it's not serious."

"May we speak alone?"

"Of course. Of course. This way, please," he said, then over his shoulder, "Coffee and cookies, Pamela."

Andy led Nelson down the hallway that opened into a vast office at the corner of the building. Windows on both sides looked down at the cars and trucks driving by, people going about their business, coats and jackets pulled tight against the cold. "This is what I get to look at every day," Andy said. "Isn't it marvelous? You don't get a better view than this."

Nelson didn't answer. To him, *any* city was meant to be avoided. The downtown view showed so much, yet he would take a mountain stream or a meadow with deer and elk grazing any day.

The receptionist entered the office, set a silver platter with cookies and coffee on a table, and left. Andy bent and picked up a cookie, biting delicately into one corner and briefly closing his eyes. "My ancestors—the Danes who came to this country—loved making these. My wife still makes them nearly every day and sends them along with me. 'It's tradition,' she says, 'that every good man of Danish ancestry eat the cookie.' " He smiled and took another as he motioned to the plate. "Please have some." He closed his eyes and cooed again as he slowly chewed the light pastry. "What say you, Marshal—do you think I ought to continue with tradition?"

Nelson ate the first cookie, so rich in butter that he eyed another. He decided he should not insult his host and grabbed a second one. After he'd finished it and downed his coffee, Nelson dabbed at the corner of his mouth with a napkin bearing the bank logo before taking a paper from his pocket and handing it to Andy. "I'll get right to the point—you hold the note on this section of land."

Andy grabbed the glasses dangling from a gold chain around his neck, perched them on his nose, and looked at the paper before handing it back. "It appears as if this bank has sent your office a notice to serve this rancher to vacate. Is there a problem with this, Marshal?"

"This rancher—Ulysses S. Graber—goes by the name of Lucky. He got that moniker because the man is anything *but* lucky. He lost his boy in the war. His wife to diphtheria. He's lost most of his crops to drought, and his livestock died off, except for a few scrawny chickens not even fat enough to fry. The man just needs a break—"

"Where are you going with this?" Andy asked.

"Where I'm going is that perhaps, just perhaps, you might hold off on this foreclosure notice. Give Lucky a chance to get back on his feet again."

Andy turned his back and looked out the window at the Billings traffic below. "Marshal," he said at last, "I empathize with Mr. Graber. But so many of the people you see down there have adapted to their own adversity during this Depression. Did you know Montana had another big drought last year on top of our six-year drought ten years ago?"

Nelson knew. The drought had hit northern Wyoming nearly as bad, with half the farmers going under. And that was before the crash of '29 that began this damned Depression.

"The Anaconda Mining Company—for which this bank holds a portion of the operating loan—had to cut production by ninety percent. Ninety percent!" Andy said. "Did you also know Yegan Brothers clothing—from which I buy my suits—had to innovate with the fall in the stock market? They had to expand to . . . everyday clothing. So that, even in these hard times, they thrive."

"Lucky Graber doesn't run a clothing store," Nelson said, feeling his neck warm. His face was turning red, he was certain. "He's a rancher. I don't think it would break this bank to give him an extension."

Andy turned and faced Nelson. "I have given far too many extensions over the past months to . . . deadbeats unable to pay their way—"

"Lucky's no deadbeat—"

"He owes this bank!" Andy's fists clenched and unclenched, his neck and face a reddish hue as he stepped back and took deep, calming breaths. "I have no choice. The stockholders would rebel if they knew I gave an extension to every Ulysses Graber who failed to make their mortgage payments."

"And what will you do with Lucky's ranch once you have it?" Nelson asked. "It's terribly run down. Soil is spoiled, so a buyer would play hell growing anything. And the ranch house is a strong wind away from collapsing. It'd be more trouble keeping the place than it's worth."

"I have no wiggle room, Marshal. I have to foreclose."

"But you *could* give an extension if you really wanted?"

Andy turned his back again and looked out the window.

"You gave his neighbor, Rick Jones, an extension."

"I recall Mr. Jones coming to me, yes."

"If you foreclosed on any place, Rick's should be before Lucky's. The Jones ranch actually turns a modest profit. It would sell at auction a hell of a lot quicker."

Andy faced Nelson again. "Marshal Lane, Rick Jones is at least trying to get on his feet. Making payments regularly. This Ulysses Graber is not." He threw up his hands. "I have no choice. For the bank and its stockholders, I demand you evict Mr. Graber the moment you return to Gillette."

"I have been unable to locate him. He seems to have gone into hiding."

"This is bullshit!" Andy's face turned red once again, and he stepped toward Nelson. Nelson sized him up. The man appeared soft, but his size alone would make him a powerful handful in a fight. "There are other legal ways to evict him," Andy continued. "If you cannot locate him, I *know* you can have a sale on the courthouse steps as a last resort. Do it." He turned his back to Nelson a third time and looked down at the people on the streets below, ending the conversation.

No point in pushing things further, Nelson left the office. *Arrogant son-of-a-bitch,* he thought as he stepped into the elevator.

If Andy Olssen could give Rick Jones some leeway on his note, he damn sure could give Lucky a break. Nelson thought back to his college days studying Greek, Roman, and Norse mythology. Andvari was the old Norse *careful one,* though Andy bore little resemblance to the dwarf. But the legend said Andvari possessed a magical ring that helped him become wealthy.

Did Andy Olssen possess such a ring, or was he a predator poised to pounce on those unable to pay?

Chapter 8

Nelson pulled into Gillette and drove to Probst Funeral Home to drop Gino off for burial. "Just who will be paying for the services?" a squat man in a cheap, black suit asked as he helped Nelson unload the body.

Nelson hadn't thought of that until the man asked. "The county will be footing the bill I imagine."

The man's mouth drooped. "So . . . a basic service."

Nelson nodded. "The most basic until someone comes forward to pay up besides the taxpayers."

He left the funeral director to his woes and drove to the courthouse to meet Maris at the sheriff's office—their adopted command post—as they unraveled the mystery of the dead man from New Jersey. "We have the office to ourselves because De-Myron had to go out on a theft call," Maris said as Nelson entered. "Seems someone stole some tools from a rancher north of town." She walked to the coffee pot, asking over her shoulder, "Now that we have the autopsy out of the way and Gene Bone's death officially ruled accidental, we can get on with finding Lucky Graber so's we can get this foreclosure business over with and be back in Buffalo."

"Gino Bonelli's death was a homicide," Nelson said flatly.

Maris stopped in mid-pour and looked back at Nelson with a groan. "No. You're telling me we're stuck here?" She finished pouring the coffee and handed Nelson a cup. "I don't know if you've noticed, but this isn't exactly the most scenic part of

Wyoming. Hell, it looks like all they grow here is tumbleweeds and cactus."

"There are parts of the county that are quite beautiful. I used to come over here once a season during the rodeo circuit and stumbled across some very nice country. But to answer your question, we're here until we find Lucky and give him the bum's rush off his place." He took off his hat and plopped into a chair. "Tell me you've found the man."

"Not a whisper," Maris answered. "And I've shook every tree in this burg, few though they are."

"There used to be a lot more," Nelson said, "until a tornado came through here in '28 and took a bunch out. But we gotta find Lucky soon, or we'll be forced to hold a foreclosure auction on the steps of the courthouse." He finished his coffee and dabbed at the corner of his mouth with the back of his hand. "Have you checked the bus depot?"

"I did—nothing. Lucky didn't leave town that way, though it looks like he wouldn't have enough money for a bus ticket anyway."

Nelson stood and paced in front of the desk. "What have you found out about Gino?"

"Me and Master Detective DeMyron was fixing to hit the Goings Hotel and the Montgomery to see if Gino rented a room here. I was waiting for DeMyron to come back from that theft call to check them out."

"Cross our fingers we find where he rented a room." Nelson arched his back. The ride all the way from Billings in his panel truck was less than comfortable, and he would relish a night's sleep in his motel room tonight.

He was telling Maris that he had dropped Gino's body off at the funeral home, when the phone rang. "For you," she said and handed Nelson the receiver.

"Gino's brother just called," the funeral director said. "He explained the services he needed and will wire the money via Western Union, so you won't need to *burden* the taxpayers with the burial."

"Bruno Bonelli? Did he say anything else?"

"Just that he planned on attending the funeral."

Nelson hung up. "Gino's brother will be footing the bill for putting him six feet under. Looks like Gino Bonelli will be resting in Mt. Pisgah cemetery for the duration." He grabbed his hat. "Bruno is planning on coming to Gino's funeral, so there's nothing left for me to do right now but go to my room, run hot water in the tub, and soak my aches away."

"You mean after you talk with Natty Barnes."

Nelson stopped halfway to the door, so close to making his escape . . . "What about Natty?"

"I heard from Marley down at the R&R that Natty was seen leaving town with a fancy-dressed feller not more than a week before Gino was found dead. Now where do you think him and Natty Barnes were headed?"

"I'll let you know," Nelson said, "as soon as Natty tells me."

He left the sheriff's office, exhaustion kicking in right before he caught his second wind with that little pearl of information. Why hadn't Natty mentioned that he and Gino had gone for a drive? Did Natty forget? Unlikely that something as unusual as riding in a new Cadillac would be forgotten, so he must have . . . omitted it on purpose. There was always a reason why folks didn't tell lawmen things and Nelson would get to the bottom of it.

As he headed for the panel truck, he thought about the many reasons why Natty didn't mention a ride with Gino. Nelson would later admit he had been distracted, had his guard down when his other problem ambushed him right before he reached his truck. "Marshal Lane," a voice called from the corner of the courthouse.

Nelson turned as a woman with short, strawberry-blond hair ran towards him. She held her hand on top of her cloche hat to prevent it from blowing away while pushing her flapper dress down, its skirt whipping in the wind. Her complexion reminded Nelson of gypsy women he'd known, their olive skin often matching their dark eyes, as this woman's did. Her beauty took his breath away, but just for a brief moment while she dug a stenographer's notebook out of her handbag, and he knew she'd fire questions at him.

He faced her. "Tell me I've just met Miss Jamison Romano."

"You've heard of me," the woman said. She flashed a broad smile through perfect pearlies that would melt the heart of most men. The snow had dampened the rouge on her cheeks, made even redder by the cold temperatures. Her mouth was painted into bee-stung lips that seemed to pout. Sure, he would be a sucker for her. *If* she wasn't a newspaper reporter and *if* Nelson wasn't working a case that he'd as soon not tell the press about. And *if* Nelson wasn't twenty years older than her. She met Nelson's gaze as she flapped her eyelids and smiled. Shivering, looking up at him, she said, "I've waited forever, it seems, for you to come out."

"Did you call my office?"

She chuckled, her teeth clacking, and wrapped her arms around herself against the cold. "I called your office at the courthouse in Buffalo. They said you went to Gillette, but that you never check in with them."

Nelson shrugged. "I'm usually too busy to tell my office where I am . . . I do recall them letting me know a Jamie Romano wanted to talk. Guess I didn't connect the dots until now. What can I do for you?"

She flapped her arms again and her teeth chattered when she said, "I could buy you a cup of coffee someplace warm."

"I really have to go—"

"I'll have to interview you sooner or later. Might as well get it over with."

Nelson looked skyward. "Lord, what have I done to deserve this." He turned to Jamie. "Let's go into the Gillette Café and we'll talk. But I don't let women pay."

"Fair enough," she said and followed Nelson down Gillette Avenue two blocks and into the small café.

They sat at a corner table near a window, the snow that had started an hour ago pelted the glass. After the waitress poured them coffee and left Nelson said, "Jamie, just what do you want me to say that I *can* say?"

"First off, I write under *Jamison.*" She looked around as if someone in the near-empty café could hear her. "Jamie is actually my real name. Jamison sounds . . . more professional. Serious. So I have been using that since I started journalism." She sipped her coffee daintily. "I told you a deep secret. Now you tell me one."

"Such as?"

She leaned forward, her cologne wafting past Nelson's nose. Lavender? "I learned that the victim"—she flipped pages in her notebook—"Gino Bonelli, was trespassing on Mr. Graber's land. Hunting, by the looks of it."

Nelson said nothing as he sipped his coffee.

"Well?"

"Well, what?" he asked.

"Is it true?"

"It is. But it sounds as if you already knew that."

"What I don't know is whether it truly *was* an accidental death—fool hunter crossing a fence with his gun—or whether it was a homicide."

Nelson held his cup and smelled the strong coffee. "No comment."

Jamie wrote in her notebook, saying the words out loud. "U.S.

Marshal Nelson Lane did not say that the victim died accidentally, opening the door to rule it as a homicide."

"I didn't say that."

She stuck her pencil behind her ear. "It's what you *didn't* say that's important."

Nelson knew what she'd implied. Just like he had questioned why Natty held back the fact that he and Gino had taken a ride into the country.

She sipped more coffee, then set her cup down and dabbed at her lips with her napkin. "All I want is something I can take back to my editor," she said, her voice faltering, and she looked away. "He said I haven't been part of the team . . ." She turned back to Nelson. "I've been a reporter in a half a dozen small newspapers across the country. I never lasted long at any." She swiped the napkin across her eyes. "Never had a breakout story. But this"—she rested her hand on Nelson's forearm and squeezed gently—"will be the *one* big scoop that propels me to a big newspaper. If only I had a story worth the while. Marshal Lane, you *have* to tell me something big I can bring back to my editor. I *have* to report something significant before that reporter for the *News Record* does."

Nelson studied Jamie. If she was acting, she'd be right up there with Greta Garbo. But Nelson didn't think she was playing him. He believed her when she said this was the end of the line for her journalism career. But Nelson didn't have anything he wanted the public to know. Unless . . . "Here's something you might run with."

She sat up straighter, her pencil poised over her notebook. "I'm listening."

"The victim—Gino Bonelli—was staying somewhere here in Gillette. For how long, I don't know. Ask your readers to come forward with any information about him." He stood to leave. "I know it's not much, but it's all I can give you right now."

Jamie stood as well, looking up at Nelson. *Did she just bat her eyes?* If not, perhaps Nelson *wished* she had. "You will keep me informed if and when you have something I can release?"

Nelson nodded and buttoned his coat. "Listen, I can't give you much because I don't have much—"

"The autopsy?"

"How did you know about that?"

Jamie winked. "This is a small town. There are very few secrets here. Now the autopsy results . . ."

"All right," Nelson said. "The autopsy showed Gino's death was a homicide. Not an accident. But"—he held up his finger—"that's off the record for the time being. Okay?"

She finally nodded. "Okay. But know this, Marshal, I will print anything I dig up on my own. Using my own sources."

"I can't stop you there," he said. "Just be careful. There's a murderer out here somewhere who won't want to be found out about."

CHAPTER 9

Nelson pulled into the lot of Natty's Feed Store just as Natty emerged carrying a block of mineral cake. Mac McKeen followed with a sack of feed slung over his shoulder. Toby walked beside his father, carrying a heavy sack of feed under each arm as they walked to Mac's Dodge Brothers truck. Natty set the block of cake in the back of the truck and said something to Mac before walking over to Nelson. "You here to talk with me, Marshal?"

Nelson got out, closed the door, and turned his collar up against the driving snow. "Maybe inside we can jaw, unless you want to talk out here."

"I'm all for keeping warm," Natty said and motioned for Nelson to follow.

They walked through the barn with sacks of feed for chickens piled to the ceiling, mineral cake stacked on one side of the room. The pungent odor reminded Nelson of his days as a kid on his father's Walking Chair Ranch years ago before his father lost it to this damned Depression. Before his father ate the barrel of his shotgun in desperation.

Wind whipped through the open end of the feed store, and Nelson spat out a stalk of straw that had gone airborne as he followed Natty into a small office. Chairs were arranged around the centerpiece of the room—a Franklin stove that made for a homey atmosphere.

"How's about some hot chocolate, Marshal?" Natty asked.

"The missus makes it every morning for me to bring to the store for customers."

"Sure. Why not." Nelson unbuttoned his coat and hung his hat on a bentwood coat rack beside the door. "Nasty out there. The Farmer's Almanac says this year's going to have record snows."

"My old dog says so, too." Natty chin-pointed to a three-legged cur curled up in the corner, so quiet and still, Nelson wasn't sure it was alive. "He's never wrong."

"Is that dog—"

"Breathing?" Natty said. "He is."

"And just what does he *do* to predict the weather?"

"You can just look at him and see he's *feeling* what the weather will do."

Nelson said nothing before finally spotting the rising and falling of the dog's chest.

"Marshal, for God's sake, can't you see it? Samson there lying close to the stove means this will be a long, cold winter. In years past when he lay away from the fire, it meant we'd have a mild season."

"And you don't think him lying close to the warm stove means he's just getting old? Seems like every dog I ever had gravitated to the warmth of the fire the older they got."

"Well, I never . . ." Natty grabbed two mugs hanging from hooks on the wall and turned to the pot of hot cocoa warming on the stove. "Look, Sampson is a celebrity of sorts in these parts. Ranchers come from all over to see what my critter says about the weather."

"And the ranchers don't come in here just to warm up?"

"Ah, Marshal, now look at him. You hurt Sampson's feelings."

Nelson looked at the dog from different angles but could not tell if he even raised a paw or an eyelid.

"If he wasn't so popular with folks hereabouts," Natty continued, "I'd have taken him for a ride in the country and given him the lead pill long ago. Poor old thing."

"Speaking about rides in the country, why didn't you tell me you and Gino drove off in Gino Borelli's fancy Caddy, presumably to the country somewhere?"

Natty opened the stove door and tossed in a log. *Stalling.* "When Gino first came to the café, he asked if I knew anyone who could show him around the county. So, I thought what the hay, if he was willing to give me a sawbuck just to drive him around for an afternoon—"

"Still doesn't explain why you didn't tell me. Makes me think you're hiding something."

Natty poured hot cocoa into the mugs and handed Nelson one before he said, "You never mentioned that Gino was dead that time you stopped at the R&R, and Lucky never mentioned a hunter was found dead on his ranch. I didn't think taking Gene . . . Gino, now you say, for a ride was important."

"And I would wager on that little drive in the country, you two went to Lucky's ranch. Drove around out there."

"We did." Natty held up his hand. "But that was days before Gino was found dead. Marshal . . . we drove onto Rick Jones's place as well."

"Did you have permission to be on either man's property?"

Natty waved a hand in the air as if dismissing such a ridiculous question. "If I would have asked Mac—he speaks for Rick Jones, being his hired hand—he would have allowed it. And Lucky . . . we stopped at his place, and he was about halfway ornery. Told us to go ahead and drive into his pasture just as long as we left him be." He shrugged. "He disappeared into the barn, and I figured he had a bum cow he was doctoring or something is why he was so short with me. Never acted like that before though."

Nelson sipped the hot cocoa. And puckered up. He forced himself to swallow what swirled around in his mouth before pulling the cup away and sniffing it.

"Forgot to warn you, Marshal—the missus is a mite . . . frugal. She don't believe in putting sugar in her cocoa. 'Too expensive to waste in these times,' she tells me pert' near every day." He reached onto a shelf behind him and grabbed something, then handed Nelson a small jar of molasses and a spoon. "This'll take the edge off."

Nelson spooned molasses into his cocoa and handed Natty the rest. "What did you and Gene do on your drive in the country, 'cause it sure wasn't seeing the scenic sights that Lucky's ranch had to offer?"

"We just drove around his pasture," Natty said. He scooted the dog closer to the fire, but it never woke from its sleep.

"Just drove around, that's it?"

"That's it. I'd be driving, making sure we didn't get stuck in the snow or some wash-out when Gene—Gino—would say, 'Stop!' He'd get out and wander around. Bend over now and again."

"For what reason?"

Natty stirred his mug and set the jar back on the shelf. "Didn't pay Gino no mind. All's I was thinking was how damn cold it was outside, and I stayed relatively warm in the car."

Nelson thought Natty was hiding something—stalling at best—until he realized the man wasn't that sharp, and that it'd just take some doing to pull information from him. "Did you ever ask yourself why Gino wanted to drive around Lucky's pasture, or just what he did every time he wanted you to stop?"

"Not particularly. He had a canvas satchel slung over his shoulder that he'd grab something from now and again. I just figured whatever he was doing, he was gaining information for his deer hunt."

"You said he'd reach into his bag now and again."

"He would," Natty said. "I got the impression he was putting something in it when"—he snapped his fingers—"I had what they call . . . a moment of clarity . . . what's the word?"

"An epiphany."

Natty snapped his fingers again. "Yeah. An epiphany." He grinned wide. "I just *knew* he was putting deer droppings in. I've heard of hunters checking deer crap to figure out where they'd been, what they been eating. But who was I to know, really—I've never hunted a day in my life. I'd just hate to hurt one of those beautiful animals."

Nelson finished his drink, keeping it in the back of his mind not to accept cocoa at Natty's Feed Store again, and stood. He had started for the door when Natty stopped him. "You best button your coat, Marshal. I know it's just blowing snow, but it will get progressively worse as the weeks wear on. This is going to be a historic winter, I got the *feeling.*"

"Thought you didn't have any *feelings* for the weather."

"I don't," Natty said. "But all's I gotta do is watch ol' Sampson."

Nelson looked down at the dog that had not even twitched the entire time he was talking with Natty. "Watch him do what?"

" 'Member I told you if Sampson lays close to the fire it means a harsh winter?"

"Natty—the dog hasn't moved an inch since I've been here. *You're* the one who moved him closer to the stove."

"Maybe so," Natty said. "But you notice how he didn't move *away* from the warmth." He reached down and patted the dog's gray snout. "No siree—ol' Sampson is better than any weatherman."

Chapter 10

When Nelson left Natty's Feed Store, he found Jamie Romano parked in front in her Model A, blowing warm air over her hands. She stepped out of the car and shoved her hands in her coat pockets as she approached Nelson. "I found where Gino was staying."

"Good," Nelson said. "Where?"

"Not so fast." She motioned for Nelson to sit in her car out of the weather.

After he'd gotten in and shut the car door, she nodded toward the feed store. "I see you've been talking with that blowhard."

"Natty's all right, except he's not the brightest bulb on the tree."

"Did he show you his weather-forecasting mutt?"

"Sampson?" Nelson chuckled. "Natty all but offered to sell me the dog just so's I'd know what the weather was going to be."

"He must have run out of Old Indian Weather Rocks, then."

"How's that?"

"Old Indian Weather Rocks. He claimed he got them from an Arapaho on the Wind River Reservation." She explained that Natty probably made them himself—three sticks forming a miniature teepee seven or eight inches high, with a rock dangling from a string down the center of the teepee. "The instruction that came with it said: 'Set the weather rock outside. If the rock moves on the end of the string, it's blowing. If the rock is white, it's snowing. Wet, it's raining.' Pretty foolproof."

"No, he didn't have any of those lying around. Now let's get back to you telling me where Gino stayed when he was alive."

"Marshal," Jamie batted her lashes, "a little negotiation is in order."

"Let's hear it."

"I'll tell you where he was staying, and you'll allow me to look at whatever you find."

"Can't," Nelson said. "When we look at his belongings—if there's anything left—it could be evidence. Now where—"

She motioned zipping her mouth shut. "Sorry."

"How about I arrest you and haul you before a magistrate for concealing information?"

Jamie chuckled. "I'd just tell the judge I actually know nothing. That I was using a perfectly acceptable journalistic ploy to obtain information."

Nelson knew he could make no charge stick, even if he wanted to. "All right, since we're negotiating . . . you tell me where he was staying, and when I finish looking things over, you can photograph the place, and anything that's left of his belongings."

"That doesn't give me much," Jamie said, "but a photograph of Gino's last haunt might keep public interest alive. And my editor's, too. Okay, I'll tell you. Better yet, I'll show you. Ready?"

"Not quite," Nelson answered. "I have to make a detour to the courthouse and bring my deputy and DeMyron Duggar along. After all, I'm just here officially to foreclose on a rancher and *assist* in the investigation."

"No wonder we didn't find Gino's last apartment," Maris said, shaking her head. "A rooming house." She turned in the seat towards Nelson. "For the record, we checked every motel in town and as far away as Moorcroft."

"Don't beat yourself up over it," Nelson said. "Jamie had an advantage on you—she's lived in this town for over a year and ought to know the odd places." He snickered. "But I detect . . . envy in your voice?"

Maris buttoned her coat and pulled it over the gun resting in her hip holster. "She won this time—"

"It's not a competition," Nelson said. "She just happened to find what we desperately needed—Gino's apartment while he was here in Gillette. Be glad she did."

"All's I'm saying is, you tread lightly around that woman. Or have you forgotten what a nuisance the press can be?"

Nelson hadn't forgotten. It seemed like every time he had a case that he wanted buttoned up to the public, some ambitious reporter would step in and paste it on the front page of their rag. But there was . . . *something* about Jamie that was different. Something that told Nelson she was trustworthy. Or perhaps he felt that way because he was—he hated to admit it to himself—more than a little attracted to the lady.

Nelson and Maris stepped from his truck into the biting wind and joined DeMyron and Jamie on the covered porch that ran the length of the two-story rooming house. The clanging of mechanics working on vehicles next door at Wilhelm's Service Station echoed off the maple trees lining the street that had survived the tornado a few years back.

On either side of the rooming house door, shuttered windows had been closed as if sealing out the rest of the world. Nelson was just wondering what the owner was like, when she flung the door wide. "Are you folks going to freeze your asses off out there or come on inside where it's warm?"

"Inside will be nice," Nelson said, grasping at words to describe the old lady. She barely came up to his chest, her cigarillo dangling from chapped and split lips, her hair frizzled, a bald spot on top uncovered, as if she cared little what the world thought of her.

She looked past Nelson, and one droopy eye narrowed as she glared at DeMyron. "I thought that was you, Deputy Duggar."

DeMyron tipped his hat. "Pleasure to meet again, Mrs. Raney."

"Pleasure, my wrinkled old behind." She turned on her heels and led them past the entryway. "Whyn't you folks go sit in the parlor . . ." She hesitated as she looked around. "There." She pointed. "Still hard to get used to all this space. Sit and I'll bring coffee and biscuits. Oh, and feel free to build a fire."

They walked through open pocket doors into a spacious room, with rag rugs covering nearly the entire floor. Nelson bent to the fireplace and grabbed shredded-bark kindling from a canvas log carrier before tenting cottonwood logs. He grabbed an Ohio Blue Tip from the matchbox on the mantle and lit the kindling, and soon heat from the fire had started attacking the chill in the room.

DeMyron walked to the fireplace and stood with his backside to the flames. "How did you ever manage to even get your foot in the door with old lady Raney?" he asked Jamie.

"I noticed you must have a history with her, too, the way she looked at you," Nelson told him.

"That's an understatement," DeMyron said and turned once again to Jamie. "But just how did you—"

"You just have to be . . . charming," Jamie said and batted her eyes. "Besides, I find Mrs. Raney to be an interesting lady."

"What *is* your history with her?" Nelson asked DeMyron.

DeMyron turned and extended his hands toward the fire. "We were called to the Raney ranch south of town last year. Old man Raney put his .20 gauge in his mouth and all that was left of his head was his chin and part of his nose."

"Ugh!" Jamie said. "I remember covering that. A tragedy."

"It's bound to get nastier," Maris told her. "Unless you can't handle gruesome."

Jamie waved the comment away and sat in an occasional chair next to Nelson.

"Suicide's pretty common with folks losing everything they've worked all their life for," Nelson said.

"I came along to help Sheriff Jarvis after that, though I never seen the geezer in death. But"—DeMyron lowered his voice—"even the sheriff was never certain it *was* suicide. Old man Raney had a healthy life insurance policy. With a suicide clause. That expired exactly one week before he . . . killed himself. The old lady got everything, of course. She sold the ranch for a goodly sum, I heard, and moved into town to this place." He waved his hand around.

Nelson covered the fireplace with a screen. "Lots of ranch folks move into town. Cities love it, as it increases their tax base. Even though it looked suspicious for Mr. Raney to kill himself right after the suicide clause expired, doesn't mean she had anything to do with it."

DeMyron shrugged. "We got several calls to the hospital where the old man had tuned up the missus in the months leading up to his death. I thought every time I responded there that I wouldn't have blamed her if she returned the favor somehow. Most often, she looked like she'd fallen down the stairs a dozen times. And their house had no stairs."

"Sheriff Jarvis is an excellent investigator," Nelson said. "I'm thinking if he cleared her, she ought to be innocent of killing her husband."

"He just couldn't find anything refuting her story," DeMyron said.

Or maybe he just felt empathy for her, much like Nelson felt empathy for Lucky Graber. "We're not here to question her or see if she slips up. She was gracious enough to allow us to look at Gino's room."

Mrs. Raney walked into the parlor, holding a silver serving platter with cups and biscuits. Her cigarillo still dangled from the corner of her mouth. The ash fell into a cup of coffee as she leaned over and set the tray on the coffee table. Maris noticed it, too, as Nelson picked up that cup and handed it to her.

"I bow to local jurisdiction," Maris said and handed the cup to DeMyron, who sipped it, not knowing he was drinking Mrs. Raney's ash.

When the old woman plopped down in a tattered occasional chair in front of the fire, Jamie laid her hand on Mrs. Raney's forearm. "What can you tell us about Gene Bone when he stayed upstairs?"

Mrs. Raney took a biscuit and began sucking on it. "Mr. Bone kept odd hours. I'd often get up in the middle of the night and hear him walking around. *Pacing* might best describe what he often did. But he never had anyone in his room, and he always paid the first of every week. That's why it was sad to hear he had died in that hunting accident." She bit off a corner of her biscuit and leaned close to Jamie. "Odd, it was, him hunting like that. He never wore hunting clothes. I ought to know—I did his laundry while he was here."

"How long did he live here?" Maris asked.

"Three weeks," she answered. "And I don't think he left his room more'n twice that first week." She set the biscuit down and lit another cigarillo. "Now I 'spect you want to see his room."

"If you would," Nelson said.

Mrs. Raney stood on wobbly legs and led them out of the parlor to a staircase. She gripped the mahogany handrail as she ascended the stairs. "Damned arthritis," she said, winded halfway up. "Cain't hardly climb stairs like when I was a younger. Doctor Sayles at the clinic says it's because I smoke too much, but I told him that was horseshit. Told him that if doctors smoked, it had to be okay."

When they reached the second floor, she sucked in another puff and stood panting, catching her breath before handing Jamie the room key. "You take however long you want, missy. I'm going to be downstairs knitting," she said and stumbled back down the staircase.

Jamie stepped toward the room, but Nelson stopped her. "The key," he said as he held out his hand.

Jamie hesitated. "If I hadn't found where Gino Bonelli was staying, we wouldn't be here."

"We wouldn't," Nelson said. "But we had an agreement, did we not?"

After a long moment, Jamie handed Nelson the room key. "Remember, after you're finished . . ."

Nelson nodded and inserted the key into the lock. He pushed the door open, led DeMyron and Maris into the room, and held up his hand to stop them from going farther.

"What was that about an agreement?" Maris asked.

"I promised to let her take pictures of whatever's left in the room after we gather what evidence we can. It was the easiest way to get her off our backs. Now tell me what you see in here?"

Maris walked to an efficiency desk and flicked on the small light. Eight books sat lined up on the desk, held together by rocks that served as bookends. She picked up one of the volumes, then scanned the titles of the rest. "All these books are about the mining industry. Which is not surprising, since Gino was a mining engineer."

"How about you, DeMyron? See anything that jumps out at you?"

The big deputy crossed his arms and rubbed his chin as he looked about. He walked to a chest of drawers with several maps stacked against it and thumbed through the pile. "I'd say Gino was interested in the area. All these maps are of Campbell

County." He picked up the top map and walked to the small cot in the opposite corner of the room. He unrolled the map on the cot and said, "Look here, Marshal."

Nelson and Maris looked over DeMyron's shoulder as he tapped the map. "Gino circled this area . . ." He turned to Maris. "Could you hand me the others?"

Maris grabbed the stack of maps and handed them to DeMyron. Soon, all the maps were spread out on the cot in the corner of the tiny room. "Gino circled Lucky's Ranch on each of these."

Nelson picked up one of the maps and turned to the window. He opened the shades and donned his reading glasses. "He's got Lucky's place circled, all right. But that doesn't pin anything down as to where he was interested in exactly."

"With Lucky's ranch being a section—a square mile—we might never know where he wanted to look," DeMyron said.

"Or why," Maris added.

Nelson bent and adjusted the steam register. Soon, it emitted warm heat, and he unbuttoned his coat. "I'm tempted to bite the bullet and take Natty with me to show me exactly where Gino wanted him to stop." He arched his back and stretched. "But that's a last resort, having that bullshitter riding with me all day. Unless one of you wanted to volunteer."

Maris shot DeMyron a *hell no* glance and turned to look at whatever else of interest Gino might have left. "He sure didn't plan on leaving anytime soon," DeMyron said, as he rifled through the dresser drawers. "Got all his undershirts and underwear neatly stacked in here. Socks, too."

"If nothing else," Maris said, "he was neat. Has all his letters and other items in their own bin . . . hello! What's this?" She held a slip of paper in her hand as she walked to the window for the light. "Here's a receipt from the post office. Gino mailed a certified letter the day before he was murdered."

"Does it say where or to whom it was mailed?" Nelson asked.

She shook her head. "Smudged. Can't read it."

Nelson took the receipt from her and pocketed it. "I'll drop by the post office tomorrow and find out about the letter."

They continued until early evening, sorting through Gino's papers and documents, looking for any odd notations he might have made in his mining books to indicate what he was looking for on Lucky's ranch. They had placed what they needed in paper sacks and opened the door. Nelson was surprised to see Jamie still sitting on a chair in the hallway, waiting, her camera on the floor beside her.

"Took you long enough. I thought you three had taken up residence in there. Did you leave anything for me to photograph?"

"There wasn't even much for *us* to glean," Nelson said as he held up four paper bags containing the maps and letters Gino had left behind the day he ventured out to Lucky's ranch alone. *If he* was *alone*. "You're free to take your photos now." Nelson handed the sacks to DeMyron. "Stick these in your evidence locker, and we'll look at them tomorrow."

Jamie stepped aside to allow DeMyron and Maris past her and down the stairs before peeking into the room. She dug into her shoulder bag and stuck a flash on her camera. "Looks like it'll only take me a minute to get the photos I want. Then I'll be hungry."

"I'm a bit gaunt myself," Nelson said. "Might see what the R&R has for tonight's special—"

"Marshal," Jamie interrupted, "didn't you hear what I just said?"

Nelson paused. "I heard everything you said. You're going to snap some photos, and you're hungry . . . aha. Now I see what you're saying—because we're both hungry—"

"Because we're both hungry, we could go somewhere for supper. *Together.* With the government paying. You do get reimbursed, do you not?"

"I don't understand—"

"Are you really that dense not to know when a woman is inviting you to dinner?"

Nelson felt his neck warming and worried that Jamie would see him blush. "Of course. I will take my deputy back to the courthouse and meet you . . . at the R&R?"

Jamie shook her head. "Marshal, I think I can come up with a nicer place to eat than that railroad café."

CHAPTER 11

Nelson sat upright in his chair, looking out the window of the Sage Café and watching a Studebaker sedan skid and nearly hit a parked Oldsmobile. He felt uncomfortable. Felt as if this were a date; something he had not been on for as long as he could remember.

"Don't you think, Marshal?"

"What's that?"

"I said, don't you think the roast venison would be nice?"

Nelson turned back and picked up the menu again before closing it and handing it to the waitress. "Yes. I'll order the venison."

After the waitress left, Jamie took off her hat. "This has been a long day, but at least we've come across some information about Gino Bonelli."

When Nelson didn't take the bait, Jamie leaned back and crossed her arms. "Marshal, this information sharing is two-way—"

"Who says we're sharing information?" He rested his arms on the table. "I would like to tell you more, but if some of the information were leaked to the public, I am afraid our killer would go to ground. But believe me, when I have information I think you can use, I will tell you."

Jamie guffawed. "Sure. Like the last time."

"How's that?"

"The last cop told me the same thing." She sipped her water

and Nelson waited silently for her to explain. "I was a cub reporter for the *Star-Eagle* in Newark when the Lindbergh baby was kidnapped last spring. I got wind of it and hustled out to East Armwell. The first cop on the scene—a Sergeant Masters, if I recall—assured me of the same thing you just did. Said he would keep me posted." She laughed nervously. "The long and short of it is, he never called me with anything I could print, so I got to digging. It was *me* who brought the editor the information that the ransom note was written illegibly . . . like some foreigner scribbled it. And you know what happened? The editor passed the information to *another* reporter—his pet reporter—and *he* got the credit while I got reassigned to cover the fashion scene in Newark. That, Marshal, is when I told the editor what he could do with his fashion section and scouted around for another newspaper."

"That's how you ended up here in Gillette, Wyoming?"

She nodded. "I decided to live the adventure and see the West. The *Gillette Daily Journal* had need of a reporter. 'We need someone who is hungry,' the editor told me when I applied for the job. 'Someone who will dig and dig and scoop the *News Record.*' That's why it's so important for me to come up with information the readers will like and will crave more of. So"—Jamie leaned on the table, her arms brushing Nelson's—"what else can you tell me that I can print?"

Nelson leaned back, waiting until the waitress refilled their coffee cups before saying, "I can tell you that Roosevelt will most likely beat Hoover in the election next month, or that Amelia Earhart will solo across the Pacific after her trans-Atlantic flight this spring. That help?"

"Dammit!" Jamie said, then clapped a hand to her mouth. She looked around to see if anyone had heard, but patrons sitting at nearby tables ignored her. "I need something substantial. And I have information to trade."

"Such as?"

"Oh, no. I'm not tipping my hand. But it's . . . substantial, shall we say."

He did his best to read her face, but she gave nothing away. Which was pretty much what they still had, even after searching through Gino's possessions. Though he'd never trusted the press farther than he could fling the nearest reporter, he needed all the info he could get right about now. "All right, then, here's what we found in Gino's room . . . maps of Campbell County. He'd circled areas within Lucky Graber's ranch."

"What did you make of that?"

"I'm speculating—but not sure enough that you should print it—that Gino had a geological interest in Lucky's land."

"Geological, as in some type of precious metal underground? Like gold or something? Maybe coal?"

Nelson stirred a lump of sugar into his coffee cup, thinking back to Natty's bitter-assed cocoa. "Coal is a possibility, though the nearest coal seam to Lucky's place is four miles away next to the Rawhide Ranch. Gino worked as an engineer in a silver mine in Nevada, so that's a possibility also. The other is that he thought trona was prevalent this far north."

"Trona? What's that?"

"A mineral that's refined into soda ash used in laundry detergents. Paper. Baking soda."

"That doesn't sound very lucrative," Jamie said.

"Folks down Green River way think it is. They ran some ground tests and figure there's enough underground to make money. Plan to open mining operations in another two or three years. Perhaps Gino had the same thoughts."

The waitress brought their venison on a platter along with mashed potatoes and green beans. Nelson sliced off a piece of meat and let it percolate in his mouth for moments before swallowing. "Haven't had deer cooked like this in ages. Excellent."

He put his fork down and wiped juice off his mouth. "Now your turn—what piece of information do you have that we don't?"

Jamie took another forkful of potatoes and ate it. "I know Gino Bonelli."

"You *know* him! Where did you meet him—"

"I don't actually know him personally," Jamie clarified. "I know *of* him. Or rather, I know about his brother, Bruno Bonelli, from working at the rag in Newark." She lowered her voice as she glanced around the café. "Brother Bruno got mixed up in that Castellammarese War in New York two years ago between Joe 'The Boss' Masseria and Brooklyn's Salvatore Maranzano. Rumor has it Bruno was one of the triggermen who capped Masseria in that Coney Island restaurant. And Bruno's reward was control of trucking in and around New Jersey."

"Don't tell me—brother Gino was up to his eyeballs in Bruno's business?"

"Just the opposite," Jamie said. "When I was at the *Newark Star-Eagle,* I interviewed one of Maranzano's soldiers off the record. He was adamant that Bruno and Gino were polar opposites, and that was a sore spot for Bruno. He so wanted his brother to come into the business, but Gino reviled that dark side of the Bonelli family. Ergo, he left New Jersey and changed his name. No wonder Bruno couldn't locate him." She picked up her fork again and eyed the green beans. "So maybe one of Masseria's former soldiers or lieutenants murdered Gino."

"Why didn't you share this before?" Nelson asked, perturbed.

Jamie smiled and winked. "Because it was my trading information. And I just might have more to swap."

Chapter 12

Standing by the service window at the Post Office, Nelson wanted to knock the postmaster on his keister. Or rather, the *acting* postmaster. The real one was at home nursing a broken femur after his horse had thrown him. Besides looking—and being—as sarcastic as James Cagney in *Public Enemy,* the man's attitude spoke volumes about his self-importance. With the little-man syndrome many bullies possessed, he clearly enjoyed pushing his slight weight around when Nelson asked about the certified letter Gino Bonelli had mailed before his death. "I'll need that request on an official form," the man said. Even his name—*Smitty*—shouted *knock me on my butt.* He nodded toward a counter with pens chained to it. Even in this Depression, Nelson couldn't image anyone stealing nickel pens. "Fill it out."

When Nelson finished filling out the request from, he motioned Smitty to the counter again and handed the form to him, along with the receipt they'd found in Gino's room.

Smitty glanced at it and tossed it on the counter in front of him. "I can't process this," he said flatly.

Nelson kept his temper with difficulty. "Why not? I filled out the form—"

"Mister, mister," Smitty said, rolling his eyes. "You requested to know where Gino Bonelli sent this certified letter. Yet the receipt has the name Gene Bone."

"Mister Bonelli was using the name *Gene Bone* in his professional life."

"Then," Smitty said as he tore up the request and pointed to the stack of forms again, "the form must reflect that."

Nelson had already spent twenty minutes filling out the necessary request, and he damn sure didn't feel like wasting another twenty minutes. *Calm down, Nels,* he told himself. *You are no longer a violent person since Maris taught you meditation the Cheyenne way.* He reminded himself that he was no longer the Marine who came back from the Great War busted up and barely mending, with his hearing gone from one ear and the sight gone from an eye, wanting to rend the whole world asunder. He was a different man now. As long as he remained calm, perhaps he wouldn't revert to old Nelson who drowned his troubles in a bottle.

When he'd finished with the new form, he got in line behind two ladies collecting their mail. "Here is the corrected request form," Nelson said when it was his turn in line.

Smitty looked over his half-glasses at the form and then placed it in a metal bin. "We will contact you when this is authorized."

"What you mean, when it's authorized?"

Smitty tapped his head. "Are you deaf? This form needs to go up the chain. If the information is releasable, it will come back to me—the acting postmaster—to decide if I should allow it."

Nelson rubbed his temples against a rising headache. In the old days, pounding on someone or something usually made the ache go away. He took deep, calming breaths until he regained his composure and said, "How long does that process take?"

Smitty shrugged. "Two, perhaps three weeks until it comes back here to Gillette. Then whenever I can find the time, I will review it."

"But I need the information now."

"Mister," Smitty winked, "people in hell need ice water."

Nelson felt his face flush again, his fists clenching and unclenching, the veins in his forehead throbbing. Smitty turned his back and fidgeted with something in bins behind him.

"Smitty," Nelson said.

"Yes," the man replied over his shoulder.

"That ice water . . . can be used to reduce the swelling around the facial area when one's ugly face is beaten raw."

Smitty turned to face Nelson but wisely stayed just out of reach. "Are you threatening me?"

"Little man," Nelson said, "I don't know what your problem is, but I intend walking out of here with the information I requested. This moment!"

"But I can't . . . can't," Smitty sputtered as he craned his neck to look up at Nelson. "I have to have it authorized—"

"I believe that in the spirit of inter-agency cooperation you should make an exception." Nelson pulled his coat aside to show his badge.

Smitty paled and backed away. "Even with that . . . I can't . . . can't give you that information. Even if the man is dead."

"You recall," Nelson said, "just over a year ago Al Capone went up the river for income tax evasion?"

Smitty nodded.

"I have friends in the tax section at the Treasury Department. If I mention that a certain *acting postmaster* needs to be audited for the last . . . say, five years, they will do so." Nelson leaned over the counter. "With your government job, I suspect you're in a little higher tax bracket."

Smitty nodded.

"Now, Smitty, my friend, is this something you want?"

Nelson had just walked out of the post office with the information in hand when Maris's car skidded to a stop at the curb. She stuck her head out the window and said, "I think you'd better come have a look-see."

"Tell me you found Lucky Graber."

"No, and I looked. What you need to see is Gino Bonelli's brother coming into town."

"And that calls for you driving like a crazy person?"

"It does when you see brother Bruno and his entourage. They're driving in from Denver."

"Where'd you get that information?"

"From your new bestest girl—Jamie Romano. She dropped by the courthouse looking for you and said she'd received word that Bruno and company are headed from Denver on Highway 59."

"Does he need an entourage?"

"Apparently," Maris said. "But we best hurry."

Nelson hopped into his panel truck and mashed into first gear trying to keep up with Maris as they drove towards the south end of town. They turned onto Highway 59, the only road that someone coming in from Denver could take into Gillette, and Maris pulled her car beside DeMyron's, already parked beside the road awaiting the festivities. The deputy sat on the hood of the sheriff's truck, smoking a cigarette, while he cupped a mug of coffee in his other hand. Beside him, Jamie adjusted her camera on the tripod and aimed it at the roadway. She smiled when Nelson climbed out of his truck and turned away as if nothing had happened last night. And nothing had, Nelson reasoned, except for a *light* goodnight peck on his cheek after supper.

People were standing outside their cars on the far side of the roadway, braving the cold, and dust kicked up by more vehicles approaching told Nelson this might be a community event. Whatever the hell was going on. "Tell me this is more than just Gino's brother coming into town," he said to Maris.

"It is." She nodded at Jamie, who was making adjustments to

her camera. "If you can believe her sources, that is."

Nelson walked over to Jamie. "Maybe I can drag you away for just a moment."

She looked up, twirling her hair under her knit cloche hat. "Better be quick. I don't want to miss this shot."

"What have you heard about Gino's brother," Nelson asked, "that makes some sense out of this"—he gestured at the assembled cars and people—"circus?"

"All I know is that Bruno Bonelli and some friends flew into Denver last night. And get this—they *bought* three new Lincolns for the drive up here."

Nelson whistled. "That ought to have set Bruno back a pretty penny."

"My source in Denver said Bruno shelled out nearly four thousand dollars for the cars. *Apiece.*"

"Get outta here," Nelson said. That explained the crowd. Clearly, the rumor mill was working with its usual efficiency, and folks wanted an eyeful of the rich outsiders who were probably gangsters in their fancy new roadsters. Gillette was more at home with farm trucks and tractors than new and exotic motor vehicles. Seeing new cars pass would be like watching a circus parade for many folks hereabouts. "I didn't realize running garbage trucks in Jersey was such a lucrative business."

"It is when you control the garbage all along the upper East Coast." She motioned to the south where approaching cars kicked up a plume of dust and snow. "We'll know just how wealthy Bruno is in a moment."

The first forest green Lincoln rounded the last bend in the road into Gillette, driving far faster than the forty-mile-an-hour speed limit. By the time the parade of Lincolns rolled up, thirty cars packed with gawkers had lined either side of the road eager to watch them pass.

Nelson shook out a Chesterfield and lit it as the first car

drove by. Two men sat in the front seat, their heads swiveling as they looked at everybody and everything.

The next car was driven by a man sporting a misshapen jaw, and a nose that looked as if it had been beaten flat on his face with a hammer. One eye looked askew as he—like those in the front vehicle—scanned both sides of the road while he motored past. The man's appearance screamed *bodyguard.* Did Bruno Bonelli *need* a bodyguard while he was here? Nelson doubted it, yet he knew the ways of the big city were so different than out here where deer and antelope far outnumbered people. As that car drove by, a man in the back seat looked in Nelson's direction and tipped his hat as if he could tell the top lawman among those watching on the side of the road.

Only one man rode in the trailing car as the parade made its way into town. Like the other two drivers, he watched the spectators on the sides of the road as he passed.

" 'Spect I'll follow them," DeMyron said. "My guess is those cars are driving straight to the sheriff's office to find out about Gino."

"I best go with him," Maris said. "By the looks of a couple of them, things might get nasty."

"No," Nelson said to Maris. "I'll go. I want you to find Lucky. Andy Olssen at Stockman's Bank in Billings is sure to file a formal complaint against us . . . me, if we don't serve the foreclosure papers. Andy thinks we're avoiding serving Lucky."

"But you are," Maris said.

Nelson climbed in behind the wheel of his panel truck. "I did that only to give the man a few more days to clear out his things." He called to DeMyron, "I'll follow you to your office."

They headed north on 59, the snow churned up by the big touring cars making it easy to see just where the Lincolns were headed. DeMyron was right—they pulled to the curb in front of the courthouse moments before Nelson and DeMyron arrived.

Two men who could have been brothers by their size and swarthy appearance climbed out of their car and looked around a moment, before the man with the jaw that didn't heal right and the flattened nose stepped out. He looked around the parking lot as well, then opened the back door for another passenger. This man could have posed on a fashion runway Nelson thought when the fellow stepped out. He smoothed his double-breasted gray herringbone suit and adjusted a red tie with a large Windsor knot. He donned a black fedora and slipped a Chesterfield topcoat on, the black felt collar contrasting with the gray of the fabric. He looked at DeMyron and Nelson standing beside the sheriff's truck with an expression neither hostile nor friendly that seemed to look through Nelson as the man approached.

"I take it you are Bruno Bonelli?" Nelson asked.

The fashion plate nodded, while the man with the scars stood mere feet away concentrating on Nelson as if the marshal were a threat. But Bruno looked as if he needed no bodyguard. With his stocky frame and one cheek that looked like it had swollen at one time and never went down, he gave Nelson the impression he would be a handful all by his lonesome. "I am Bruno Bonelli. Are you the law here?"

"*I* am," DeMyron said as he stepped close to Bruno. The bodyguard shifted his attention to the deputy. "My sheriff is away on family business, so I am in charge."

Nelson noticed the two bruisers from the front car had positioned themselves so they could watch the entire parking lot. The bulges in their coats suggested pistols in shoulder rigs, all of which made Nelson jittery. "Mr. Bonelli," Nelson said, "tell your . . . associates they are making me nervous. I'd like them to come up front here where I can keep an eye on them."

"And just who are you?" Bruno asked, a faint Italian accent coming through.

Nelson pulled his coat aside and tapped his badge. "I am the U.S. marshal for the state of Wyoming."

"Marshal," Bruno said, "my brother's death is a federal matter?"

"I was on this side of the state on other business when his death occurred, and I'm just helping Deputy Duggar. Now, about your men . . ."

Bruno cracked a smile. "Are you expecting us to cause you trouble?"

"Are you seeking trouble?" Nelson said. " 'Cause the way they're spread out, they're expecting *something* to happen."

Bruno twirled his hand over his head, and the two outriders approached. "These are good boys, Marshal," he said and tapped the nearest one on the shoulder. "Angelo here—we call him Angel because he is so nice—has been with my . . . firm for two years. About the same time as Lazarro here came on board." Both men stood slightly shorter than Nelson, and he figured he outweighed them both by thirty pounds, though the scars on their knuckles told him a few pounds wouldn't make any difference if they chose to pounce. As they stood flanking their boss, they exuded an air of efficiency. If thugs can be efficient. "Lazy here—don't ask how he got his name, there's not a lazy bone in his body—is a good boy."

Nelson couldn't help but wonder what arsenal they packed under their coats. "And that other feller slinking by the car," he said and motioned to another man beside the last Lincoln.

"Sal," Bruno called out. "Come on over, and we'll introduce you to these fine local lawmen."

A dandy sauntered over—hatless, his black hair pasted down with brilliantine and parted in the middle—putting his comb in his pocket as he neared. Not nearly as tall as the others, his lithe frame reminded Nelson of an Olympic runner. Athletic. He'd remember that.

The man smiled wide as if to show off four glistening gold teeth as he thrust out his hand. "Just call me Sal—Salvatore is my Christian name." He crossed himself. "By the way, is there a dance hall here, because I feel like cutting a rug?"

"We have a billiard hall and bowling alley," DeMyron said. "McAnany's. Just down the block."

"We're not here for entertainment!" Bruno said, and Sal slunk back several paces.

Bruno stepped around Nelson and said to DeMyron, "We're here to learn about my brother's death."

"Perhaps it would be better if we could talk inside my office," DeMyron said, "out of the cold."

"And just where *is* your office? I was told this is the address."

"Upstairs." DeMyron nodded toward the courthouse.

Bruno smirked. "How quaint to have the sheriff's office in an old . . . farmhouse."

"It's the old Daly mansion," DeMyron spit out, immediately taking offense at Bruno's condescending tone. "The family donated it to the county out of the goodness of their hearts. We hicks do that now and again—help one another out."

"Of course," Bruno said and turned to his men. "You three stay here and look after the cars while Gavin and me talk with the lawmen inside."

"You think you need another man along?" Nelson asked as he motioned to the scarred man staying close to Bruno.

Bruno seemed to ponder that. "Gavin Corrigan here is like my . . . sounding board, and he looks after me. Follows me around like a stray puppy, don't you?"

Gavin nodded but said nothing.

"He likes to be close, not that anything could ever happen here in this town." Bruno waved his hand around, then spoke to Gavin. "I'll be all right with the marshal and Deputy Duggar. Wait here by the car."

Unlike with the other three men, Nelson could not detect an imprint of a gun on Gavin. Either he wasn't packing heat, or he was very good at concealing it. Or, Nelson suspected, the man didn't need a weapon.

They were starting toward the courthouse when Maris pulled to a stop next to Nelson's truck and climbed out of her car. Bruno's men—with the exception of Gavin Corrigan—stared at her as she approached the courthouse.

"Why don't you stay out here," Nelson said. "Watch the horses, so to speak."

"Marshal," Bruno said, "is this lovely creature *actually* a law officer?"

"She is."

"Fascinating," Bruno breathed. "I have heard of women being policemen but never met one who . . . made arrests. She does make arrests, no?"

"She does," Nelson answered. "And cracks heads now and again, though her sweet and unassuming nature makes it a chore for her to do so. The sheriff's office?"

DeMyron led them into the courthouse and upstairs. Bonnie Matchuk looked up from her desk as they entered and put down her issue of *True Confessions* to eyeball Bruno. She flashed a smile that the Italian ignored as he followed Nelson into the sheriff's inner office.

As Nelson closed the door, Bruno took off his topcoat and hung it and his hat on the bentwood coat rack before sitting in one of the chairs situated around the sheriff's desk. "Mind?" he said, producing a silver cigarette case from his inside pocket. "Doctors tell me this is probably not good for one's body." He chuckled. "But what do they know?"

He shook out a cigarette and offered one to Nelson, who waved it away. "Don't smoke too often?"

"Now and again I do," Nelson answered.

DeMyron had seated himself behind his desk. He leaned over with his hand outstretched. "I do, but I'm not sure I can handle those."

Bruno laughed. "Then by all means, you need to . . . expand your horizons. These are French *Gauloises,* the mildest Turkish tobacco you will ever smoke. Please, Deputy. And Marshal . . ."

Nelson finally took one, and Bruno handed DeMyron the case.

Bruno lit up for them all and spent a moment watching smoke rings filter toward the high ceiling. "Now, Deputy, I expect some answers. All I knew when the policeman came to my door in Newark was that Gino died in a hunting accident."

DeMyron rested his elbows on the desktop and tented his fingers together. "Everything pointed to Gene—"

"You mean Gino."

"He was going by the name Gene Bone."

"As apparently he has for years," Bruno said. "Gino didn't want to become involved in the family business. Even when I offered to give him a full ride to Cornell, he turned me down and went on his own dime to New York City College." He shook his head. "I think he was a little angry at me for running interference for him during the Great War."

"How's that?" DeMyron asked.

"Gino tried to enlist. Tried to get over to France to fight, but he is . . . was . . . my only brother. I could not let him go to war and risk dying."

"So, you stifled him?" Nelson said. "And he pushed back."

Bruno flicked his ash into an ash tray in the shape of a tiny tire atop DeMyron's desk. "He'd changed his name by the time he graduated college, though I did not know what it was until a few days ago. All I knew was that he came out here somewhere for post-graduate study." He turned his head, grabbed a silk handkerchief sticking out of one cuff, and dabbed at his eyes before turning back. "After that, I lost track of him, even though I had . . . contacts looking for him."

DeMyron explained that Gino was living and working in Tonopah, Nevada, before coming to Gillette three weeks ago. "He worked for some silver mine that seems like it was going under."

"That doesn't surprise me," Bruno said. "But tell me about this hunting accident that killed him."

DeMyron explained how Gino was found frozen, one leg draped over a pasture fence, his gun apparently discharged lying on the ground beside him.

"Gino never hunted," Bruno said flatly. "He couldn't bring himself to kill a creature as beautiful as a deer." Bruno dabbed at his eyes again. "The kid was never . . . like me. In many ways he was *soft.* But I guess that was his charm."

"And compassionate?" Nelson added. "Human, if he could not force himself to kill an animal. When I served in France during the Great War, there were men—brave men—conscientious objectors. Men who would not take up arms against others but who served in some of the more dangerous roles as couriers. Men who went behind enemy lines to reconnoiter." Nelson put his hand on Bruno's shoulder. "There's nothing to indicate that Gino was soft in any way."

"Thank you for that," Bruno said. He swiped his handkerchief across his eyes once more before he sat up straight and spoke to DeMyron. "Tell me what *really* happened to my brother."

DeMyron looked at Nelson, who said, "Gino was murdered. I took his body to the medical examiner in Billings. Gene . . . Gino was shot with a .30 caliber rifle of some model."

"What do you mean 'of some model'?"

"Gino's gun, a Remington .30—"

"Autoloader," Bruno said. "I gave it to him on graduating college. Figured he might need some protection if anyone connected him to me. How do you know it wasn't his gun that killed him?"

Nelson walked to the rack of Winchester lever action rifles in a gun holder screwed to the wall and took one down. He jacked the lever and caught the cartridge case before it fell to the floor. "This .30 caliber round has a lead bullet. Pretty soft. So soft that it would get deformed if shot in Gino's autoloader. Those Remington autos prefer a hard-jacketed bullet for functioning." He thumbed the round back into the rifle and replaced it on the rack. "If a man shot a soft lead round in that auto, it might malfunction."

"So, you're basing your homicide ruling on that?"

"That and the spent cartridge case." Nelson sat across from Bruno as he explained. "Deputy Duggar here found a spent case in the snow right beside Gino. Too close. The case was tossed at Gino's *feet* so it would be discovered easily. But I can tell you that a hard-kicking rifle like that throws the cartridges several yards away. Whoever killed Gino knew little about guns."

Bruno sat silent for a moment before saying, "I believe you when you said he was murdered. But why?"

"We don't know why," Nelson said. "We do know that he went to a local rancher's place days before his death—"

"For what reason?"

Nelson shrugged. "We don't know that either, positively."

Bruno moved to the edge of his chair. "Then what *do* you know? Do you even have any suspects?"

"None," DeMyron said. "And we've beat the pavements looking for anyone who might know something."

Bruno stood. He walked to the stove in one corner and rubbed his hands together close to the heat. "Surely there had to be something in his car that might help . . . I know the kid would have had a car. Gino was afraid of flying and drove wherever he went."

"His Cadillac hasn't been found," Nelson said.

Bruno threw up his hands. "There you have it. Gino was killed for his fancy car. You find that and you find his killer."

Nelson stood and walked to the window. A light snow had begun and, for a change, without the accompanying wind. A lull? He faced Bruno. "I do not think Gino was killed for his car. If that happened, the killer wouldn't stick around and take the time to stage the scene."

Bruno put on his hat and coat and turned down the collar. "Here's what *I* know, Marshal. I know that I have men at my disposal who can be very . . . persuasive in talking with people who know something but choose not to say. They have their own special way of eliciting information."

DeMyron slammed his hand down on the desk. "I'll be damned if you're going to run roughshod over folks in my county!"

The door burst open. Lazy Stefano ran into the room and over to Bruno's side. The bodyguard, Gavin, followed him. In their wake, Bonnie said, "I couldn't stop them—"

"That's okay," Nelson said.

"I thought something happened," Lazy said. "Gavin said he'd handle things, but I got worried, Boss—"

Gavin leaned against the wall, cunning eyes looking over the scene but apparently not particularly worried.

DeMyron stepped around the desk and grabbed Lazy's arm. He jerked away and stepped back into a boxer's stance.

Bruno stopped him. "Stand down."

Lazy relaxed. Bruno said to DeMyron, "Were I you, I'd not grab his arm again. Or grab any of my men."

"Then tell them not to butt in where they're not wanted."

Bruno took Lazy by the elbow and turned him toward the door. "Marshal—and Deputy—as I stand here in your office, know that I *will* find out who killed my brother. That is my word that you have." He led Lazy out of the office. Gavin gave the room a last keen-eyed glance, then left as well.

Nelson shook out a cigarette—a good old Chesterfield—and passed the pack to DeMyron. They lit up, Nelson feeling his heart return to normal, for he had recognized the danger Bruno and his men posed. "I'd tread lightly around those people. At least three are packing guns in shoulder rigs."

"They can't be any more dangerous than a five-hundred-pound steer at any given rodeo I've been in."

"Think again," Nelson said. "Cattle can't shoot at you."

Chapter 13

Nelson woke the following morning to four inches of fresh powder covering his panel truck parked outside his rented cabin. Just what he needed after yesterday's long drive. After keeping an eye on Bruno Bonelli and his thugs to see where they were staying, Nelson had driven into the country once again, shaking the trees, hoping Lucky Graber would fall out. But he never did, and everyone Nelson talked with knew nothing. Or they knew but did not trust a federal marshal. Nelson was getting desperate. He needed to find Lucky and serve him. Andy Olssen had called twice yesterday, but Bonnie Matchuk had deflected him, the secretary insisting that Marshal Lane was tied up. "Nonfeasance is what it is!" Andy had shouted right before he hung up on Bonnie. It was just a matter of time before Andy contacted the U.S. attorney to file an official complaint.

Nelson stepped around back of the line of cabins to the two-holer and shut the door. As frigid as it was, he was grateful that the owner of the motor lodge had lined the wooden seat with sheepskin and had a Sears and Roebuck catalogue for patrons to use rather than softened corncobs.

After tending to his morning business, Nelson left and walked to his bungalow, where he grabbed the broom from inside to clear the snow off the panel truck's windows. He headed to his truck, then halted. Someone had walked up to the truck within the last hour, if he was guessing the age of the tracks correctly. Maris? She was staying in the cabin next to Nelson's, but he hadn't heard her come in last night.

He walked to her truck parked in front of her own cabin but saw no boot prints. *She had not approached his truck.* He thought a moment—but only a moment—about waking her and asking for certain if she'd gone to his truck for some reason, then reconsidered. He'd just as soon face all of Bruno's men in a wild donnybrook than have to grab a whip and a chair and wake Maris up when she didn't want to be woken up. Especially if she'd found a man to bring home last night to keep her warm.

He turned his collar up as he broomed the snow off his windshield. The driver's-side window was mostly clear, which bothered him. Had the wind blown the powder away, or had the few remaining snow smears been left by someone's gloved hand? He shook his head and climbed into an icy cold driver's seat. He pulled the choke out all the way and inserted the key in the ignition, then paused. Why *had* someone approached his truck?

He stepped out and looked around at the other seven cabins all in a row. Cars were parked in front of the cabins at the far end, and the middle ones were empty this time of year. No sign that anyone from those cabins had walked to his panel truck. He felt almost foolish when he lay on the ground for a look underneath, thinking he'd seen too many movies and read too many stories about gangsters planting bombs in the vehicles of their enemies.

Nothing. No bombs planted, nothing to indicate the truck had been tampered with. He got to his feet and stood there, not moving. Someone *had* walked right next to his truck, and that gave Nelson an uncommonly odd feeling as he looked around again before climbing back into the panel. He hit the starter, and the big V-8 engine grudgingly coughed to life. He pushed the choke in ever so slightly until the motor hummed smooth, and then he sat for a moment warming his hands with his breath.

Nelson had left orders with Maris yesterday to bang on his door if she came across Lucky, so he could only assume she hadn't. Would Lucky be foolish enough to drop by the R&R for a quick game of cards? Nelson hoped so, and he headed to the café.

He didn't see Lucky's Model T as he turned the corner, but that didn't mean the rancher wasn't inside, sitting across from Natty Barnes with a winning hand. He could've parked a ways away just in case Nelson or Maris came around to serve him his papers.

Nelson parked a few doors down from the R&R and walked into the café. Natty sat at the head of a table, sipping coffee across from Mac McKeen. Toby stood slack-jawed and looking lost behind his father.

But it was Andy Olssen who caught Nelson's attention. The Billings banker looked out of place seated in a chair undersized for his frame, ditching his suit for denims and a cord parka. He spotted Nelson, and his jaw muscles worked overtime. He bent and said something to Natty, who said to Mac, "You and the boy better get back to Rick's ranch or he'll fire both your asses."

"I don't have to be back for a while—"

"Then take your damn kid up to Wilhelm's Tire Station," Natty said. "They ought to have more wheel weights saved for him by now."

"But I don't want to go to the service station," Toby said. "Andy just paid me, and I want to go and buy a Snickers—"

"I don't care what you want." Mac glanced nervously at Nelson and downed the last of his coffee. "Natty's right—we best not let Rick think we're sluffing off. We'll stop and get those wheel weights, and on the way out of town we'll drop by Pines Grocery to buy your candy bar."

Toby glared at Nelson in passing, as if the marshal were the cause of leaving a warm café early and stomped outside after his father.

"I was just about to hunt you up, Marshal," Andy said. "Have you served Lucky Graber yet?"

"I didn't come in here to talk with you, but if you give Natty and me a few moments private like, I'll answer any questions you have."

Andy wiggled out of his chair. "I'll be in the pie room. You *will* let me know when you're finished?"

"Of course," Nelson lied. He waited until Andy had left the room before sitting across from Natty. "Didn't know you and the banker were acquainted. And why'd he give Toby money?"

Natty reached into his coat pocket and laid four lead fishing lures on the table, each painted a different color scheme. "Kid smelts wheel weights and molds lures to sell. Hell, it's about the only money Toby earns. Mac takes everything Rick pays the kid for helping around the ranch. Mac says it's to help out 'with household expenses,' but I know that a bunch of cock-and-bull. Andy bought a few lures this morning out of the goodness of his heart."

The last thing Nelson associated Andy Olssen with was doing something out of the *goodness of his heart.* He picked up a lure, turning it over, holding it to the light. As slow as Toby was, he had an uncanny talent for molding and painting lures. *Professional.* The kid could make some serious money even in these hard times if he only had someone with ambition guiding him. Which Mac McKeen did not have. Nelson made a note to buy some lures himself when this case was wrapped up and he was headed back to his favorite ice fishing hole.

Natty whistled and held up his cup. "Marley, girl. Refill for me and a cup for my good friend the marshal here." He put the lure back in his pocket. "You might buy some now and again, too, just as a nice gesture to the kid."

"You read my mind," Nelson said.

Marley walked to the table with a coffee pot and cup. She set the cup in front of Nelson and filled it. She refilled Natty's mug and sashayed out of his reach as she retreated behind the counter. "Now what's so important that you had to ask Andy to leave?" Natty said.

"I didn't know you and he were friends."

"We're . . . business associates. His bank owns the note on my feed store, like his bank owns the notes for many businesses here in Gillette. I called last week, needing more operating capital, and he agreed. He brought the revised note down for me to sign, and the cashier's check hisself, since he wanted to look you up anyway. Again, Marshal, what do you need with me?"

"Did you hear that Gino Bonelli's brother and some of his thugs rolled into town yesterday?"

"Who hasn't? A photo was pasted across the front page of the *Daily Journal* this morning showing those three big Lincolns roaring into town. Why?"

"I had to tell Bruno his brother was murdered."

"So?"

"So, one of the last ones to see Gino alive was you when you drove him out to Lucky's and Rick's places."

"And you think one of those fellers will think I knowed what happened?" Natty propped his boot up on a chair and sipped his coffee. "Well, I don't know nothin'."

"Doesn't matter what you know," Nelson said. "What matters is what they *think* you know."

Natty winked. "If that happens, I got the law to help protect me. But tell me for my own knowledge, just what do you know about this Bruno Bonelli?"

"Not a lot." Nelson stood and stretched. "But I intend finding out as soon as I get to the sheriff's office. As for being there to protect you, do you know how big this county is?"

" 'Course I know—five thousand square miles, give or take."

"Just remember that if you're in trouble and call the law to help, we might be just that far away."

Natty brushed the threat aside. "I can handle myself."

Nelson leaned across the table. "These men are thugs. Gangsters. They have a different way of . . . interrogating people to extract information from folks."

"Are you finished, Marshal?" Andy said as he walked back into the room, licking blueberry pie filling off his fingers. "Because I have other stops to make."

"I am," Nelson said, bracing for what was coming next.

"Tell me you'll serve Ulysses Graber today?"

"Can't promise anything," Nelson said. "He seems to be avoiding service."

"That's what I thought." Andy's pale complexion showed the crimson of rage filtering from his neck all the way to the throbbing veins in his forehead. "I gave you the benefit of the doubt. Thought you were actually making an effort to find Mr. Graber. I held off placing a call to the U.S. attorney. But now . . . now I am going to have to file a formal complaint. Do you know Mr. Witherspoon?"

"I do," Nelson said. He had clashed more than once with the guttersnipe attorney from Chicago, who had been pressured to move to Wyoming to give the hicks of the state the benefits of his big city criminal expertise. Nelson had arrested poachers that Witherspoon dropped charges against, brushing aside Wyoming's desire to protect its environment and its animals. Including letting Dan Dan Uster go free, whom Nelson suspected of poaching dozens of trophy animals for his hunting clients. And of poaching a man or two along the way as well.

Just the mention of that pompous ass Witherspoon caused Nelson's heart to race, but he might not have to worry about the man for long. Nelson had heard on good account that—should Roosevelt be elected this fall—Witherspoon was in line to be his attorney general. And Nelson suspected the last thing Witherspoon would do before closing his office in Casper was to lobby the new administration to appoint a new U.S. marshal for Wyoming. In the pit of his stomach, Nelson knew that was all right, too—it would give him an excuse to spend just as much time as he could on a trout stream or bass pond or hunting that elusive big buck mulie he'd spotted several times above his Buffalo cabin. It would give him a chance to try some of Toby McKeen's homemade lures.

"Are you going to be available for a phone conversation with Mr. Witherspoon this morning?"

Nelson felt his temper begin to get the best of him as he stepped closer to the banker. With Andy's youth and size, the man would be a powerful opponent if it came to fists. Yet Nelson saw in Andy Olssen all the bullies he had ever come across. All the officers pushing enlisted men around just because they could. All the criminals thumbing their noses at the law because people like Bobby Witherspoon felt their crimes didn't warrant prosecution. Nelson breathed deeply, composing himself, Witherspoon in the back of his mind. If the U.S. attorney were going to lobby for Nelson's removal from office, it would be for something substantial, like kicking the dog shit out of some Billings banker. "Andy, you can call Witherspoon this morning. Even tell him to call the sheriff's office if you like. But you know what—I *probably* will not be available for any phone conversation. I have other responsibilities besides finding Lucky Graber. But feel free to tell him he's invited to drive up from Casper and tag along as I look for Lucky."

Chapter 14

"Elusive is about an understatement," Maris said. She took off her jacket and draped her gloves over the register to dry them, looking like she hadn't slept any. Which she wouldn't have if she had *entertained* some hapless cowboy last night.

"You look beat. You get any sleep last night?"

Maris smiled as she took a small green box from her handbag. She began dabbing pink-colored Nadine face powder on to cover her drooping cheeks. "I got . . . a little. But if I were smart—"

"If you were smart, you would have left the local men alone for one night and got some shut eye," Nelson said.

"You're always so . . . direct." Maris closed her small compact mirror and put it back in her purse. "I like that in a man."

Nelson felt himself blushing when Maris said, "Don't worry, Boss. I'm not going to jump your bones. But you might jump mine because of yesterday."

"How's that?"

"I did not find Lucky, and I know you wanted him found in a bad way. I staked out his ranch until I about froze my toes off. I had to come back to town just to thaw out. Damned if I didn't go back out later and see where he had sneaked back to his house while I was gone."

"I take it he wasn't inside though?" Nelson said.

Maris shook her head and grabbed her pouch of tobacco from her back pocket. She stuffed her cheek and said, "I figured he might be there, as the mail was gone from his box by the road when I returned. I remembered him threatening me with that old Savage lever gun of his. The last thing I wanted was to get ventilated by some rancher's .30-.30, so I put the sneak on the house. When I finally figured out he wasn't inside, I went in. Lucky had come back and grabbed some clothes by the looks of his dresser. His shaving mug and brush were gone and his toothbrush missing." She laughed. "Didn't realize he had enough teeth left to worry about."

"Tell me you were able to track him. At least get a direction—"

"You know I'm no tracker." She held up her hand. "I know the stereotype that all us *injuns* are trackers, but not me. If we'd had the fresh snow we did last night, I might have been able to. But I followed Lucky's tracks best I could leaving his yard. Lost them along with the other vehicle tracks once they got onto the county road."

Nelson slammed his hand on the desk. "Damn. I wish you'd have got hold of me. I would have tracked the man."

"I was fixin' to," she said, "until I stopped at the Dooley and Holmes station. Mac's kid was getting right dirty sifting through some wheel weights when Mac told me you was about to get into it with Andy Olssen. I didn't particularly want to show up and calm you down before you could whup that fool, so I went back out to Lucky's again. I expected a bloody Andy Olssen to be on the front page of the *News Record* or the *Gillette Daily Journal* when I returned."

Nelson cracked the heat register. It emitted more steam, cutting through the chill of the office. "I felt like planting a fist into those perfect pearlies. But I have enough trouble with him fixin' to complain to Witherspoon that I've been refusing to serve Lucky foreclosure papers."

"We're doing the best we can."

"But we can do more," Nelson said, sniffing the burnt coffee in the pot and returning it to the hot plate, cursing to himself. *DeMyron's beat me to the office this morning again.* "I'm afraid I'm going to have to have a foreclosure sale on the courthouse steps sooner than later." He hit the desk again. "Why the hell didn't Lucky use the time I gave him and move off his place? Would have been a hell of a lot easier for all of us." He shook out a cigarette and offered Maris one. "Did you by any chance take a look in my panel truck last night?"

"Why would I do that?"

Nelson shrugged. "No reason. But when I came out this morning, someone had walked up to my truck and brushed the snow off the driver's side window like they were looking for something. I couldn't tell if the boot prints were yours or not. I was thinking of rousing you and asking about it—"

"Glad you didn't," Maris said. "I had a . . . guest last night."

"Anyone we know?"

Maris wagged her finger. "We agreed I wouldn't discuss my private life."

"You're right," Nelson said. "We did." The thing that always surprised Nelson was how quickly Maris could connect with a man needing a woman. She wasn't a beauty, though even Nelson had been tempted some years ago to have a relationship with her in a moment of weakness. She certainly wasn't charming for a woman, with her tobacco chewing and spitting wherever she pleased. But there was just *something* that attracted men to Maris, and he wasn't surprised she'd found a *victim* last night.

DeMyron walked through the door brushing snow off his coat. He poured some of the thick liquid he called coffee and sat behind his desk. "Just came from Rick Jones's ranch. I tried to get him to fill out a statement. He refused. But with his injuries after Bruno's thugs worked him over, I'm sure the judge will issue an arrest warrant for felony assault."

"What injuries?" Nelson asked.

"Mac said that guy Lazy Stefano did a soft shoe on Rick's head there at the ranch as he was working in the barn, and I'll put his name on my affidavit."

"Do you know where Lazy is now?"

"Eating lunch at the R&R. Soon's the judge signs the warrant, I'm going to arrest him."

"I'd better come along," Maris said. "That Lazy's a big ol' boy and might not cotton to being arrested."

"He can't kick any harder than a bulldogged steer," DeMyron claimed once again and headed out the door.

After nearly ten minutes—for which Sheriff Jarvis will be angry about the long-distance charges to the county—Nelson connected with Magnus Koats, a captain with the New Jersey State Police. "My secretary tells me you're looking for information on Bruno Bonelli," Koats said.

"I am," Nelson answered. "The deputy here talked with Lieutenant Quinn of the Newark PD a few days ago, but he didn't have much information."

Captain Koats chuckled on the other end of the line. "That doesn't surprise me. Bruno has most of the city law kowtowed or on his payroll. I assume you're checking because you somehow had a run-in with Bruno or his thugs way the hell out in Wyoming?"

Nelson explained how Gino Bonelli had been murdered, and how Bruno and some of his men roared into town and began pushing their weight around.

"That's Bruno. Let me tell you something, Marshal—Bruno Bonelli has garbage collection sewed up along the upper East Coast. He did it by being the most ruthless son of a bitch in town after he was given the business following that Masseria hit at Coney Island. My troopers have stopped numerous trucks bearing the *Bonelli Trucking* logo and found moonshine. Not the good stuff—that would take too much effort. I'm talking about rotgut bathtub gin that's more wood alcohol than mash and that kills drinkers more often than not."

"Why isn't he in lockup?"

"Remember I said he was ruthless? I should have said his *men* are ruthless, at Bruno's orders, we're certain. They're the ones that make witnesses disappear. Evidence go missing from police lockers. People wind up in emergency rooms telling investigators they remember nothing they said the previous day. And they intimidate police department lieutenants."

"You're saying I need to be careful around Bruno and his men?"

"Depends on who he brought out west," the captain said.

Nelson ran the names of Bruno's thugs by the captain, and Koats whistled. "Angelo Gallo and Lazarro Stefano are your run-of-the-mill thugs. They'll do whatever Bruno orders. Both of them are in line for lieutenant positions in Bruno's organization. But only one will move up, so they're constantly trying to impress the boss with *their* ruthlessness."

"I'll remember that."

"Also, Angelo likes his wine and booze. A lot. My guys have arrested him four times in two years for driving drunk. Bruno got so tired of Angelo getting arrested for it that Angelo only drives when it's absolutely necessary."

"I'll remember that as well."

"Now as to Sal DeLuca," Captain Koats said. "He has the potential to be an enforcer, but his value to Bruno is his charm. If there's a woman within a hundred miles that he can beguile into giving him the information he seeks, he will."

"I noticed how dandy he dresses," Nelson said. "Looks like he came off the front cover of a fashion magazine."

"That's Sal. But he's about as charming as a carbuncle to men. Watch your back—he favors a thin stiletto when he needs to get his point across."

"How about Bruno's bodyguard, Gavin Corrigan?" Nelson asked. "Sticks to his boss like flies on a gut wagon, but I didn't spot him carrying a gun."

"That's 'cause he doesn't need one," the captain said. "I assume you've noticed all the scars across that lovely, misshapen mug of his? He's earned every one of them. He's Bruno's bodyguard because Bruno won a hundred bucks on the Irishman."

"I don't follow you."

Captain Koats chuckled. "Word on the street was that Bruno and Salvatore came out of a speakeasy in Manhattan late one night when they spotted three Russian thugs jump Gavin in the alley. Sal bet Bruno a hundred bucks Gavin wouldn't last five minutes. Bruno saw something in Gavin that made him take the bet, and he upped the odds five to one. Before those five minutes were up, Gavin had laid out all three bruisers. Crippled one, and NYPD had to investigate the two dead Russians. Bruno hired him on the spot." The captain's voice grew serious. "Gavin Corrigan might not be as big or intimidating as the others, but I'm telling you the man does not know the meaning of pain. Or of quitting. *That's* the one you need to be cautious around, Marshal."

"What does the New Jersey police have on Bruno and his men?" Maris asked after Nelson disconnected with the captain.

"They've had extensive contacts with them. They just haven't been able to make anything stick," Captain Koats had told Nelson.

The phone rang, and Nelson answered. He stayed on the line mere moments before hanging up and giving Maris the bad news. "A Johnson County deputy will meet you this afternoon and hand you the rancher's statement . . . the one who found Gino's car."

"Didn't know it'd been located," Maris said.

"It has been, and you get an all-expense-paid trip to the county line."

"Shit!"

"Is there something pressing that prevents you from doing that?"

"I had a date this afternoon to go to that pool hall and shoot a few games."

"A date like you had last night?"

She nodded. "Eventually. After we hit the pool hall. At least, that was our plan."

"I guess you'll just have to postpone your little romantic interlude. Unless you think it's more important—"

"I'll go."

"I can get word to the young feller that you didn't stand him up but that I assigned you extra duty. Fair enough?"

Maris looked away.

"I am willing to do that just so he doesn't . . . lose interest. Who is it?"

She remained silent, looking at the ceiling, the floor, the wall, every place but at Nelson.

"Maris," Nelson said, "is there something about your new boyfriend that you're not telling me?"

She kicked at a piece of paper with the toe of her boot.

"Maris . . . just *who* is this new beau?"

"Sal," she whispered.

"What was that?" Nelson said. "I didn't quite hear you."

"It's Salvatore DeLuca. That's who I was with last night."

"Sal—Bruno's man! Whatever possessed you to get involved with someone like him?"

Maris grabbed her gloves where they lay warming on the

register. "He came on to me last night when I was at the bowling alley."

"And what, you just couldn't resist him?"

"He's charming."

"I'll bet he is."

"He's probing—"

"I'll bet he's that, too," Nelson said.

"I mean, he came on to me to ask questions. A *lot* of questions about the investigation. About you. About DeMyron. About me."

"And you told him all about us and how we're coming along?"

"Nelson," Maris said as she put her coat on, "give me credit for something. You might say I *let* him come on to me. And what happened in my room later."

"But why?"

Maris grinned. "Because I intend finding out all about him and those men Bruno brought along. And when I do," she winked, "we'll have a better handle on how to handle these boobs."

Nelson thought about that. It was a dangerous game Maris played. If she were successful, she and Nelson would know Bruno's next move and be prepared. If she were caught double dealing, she could end up looking like Rick Jones after those New Jersey thugs finished with him.

Or worse.

Chapter 15

DeMyron sat behind the desk when Nelson walked into Sheriff Jarvis's office, while Rick Jones sat in front holding a wet towel to his head. He rubbed at his swollen lower lip while he looked up at Nelson through an eye that was fast closing.

"What the hell—"

"This is Lazy Stefano's work I was telling you about," DeMyron said. "He roughed up Rick again behind the Farmer's Co-Op not an hour ago."

Nelson dropped into a chair beside Rick and bent to study the rancher's face. "You mouth off to Lazy or something?"

"Me?" Rick said and winced as he put the towel to his mouth. "I don't lip off to anyone. DeMyron can tell you that. No, Lazy stopped me as I was going into the Co-Op office and said he wanted to talk with me. Again. As if yesterday wasn't enough."

"Talk to you about what?"

"Lucky. That gangster hustled me around back of the office when, *pow!* He popped me in the kisser. He caught me when I was going to fall and hit me again."

"I don't understand," Nelson said. "What did he want from you?"

"He thought that Rick here knew more than he let on about Gino's murder," DeMyron said, holding up the statement he was writing for Rick.

"That's right, Marshal," Rick said. "He said all us ranchers know *everything* that goes on around our spreads, and he just *knew* I had information about Gino's killer."

Nelson stood and leaned over DeMyron's desk to read the statement. "Says here Lazy knocked you to the ground and was cocking his leg back to kick hell out of you when a couple farmers heard the commotion and came around. Found you on the ground."

Rick laid the towel aside. "That's right—two farmers down from Broadus, Montana, it were. Big fellers. Bigger 'n Lazy and he musta figured his odds were none too good, so he lit out. 'We'll talk again,' he yelled and ran off."

DeMyron tapped the statement. "With this and the previous assault, I have something I can take to the judge and get an arrest warrant issued. Bruno's thugs have been pushing their weight around town a little too much for my liking."

The moment DeMyron left to see the judge, Nelson closed his eyes and leaned back in the sheriff's chair. Nelson had advised Rick to arm himself in case Bruno's men retaliated for swearing out a complaint. "I'll just keep to the ranch and be more cautious until those fellers move on," Rick said. "At least there I have Mac and Toby as witnesses. Bruno's men wouldn't dare come to my home." But Nelson knew they just might. With not a single-digit IQ between Toby and his father, they wouldn't make much for witnesses, either.

Nelson's mind drifted in and out of sleep, his thoughts returning to Dan Dan Uster as they often did when he was on the verge of nodding off. Amidst all the turmoil of finding Lucky Graber and the death of Gino Bonelli, Dan Dan had come sneaking his way back into Nelson's memory. The poacher remained Nelson's only obsession in life. "Just leave me the hell alone," Nelson mumbled under his breath. "Why not just fall off a tall cliff somewhere and break your neck."

But he really didn't want that, and why not, he asked himself.

Because I want my hands around your throat. I want to pummel you all the way to the lockup and bring you before some prosecutor besides gutless Bobby Witherspoon. In the back of Nelson's mind, he feared someone—or something—would get to Dan Dan first and deny Nelson the pure pleasure of dragging him to justice. Or beating justice into him for all the poaching and thievery he'd done.

As he half dozed, Nelson imagined what it would be like dragging Dan Dan kicking and screaming in front of a judge. He could almost see it. Could almost hear . . . *kicking. Screaming.* Coming from the direction of the jail downstairs.

Nelson woke and leapt to his feet, as fast as a fifty year old with bronc-sore knees and a piece of shrapnel in his leg could leap. He ran to the door just as he heard DeMyron yell profanities at someone and slam shut the door of the holding cell.

DeMyron *clomped* up the stairs, taking great gulps of air as he paused just down from the landing outside the sheriff's office. The brim of his Stetson had been torn and sat at an odd angle, while one shirt pocket had been ripped all the way down to the waist.

"That sounded like Lazarro Stefano," Nelson said.

DeMyron used the handrail to climb the remaining stairs. He stood there looking at Nelson. "Whoever the hell nicknamed that man *Lazy* oughta be shot."

"I take it he didn't come easy?"

"That's an understatement," DeMyron said. "The next time I say a man can't be as big a handful as a rangy steer, just shoot me." He tossed the sheriff's copy of the arrest warrant on the desk. "I could use a cup of coffee—"

"Allow me," Nelson said, recalling the last time he'd sniffed DeMyron's mud. "I'll make it. You just sit back and regain your composure." He handed the deputy a bandana to wipe blood off above his eye where Lazy's fist must have cut him. "Better yet, I'll buy a late lunch at the R&R."

By the time they finished lunch and headed back, two of Bruno's fancy Lincolns had pulled to the curb in front of the courthouse. Nelson looked around but couldn't see the thugs, and the hair rose on his neck as he and DeMyron walked into the building. They tramped upstairs and entered the sheriff's office . . .

. . . and Nelson's hand shot to the slab-sided pistol on his belt.

"No need for that, Marshal," Bruno said. He sat in a chair beside Angel Gallo, while Gavin Corrigan leaned against the far wall, silent, his arms hanging loosely at his sides, taking in everything but saying nothing. Bonnie Matchuk was in her usual place at her desk, apparently unharmed, but white faced and silent.

Angel stood abruptly and said to DeMyron, "What the hell did you do to Lazy?"

Bruno rose instantly from his chair and stepped between his man and DeMyron. "I think there's been enough violence for one day. Sit down."

Angel paused for a moment before sitting again, his eyes never leaving DeMyron's.

"How'd you get in here?" DeMyron demanded.

"How?" Bruno said. "We walked through that door, of course."

"I know I locked it when me and the marshal went to lunch."

Bruno shrugged. "I have no answer for you, except you are mistaken." He held out his hand, and Gavin passed him a slip of paper. He unfolded it and handed it to DeMyron.

DeMyron read it, and his fist knotted at his side while he passed the paper to Nelson. "It says you made bond for Lazy."

"That is correct," Bruno said. "I posted bond for that trumped-up assault charge against Rick Jones. And for resisting arrest. Now is there anything else, deputy, or can I have my man now?"

"Payment for a uniform ripped to shreds would be nice."

Bruno smiled and reached inside his coat pocket. He pulled out a wallet and handed DeMyron a fifty-dollar bill. "That should cover it, don't you think?"

When DeMyron didn't take the cash, Bruno said, "I would swear this is more than you ever made in the rodeo circuit."

"Is there any federal statute that can hold Lazy?" DeMyron asked Nelson, ignoring the money in Bruno's hand.

Nelson shook his head. "Everything Lazarro's done in this county has been a violation of state statute—"

"But he's not going to *make* his court date," DeMyron pleaded with Nelson. "He'll waltz right out of that cell, and come his court date, he won't show." DeMyron turned to Bruno. "Will Lazy make it to court?"

Bruno exaggerated a shrug. "What people in my employ do is upon them. If he does not make it back, then the bond will be forfeited, and I'll lose my money. And, deputy, nothing you charged Lazy with is a felony, so if he crosses the Wyoming state line, he is a free man, no?"

DeMyron stepped toward Bruno. Gavin came off the wall and moved closer to DeMyron when Nelson grabbed his arm. "Best let your prisoner out, deputy," Nelson said. "Nothing you can do about the situation except to follow court orders."

DeMyron glared at Bruno a final time and left the office to free Lazy from the holding cell.

With the door shut behind DeMyron, Nelson said to Bruno, "Your man was fortunate this time, being arrested for just simple assault. Must have had to slip the judger a sizeable amount to get it reduced from a felony."

Bruno shrugged.

"You might have won this time, but I would tread lightly if you go back and threaten Rick Jones for filing a complaint."

"This was a simple misunderstanding, is all," Bruno said. "A one-time occurrence."

Nelson stepped closer to Bruno. From the corner of his good eye, he saw Gavin come off the wall once again, ready to protect his boss. The Irishman's gnarled knuckles scraped against his pant leg as he eyed Nelson intently. "I understand people back in your state have come up missing," Nelson said. "Witnesses in more than one of your trials have never appeared for court."

Bruno waved a hand in the air. "So I have heard. Fortunately for me, they did not stick around to testify to . . . made-up charges against me."

"Rick Jones thinks your men will retaliate for pressing charges. Know this: Rick Jones is armed. And fearful for his life. I've seen him shoot," Nelson lied. "I'd like to say I'd hate to bury one of your men here in Campbell County, but . . ."

"But," Bruno said, "you just can't bring yourself to say it?"

"You read my mind," Nelson said. "I really wouldn't hate it that much, the way things are stacking up with your men."

Nelson sat on a stool watching Maris process Gino's car for evidence. "Tell me you found something we can use."

"Fingerprints," Maris said, proudly holding up a blank recipe card with tape stuck to it. She passed the card to Nelson, and he donned his reading glasses. The prints she'd lifted from the car showed different fingerprint patterns that made no sense to Nelson.

"Doubt if they'll be of much use," Nelson said.

"Then why did you send me to that fingerprint class if you think it's all useless?"

"Because maybe—just maybe—some miracle will occur, and

we'll be able to match one of these to a suspect." He stubbed his cigarette out on the floor of the sheriff's garage. When Maris followed the wrecker into town, she'd had him back the car in the sheriff's garage where she could process it out of the weather. "Just don't hold your breath." He stood and walked around the car. Mud and snow had caked the fenders running all the way up the sides where either Gino or his murderer had driven the car after the theft.

"And something else," Maris said. "When I went to Johnson County with the wrecker to pick the car up from that ditch, it looked like it had been there for a while. Anyone passing by and seeing it could have opened the door to peek inside. That means any prints on the car might not belong to Gino *or* his killer."

"Then tell me the killer left *something,*" Nelson said. "An identification card. A letter from Mom. Anything."

"Nothing that obvious," Maris said. "The Caddy ran out of gas right outside Buffalo. That rancher saw it sitting on the road for two days before he reported it." She held up a piece of green-colored metal. "This is all I have to show for missing out on my date. A broken door handle. Looks like someone pulled too hard on it getting out, and it just snapped."

Nelson turned the broken metal over in his palm. "Either these Cadillacs aren't made so good, or some stout bastard broke this."

He was handing Maris the door handle to enter into evidence when movement through one garage window caught his eye. He stared at the window. Once again, a blur filled the windowpane for a brief second before disappearing.

He unsnapped the retaining strap on his holster and placed his hand on the butt of his .45, then tiptoed to the walk-in door and carefully turned the handle. He peeked out and saw a streetlight shining down on Natty Barnes crouching under the window. Seconds later, Natty jumped up again, looking into the window for a heartbeat before coming back down to the ground.

Nelson eased out of the garage toward Natty. "You're going to hurt yourself," he said. "Unless you can beat gravity."

Natty jumped, his hand going to his chest. He leaned against the side of the garage. "You're going to give me a heart attack, Marshal," he wheezed.

"You're going to give yourself one if you continue those . . . antics. Just what *are* you doing?"

Natty looked around quickly, then said, "Can I come in?"

"Sure." Nelson snapped his holster strap closed again as he held the door for Natty. "Now what were you doing out there—"

"Sheriff, you gotta protect me."

"Protect you from what?"

"Those goons—Angelo and Lazarro. They came to the feed store this evening just as I was fixin' to lock up." He spotted a coffee pot atop a Franklin stove in one corner of the garage. "Mind?"

"If it'll calm you down," Nelson said, "drink the whole pot."

Natty tipped his hat to Maris as he walked to the stove and blew dust out of a tin cup hanging on a nail in the wall. He filled the mug and cupped it in his trembling hands while he sat on a milk stool in the garage bay.

"Now what's this about Bruno's men?"

"The one that DeMyron got into it with—that Lazarro—stood in back of me while that Angelo grilled me. *Somehow* they knew I showed Gino around the county. They *knew* I drove him all around Rick and Lucky's places a few days before he died."

"Did they threaten you?" Maris said as she bagged the door handle as evidence. "Because if they did, that's a crime."

"They didn't," Natty answered. "Not directly. But with those two standing within arm's reach, I knew I was a goner if they so wished it." He laid his hand on Nelson's forearm. "I'm telling you, they wanted to know all about what Gino and me was doing that day."

Nelson took his pack of cigarettes out of his shirt pocket and passed it to Natty. The man's shaking hands finally snatched a cigarette, and Nelson lit a match, bringing it to Natty's lips. "Now take a few breaths. Calm down, and tell me exactly what you told them."

After a deep draw of the smoke and a sip of the coffee, Natty said, "I told them Gino asked me to stop now and again as we were driving the fields. Said he got out and took something from his bag. I didn't pay any attention. Just like I told you before." He shuddered and took in another draw of smoke. "Bruno's men didn't believe me."

"Go on."

"I told 'em Gino got out of the car and picked up something every time we stopped. Stuffed it—I don't know what it was—in that bag over his shoulder. None of my business, but I thought he was collecting plants or something."

"But you don't know?"

Natty shook his head.

"You said Angelo and Lazy didn't believe you. It would seem they should have treated you like they treated Rick Jones. How'd you get away without a scratch?"

Natty flicked ashes onto the garage floor. "I feel real bad—"

"About what?" Nelson asked. "Just what the hell did you tell them?"

"I told them Gino was most interested in Rick Jones's ranch," Natty blurted out. "Not so much Lucky's place. And that Rick would know all about it."

"But you told me before that Gino asked you to drive him around Lucky's place specifically."

"That's true, Marshal." He snuffed his cigarette out with the toe of his boot. "But I had to tell them *something,* or they would have cracked my skull. If I told them Gino was interested in

Lucky's run-down place, they wouldn't believe me."

"So, you threw Rick under the bus?" Nelson said.

Natty stared at the floor. "I had to, or they'd put some hurt on me."

"And now they'll come hunting Rick up for another session of wall-to-wall counseling?"

Natty nodded.

"You ought to crawl in a hole," Nelson said and held the door for Natty to leave.

Chapter 16

"I hope we get there before those peckerwoods do," DeMyron said. "The way they roughed up Rick the last time, I'm afraid it was only a prelude to more painful things for him."

"Natty's got about as much guts as a turnip, telling those boobs Rick was the one they needed to squeeze," Nelson said as he veered around two doe antelope crossing the county road.

They passed Lucky's empty mailbox, snow drifting across the drive with no sign of activity in or out. They drove the last half mile of county road and turned onto Rick Jones's long driveway. Trucks—maybe cars, too, Nelson couldn't tell—had busted through the drift going into Rick's. "Lot of outfits coming and going here," DeMyron said as they topped the last short rise and headed down into Rick's ranch yard.

Ranchers in this part of the country usually stepped out to greet whoever pulled into their place, but no one showed. No one walked out to meet them as they pulled through the ranch yard. Nelson parked in front of the house next to Jamie's Model A. "What's she doing here?" Nelson asked, not expecting an answer, for he had gotten a feel for the reporter sticking her nose in where it didn't belong. Jamie struck him as a reporter who would throw caution to the wind to get her story. Did she do that here?

"Something's wrong," DeMyron said. "Rick ought to have come out and met us."

"Unless he's busy. I saw some bales in that west pasture of

his that should have been gathered by now," DeMyron said.

But Nelson didn't think Rick was gathering bales in his west pasture. His gut told him DeMyron was right—something *was* wrong here—and he unsnapped his holster as he climbed out of the truck.

Nelson moved around the vehicle and spotted blood staining the snow on the steps leading to Rick's front door. DeMyron saw it, too, and drew his gun a moment before Nelson did. Nelson motioned for DeMyron to stay behind cover of the truck while he approached the front door.

He put his ear to the weathered slab of wood. Men talked wildly amongst themselves, their voices too muffled for him to recognize.

Nelson backed away and motioned for DeMyron to join him on the porch. "At least two men inside," he whispered. "I tried the knob—it's unlocked. When we go into the room, I'll go left, you go right, 'cause I don't know who they are or where they are. But with this much blood, somebody's hurt bad."

DeMyron lowered his revolver as he stood behind Nelson. The marshal counted with his fingers—*three, two, one*—and they burst through the door.

Jamie sat in a chair across from Rick, a bowl of water and a cloth balanced in her lap. Startled, she looked up at Nelson and DeMyron with their pistols drawn. "I'm thinking you two are just a little late. You can lower your guns."

Mac McKeen stepped from another room with Toby following. Mac cradled a Marlin lever gun in the crook of his arm. "Sorry about the rifle, Marshal. When I heard your truck, I wasn't sure if they came back for another crack at poor Rick." He handed the weapon to Toby. "Put it behind the door."

"What's going on here?" Nelson asked.

"You can see what's going on." Jamie dipped the cloth into the water, then leaned over and gently dabbed Rick's head.

"Man's been beaten. Again."

Jamie wasn't exaggerating. Rick's lips were bloated and split, and one eye had swelled shut despite snow wrapped in a bandana that Rick held against it. One of his hands rested gingerly on a table, two fingers sitting at an odd angle—broken. He hugged his torso with his other arm, his breathing wheezy and labored. Broken ribs, Nelson guessed.

DeMyron holstered his gun and grabbed a notepad from his pocket. "What happened, Rick?"

"I don't remember anything."

"What?"

"That's right." Rick winced in pain. "I don't remember nothin'. Including the first two times Bruno's thugs beat me. I ain't sayin' a damn thing."

"But *I* will." Mac pulled up a chair. "It was that Lazy Stefano and Angel Gallo. Me and the kid was out in the barn when we heard the commotion—"

"Shut up, Mac!"

"Rick, these gangsters can't be going around the country beating hell out of folks. Just be quiet and let Jamie patch you up." He turned back to Nelson and DeMyron, who stood with a stub of a pencil poised above his notepad. "Like I said, I heard a commotion, so I come running. The taller one—the one they call Lazy—was knocking Rick around while Angel held his arms from behind."

"That right?" DeMyron asked.

"I don't remember nothin'," Rick repeated.

"Pa's right," Toby volunteered. "Soon's they seen us come bustin' through the door, they stopped. I wanted to kick hell out of 'em myself, but Pa wouldn't allow me."

"You'd just ended up beaten, too," Mac said. "Toby's right, though—they stopped when we came into the house, but I don't think it was 'cause they was afraid of us. I think it was because they didn't want any witnesses to what they was doin'."

"Rick," Nelson said, leaning close, "*if* someday you could remember what they wanted from you, what would it be?"

Rick had to turn his head to look at Nelson with his good eye. Or at least the better of the two that wasn't swollen completely shut yet. "They was convinced that me and Gino Bonelli had some scheme going on. 'That Natty Barnes hauled Gino out to your place, and he was mighty interested in your land,' Angel kept yelling. 'Either tell us why, or we'll *really* give you a thrashing.' They even suggested me and Gino had a falling out in some business dealing of ours and that *I* killed him."

Nelson glanced at Jamie. "Where do you fit in?"

"The Cottonwood Motel," Jamie said as she dipped the cloth in the water and wrung it out. "Bruno Bonelli rented the entire motor lodge—that new one that just went up."

"I knew that, but not that Bruno rented the entire motel."

"Well, he did," Jamie said, "after the manager had to evict a couple from one of the rooms."

"What's the motel got to do with you?"

"I was . . . staking it out," Jamie answered. "I knew it was just a matter of time before they'd stir up something big, and *wham! I'd be there to get the story.*"

"You're not telling us anything we didn't already know," Nelson said, beginning to get frustrated with Jamie's roundabout way of relaying information. "How did you wind up here at Rick's ranch?"

"I'm coming to that." She reached over and laid the wet rag atop Rick's balding head. "Hold that there, and I'll get some more snow in a minute and put it on top." She dried her hands on a flour sack towel hanging off the chair. "I saw Bruno talking with his thugs in the common area of the Cottonwood. Things were getting heated. One of them said Natty Barnes told them it was Rick's land that Gino had been interested in, not Lucky's ranch. Next I knew, they all ran out and thundered away in one of those fancy cars of theirs. 'Jamie, girl,' I says to myself, 'they's not driving crazy like that just for the heck of it. If you follow them, there'll be a story.' "

"You're lucky they didn't hurt you, too. When exactly did you arrive here?"

Jamie cocked her head and looked Rick over. "About the time they closed his left eye and split his chin. It took me a while to get here; my Model A's not quite up to Lincoln speeds. By the time I did, they'd already dragged Rick from the porch steps and inside the house. They ruined my film before dragging me in here with Rick."

"How's that?"

"When I got here, they were just hauling Rick inside. I gave them a few minutes, hoping they'd come out so's I could get a picture of them, but they never did. So, I sneaked inside the house while they were working Rick over. Snapped a photo of them. I thought I could duck out fast enough. But they heard the shutter click, and Lazy snatched my camera and opened up the back. Exposed the whole roll of film and tossed the camera aside." She nodded toward a coffee table in front of the couch, and for the first time Nelson registered the broken camera body with pieces dangling off. "I don't know if the newspaper even has another camera to lend me."

DeMyron squatted in front of Rick. "We have enough this time, we can charge them with aggravated assault. A felony. They won't be getting out of the hoosegow so easily."

"But they will get out eventually," Rick said. "And they'll come back."

"Me and Toby can stay with you if you go ahead and file charges against them," Mac said. "We're both pretty good shots with that old rifle—"

"Thanks," Rick said, looking around the room. "Thanks to

all of you. But I just want to run a few cows and hogs. Let the missus plant her garden in the spring . . . thank God she's in Rawlins visiting her sister." He stood on wobbly legs and headed for the door. "I'll be all right soon's I get some snow on these lumps. And come calving time, I won't even remember that Bruno's thugs beat hell out of me. No, DeMyron, I won't file charges. And I withdraw my complaint from a few days ago."

"At least they won't be shooting anybody soon," Mac said.

"Why do you say that?" Nelson asked.

"Toby."

Toby grinned as he bent and brought out a sack brimming with ammunition. "They was so occupied with Rick, they didn't even see I stole every one of their bullets from their holsters that they's hung off the couch when they went to work Rick over. Yesiree . . . there's a passel of fish weights in that ammo."

Chapter 17

"There's no way we can convince Rick to go ahead and press charges, is there?" DeMyron said.

Nelson shook his head and grabbed first gear to coax the truck over a hill. "The man is plumb scared. Can't blame him none—thugs like Lazy and Angel have a habit of returning to settle scores. Even years later."

"How about you, Marshal—would you have pressed charges if you were Rick?"

"You're asking me if I was Rick's size, would I have cowered? If I didn't have a mean bone in my body and probably hadn't been in a fight my entire life?"

"No, I mean right now—if they came and worked you over right now, would you press charges?"

"First off, there'd be pieces of *all three* of us lying around. With two of those bruisers jumping me, they might get a meal, but I'd damn sure get a snack. They'd know they were in a fight, but there'd be no pressing charges later. I'm afraid I'd have to bide my time until I could get them each alone," Nelson said, rubbing knuckles that had been broken more than a few times in fights. "And then . . ." He ran his finger across his throat.

"I wouldn't beat them if I had the chance."

"Oh?" Nelson asked.

"Sure. I'd just want to kill them right off," DeMyron said. "Not give them a chance to go to the press with their tale of the local law dog beating up a couple of law-abiding taxpayers."

"For the record," Nelson said, "I didn't hear that."

"Tell me you haven't thought that a time or two," DeMyron said.

"I have, but that's all it was—a thought. As much as I'd like to be judge, jury, and final arbiter, I know we can't."

"Even if you came across Dan Dan Uster in the woods with no one around?"

Nelson had fantasized more than once about finding Dan Dan in the wilderness. Alone. With no witnesses. Would Nelson succumb to his want, his *need* to kill the man outright? It was still something Nelson wrestled with and had no answer for. "It would be tempting. Dan Dan is suspect in at least three murders and was complicit in that sex trafficking case I had this spring over by Thermopolis. I honestly don't know if I could control my impulse to see justice finally administered to him or not. But for lawmen like us, that better be all we do—*dream* about it."

"I just think I couldn't stop myself."

"Tell me, DeMyron, what did you do before Sheriff Jarvis hired you?"

"You know what I did—I travelled the rodeo circuit. I was pretty good, too, before—"

"No," Nelson said, "before that, what did you do?"

"I was a ranch hand, of course. Only thing I've ever knowed before Sheriff Jarvis took a chance with me."

"So, you were a cowboy?"

"What kind of silly question is that?" DeMyron asked, digging his packet of Mail Pouch tobacco out of his shirt pocket. "I was raised on a ranch where my pappy rode for the brand. And every spread I worked for since I was a cowboy. Why do you ask?"

"Because I was a cowboy. Once. Many years ago," Nelson

said. "And as a cowboy, we had certain rules . . . no, a certain *code* we lived by. I keep telling myself that code wouldn't allow me to just pop Dan Dan Uster in the head with my gun even if I *could* get away with it. I keep telling myself that cowboy code . . ." Nelson stopped the truck abruptly on the county road at Lucky's mailbox. "Crap," he said and pointed to fresh tire tracks. A vehicle had broken through the snow during the time Nelson and DeMyron had been at Rick's, and the tracks disappeared over the hill toward Lucky's ranch house.

"Maybe Lucky sneaked back to his place for more clothes or supplies," DeMyron said. "I'm no fan of you serving foreclosure notices, but the quicker you can get him served and off this place, the sooner you can help with Gino's murder investigation."

DeMyron didn't need to state the obvious. Even though Gino Bonelli's murder was Campbell County jurisdiction, Nelson had consented to assist DeMyron. Besides, Gino's murder was a damn sight more interesting—and more satisfying—than kicking a man down on his luck off his property.

Nelson slowly followed in the ruts the other car or truck had driven, careful not to telegraph to Lucky that someone approached. As he inched around the curve in the driveway, he spotted a long-hooded Packard parked in front of Lucky's barn.

"Unless Lucky got really lucky," DeMyron said, "I'd wager that's not his car."

"No shitske," Nelson said and cut the motor. He let the panel truck coast toward the barn just as Andy Olssen emerged from the swinging doors. Another man walked beside him. They stopped when they spotted Nelson's truck. "Not that SOB."

"Andy Olssen?"

"Him, too. I was talking about that man at his elbow. Darby Branigan."

"Never run into him before," DeMyron said.

"You're lucky," Nelson said. "He's pure trouble. Man's an engineer who claims to be an expert in silver and gold and copper and everything else that comes out of the ground."

Andy and Darby stood waiting for Nelson to climb out of the truck and approach them. Nelson didn't move, just kept talking to DeMyron. "Rumor was that Darby shot and killed two Mexicans south of the border at a mining operation right after the Great War. He said they jumped his claim, though he hightailed it out of Sonora before the Mexican police could conduct much of an investigation. Now he hires out to whoever pays the most money."

"I still don't see the problem—"

"If Andy hired Darby, it means he thinks there's *something* valuable underneath Lucky's land to be had. Darby will finagle around and sew up any mineral rights and hire up the crew no matter what it takes."

Nelson opened the door, then said over his shoulder, "Some advice—Darby wears that Colt Army low in that cut-down holster like he thinks it's the Wild West all over again. I heard he tried to goad a couple cowboys into a gun fight like it was high noon in Cody last summer. Unsnap your holster. Just in case. And don't show an ounce of back-down with that bastard."

Nelson slid his hand inside his jacket and unsnapped his own holster as he climbed out of the panel truck and approached the two men. "Just because Deputy Duggar is a nice feller, you two won't get arrested today."

"I don't think you could arrest me any day," Darby said.

Nelson ignored him and turned to Andy Olssen. "Tell your loudmouthed bulldog to keep out of our conversation."

Darby moved toward Nelson, who said, "Another step and you'll be eating tripe and crackers in the hoosegow tonight."

"Darby," Andy said, "why don't you go sit this one out. Maybe the porch, if you don't fall through."

Darby glared at Nelson for a long moment before turning on his heels and strutting towards the ranch house and the porch that was falling down on two sides.

"Now what's this about us getting arrested for . . . what, Marshal?" Andy asked.

"Trespassing."

"Trespassing!" Andy blurted out. "On my own property—"

"It's not your property yet," DeMyron said, his gaze fixed on Darby where the engineer-for-hire sat nervously on the porch, hand resting on the Colt thumb-buster.

"It will be mine as soon as you do your job and give Lucky Graber the boot offa here."

"My point is, I haven't yet."

Andy's fists balled up, and he shifted his weight from foot to foot, while Nelson kept an eye on Darby Branigan sitting on the porch steps. "Did not Bobby Witherspoon call you directly—"

"Andy, Andy," Nelson chided. "I would have just *loved* to speak with Little Bobby, but I was out. Doing police work. And no, I have not found Mr. Graber as yet." Nelson fished a pack of cigarettes from a pocket. He shook one out but didn't offer Andy one. Nelson's tone grew serious as he tucked the pack away again. "Just what are you and that mercenary bastard doing on this ranch?"

Andy smiled and waved his hand around the ranch yard. "Like I said before, as soon as you serve Lucky notice, this will be my property . . . the property of Stockman's Bank of Billings, that is. You might say I was getting an advance look at things." He glanced around the yard and then motioned to the house and barn. "You were wrong about this place—I'll get rid of both those run-down buildings and burn the outhouse to the ground. Bring a new Sears and Roebuck catalogue house here and hire some out-of-work carpenter to put the kit together. This place will sell like hotcakes."

"At what expense?" Nelson said, not believing for a moment that Andy was interested in the ranch for resale. "By the time you invest all that and add it to the price, no one will be able to afford it. In case you haven't noticed, the ranch is not much for raising livestock or crops. You've been in the property business long enough to see just by *looking* at the place that Lucky ran it into the ground."

Andy looked away.

"You didn't come here to see what generous improvements you could make for a quick resale, now did you?"

"I don't know what you're talking about."

Nelson chin-pointed to Darby. "Branigan. The man doesn't know the difference between a horse and a cow. He does, however, know the mining industry. Which is why I suspect you hired the likes of him."

Andy forced a laugh and withdrew a silver cigarette case from an inner pocket of his coat. "You do have an imagination, Marshal. Like you said, I've been in the property business long enough to know there could be nothing underground *here*. On *this* place." He jerked his thumb over his shoulder. "Mr. Branigan is accompanying me while I look at other foreclosure properties my bank will soon acquire." He lit his cigarette and watched the wind carry the smoke away. *Stalling*, Nelson thought. "That's as soon as you do your job and serve the notices."

He motioned for Darby, and the two men climbed into Andy's car. Darby stared at Nelson until they turned the car around and started up the long drive.

"You think Andy was telling the truth?" DeMyron said, finally relaxing and snapping the retaining strap on his holster. "You believe Darby Branigan is along to look at other ranches with Andy and they just happened to stop here?"

"I doubt anything Andy Olssen does is by chance, but I aim

to find out," Nelson said. He began following the footprints of the two men from where they'd stepped out of Andy's car. They hadn't bothered looking at the house or inside the barn—something Andy would have been interested in for resale purposes if he were telling the truth—but they *had* walked in back of it and stopped, as if looking out onto Lucky's pasture. Which wouldn't be Lucky's once Nelson located him and slapped eviction papers on him.

"Either they weren't too interested in the place," DeMyron said, "or we surprised them before they could wander around much."

"I think the latter," Nelson said. "If you can find the manpower, I'd suggest you station a man where he could watch for their return."

DeMyron chuckled as they headed back to the panel truck. "You know better, the sheriff's department being just me and Sheriff Jarvis. We have a posse we call up when things get real dicey, like when the sheriff wants more men to take down a still or when somebody gets lost. But until the sheriff returns from Phoenix—you're looking at the entire force of the Campbell County SO." He shrugged and opened the passenger-side door. "But I'll see if there's a posse member who'll volunteer to sit on the place."

They got in the truck and drove off. When they reached the county road, they had to wait for a rarity—another vehicle passing, a tan Chevrolet truck hitting on five of its six cylinders, smoke billowing out its rusted exhaust pipe. As the Chevy passed Lucky's mailbox, it skidded to a stop, the driver fighting the wheel to keep the vehicle out of the ditch. Gears mashed loud as the driver threw the Chevy into reverse and stopped in front of Nelson's panel truck. A man bailed out and Nelson grabbed for his pistol, but DeMyron stopped him. "Vilas Hall. Rural postman. This part of the county is his route."

Nelson moved his hand away from his gun and rolled down the window. "DeMyron," Vilas said, and stuck his head inside. "I tried catching you 'fore you left town. That hair cream that smells *soooo* sweet that you ordered from that fancy place in Chicago came in—"

"Never mind," DeMyron blurted out. "I'll catch up with you later. But you didn't stop us for that?"

"Looking for the marshal," Vilas said. "You must have Smitty at the post office right scared or something. He brought in all us rural carriers the morning you had words with him and ordered us to rack our brains to see if we remembered anything unusual around Lucky Graber's or Rick Jones's ranches." He smiled wide. "And I did. Just now as I was coming up on Lucky's mailbox. I stopped that day and was putting another notice from Stockman's Bank in the box. I seen Lucky had thrown a tarp over the back of that ratty wagon of his and was whipping his poor old mare for all she was worth across the pasture towards Rick's place."

"I don't follow you," Nelson said. "What day are you talking about?"

"The day Gene . . . Gino was found murdered. Two days before he mailed that package you was checking on." Vilas hooked his thumbs in his bib overall straps and rocked back on his heels. "If I have my directions right, and by the talk around town, that would have put the path of Lucky's wagon close to where Gino's body was found."

Chapter 18

Maris had eaten supper by the time Nelson and DeMyron pulled up in front of the courthouse. She stepped from her own truck, patting her belly and picking her teeth with a matchstick. "You two ladies finally made it back from your little drive in the country," she said, "while I've been holding down the fort."

"Holding down the fort as in, actually working?" Nelson asked.

"I talk better when I'm warm and can wrap my mitts around a hot coffee cup."

"You two have a visit without me," DeMyron said. "I'm turning in *one* night at a normal time." He got out of Nelson's vehicle, walked to his sheriff's truck and drove away.

Bonnie had gone home for the day when Maris led Nelson upstairs and unlocked the door to the sheriff's office. Inside, Nelson ladled water into a pot to heat for coffee while he explained how Bruno's men had beaten Rick Jones and about catching Andy Olssen and his hired mining engineer on Lucky's property.

"That was the other thing I've been fielding," Maris said. "Calls from your *good friend* Bobby Witherspoon. He called four times while you were out, and each time he demanded to speak to you. The last time, he threatened to have me kicking rocks looking for another job . . . he claimed you were by the phone all along and that I was lying for you." She laughed. " 'I can lie for myself, I don't have to lie for my boss,' I told him, but that only seemed to infuriate him. Which was my desired effect."

Nelson sighed. "I'll eventually have to take his call and convince him we really haven't been able to locate Lucky."

"I'll let you know as soon as he's spotted, but I came up short with everyone in town I talked with."

Nelson stripped off his coat and hung it on a chair back, then sat. "I asked Vilas to keep his eyes peeled. The postal carrier said Lucky's bound to be close. Every day that Vilas delivers the mail, it's gone the next day, so he knows Lucky checks the box."

"Bruno's men might locate him first," Maris said.

Nelson laughed. "Good luck with that. Lucky's been able to evade us, and Bruno's thugs will have less luck. But I am sure they'll notify you just as soon as they find him."

Maris's smile faded. "That's precisely what I expect."

"I'm listening."

"My newest . . . acquaintance, Sal DeLuca . . . did I tell you the man is super paranoid?"

"I suspect most goons in his business are paranoid if they intend to stay on this side of the grass for very long. What about him?"

"Seems like he can't get enough of my charming company." Maris took off her boots and stuck her bare feet close to the heat register.

"You don't have any socks."

"No," she said, "I don't. I ran out so quick I forgot them."

"You lost me."

"I lost them running out of Sal's motel room when Bruno and that nasty-ass bodyguard suddenly came back. I had to dash out of Sal's room without them. Sal called here earlier in the day and wanted—*needed*—to see me, he said. 'Come to Room 118 at the Cottonwood Motel. Come quiet . . . the boss is slinking around town somewheres.' Of course, I went, figuring I was irresistible, and he needed an afternoon . . . *get together.* Started taking my boots and socks off when he stopped me. He wasn't interested in getting . . . intimate. I got hurt feelings when I realized all he called me over for was conversation. Specifically, information as to where you and DeMyron had drove off to." Maris laughed. "The man tried his best to be subtle, but it was obvious what he wanted from me."

"You played along, of course."

"Does a fat baby fart?" Maris said. "I told him you two were headed to the country *somewhere,* but I didn't tell him you were going to Rick's ranch. In the course of him prodding me—not like he's done the last few days, alas—he let it slip that Bruno and the other thugs were staking out Lucky's place. Seems like Angel and Lazy leaned on Rick hard enough that they believed him when he said he knew nothing about Gino looking over his spread. That left Gino and Natty driving around *Lucky's* ranch."

"They figure Natty was lying to them?"

Maris nodded and put her boots back on. "If I were Natty Barnes, I'd be looking over my shoulder, 'cause Sal said those two enforcers of Bruno's are pissed. They *know* Gino was interested in Lucky's place. And they *know* Lucky knows just what happened the day Gino was murdered. And they *know* Natty can tell them just where Lucky Graber is hiding."

"Perhaps I can save Natty from getting his butt beat," Nelson said, "not that he deserves saving for the way he threw Rick under the bus. I think it's time for me to have a real heart-to-heart with *gentleman* Bruno Bonelli. As soon as I call Captain Koats again."

Nelson walked into the Cottonwood Motel, the high vaulted ceiling rimmed with stuffed game mounts reminding him of a hunting lodge. An antelope head stared down accusingly at anyone entering the common room, as did an equally accusing white tail deer, its six-by-seven antler spread surely noted in a record book somewhere. A cinnamon bear rug occupied the floor in front of the fireplace; a mountain lion perched above the mantle as if ready to pounce on folks warming their hands at the fire.

The room was empty of people except for Gavin Corrigan and Bruno sitting by the fireplace. Bruno nodded to Nelson and motioned to a seat in front of the hearth. "I miss this," Bruno said, rubbing his hands together. "I grew up on a farm in rural upstate New York—"

"Until your folks died in a buggy accident when you were fourteen." Nelson stood beside Bruno and held his own palms to the flames. "At which time you ran off to the city to seek your fame and fortune working for connected *businessmen*. Men who needed a stout young feller to impose their will on people like errant shopkeepers in arrears of their protection money. Bookies trying to stiff the bosses. Ladies of the night who held out on their . . . handlers."

"You *have* been checking up on me."

Nelson shrugged. "Comes with the territory. It's how I know those scars on your knuckles weren't earned by hard work."

"Oh, it was hard work, all right." Bruno motioned to Gavin. "I'll be fine. See if you can round up some tea." He turned to Nelson. "Tea fine with you?"

"I'm not much of a tea man, but if it's hot I'll drink it."

"That's right, a farm boy like you grew up with a coffee mug in your hand." Bruno laughed. "I'll bet all the ranch hands on the Walking Horse lived through the day with strong coffee in their gullets. Please sit."

Nelson joined Bruno on the couch, careful not to ruffle the buffalo hide hanging over the back. "So, you've been checking up on *me*?"

It was Bruno's turn to shrug. "Comes with the territory. I did find out some interesting things about you."

"Such as?"

"You were wounded in France as part of the . . . Fifth Marine Brigade, was it?"

"Go on," Nelson urged, interested to know just how much research Bruno had done on him in such a short time.

"You were wounded at Belleau Wood. Lost the use of one eye. An ear." Bruno nodded at Nelson's leg. "You took a piece of artillery shell to your hip. It's why you have that slight—but distinguishable—limp."

"A German *kriegsmortar,*" Nelson said. "The round blew up damned near at my feet."

Gavin came back into the common room balancing a tray in his hands. He looked at Nelson—no, looked *through* him. He set the tray on the table in front of the couch for the briefest moment before slithering back behind them to where he could watch his boss.

"Must have been a long, boring recovery at Portsmouth." Bruno skimmed loose leaves into a closed, silver-colored basket and let it steep in the hot water. "That was before you met your wife. God rest her soul." Bruno crossed himself like a good Catholic while his face changed as if he were genuinely sorry Helen had died eight years ago.

"That's right," Nelson said, "and you lost your own wife in a train derailment."

Bruno's mouth turned down. "Betsy was such a kind soul. To die so young was a tragedy." He turned on the couch to face Nelson. "But you haven't paid me a visit this morning to share how much we've each found out about our . . . enemies? Is that what we are, Marshal, enemies? Or are you using insights from your college psychology minor to see what makes me tick?"

Nelson thought about that. On the one hand, he wanted to know Bruno better, yearned to know the man who had grown to run a criminal enterprise all along the eastern seaboard. On the other hand, his gut feeling tempted him to pummel the man for ordering the beatings of Natty and Rick Jones, for surely Bruno's thugs didn't raise a hand against anyone without Bruno's okay. Or had they acted alone? "Rick Jones was beaten at his ranch yesterday by your men Lazarro and Angelo."

"Did he say that?"

"He refused to speak of it. But his hired hand told us what happened."

"His hired hand cannot press charges, you know that."

"Makes no difference," Nelson said, anger brewing at Bruno's calm demeanor. "A man, a citizen of this county, was beaten for no reason."

"Sugar?" Bruno said as he put two lumps in his tea and slid the sugar bowl toward Nelson. "I neither ordered nor authorized Lazy and Angel to go to Mr. Jones's ranch and hurt him, if in fact they did. Those boys just get a little . . . rambunctious. Exuberant I call them. I am afraid they try too hard to impress me—"

"Like they're in competition for the next lieutenant slot in your organization."

"Lieutenant? You make it sound as if I am the general of some mighty force and I have captains and lieutenants under me."

"Don't you?" Nelson asked. He motioned toward Gavin, leaning cross-armed against a wall twenty feet away. "If I make a move toward you, I am more than certain that man would—"

"Do what it took to protect his boss?" Bruno sipped his tea, and a wry smile crossed his face. "No less than your deputy Maris Red Hat would do what it took to protect you."

Nelson drank his own tea, thinking even sugar and cream wouldn't make it tasty. He needed a strong cup of joe. But then, maybe it was the company he was presently keeping that made it unpalatable.

"This brings us back around to the question of whether or not we are enemies," Bruno said. "I would like to think we have the same goal—finding out who murdered my brother and bringing the killer to justice."

Nelson set the cup on the tray and stood. "In that, we have the same goal. But our methods are different."

"That they are."

"When the killer is found, he—or she—can only have justice meted out *my* way."

"We shall see," Bruno said.

"One last thing," Nelson said. "Natty Barnes."

"What about that little man at the feed store?"

"He's a slug for siccing your dogs on Rick Jones when the poor bastard didn't know a thing about your brother. But I want him left alone."

"He hasn't been touched," Bruno said.

"Not yet. I do not want to hear that one of your men, in their desire to impress you, roughed him up. Or Lucky, when he finally returns to his ranch."

Bruno smiled. "You have done your homework, Marshal. One of my men watches the Graber ranch, I'll admit. Just in case this Lucky Graber returns, for I believe he is the key to finding out about Gino's murder."

Bruno stood, and Nelson was quick to size him up. With his heavy shoulders threatening to burst through his casual jacket, he would be a worthy opponent in a fair fight. But his kind, Nelson knew, rarely fought fair. Of course if it came to that, Nelson knew how to fight the *other* way as well.

"You have my word, Marshal—just to ensure good relations with local law enforcement—that Natty Barnes will not be touched," Bruno said. "It would seem he knows little about my brother anyhow."

As Nelson left the Cottonwood's common room, he watched Gavin Corrigan out of his good eye. If the thug jumped him, Nelson was certain Gavin knew enough about him now that he would come at him from his blind side. Attack his bad leg, and that would be bad news for Nelson.

CHAPTER 19

Nelson headed for Natty's Feed Store to tell him he'd talked with Bruno and actually believed him. In his perverted way, Bruno's own code of honor assured Nelson that Natty wouldn't be harmed.

As he headed across the highway, Maris's truck slid around the corner kicking up snow, passing a covered buggy, the horse sun-dancing in the traces as Maris passed, the woman fighting the reins to get the gelding under control. Nelson stopped the panel truck just as Maris's vehicle skidded in the fresh snow and nearly clipped Nelson's. She bailed out and slipped on the ice, her hat rolling across the road as she fell.

Nelson got out and offered her his hand, but she slapped it away, looking around to see if anyone was watching. She used the fender of her truck to stand and said, out of breath, "There's been another killing." She brushed snow from her jeans. "At Lucky's ranch."

"Take a breath," Nelson said, "and tell me what's going on."

She bent over and sucked in big gulps of air. "Rick Jones called the SO. There's a dead man in Lucky's barnyard."

"Lucky?"

"He couldn't tell. Only thing he knew is, Toby came running back from Lucky's and said there was a man lying dead beside Lucky's old tractor. DeMyron was washing his clothes at the sheriff's garage when the call came in, and he headed out there right away."

"Then we better get there before he screws up the crime scene. Park your truck. I'm thinking you're in no shape to drive—"

"I am *not* drunk."

"I didn't say that," Nelson said. "But the way your shirt is a button off and you forgot to zip your jeans, I'm thinking you just came from Sal DeLuca's room."

"Or he from mine," Maris admitted. "I'll park this thing."

When they arrived at Lucky's ranch a half hour later, DeMyron had parked his sheriff's truck blocking Mac McKeen and Toby from driving their Model T into the crime scene and destroying any evidence. *At least DeMyron's was learning something,* Nelson thought. "See what Mac and his kid have to say. I'm going to grab DeMyron and look over the scene."

Maris peeled off toward Mac's Model T while Nelson walked to DeMyron's sheriff's truck and climbed in. "What do we have?"

DeMyron pointed to the body lying face down in the snow fifty yards away in front of the house. "All's I know is, Mac and his boy showed up right after I pulled into the yard. I'm thinking they were a little scared to come any farther. Maybe something to do with all the blood."

"So, we don't know who the victim is?"

"We do not," DeMyron said. "I didn't want to approach and disturb anything until you got here. You're a lot better than me at deciphering tracks. But my money's on Lucky sneaking back to his ranch and running into one of Bruno's thugs."

Nelson buttoned his coat and turned up his collar. "Let's take a look."

DeMyron fell behind as Nelson slowly walked toward the victim, looking at the ground, picking up telltale signs as to what happened. Toby had gotten out of the Model T, apparently feeling safe enough to gawk now that the law had arrived, and his worn-to-hell boots made little impression despite the kid's bulk as he approached the dead man. He eyeballed the body for a couple of seconds, then turned and walked away.

Nelson stopped five yards from the corpse and squatted on his heels while DeMyron looked over his shoulder. "I give you Lazy Stefano."

DeMyron whistled. "I'd like to say I'm sorry, but I'm not."

"We still have to treat this as any other murder. Wait here."

Nelson walked a loose circle around the body. He could just see Lazy's tongue protruding, swollen, making the corpse look like he was licking the snow. One hand had frozen close to his side, the fingers broken and sticking out at odd angles. A revolver lay in the snow a few feet from where Lazy had fallen. The tire tracks of Andy Olssen's Packard—wider than most cars hereabouts—showed where it had driven around the ranch yard before leaving, and Nelson wished it had snowed *more* last night. He couldn't age the tire tracks, couldn't say if they were fresh or not. Couldn't say if the tracks were made the last time Andy and Darby Branigan were here.

Nelson walked a few yards away from the body, halting when he spotted fresh tire tracks that led to the barn. He motioned for DeMyron to follow him and started toward the dilapidated structure. Inside was Lazy's Lincoln, backed in and positioned so the driver could look out the open barn door at the house and the ranch yard. A single set of footprints showed where Lazy had gotten out of his car and walked to where he now lay.

"Any theories?" DeMyron asked.

"Didn't learn much from the tire tracks. Those"—Nelson pointed to tracks entering the yard—"are probably from yesterday when Andy Olssen and his engineer drove in here. And Mac's Model T tracks show that he turned right around and took off when he saw the body."

"What do you make of Lazy's car backed into the barn like this?"

"You tell me," Nelson said, forcing the deputy to think for himself.

DeMyron glanced over at the Lincoln. "Bruno's men were . . . assigned to watch for Lucky to come back. Lazy backed in far enough to hide the car and still watch the house." He shook his head. "If I were supposed to watch the place, I'd have thrown a sheet over myself and lain in the snow on top of that hill over yonder." He pointed to a rise a hundred yards away. "Like I do when I'm hunting coyotes."

"*You* would do that, but you got to remember these are city boys. The most discomfort Lazy here could have stood was sitting in his car in the barn. He'd last about five minutes watching the place lying out in the snow."

DeMyron chuckled. "Well, he's lying in the snow now."

Nelson couldn't argue with that as he left the barn and walked back to the corpse. He tried rolling Lazy over, but the dead man's departing body heat had melted the snow beneath him, which had since stuck him to the ground. "Take his legs and help me," Nelson said to DeMyron.

Lazy's jacket stuck to the dirt. They jerked, and the cloth ripped, leaving some material behind as they laid the body on its back. Nelson knelt beside the corpse and bent closer. Lazy's eye socket was broken, and his jaw sat at an odd angle, also probably broken, along with fingers of his left hand.

"Lazy was a stout feller," DeMyron said, looking over Nelson's shoulder. "It took some power to work him over like that. What do you make of his fingers busted back?"

Nelson pushed Lazy's left coat sleeve up but saw no wristwatch. When he pushed up the right sleeve, a Bulova sparked in the bright sunlight. "Lazy was left-handed. His left fingers are broken. His gun in the snow." Nelson stood and arched his back, stretching. "Someone—powerful, like you pointed out—fought with Lazy. He drew his gun. His attacker grabbed his hand. Broke his fingers."

"Before shooting the bastard, I'd wager," DeMyron said, staring at the hole in Lazy's midsection.

Nelson squatted beside the corpse again. "Mushroom soup."

"What's that?"

"Mushroom soup. Lazy ate some not too long before he was killed." Nelson flicked aside pieces of mushroom from Lazy's silk shirtfront and unbuttoned it. Unburnt flecks of powder dotted the fabric. "Close range."

"Any guess of weapon?"

Nelson shook his head. "High powered handgun. A .45 Colt." He tapped his holster. "Or an Army Colt .45." He nodded at DeMyron's single-action thumb-buster in his hip holster. "Or any deer rifle. We'll know more when we get Lazy to autopsy."

Maris walked over with Mac and Toby beside her. "Tell him what you said," she told Toby.

Toby buttoned his long overcoat that reached to his knees and pulled his cap down over his ears. He stared at the ground and kicked a piece of ice with his boot toe. "I come over here this morning—"

"Why? Did you think Lucky might return?"

Toby shook his head. "I came over, Marshal, 'cause I figured he *weren't* coming back anytime soon. I been coming over every other day or so to make sure Lucky's old mare has hay and bust the ice off the water tank." He looked at Lazy's body and quickly turned away. "That's when I seen him. I walked on over to him, lying there. Figuring maybe he just fell or had a heart attack or something. Soon's I seen he was a goner, I hightailed it back home and got Pa."

"I didn't believe him," Mac said. "Dead man. I was sure the kid was making things up."

Nelson told Maris, "Follow Toby and Mac to Rick's place and get a written statement from them—"

"Marshal," Mac said, turning his back so Toby wouldn't hear. "The kid cain't write and spell so good."

"Deputy Red Hat can write it for him, then."

"You going to wait for the coroner?" Maris asked.

"Not much he can do," Nelson said. "We can load Lazy up in DeMyron's truck and haul him to town. But it's DeMyron's call."

DeMyron shrugged. "The marshal's right—nothing the coroner can do except verify he's dead. Which I think I can look at a man with a hole in his gut and his last meal leaking out of said hole and call him dead."

Nelson patted Maris on the back. "Then later today or tomorrow you get an all-expenses paid trip out of town."

Maris smiled. "About time I got to live large on the government's dime. Where'm I going?"

"Billings," Nelson said. "You are going to cart Lazy there for a visit to the medical examiner."

Chapter 20

Nelson found Bruno and Sal DeLuca and Angel Gallo dining at the Gillette Cafe. He almost didn't spot them right off with their new clothes. They had discarded their double-breasted suits for jeans and flannels, and three suede leather coats hung on the coat rack by the door. Angel still had the store's *B. H. McCarthy* tag dangling from a lapel where he hadn't cut it off.

It took Nelson a moment longer to spot Gavin Corrigan seated at a corner table apart from his boss, yet close enough to respond if needed. Bruno looked up for a brief second before saying, "As you can see, Marshal, there's not enough room at the table for another."

"I'm not here to eat. I am here to have a word with you."

"Talk away if you can make it quick."

"I'd rather talk in private."

Bruno waved the air with his glass of tea. "I have no secrets from my associates. Whatever you have to say, you can say with them present."

"All right, then," Nelson said. He grabbed a chair and turned it around, draping his arm over the chair back, ready to gauge the reactions of those at the table. "Your man Lazarro was watching Lucky Graber's place in case Lucky returned."

"I won't comment on that," Bruno answered, "except to say that would be trespassing, and my men don't break the law. Why, has that Deputy Duggar rousted Lazy again?"

"Lazy is dead," Nelson said flatly, watching the men at the

table, and Gavin from the corner of his good eye. Sal had no change in his flat expression as he twirled spaghetti on a spoon before stuffing his pie hole, while Angel merely broke off a corner of garlic bread and dabbed sauce on his plate.

Bruno's hands trembled, and he set his fork and spoon down. "How did it happen?"

"As I said, he was at Lucky's ranch. Hiding in the barn. Watching the house. It appears he left his car, probably to check out his killer who had come onto the place. There was a fight. I would say he went for his gun, and his attacker broke Lazy's hand right before he either hit or kicked Lazy in the head. Before Lazy could recover, his killer drilled him."

Bruno slapped Angel on the back of the head. "What the hell are you smiling about?"

"I can't help but smile, boss. With Lazy gone—"

"With Lazy gone, you figure you're next in line?" Bruno said.

Angel shrugged.

Bruno took his kerchief from his pocket and dabbed perspiration from his forehead. "Who did this to Lazy?"

"I don't know yet," Nelson answered. "I was hoping you'd have some ideas?"

Bruno's eyes darted to Angel for a brief moment before he looked at Nelson again. "Lazy was a cautious man," Bruno began. "Actually, he was a paranoid man. People in our business tend to develop that if they want to stay alive. He would not let just anyone get close enough to grab him, let alone hit him. I doubt anyone could distract him long enough for him to get shot."

"And yet he was," Nelson said.

"And yet he was," Bruno repeated and looked directly at Angel. "Unless Lazy knew his killer. Unless his killer was someone he was used to talking with, up close."

Angel's smile faded. "Whatcha looking at me for, boss?"

"I think he feels you had the most to gain from Lazy's death," Nelson said.

"Boss, I wasn't within twenty miles of that place. I left Lazy last night, and I didn't figure on relieving him on lookout until this afternoon."

"Tell me, Marshal," Bruno said, "were Lazy's injuries—at least those not connected with his gunshot wound—made by a physically powerful man?"

Nelson nodded, keeping his eyes on Angel. The bruiser sat back in his chair, his foot tapping nervously as he looked away. "Lazy's attacker would have been strong, for certain."

"Then you may have your killer already."

"Angel?"

"Deputy Duggar," Bruno said.

"I don't follow you," Nelson lied, thinking back to his recent conversation with DeMyron about what they would do if Bruno's boys came after them. It was plausible the deputy had gone off the reservation and killed the thug, especially after Lazy had fought DeMyron so hard when the deputy arrested him. And DeMyron was a little more than pissed that Lazy had made bond so easily.

Bruno clearly thought so, too. "I heard from a good source that your Deputy Duggar used to be a rodeo man. Bulldogging five-hundred-pound steers. Riding saddle bronc. Bulls. And along with that, a working ranch hand."

"What's your point?"

"A man that strong could get the upper hand against Lazy. He did the other day when he arrested him. And the deputy always carries a gun."

"You all carry guns as well."

"We do not—" Sal began.

"Sal, Sal." Nelson wagged a finger. "Next time you select a gun to carry, make sure it's small enough to be hidden under your armpit."

"Your man, Deputy Duggar . . . he had words with Lazy," Angel blurted out. "Goaded him into resisting arrest. Roughed him up before tossing him in jail."

"It's debatable who roughed up who," Nelson said, fighting to blot out of his mind what DeMyron told him yesterday: that he could kill a criminal if it meant a safer place for citizens. Did DeMyron's idea of rough justice bleed through when he found Lazy at Lucky's ranch? "And like you said, *your* man Angelo had a lot to gain with Lazy dead. That's if we're pointing fingers."

"I don't think he killed Lazy," Bruno said, kicking Angelo under the table, "though they were rivals in my . . . business. Marshal, I am not entirely convinced Deputy Duggar was so brazen as to kill Lazy either, especially since I doubt Lazy would have allowed the deputy to get close, given the bad blood between them." He laid his fork on his plate, his appetite obviously gone. "So that leaves us with the only one it could be—Lucky Graber himself. He could have returned—"

"Lucky's a small man," Nelson said. "Almost frail. At least that was my impression the few times I met him."

"All the more reason to suspect him."

"How so?"

"Lazy was a big man. He would not feel threatened at all if a small man walked up to him for any reason. In fact, he would have welcomed Lucky's approach, as Lazy would finally have him within his grasp to . . . talk with."

"Just how would a little feller do the damage he did on someone like Lazy? You're right—your man was anything but small."

"Perhaps—just perhaps, Marshal—your rendition of things is out of order. What if Lazy was shot first?" Bruno held up his hand. "I know what you're wondering—why bust up Lazy after he was dead? And I say to you, I've known men who went berserk *after* they killed another. Went nuts and just kicked and kicked and kicked the dead body." He shot a furtive glance toward Gavin at his table in the corner. "Can you not see this Lucky Graber—his ranch held hostage by a fancy Billings banker—losing it and killing the first man he caught on his place—Lazy. Can you not see Lucky venting his frustrations after Lazy was on the ground dead?"

Nelson thought back to Maris's encounter with Lucky and how he had gone nuts on her. Threatened her with his rifle. And Nelson remembered that day in the R&R where Lucky's temper nearly got the best of him.

But if Lucky were the killer—provided he was actually still alive—where the hell was he hiding?

Chapter 21

"Your bedmate had nothing to say about Lazarro Stefano's murder?" Nelson asked.

"Nada," Maris said. "I didn't want to press Sal on it too much, especially since he was trying to get information out of *me* at the same time. All I know is that it's making Bruno's men nervous. First Gino's death that hasn't been solved, now Lazy's." She warmed up Nelson's coffee before sitting back behind Sheriff Jarvis's desk. "There's something else that's been bothering you about Lazy," she said, "or else you wouldn't have let your coffee get cold just staring at it."

Nelson set his cup down and stood, pacing in front of the desk like he was preparing to address a jury. "I was only lukewarm to DeMyron being the killer yesterday, but what he said just got me edgy."

"Let me ask you this," Maris said. "If DeMyron were the killer, could he have walked up on Lazy? By what Sal said, Lazy was the most cautious one of Bruno's men."

"Unless he didn't feel threatened," Nelson said. "I thought of Lucky when I thought of that—smaller man. Non-threatening to someone Lazy's size. And what if Lazy *didn't* feel threatened when DeMyron approached him. He wouldn't expect to get shot right off by a lawman—"

"Stop it!" Maris said. "DeMyron might have wanted to do just what the killer did, but it doesn't mean he's the one who popped Lazy. Besides, there are other suspects you're forgetting about."

"Oh?"

"Sure," Maris said, then, "Will you have a seat and drink your coffee. It's way too early in the morning, and you're making *me* nervous."

Nelson did as his deputy suggested and settled back in the seat cradling the coffee mug. "Who are these other suspects you're talking about?"

"Who did you catch trespassing at Lucky's ranch less than twenty-four hours before Toby found Lazy dead?"

"Andy Olssen," Nelson breathed. "I thought about him and Darby Branigan. Andy's tire tracks were at the scene, but I couldn't tell if they were from before or not. Besides, I wouldn't figure him for murder."

"Maybe it wasn't murder. At least not outright," Maris argued. "Maybe Andy and Darby stopped at Lucky's ranch again when Lazy spotted them. Confronted them, and Andy put a hurt on him. By the size of Andy, I would say he's big enough he could have twisted Lazy in a pretzel without breaking a sweat."

"That would mean Andy would have to get his hands dirty. Besides, he doesn't pack a gun."

"Maybe *he* didn't pull the trigger," Maris said. She opened a box and rooted through a stack of small paper bags, chose one, and dumped what it held—a deformed bullet—onto the desk. "When Dr. Barr cut into Lazy's chest at autopsy, this is the only piece of bullet fragment she could find. Soft. Part broke off when it hit his sternum and exited his back. She couldn't speculate on it being from a rifle or handgun, though. Even you said it could have been either. Darby Branigan packs a hogleg, and he's been with Andy."

"I don't know—"

"Darby's killed before, you said, if the stories from his time in Mexico are accurate."

Nelson hefted the bullet. His thumb dented the soft lead, and he put it back into the paper sack. "Darby carries a Colt Army revolver. I haven't used one of those for years, but last I recalled, they favor softer lead bullets."

"Shit!"

"Shit, what?"

"Darby's not the only one who packs a Colt Army," Maris said.

"Shit is right," Nelson said. "We're back to looking at DeMyron."

She stood abruptly. "Shush. Here he comes now."

DeMyron walked through the door and set a plaster cast on the desk as he caught Maris's eye. "You're not the only one who knows something about gathering evidence."

She stood and brushed dirt from the cast onto the floor. "So it's plaster of Paris—"

"Dental material," he corrected. "Dentist down the street let me have a box. Used for casting for dentures—"

"I know what it's for," Maris interrupted. "What I don't know is what this casting is *of*."

"A footprint, of course." DeMyron draped his coat on the elk-horn rack beside the door and grabbed a paintbrush from his pocket. "Rather, it's two footprints," he said as he brushed the last of the dirt into the garbage can. "From right outside the point of entry."

"Point of entry for what?" Maris asked, her curiosity piqued as she looked down at the casting.

"Pearl's Drug Store. It got broken into last night, and this set of tracks was *right* under the window the burglar climbed in."

"What was taken?" Nelson asked, knowing Pearl's had everything from hard drugs to chewing gum.

"Booze," DeMyron said. "Plain old hooch that old man Pearl claims he keeps just for when doctors prescribe it for medicinal purposes." He laughed. "I always suspected Pearl himself took a nip of his *medicinal* alcohol more often than not. I saw a whole pack of prescription notes just ready to be filled out on the counter."

Nelson had seen the tan-papered prescription notes back when he was still drinking, and he'd asked a pharmacist in Buffalo to issue him a prescription for alcohol. For a cough, Nelson had lied. Even though he'd had to pay three dollars for the prescription and another three for the pharmacist to file it with the government, it had been worth it just to get his hooch for the day.

"Except he has permits issued by the government," Nelson said. Pharmacists and doctors were allowed to prescribe alcohol for *medicinal purposes.* Some drug stores—like Walgreens across the country—had added hundreds of stores since Prohibition began. It was not uncommon for local pharmacies to be stocked as well as any liquor establishment prior to the Volstead Act.

DeMyron took out his pouch of Bull Durham and deftly rolled a cigarette. "I figure our burglar is an alcoholic. Took all the hooch that old man Pearl had stashed under the counter. Enough to last for some time. And . . . the burglar is very cagey."

"You can tell that just from the footprints?" Maris chided. "Amazing."

"My dear Deputy Marshal, even us local hicks can figure some things out." He held the casting up and grabbed a pencil, pointing with it while he spoke. "This man—and I figure he is a male by the size and depth of the prints—slipped something over his shoes to mask any identifying marks. I'm thinking maybe nylon stockings. As you can see, there's almost nothing that might identify the burglar's boots."

"Then why the hell did you take the time to cast them?"

Maris asked.

DeMyron set the casting down on the desk. "I guess I thought there might be more to ID the suspect once I got an impression made."

Nelson leaned over and looked at the casting. The smoothness and the shape nagged at him. Most tracks left by men walking showed at least some faint design, even moccasins. He had seen the vagueness of that print somewhere, though he couldn't recall where. And right now, he had other things to do before the sun came up.

Chapter 22

The bloody snow hadn't been whisked away by the wind, reminding Nelson of Lazarro Stefano's body lying twenty yards from the barn where his car had been backed in. He paused and closed his eyes, once again thinking how Bruno's thug had been killed. Nelson breathed deeply, coming up with the same scenario: someone Lazy trusted or was not alarmed by had gotten close enough to attack him.

But the *why* continued to eat at Nelson, and the suspects came to mind once again. DeMyron, because Lazy had resisted arrest and because DeMyron would have little remorse killing someone who deserved it. The cowboy code? Nelson had no answer, but other more likely suspects pushed DeMyron down on the list. Angelo Gallo could now rise to the top of Bruno's organization, with Lazy no longer competing for the top spot. If Captain Magnus Koats was right about Angelo's victims in New Jersey, the thug would have had no trouble killing Lazy, either. Just another day at the office. Gavin? If he thought Lazy was about to do something that would reflect bad on his boss, he would be capable.

When Maris first mentioned Andy Olssen as a suspect, Nelson pooh-poohed it, thinking the fancy Billings banker incapable of murder. But if Andy was comfortable foreclosing on so many ranchers, kicking them off their land, leaving them and their families without a home . . . if he could do that with not a shred of remorse or empathy, he could be capable of murder.

More likely Darby Branigan. Nelson knew little of him except that he was a bully, bragging to folks how he had killed Mexicans south of the border, and wearing his Colt Army low like he would quickly use it again if provoked. But Nelson didn't figure Darby to be Andy's protector—the man was big enough that his *size* was his own protection. Had they worked together, with Darby doing the shooting after Andy roughed Lazy up?

And Lucky Graber—he grated on Nelson the worst, perhaps. The man had gone missing just before Bruno and his entourage motored into Gillette. He surely would have known all about Gino's death and would have gotten wind of Bruno and his men coming into town. Nelson and Maris had scoured Campbell County for him but failed to find any trace of Lucky. Had he gone into hiding, or had one of Bruno's men found him that first day? Nelson didn't think so, for—up until yesterday when Lazy was murdered—they had placed a man at Lucky's ranch to watch for his return. But would Lucky go into hiding and leave the care of his mare to Toby, either by arrangement with the kid or just by happenstance? Most ranchers wouldn't leave their livestock without food and water, particularly their horses. He made a mental note to talk with Toby and ask him if he, in fact, had agreed to look after Lucky's mare.

Nelson had started for the barn when he heard a car approaching. Jamie Romano fishtailed down the driveway into the ranch yard. She skidded to a stop beside Nelson's panel truck and waved frantically from the window of her Model A. He paused before the open barn doors and waited for her to climb out.

She shut the car door with a *thunk* and hurried over to him. "Nelson, I'm glad I caught you before you rode off."

"How did you know I'd be here, let alone that I'd be riding?"

"A reporter's sources are never revealed," she said and laughed. "All right, Deputy Red Hat said you'd gone out to Lucky's ranch. Do you really think he's dead?"

"Whatever I say will just get in your newspaper, so I have no comment."

She slipped her notebook and pencil back into her handbag. "Okay then, off the record—do you think Lucky's dead?"

"I don't know," Nelson said. "He hasn't been seen in a week."

"I heard Bruno and his gangsters have taken an interest in him," Jamie said.

"Bruno thinks Lucky knows what happened to his brother Gino. He figures if Gino was on Lucky's property, Lucky has to have known how Gino died. I aim to find out just what happened to Lucky."

"So you think he's still here on his ranch?"

Nelson nodded. "Either dead or in hiding."

"How do you expect to find him?" Jamie asked, putting her collar up against the wind. "This place is pretty big."

"The postal carrier saw Lucky head cross pasture in his wagon the day Gino was discovered dead. This is something I should have done long ago, but I was a little busy with other things." He motioned to the bloody snow where Lazy was killed.

Jamie grabbed her pencil and notebook once again. "On the record: are there any suspects in Lazarro Stefano's murder?"

"Ask Deputy Duggar—it's his case. I'm just helping out until I find Lucky."

Jamie stowed her notebook again. "DeMyron wouldn't tell me anything about Lazarro's murder either. Heck, when I interviewed him about the burglary at Pearl's Drug Store, he said he has a suspect but would tell me little else. Certainly nothing I can use for a story."

"That's news to me that he's developed a suspect already."

"You'll tell me who it is when he makes an arrest?"

"Again, it's DeMyron's case."

"You're not helping any," Jamie said.

"Okay. Okay. I'll put in a good word, tell DeMyron when he makes that arrest to contact you before the *News Record* reporter lassoes him for comments," Nelson said and headed for the barn.

"Where are you going?"

"The barn. Come along if you want."

Nelson walked through the barn doors and over to the cracked and weathered saddle he'd seen hanging over the top rung of a stall. A snaffle bit hung by a nail nearby, and he grabbed both. "Hand me that blanket."

"That!" Jamie said. "It's dusty and . . . it smells."

"Of course it smells," Nelson said. "It's a horse blanket. Now grab it and follow me if you want to be of any help."

He shouldered the saddle and walked out of the barn to the corral, where Lucky's mare trotted over, expecting a treat. He reached into his shirt pocket and gave the sorrel a carrot.

"That's your ride for today?" Jamie asked, holding the blanket away from her.

Nelson stroked the horse's muzzle. "She'll do me just fine."

"Is there room for two people on her?"

"Jamie," Nelson said, "that sorrel has to be pushing twenty years. It'll be all she can do to cart me around even if I don't push her."

"Can I at least quote you as to where you're riding?"

"I'm riding to where Gino was found dead."

"Why?" she asked. "Was there something you missed?"

Nelson shook the dust out of the blanket before draping it over the mare's back. "There is always something to be missed," he said, eying the mare, thinking this might be a mistake before giving her the benefit of the doubt. She wasn't Nelson's mule. But she'd do for today.

Nelson stood in the stirrups and looked around as he gave the sorrel another carrot. He had meandered back and forth on Lucky's section of land, riding to cut any recent sign in the snow. Especially wagon ruts. But with the ground frozen for the past month and the blowing snow covering any wagon tracks made last night, he wasn't optimistic that he would find anything.

As he rode toward the place where Gino's body had been found, movement along the fence line caught his eye. Toby stood beside Mac's Model T truck, bending over a broken fence post. He looked up and frowned when he saw Nelson.

"Lucky's old mare hasn't been ridden in a long time," Toby said. "I don't think Lucky would like that."

"You wouldn't know if he's still around here to disapprove?"

Toby turned his back and bent to the fence post once more. "I can only hope he is. He's a good friend. Maybe my only one."

"Lucky didn't ask you to look after his mare, by any chance?"

Toby looked sideways at Nelson. "Why do you ask, Marshal?"

"Because you've been a good neighbor, stopping by Lucky's every other day, feeding and making sure this old girl has ice knocked off the water tank. I ask you because I wonder if you know where Lucky is, and if he asked you to tend to her."

Still bent to the fence post, Toby said, "I don't know where Lucky is. I think I am like you said . . . a good neighbor."

Nelson stepped down from the horse, dropped the reins, and walked toward the fence. He pulled his gloves on tighter. "Let me help you with that."

"I don't need help, Marshal."

"But the ground's froze."

Toby wrapped his arms around the busted post and grunted as he lifted with his legs. The post came out of the ground, and he tossed it aside. "I hope you find Lucky," he said as he stood panting, wiping sweat from his forehead. "He's a nice man."

"Where do *you* think he went?"

Toby shrugged and took a new fence post from the back of the truck. "Where do *you* think he went?"

Nelson nodded to the west. "I'm thinking he went thataway a week ago, right after I confronted him in the café."

Toby looked in the same direction and pulled his coat around his bib overalls. "Went where?"

"Don't know. But Vilas, the postman, saw him with this old mare hitched to his wagon headed thataway the day Gino Bonelli was found dead." Nelson pointed to the west again. "If you're his friend, I was hoping you might know where he went."

"So you can boot him off his place?" Toby kicked snow off his worn-out boots before dropping the new fence post beside the hole. "If you do find him, tell him Toby misses him. And, Marshal, you might give the mare an extra dollop of hay when you bed her down for the night."

Chapter 23

Nelson got back into town some while later and was nearing the courthouse when he saw two new Lincoln touring cars parked in front. Only one man in Gillette could afford those. As Nelson pulled into the parking lot, he saw Mac McKeen leaving the courthouse, dragging Toby along by the arm. The boy had a large welt on his cheek, and his split lip bled onto the front of his bib overalls. Mac hauled Toby into their farm truck, then climbed into the driver's seat and mashed gears as he fishtailed away. Nelson heard loud cursing coming from inside the truck a moment before it disappeared around the corner of Main Street.

Nelson parked beside DeMyron's sheriff's truck and climbed out. He went into the courthouse, mounted the stairs to the suite marked *Sheriff's Office,* and was passing Bonnie's desk when she said, "*Psst.*"

Nelson stopped. "What was Toby and Mac's problem?"

"Toby got a little roughed up by Bruno Bonelli's men," she said. "They're inside Sheriff Jarvis's office with DeMyron."

Nelson expected the worst as he entered the small room. Bruno and Sal DeLuca sat to one side, with Gavin Corrigan doing his usual best to hold up an opposite wall while he watched his boss. "Here, sign this," DeMyron said, pushing a piece of paper across the sheriff's desk.

"Don't know if I can," Sal said. "The kid about broke my neck."

"Do your best," DeMyron said.

Sal took the pen and slowly, painfully signed DeMyron's form.

"What's going on?" Nelson asked.

"That McKeen kid," Bruno said. "Got a little . . . overzealous with Sal here."

"About what?"

Bruno chuckled, but Sal did not as he handed DeMyron the form and pen back. "We were down at the R&R for a late lunch when the kid comes in and sits down. The waitress with the nice tush . . ."

"Marley," Sal said.

"Sure," Bruno said. "Marley. She and the kid got to talking when Sal wanted to order a piece of pie after the fine buffalo stew. When she didn't hear, Sal whistled at her, and the kid went ape shit. Yelled that Sal was disrespecting a woman and jumped him."

"He caught me by surprise," Sal said, "or I would have laid him out right off. But he put me in a chokehold so bad, Gavin had to get the kid off me."

"And after Toby's hold was broke?" Nelson faced Gavin. "Is that when those knots on the kid's face came about?"

Gavin smiled. "I do what's me pappy showed me to do. But I took it easy on the kid."

Nelson bent and looked at the statement form. "So now you're pressing charges for assault? On a sixteen year old who's more than a little slow?"

"Marshal," Sal said and rubbed his throat, "the kid's as big as me and strong."

"That's fair enough." Nelson sat on the edge of the desk. "You know how I doubted Lazy would be coming back for his court date on DeMyron's assault warrant?"

"I remember," Bruno said. "What's your point?"

"My point is," Nelson answered, with an exaggerated wide

smile, "I doubt Sal here will want to come back from New Jersey to testify against Toby."

"Marshal's right," Sal said to DeMyron: "Might as well rip it up. But, Marshal, a kid can't be running around attacking people."

As if you don't do just that for a living? "I don't understand. I spoke to Toby this morning, and he was all right."

"Well, he was sure worked up about something," Bruno said.

About his friend's disappearance? "When's Toby's court date for the assault?"

"Guess we're not pressing charges. Are we, Sal?"

"Guess not, Boss. Even if I did stick around to testify, it would be embarrassing to tell the judge Gavin had to rescue me from a . . . kid. Even if he is as big as me."

Bruno put up his hands. "So you see, Marshal, we're not as bad as Captain Koats says we are. We just want to get along with people here until we find my brother's killer, then be out of your hair. I take it you didn't find out anything today?"

"Does everyone in town know I went back to where Gino's body was found?"

"I notice that you always say 'where Gino was found,' " Bruno said. "As if he wasn't killed there?"

"I don't know *where* he was killed. There was blood at the scene, but we're not ruling out he was murdered some other place and transported there," Nelson said, an image in his mind of Lucky in the wagon, headed across his pasture the day of Gino's murder.

"I am getting impatient," Bruno said, "about Gino as well as Lazy. He might not have been family like you think of it, but Lazy was *family* in *our* way. You will let me know how your progress is coming?"

"Not if you plan on dishing out your special kind of justice," Nelson answered.

"Then there is nothing more to discuss," Bruno said a moment before leading Sal and Gavin out of the office.

Nelson waited until he heard their cars drive off before relaxing and snapping his holster closed. "What's up with Toby?" he asked as he picked up Sal's written statement. "I would have thought the kid didn't have a mean bone in his body."

"Me, too," DeMyron said. "I talked with him in his cell at the city jail after I hauled him in, and he admitted what Bruno said—that he thought Sal was disrespecting a woman in the R&R. Toby's mother died when he was just a little pot licker, and he's sensitive around women, according to Mac."

"And I'm sure me prodding him about Lucky didn't help any," Nelson added. "No wonder the kid was worked up."

The phone rang, and DeMyron answered. He got a serious look on his face and handed it to Nelson while he covered the speaker with his palm. "Hold onto your butt, big man."

An unpleasantly familiar voice crackled from the mouthpiece. "Bobby Weatherspoon here," the U.S. attorney said. "I know you're there because the deputy said you were."

Nelson breathed deeply before he raised the phone to his ear. "This is about Lucky Graber, isn't it?"

"Marshal Lane," Witherspoon said, "we have a dozen Lucky Grabers around the state doing their best to avoid service."

"But only one with his note held by Andy Olssen of the Stockman's Bank of Billings?"

"Bingo," Witherspoon said. "There better be a good reason why you haven't evicted him off his property."

"We haven't been able to find him." Nelson added, "Believe me, I have froze my butt off looking for him today alone."

"There's another way," Witherspoon said. "Put an ad in the paper announcing a quick sale of the Graber ranch. The only one with money who's interested in the property is bound to be Stockman's Bank. Andy Olssen will buy it, and we'll have him off our backs. Are we clear?"

"As clear as that stock tank on Lucky's ranch."

Nelson placed an ad in the *News Record* that he would be conducting a sale of Lucky's ranch on the courthouse steps in forty-eight hours, then drove to the R&R. The supper traffic was thinning out, with only one railroader left in the café. Marley smiled wide as she walked over to his corner booth with a coffee pot and cup "What'll it be, Marshal?"

"Peach pie and information."

"Information about what?"

"Toby," he answered. "Please sit down. You need a break."

"After the commotion today that Buster figures I started, he's watching me closely—"

"Let me worry about your cook. Besides, business is slow right now," Nelson said. "Your feet deserve a rest."

Marley fetched the pie slice, then sat across from Nelson and poured two cups of coffee. "It's about the fight here earlier today, isn't it?"

"It is." Nelson told the waitress what Bruno had said about the altercation.

"That about sums it up," she said. "I don't know what got into Toby, but he just seemed to snap."

"Bruno claimed Toby went off when Sal whistled at you."

"He had to whistle to get my attention. We were near-full then with a lot of people gabbing. As much as I'm flattered that Toby came to my rescue, there was no disrespect to it."

"Then I'll drop it." Nelson cut into his pie and let the first sliver of hot peach slide *slooowly* down his throat.

"Anything else?"

"Lucky Graber," Nelson said. "The last anyone saw him was when he was in here playing cards with Natty and Mac last week."

"I know." Marley reached across the table and dabbed peach off Nelson's chin with a checkered napkin. "Natty and Mac were worried when Lucky didn't come in for their usual Monday coffee and card game. Mac feared Lucky might have fallen into that canyon on his place."

"Canyon?"

Marley shrugged. "I guess. They said there's a deep canyon on the west end of Lucky's ranch that runs north into Rick Jones's place. According to what Mac was sayin'."

Nelson hadn't ridden that far today. He'd stopped where Gino's body had been found and backtracked towards Lucky's ranch, looking for wagon ruts that might have indicated where the rancher would have gone the day Gino turned up murdered. Or if Lucky had, in fact, transported Gino's corpse to where the McKeens found it.

He ate the last bite of pie and thanked her. He stood and dropped a dollar on the table when she said, "I almost forgot. Andy Olssen asked me to give you a message when I saw you. Him and some husky feller with a gunslinger's rig on stopped in for breakfast."

"I bet it's a doozie. What did he say?"

"He said, 'Tell Marshal Lane I'll see him Friday on the steps of the courthouse.' "

CHAPTER 24

DeMyron stopped alongside Nelson's bungalow as he was unlocking the door. "Want to go along while I talk with Angelo Gallo about Lazy's murder?"

"Think he'll talk?"

"Don't know," DeMyron said. "But I at least have to try if I'm going to eliminate suspects. And if we can talk to him when he's not around Bruno and that bulldog of his, Gallo might just tell us something."

"Sure. I'll go along, soon's I make a detour."

He walked to the cabin next to his and rapped on the door. He got no answer and rapped louder until Maris cracked the door open. Her hair looked as if she had stuck it in a butter churn, and mascara was smeared across one cheek. She squinted through one eye, the other shut tight against the morning sun. "You know what the hell time it is?"

Nelson fished his Waltham out of his jeans. "It is a quarter past seven. Why?"

She wrapped her coat around her before stepping out. She held her finger to her lips and said, "Sal is in there. His neck and back was hurting from that little scuffle with Toby McKeen. I gave him a . . . massage, and it seemed to help—"

"Poor baby," Nelson said. "Could you give me a massage . . . I hurt my backside riding so far on Lucky's old mare yesterday—"

"The hell I will! Now what are you rousting me so early for?"

Nelson motioned for Maris to step away from her door and lowered his voice. "When Sal wakes up from his beauty sleep, get him talking about Angelo. We need to see if he thinks Angelo could have killed Lazy." He chin-pointed to DeMyron. "We're driving over to the Cottonwood to talk with Angelo about Lazy's death. Then"—Nelson swiped her mascara smudge with his bandana—"go to the post office. Talk with that acting postmaster, Smitty. If he gives you any grief, tell him I'll talk with him later."

"About what?"

"Gino mailed a package the day before he died. I want to know where it went and to whom."

"This sounds like a *really* exciting assignment. Is there anything else this damn early in the morning?"

"Matter of fact," Nelson said, "there is. After you go to the post office, drive on over to the feed store and talk with Natty—confirm Gino took him to the cleaners that last card game before he died. I want to know what happened to the hundred dollars Natty claims he lost to Gino that we never found on the body."

Maris went back into her cabin and shut the door while Nelson turned and climbed into DeMyron's truck. "By the way, any leads on your Pearl Drug burglary?" he asked as DeMyron drove away from the motel.

"None," DeMyron said.

"I thought Jamie Romano said you had a suspect?"

"I have a bunch of suspects," DeMyron said, "and they all rolled into town in new Lincolns a week ago."

"Bruno's men? I would think they would be above something as amateurish as breaking and entering some country drug store."

"Tell me, were you ever hooked on the booze . . . when it was legal, of course?"

"Never," Nelson lied. But he had been hooked. More than hooked, it had dominated his life. He got to drinking when he was recuperating in Portsmouth Naval Hospital after the war, even before he met his nurse, Helen, whom he later married. When he was released and they moved back to Wyoming, he would get his drink with a pharmacist's prescription or from a moonshiner, always thinking he was fooling Helen, never realizing she knew every time he came home stinko. Never realizing the damage his drinking did to her until she died young. "Never had the urge. Why?"

"Because it's that urge that I think made one of Bruno's men steal all of Pearl's medicinal hooch."

"How'd you jump to that astute conclusion?"

"Think about it," DeMyron said. "Where they come from, there are thousands of speakeasies. Thousands of places a man can get a drink. But not so in these parts. Sheriff Jarvis and me have shut down all the stills—"

"You never shut down *all* the stills," Nelson said.

"Those we know about, we have. And if we can't find the rest, big city slickers from the East Coast sure can't."

"Still doesn't explain why you suspect one of them."

"Sure it does." DeMyron stopped to let a Diamond REO truck stacked twelve high with chicken cages lumber across the road. A stiff wind passed over the truck, feathers fluttering to the ground like a mini blizzard. "Let's say you're used to a drink whenever you want it. Like they are back home. Then suddenly, you're thrust into an environment where there is no booze at all to be had. Not even the nastiest bathtub gin. You get nervous. You get skittish. If your habit is bad enough, you might even go through withdrawal. Or be so irritable that you go off the deep end and go after your co-workers like Lazy—"

"Lazy wasn't one of Bruno's co-workers. He was a garden variety killer working for a gangster."

"You know what I mean. I could see one of them—maybe Angel—snapping as he's talking to Lazy at Lucky's ranch. They start to argue. Neither has love for the other, and *snap!* Angel goes off the deep end and kills Lazy all because he needs a drink." Still waiting for the chicken truck to pass, DeMyron took the opportunity to stuff his cheek with tobacco. "I think all this is connected. I think one of Bruno's thugs broke into Pearl's for booze, and that person might have killed Lazy in an argument."

"That is one hell of a theory," Nelson said as the road cleared and they started up again. "Let's see if Angelo agrees."

A short while later, they pulled into the parking lot at the Cottonwood Inn. Though Nelson saw no one looking out at them, the hair on his neck told him they were under observation from the second they got out of the truck and walked inside. They entered the common room, where Bruno sat near the fireplace, shadowed by Gavin Corrigan leaning against a wall, his arms crossed. "We seem to meet up more often than I like," Bruno said to Nelson. "Did you like the tea so much you came back for another cup?"

"We're not here to talk with you," DeMyron said. "We need to talk with Angelo."

"Angel? What has he done?"

"We just need to talk to all suspects in Lazarro's death," DeMyron answered.

Bruno's face turned crimson, and he stepped toward DeMyron. "You . . . you think my Angel killed Lazy? How about you? You had as much reason as anybody to kill him."

"What reason would I have—"

"Lazy fought you when you arrested him. Made you look the fool. A proud . . . cowboy would have reason to want revenge. Is that not the cowboy code, Deputy?"

"That's enough." Nelson stepped between them. From the

corner of his good eye, Nelson saw Gavin drop his arms and step away from the wall. "I figure on talking with DeMyron in my own time. My own manner. For now, we need to talk with Angelo. We can do it here or haul him to the sheriff's office."

Bruno backed up and took calming breaths, then told Gavin, "Tell Sal to wake Angel up—"

"Sal's not here," Gavin said. "I don't think he came back last night."

"Well, where the hell is he?" Bruno said.

"Don't know."

"Go wake up Angel." Bruno waved a hand in the air. "I'll be all right."

When Gavin had disappeared down the hallway of rooms, Nelson said, "Your man seems a little nervous leaving you here with us."

"Gavin is like me—he doesn't trust the law. Especially since my brother and one of my men have been killed with absolutely no information about the murderers." He glared at DeMyron.

"Like I told you before," Nelson said, "we both want to find out who killed Gino and now Lazy."

Gavin returned to the common area, followed by Angelo Gallo rubbing his eyes and scratching his crotch through his purple and white undershorts. "Gavin says you insist on talking with me this damn early."

"Come outside," DeMyron said.

"In my skivvies?"

"You can go to your room and put on some pants if you want."

Angel looked to Bruno, who nodded slightly. "Get your pants and coat on and go talk with them."

Angel walked back down the hallway and returned a few minutes later, dressed. He put on his coat and followed DeMyron and Nelson outside. "Now what is this crap Gavin told me about being a suspect in Lazy's death?"

"You and Lazy were not exactly the best of friends," DeMyron said. "In fact, you were competitors for Bruno's attention."

Angelo shrugged. "Can't say I'm sorry he's gone. He was a bastard to get along with. But we've hashed this out already."

"Then you could tell us where you were when Lazarro was murdered," DeMyron asked.

"No big secret now. We were watching for Lucky Graber to come back." Angelo exaggerated spitting on the ground. "That rancher knows *just* what happened to Gino. Lazy relieved me the morning he was killed . . . about the time I was driving back to town."

"Anyone vouch for that?"

Angelo smiled wide, showing front teeth missing. "Sure. Just ask Bruno and Gavin. They'll back up my story."

"I bet they would," DeMyron said. "And how 'bout two nights ago . . . did you happen to stop at Pearl's Drug Store after he closed up?"

"What the hell you talking about now?"

"The drug store keeps . . . kept booze certified for medicinal use," DeMyron said. "How much do you like to drink?"

Angelo shrugged. "I like a nip now and again as much as the next man. But"—he waved his arm around—"there's none to be had in this one-horse town."

"So you admit you have a booze habit?"

"Deputy," Angelo said, "I do not have a booze habit. And that's a good thing, because Bruno threatened any of us if we took a drink while we were here, he'd cut us off at the knees. Or have that mean little bastard Gavin cut us off." He scratched his groin again as two sedans drove slowly by, gawking. "Bruno can vouch for that, too."

"The nerve of Bruno, accusing me of killing Lazarro." DeMyron steered with his elbows as he deftly rolled a cigarette while driving toward the café. "But that was a nice deflection—telling the gangster that you intended talking with me about it."

"It was no deflection," Nelson said. "I needed to talk with you about it sooner, but we've been a little overwhelmed lately."

DeMyron pulled to the side of the road and put the mixing stick in neutral before turning in his seat to face Nelson. "Let's get this over with now so I can get back to solving these two homicides."

"Okay," Nelson said. "Where were *you* at the time Lazy was killed?"

"Where was I?"

"I asked you first."

"Why even ask such a question?"

"To eliminate all possible suspects."

"I'm a suspect?"

"You having a good reason to pop Lazy."

DeMyron struck an Ohio Blue Tip on the dash and lit his cigarette. "I was in my office until about ten o'clock, then went to the fairgrounds. I'm halter breaking one of those wild mustangs from the Red Desert that lady adopted from the government. It's wild as a corn crib rat. I'd just arrived back at the office when I got word of Lazy's death."

"You must have hated him pretty bad, the way he roughed you up when you arrested him."

"I would have loved a rematch," DeMyron answered, "some time when I wasn't wearing this." He tapped his sheriff's star.

"Anybody see you at the fairgrounds, or when you came back to town?"

"It was too cold for anybody else to be there. I didn't run into a soul at the fairgrounds or on the drive back here. Much as I wanted to, I had nothing to do with Lazy's death. You'll just have to trust me."

Right now, Nelson thought, *I don't trust anyone fully. Not even DeMyron Duggar.*

CHAPTER 25

DeMyron held the door to the café for Nelson just as Darby Branigan and Andy Olssen headed outside. "We've been meaning to talk to you," Nelson said to Andy.

"I've been meaning to talk with you, too, about the quick sale of the Graber place tomorrow."

"*After* I talk with you and your engineer about Lazarro Stefano's death at Lucky's ranch," Nelson said. Then to DeMyron: "Why don't you take Darby around the corner and interview him while me and Andy here have our own little visit."

"Can we at least go back inside where it's warm, Marshal?"

"Love to," Nelson said and followed Andy into the cafe. As usual, Marley was working as the sole waitress, and the place was only half crowded with noon customers.

"The special, Marshal?" she called over. "Buffalo stew and cornbread."

"Sure," he answered. "And a big mug of hot cocoa this time." Then, recalling Natty's wife's cocoa, he added, "Make sure it's sweet enough."

Nelson took off his coat and draped it over a chair at a table away from two other people sitting in a corner booth. He turned his chair so he could gauge Andy's expression. "Where were you yesterday morning?"

Andy shrugged. "I was in town. Is this even important?"

"Lazarro Stefano—one of Bruno Bonelli's men—was murdered yesterday."

Andy scooted his chair back, and his eyes darted toward the door as if he intended running out. "I read about it in the *News Record* and *Gillette Daily Journal* both. So this must be important."

"Obviously."

Marley brought over Nelson's meal, then left again. "Okay, Marshal. Okay," Andy said when she was out of earshot. "Let me think . . . I drove south of town to look over two ranches we just . . . acquired—"

"Did you have Darby Branigan with you, by chance?"

"Not then," Andy answered. "Later in the afternoon we had a meeting. Just us two."

"Anyone vouch for where you were?"

Andy looked up to the copper-plated ceiling as if his answer was there. "No. The places I was . . . well, the ranchers had moved off of their own free will, so no one was around."

Like Lucky's free will, Nelson thought. "No one can attest to where you were yesterday morning, then—"

"Natty Barnes," Andy blurted out. "I saw Natty later in the morning with Mac McKeen and that half-wit kid of his. I brought papers by the feed store for Natty to sign." He paused for a long moment before adding, "Mac's kid hit me up to buy more lures, so I know he'll remember it even if he is a little . . . slow. They're still on my floorboard where I threw them if you want to look at 'em."

"That won't be necessary," Nelson said. "That little meeting's easy enough to verify where you were." He took out a notebook and a pencil stub and wet the pencil tip with his tongue.

"What are you writing down?"

"That Natty and Mac and Toby saw you."

Andy blew out a loud sigh. "You *do* believe me, then?"

Nelson nodded. "I believe you were at the feed store *later* in the morning." He underscored his notes and held the notebook so Andy could sneak a look. "But you have no alibi for *early* morning when Lazarro was most likely murdered."

"Now see here, Marshal—"

"No, *you* see here, you pompous, overgrown bully. You complained to the U.S. attorney that I purposely failed to evict Lucky Graber from his ranch. I have no recourse now but to stand on the courthouse steps tomorrow morning and conduct a quick sale of Lucky's property. All right—I took a hit. Might even lose my job when all the dust clears. But"—Nelson tapped his notebook—"there have been two homicides recently, both related to property that you are hot to foreclose on. If you are involved—even the tiniest bit—*I'll* be the one who bullies you straight into a federal lockup."

Andy started speaking, but Nelson held up his hand. "It's bad enough I'll have to listen to you tomorrow morning. Right now, I want to enjoy my lunch. Which doesn't involve you sitting here at my table while I eat. Now scat!"

Andy stood abruptly, knocking his chair onto the floor. He stalked toward the door, nearly colliding with DeMyron coming into the café. The deputy glanced at Andy as he walked past him to Nelson's table and sat while Andy scuttled outside, the door swinging shut behind him.

"Looks like your interview went well?" DeMyron said.

"Andy thinks he's a prime suspect." Nelson smiled, recalling how flustered Andy had gotten at Nelson's accusation. "He was at the feed store late yesterday morning."

"I hear a *but* in there," DeMyron said.

Nelson nodded. "But he has no alibi for early morning. He could have been out, looking Lucky's place over, when Lazy jumped him and still made it back to town to establish an alibi."

"Andy never carries a gun," DeMyron said. "Darby Branigan told me that again a moment ago. I got the impression he feels a little . . . contempt for Andy. Says any man not willing to pack heat and defend his views is no man to Darby."

"Tell me Darby had no alibi for early yesterday morning," Nelson said as he sopped up stew with a slab of buttered cornbread.

"Darby blew a tire and hit the curb driving out of town. Bent the rim. He was at the White Eagle Service Station until about nine o'clock before they could mount and balance a new tire on a rim they rounded up. That's his alibi."

"Don't think he needs one." Nelson wiped stew that had dribbled onto his chin. "By that time, Lazy's body was already half frozen to the ground. Unless . . ."

"Unless what?"

"Unless Darby was at Lucky's ranch *really* early . . . before the sun came up. With the weather like it has been, it was hard to determine just how long Lazy had lain on the ground ventilated like he was."

"Then where does that leave us with those two?" DeMyron asked.

Nelson pushed his empty bowl back and resisted the urge to pat his stomach. "That leaves us with two *faintly* possible suspects. Andy has no provable alibi for the time of the murder. He could have been snooping around Lucky's place again when Lazy confronted him. And he's damn sure big enough to bust the thug up. But . . . he doesn't carry a gun. And Lazy was shot with either a rifle or a large caliber handgun like Darby carries."

"Who probably had an alibi for the time of an extra-early murder as well."

Marley came over, and DeMyron ordered a donut and coffee. "Andy *could* have armed himself," he said as she moved off. "Maybe he carries a gun we don't know about."

"Possible," Nelson said. "Sounds like a good reason for a late-night investigation into Andy's car while he's staying in Gillette."

"Are you suggesting me—or someone looking a lot like me—break into Andy's car and see if he's got a gun stashed there?" DeMyron asked with a grin.

"If it happens here in the county," Nelson said, "it would be your case. Way out of my jurisdiction."

When Nelson got to the sheriff's office, Maris was not there, and he speculated she was doing some investigating work *under the covers* with Salvatore DeLuca as her target. Or was she *his* target as she tried learning how the twin investigations were progressing?

Nelson left his coat on, figuring he wouldn't be here long. Either Yancy was at the Wind River Tribal office to take a call or he was—like Maris—doing his own version of teepee creepin' around Ft. Washakie. Nelson picked up the phone and dialed.

"Wind River Police," Yancy said after just the first ring.

"You living at the tribal office again?" Nelson asked.

Yancy Stands Close, the tribal police chief for several months now, laughed. "What else do I have to do but sit around and answer the phone, hoping it isn't some jealous husband wanting my butt again? I thought you were going to Gillette for an over-nighter?"

Nelson explained that his efforts to quickly evict Lucky had run afoul, ruining his fishing trip. Something to do with two dead men disrupting his plans. "You sold your cows last fall, didn't you?"

"You know I did. Why, are you running low on meat, 'cause I have two steers fattening up in that pasture I'm leasing from the tribe?"

"Not exactly. Tell me, did you salt the money away or did you blow it on wine, women, and song?"

"Nelson," Yancy said, "I am a reformed man. I opened an ac-count at the bank in Lander after I sold the cows. I took a chance on the bank, and my money is drawing interest, low though it is."

"What if I told you I ran into another investment opportunity for you?"

"During this Depression there's not many opportunities out there."

"I have one," Nelson said. "The chance to own a section of land with your name on the deed right here in Campbell County. Absolutely worthless land as it now sits after the rancher ran it into the ground."

"What would I do with land all the way over there?" Yancy asked, and Nelson could hear disbelief in his voice. "Especially if it's so rundown?"

"Sell it when the market comes roaring back. Someday. You could get the land for a song tomorrow."

"Already this isn't sounding good," Yancy said.

"Have I ever steered you wrong?"

Yancy sighed loudly. "Let's have it."

Nelson explained that Lucky's ranch was fixing to be sold for pennies on the dollar at a quick sale tomorrow morning. "All you have to do is be here at the courthouse as the sale is going on. Pay the filing fee and assuming fee at the clerk's office, and you will be a proud landowner."

"Nelson, did you not just tell me the land was worthless? That this rancher ruined the spread?"

"He did," Nelson answered. "He did. It's in bad shape. Utterly worthless."

"And this is a good investment how?"

"That, I don't know yet. But there's a reason the banker holding the note wants it. He could have foreclosed on a dozen ranches in the county that could turn a profit instead of this one."

Yancy had started objecting again when Nelson said, "Relax.

You don't have to keep the ranch forever. Just until Lucky—the original owner—gets back on his feet. Unless, of course, he'll never get back on his feet because he's dead—then you lose your money for certain."

"What a deal," Yancy said.

Chapter 26

Nelson drove past the feed store, then turned around and parked out front so folks would see his panel truck there. It wouldn't hurt any if Bruno's thugs knew Nelson was checking up on Natty's well-being.

He paused before going in. The fur buyer from Casper had parked his truck in front as well, coyote and fox hides stacked neatly in a pile, bobcat hides along with one mountain lion pelt lying beside the others. *Somebody's making some money,* Nelson thought and entered the feed store.

"Marshal!" Natty yelled from the next room. "I seen you come in—I need your opinion."

Nelson stepped into the next room, where mineral cake and sacks of oats were piled five high. In the center of the room stood Natty with his arm around Toby. A small man sporting a world-class handlebar mustache sat on a stack of feed sacks, his scratching and itching telling Nelson this was the fur buyer, constantly exposed to fleas from fresh hides he inspected.

Except the hide he was haggling over in the middle of the floor was several days old, by the stiffness of the pelt. "Marshal, this ought to be worth fifty bucks for Toby—twice what a bobcat will bring. Whatcha think?"

Nelson didn't want to get in the middle of heated negotiations on a hide, but . . . something about it piqued his interest, and he bent to the animal skin. "I'll be damned," he said. "We haven't seen a wolf in these parts for years. Where did you shoot this one?"

"Down on the Powder River," Toby answered proudly.

"Damn," Nelson breathed again. Growing up on a ranch butting up to the Big Horn Mountains, he had often spotted wolves hanging around the herds. Each time one got within rifle range, he would shoot at it, even hitting one now and again. Every other hand on the Walking Horse would kill them on sight as well. Still, they proved elusive and adaptable, slipping in and killing a cow now and again. And the wolves wreaked havoc during calving season.

The fur buyer picked up the mottled gray pelt and blew on it. "This old wolf is definitely haired up nice." He turned to Toby. "Only thing wrong is the way you skinned it. Left too much fat on, though I'd forgive that if you intended fleshing it out later. And this big ol' exit hole from your rifle will bring the price down a mite. Thirty bucks is all I can offer. That and the price you got for bounty—"

"The Wool Growers Association wouldn't give me anything for a wolf. They said they pay out only for coyotes," Toby said as he ran his hand over the thick gray shoulder hairs, brown underneath. "I never skinned a wolf before. I done coyote and fox, but this is my first wolf. It ought to be worth . . . forty dollars, don't you think, Marshal?"

Nelson laid the pelt on the floor. "That's between you and the fur buyer."

The thin old man twirled his waxed mustache and eyed the pelt. "You drive a hard bargain, kid, but I'll give you forty dollars. That's if the game warden has no objection."

A man had entered the room from Nelson's blind side, and he turned to face him. "I heard you were hot after a poaching ring over by Sheridan," Nelson said to the game warden.

"Not a ring," Marcus James answered as he stripped off a

glove to shake hands with Nelson. "One poacher—your old enemy, Dan Dan Uster. Thought I had him cornered at the edge of a canyon above Dayton. But he just disappeared, and I lost his tracks. I thought about calling you to help me find him."

Nelson chuckled. "I've been a bit busy with my own things right here. What brings you all the way to Gillette?"

"That," Marcus said. "The state wants to know all about their wolves roaming around. Or at least the Cattleman's Association wants to know."

"I've heard a pack has been playing hell with ranchers in the Big Horns around Buffalo and Sheridan."

Marcus nodded. "This old lobo might have been driven out of the pack and made his way to the Powder River, where the kid shot it." He picked up the pelt and blew on it like the fur buyer had before setting it back on the floor. "Last wolf we verified over here got hit by a truck crossing the road last year. But *you* didn't come here to stare at some wolf pelt . . ."

"I didn't," Nelson said. "Me and Natty need to visit about something else." He motioned to Natty. "Your office for a moment."

When Natty had shut the door to his office behind them, he turned his back to the stove to warm himself. "This an official visit?"

"Let's say it's a visit to keep you in one piece. I figure if Bruno's goons saw my truck parked outside, they might think twice about getting their little piece of revenge. Any of them come around since our last visit?"

Natty grabbed two mugs from a rack on the wall before turning to the pan on the heat stove. "Haven't seen any of them. Your warning must have had an effect." He poured each of them a mug of hot cocoa and handed Nelson one.

"You still got molasses or sugar?" Nelson asked, remembering the last time Natty served up a cup of hot cocoa.

Natty's eyes darted to a Chase and Sanborn can on the shelf. "Got sugar in there, but I wouldn't," Natty said. "The missus made it sweet enough."

Nelson used a spoon to ladle in two heaping teaspoons of sugar, then—because the concoction had been so *ungodly* bitter last time—scooped another and stirred. "I'm thinking that maybe it's not so wise to have Toby hanging around. After all, he did find Lazy dead, and they can connect him to Rick Jones. It just might not be safe for him. They might figure he knows more than he's saying, too."

"He's a big boy," Natty said. "Kid can look out for himself. Besides, I pay Toby every Wednesday when the freight truck makes a delivery. Kid can unload cake and feed faster than any grown man. He's not afraid of work."

"You pay him by the hour, I'd assume?"

"I do," Natty answered.

"That's why you hire him when there's a dozen grown men that would love day-labor work. Toby costs you less than anybody else."

Natty shrugged. "So, I'm a businessman. I have to make ends meet, too. It's all me and the missus can do nowadays to get by. If it wasn't for the seventy-five dollars a month she gets for teaching school we'd go hungry some weeks."

Nelson had no answer for that. In these times, a businessman like Natty had to cut corners any chance he got.

Nelson tested the hot cocoa, found it cool enough to drink, and took a deep swallow. And nearly gagged as he fought not to spit the drink out. "What the hell did your wife do to this?" he asked when he'd choked down the cocoa. "It's only about a dozen times sweeter than pure honey."

"I tried warning you."

"But the last time . . . I needed a couple spoonfuls of sugar.

Now . . . I can't drink this."

"Sorry, Marshal. I told the missus last time how you couldn't hardly choke it down, it was so bitter. She said she better sweeten it up if a genuine U.S. marshal was going to sample her cocoa again."

Nelson set the mug on the edge of Natty's desk. "You remember telling me how Gino took you to the cleaners in a poker game a couple days before he was found murdered?"

"A hundred dollars cleaning, it was," Natty said, then added, "and it took him no time at all. If you hadn't found out he was a mining engineer, I'd have sworn he was a professional gambler."

He finished his drink and turned to the pot for a refill. "Your deputy Red Hat already stopped by asking me the same thing, and I told her the same thing—Gino's death must have been a robbery if he had no money when you found him. Those hundred dollars and some change is reason enough to kill anyone if a man's down on his luck."

"Then tell me, have you seen anyone floating around money like that? Here? Maybe at the R&R?"

"Just Bruno's thugs," Natty answered as he sipped. "They always flaunt a lot of money. But they didn't come into town until several days after Gino's murder, so they couldn't be suspects, right?"

Nelson settled back in Sheriff Jarvis's chair and asked Maris, "What did you find out when you talked with Smitty?"

She took off a boot and sock and began digging at a toenail with her pocketknife. "Bruno's thugs paid him a visit there at the post office." She held up her hand. "But he won't identify his attacker to press charges. Says he wants to be able to eat solid food. Can't blame him none."

"Let's hear it."

"Smitty said he felt like he'd gone ten rounds with Jack Sharkey. He claimed he had a couple broken ribs and was peeing blood, but there were no injuries to his face. Bruno's goon was careful not to give him any scars he could take to the law as proof, not that he intended to after Gavin's little talk."

"He's positive it was Gavin Corrigan who worked him over?"

"More than positive. The Irishman came to the post office right at closing time yesterday. Said, 'I have it under good account that Gino Bonelli sent a package out two days before he was murdered,' and asked where it was sent. When Smitty balked, Gavin drove his fist so far into Smitty's gullet, sure it was going to come out his backside. When he couldn't answer, let alone breathe, Gavin asked again where Gino sent the package. When Smitty still didn't tell him, Gavin landed a couple more punches that busted Smitty's ribs."

All Nelson needed was one good case to take before the judge to plead that Bruno's thugs—all of them—needed to be denied bond if they were charged. He needed one good witness that had the guts to stand up—unlike Rick Jones, who had folded when Bruno's men talked to him in their own special way. "You couldn't convince him to sign his name on an affidavit?"

"He didn't want *anything* to do with filing assault charges. He saw what Lazy and Angel did to Rick Jones, and the way they threatened Natty. A few more blows and Smitty finally broke down and told Gavin about *one* of the two packages Gino sent two days before his death."

"Two packages? All Smitty told me about was the one Gino sent to some place over in the Black Hills in South Dakota."

Maris set her pocketknife aside and grabbed her notebook from her back pocket. "One package went to a research lab in Reno, Nevada. That's the one Smitty coughed up. But he was pissed enough knowing he'd spend money to have the sawbones set his ribs that he didn't divulge any information about the *second* package. That one went to the School of Mines and Technology in Rapid City, to"—she scanned her notes—"Emily Baker, whoever that is."

"You'll find out."

"What?"

"Tell me about the package to Reno first. What do they research?"

"How the hell should I know?" Maris picked up her pocketknife again and eyed a different toe. "You're the one with a college degree. You tell me. Or," she winked, "give me some more per diem to entertain Sal DeLuca and I'll get him to tell me what kind of a research lab it is."

"Why would he know?"

"Because he whispered kind nothings in my ear last night, telling me Bruno hired a private detective to find out that very thing—what Gino would have sent to that laboratory in Nevada not two days before his death."

"Not long after Natty drove him around Lucky's place," Nelson said.

Maris nodded. "As soon as the PI tells Bruno what the package contained that Gino sent to Reno, I'll get it out of Sal—"

"We can't let Bruno get that close to the truth, whatever it is, or we're sure to have another murder to investigate."

"How're you going to stop it?" Maris asked.

"I'll call the sheriff in Reno and ask him to order the lab to refuse any inquiries."

"I thought you were sending me down there?"

"Not there," Nelson said. "I want you to find out what was in that package Gino sent to the School of Mines. You do want an all-expense-paid trip out of state?"

Maris frowned. "But not Reno?"

"I can handle the research lab. I need you to drive over to South Dakota."

"And you're not worried about Bruno finding out about the one to Rapid City?"

"Did your paramour Sal say they knew about *that* package?"

"He didn't."

Nelson nodded. "Smitty was telling the truth, then—he didn't tell Gavin about that one." He fished in his pocket and handed Maris a quarter. "Stop off at Spearfish, will you—they have the best rock candy you could ever want."

Chapter 27

A faint rap on the office door, and Nelson cracked it just enough to see Yancy Stands Close stomping snow off his feet. Nelson let him in and locked the door behind him. "We alone?" Yancy asked.

Nelson nodded. "I sent Maris to Spearfish and Rapid City, and the only deputy here in Campbell County is snooping around Bruno Bonelli's men. He figures one of them broke into Pearl's Drug Store and stole some medicinal hooch. I told the sheriff's secretary she could have the morning off."

"Then the least you can do is offer a man coffee for driving six hours in my old beater Chevy truck that has no heat."

"I'd do better than that if I could—I'd buy you a steak dinner if it wasn't so important folks didn't see us together." Nelson poured Yancy a cup of coffee. "You weren't seen coming in here, were you?"

"Folks walking by didn't pay me any attention. I'm sure they figured I was just another Indian who got in trouble and was paying his fine at the courthouse." Yancy took off his Stetson, and his braids fell out, one lying on his back, the other on his chest. He straightened them and the bone hair ties keeping them neat. "You really think this will work?"

"I do."

"Good, 'cause if it don't, my life savings from selling those cows will be down the drain. What's your plan?"

Nelson explained that it was imperative Yancy *not* go to the clerk's office this morning and inquire about paying Lucky's mortgage until after he saw Nelson and Andy Olssen standing on the courthouse steps. "If Andy even suspects someone else is interested in Lucky's place, he'll pay off his *own* mortgage note and take over the ranch."

"That makes no sense." Yancy took out his pouch of Bull Durham and a cigarette paper and trickled tobacco into it. The tobacco slid out one end, and Yancy licked the paper that was nearly devoid of tobacco.

"Here," Nelson said and handed Yancy his pack of Chesterfields.

"Never could get the hang of rolling a smoke." Yancy lit one and handed the pack back to Nelson.

"Keep it."

"Thanks." Yancy blew perfect smoke rings toward the ceiling. "Like I said, it makes no sense this Andy holding the note, then buying the ranch if he figures someone else is interested."

"Andy Olssen plans on picking the place up for a song. He'll outbid anyone else who wants it. He's got enough money of his own, he could just buy the note, but he's too greedy. Wants it on the cheap."

"You never said what's so special about this section of land, anyway?"

Nelson ladled water into the pot from a large brown crock and grabbed the can of coffee grounds. "There's gotta be something there, but I don't know what it is just yet. All I know is that Gino Bonelli was a mining engineer with a keen interest in that land. And Andy Olssen hired his own engineer, so there must be some compelling reason to kick Lucky Graber off. As soon as I find out what the samples were that Gino sent away to a lab in Nevada, I might know more."

"Without seeing the place," Yancy said, "I'd bet there's coal underground. Lot of mines hereabouts. And a lot that went belly up before they even panned out."

"I thought of that, too. Some places here in Campbell County you can almost pick up lumps of coal off the ground. I even thought about oil on Lucky's place, but none has developed around here—"

"There's that well some company sunk over by Rozet nearly ten years ago."

"A wildcat well," Nelson said, "that failed to show black gold. We'll worry about that after we—you—take possession of Lucky's ranch."

Nelson stood on the courthouse steps clutching a paper with the land description on it. A few steps down, Andy Olssen stood beside Darby Branigan, the latter with his Army Colt slung low like this was high noon, glaring at Nelson as if he were going to fight for the property.

"Let's get on with it," Andy said. "I'm hungry. I want a bite to eat before I go out to my new ranch. Just to see what my Stockman's Bank owns."

Nelson had checked with the clerk of courts before the sale. Andy had registered *himself* as the bidder on the property with no mention of Stockman's Bank.

Yancy—his braids bouncing on his chest for all to see and flashing a beaded Arapaho headband—brushed by them, but Andy paid him no mind. *Just another Indian.*

"You know what you'll have once the sale is over," Nelson said. "A dry piece of land with little redeeming qualities."

"Just the same, call the sale—"

"It's not quite time yet." Nelson dug his watch out of his pocket. "A few more minutes to give anyone else time to pay the note."

"Come one and call the sale," Andy said. "My bid's the only one, and you said yourself no one else is going to want that dried-up piece of real estate."

The clerk emerged from the courthouse. She walked up to Nelson and handed him a slip of paper while looking smugly over at Andy before hustling back inside.

"Time!" Nelson shouted and looked around. He unfolded the piece of paper the clerk had handed him. "The ranch of Lucky Graber—known on the deed as Ulysses S. Graber—is hereby passed to the new owner." Nelson paused and looked at Andy and Darby. "Yancy Stands Close."

"What?!" Andy cried out. "What the hell is this—"

"Seems that Mr. Stands Close has paid off the note and is now sole owner of the Graber property."

"What! Who the hell is this Yancy Stands Close?"

"I am." Yancy stepped out of the courthouse, a thick cigar held in his fingers. He stopped in front of Nelson and handed him the clerk's receipt.

"You can't do that," Andy said. "You . . . you—"

"It appears as if he has," Nelson said, "paid the note off in full."

Darby hitched up his belt and said to Yancy, "I don't know what your game is, Indian, but you don't deserve to buy the ranch out from under Mr. Olssen."

Nelson stepped between them and laid his hand on Darby's chest. "I'd back away, were I you. This is no business of yours."

"Maybe I'll make it my business."

"And maybe I'll make more business for the hospital when I stomp a mud hole in your ass. Or worse"—Nelson pulled back his jacket to reveal his own pistol in a belt holster—"make more business for Probst Funeral Home and Mount Pisgah Cemetery if you even try skinning that hogleg."

"Are you threatening Darby?" Andy asked.

Nelson faced him. "You bet I am."

"I wonder what Bobby Witherspoon will say about this? I

intend calling him right damn now."

"He'll say," Nelson said, "that I finally rid the government of any more involvement in the Lucky Graber Ranch."

"This is horseshit," Andy said.

"Why is that?" Yancy said, a slight smile tugging on the corners of his mouth. "I had every right to pay the note for the foreclosure amount, as anyone else would. You should be happy your bank lost no money on that worthless piece of Wyoming land."

"I'll . . . I'll buy it from you. Name your price."

Yancy seemed to be mulling the offer over. Then he said, "I think I'll pass. I always wanted a ranch that I can turn into my own piece of heaven."

"I've got attorneys," Andy spit out. "We'll see about this—"

"Bluster all you want," Nelson said, handing the receipt back to Yancy, "but the sale is final, and the bank has reclaimed its money. Just like you wanted."

"Now who's at the door this time of night?" Maris asked. "Can't be anything good." She unsnapped her holster and walked to the door of the office with her hand resting on her gun butt. She flung the door open. Yancy stood there, giving her an exaggerated once-over.

"You still look hot, woman."

"Get in here." She dragged Yancy in by the arm and looked up and down the hallway before closing the door. "Anyone see you come in?"

Yancy guffawed. "I'm an Indian. I can be real quiet when I need to be, or did you forget?"

Nelson rose from his chair, not sure if he should get between them, finally concluding theirs was harmless banter between former lovers.

"I didn't forget how you'd come sneaking into a lady's room—"

"You invited me in each and every time—"

"But now I hear you have a new squeeze—a tribal councilman's daughter half your age?"

Yancy shrugged. "Jealousy—that's good."

"I'm not jealous."

"Whatever you say," Yancy shot back. "But I don't ask about your lovers. I'd have thought you possessed better taste than to sleep with that gangster Salvatore DeLuca."

"Funny you should ask about him," Maris said. She grabbed a cup and poured Yancy some coffee. When she noticed him taking his bible out to roll a smoke, she slapped his hand. "It's painful to even *watch* you roll a cigarette. Here." She grabbed her pack of cigarettes from her shirt pocket. "Have a Lucky Strike. Besides already being rolled and licked at the factory, they're also good for you. At least according to the ads."

Yancy dug an Ohio Blue Tip from a small metal box beside the stove and lit the Lucky, holding the smoke for a long moment before exhaling. "I think you're right—this *is* good for me."

"It's nice to extol the health benefits of cigarette smoking," Nelson said, "but I want to hear about Sal DeLuca."

Maris sat in a captain's chair next to Nelson and draped her hat over her knee. "Sal followed me to Rapid City. Or he tried to."

"Why would he ever want to do that?" Yancy asked.

Maris took a deep breath. "Sal caught up with me at my motel room this morning right before I left. He said he felt real frisky and that Bruno and the others were out doing . . . *things*, but wouldn't tell me what. He wanted me to sneak in his room for some fun. I told him I had official marshal's business out of town, and I couldn't meet him until tonight at the earliest."

"Did he get angry?" Yancy asked. " 'Cause those Italians get a lot madder than us level-headed Indians."

"He didn't get mad. He didn't even act like it bothered him. Oh, he asked what the marshal's business was, but he didn't show any emotion when I told him I couldn't tell him. That's why I was so surprised when I first caught sight of his Lincoln right out of Moorcroft, keeping about a quarter mile behind me as I headed east. Not a lot of Lincolns in these parts." She chuckled. "For being a professional gangster, he sure don't know crap about tailing somebody. He hung back, just not far enough."

"Did he follow you when you went into the School of Mines administration building?" Nelson asked.

"He never made it that far." Maris took the pack of Luckys back from Yancy and shook one out. "I stopped at that little candy shop you told me about and got your rock candy . . . I forgot the bag out in the truck. What's left. I sort of had a few pieces on the way back to Gillette."

"Not to worry," Nelson said. "We'll get it later. But for God's sake tell us what the hell happened with Sal?"

Maris blew smoke rings, drawing out her explanation like she enjoyed keeping Nelson and Yancy guessing. A smile broke across her face and she said, "What's the odds that Sal—or any of that New Jersey big-city bunch—*ever* drove icy mountain roads?"

Nelson looked at Yancy, who shook his head. "I give up . . . what's the odds? And what's that got to do with Sal?"

Maris grinned. "It has everything to do with him." She dug her pocket watch out and opened it. "He's probably getting pulled out right about now."

"Maris—"

"All right. All right, I'll tell you. When I came out of that candy shop, Sal was sitting a block away watching me. So, I fired up the old Chevy and drove *slowly* into Spearfish Canyon."

"What's with that?" Yancy asked. "Nice scenic drive, but a little out of the way if you're going to Rapid City."

"I'm getting there," Maris said. "When I started the Spearfish Canyon drive, it was an icy mess. Just like I figured."

"Usually is this time of year," Nelson said.

"That's when I sped up. But ol' Sal, he was about a block behind me by then and trying to catch up. The faster I drove that winding damn road, the more certain I was that he'd never driven *anything* on roads like that. I got to tell you, Nels, I pushed the limits of that old government truck until about a half mile past Bridal Veil Falls, when I saw Sal lose control of his car and slide off down a steep ravine."

"Your new boyfriend might have killed himself driving off the edge of the road like that," Yancy said. "There's some mighty steep canyons on that drive."

"He didn't," Maris said. "After I cleared the next curve, I parked and walked back, sneaking through the trees . . . I'm Indian, too, and can be as sneaky as you."

"I know you can," Yancy said and winked, holding out his hand for another cigarette.

"What the hell, did I adopt you?" Maris said and tossed Yancy another Lucky.

"So you sneaked back towards Sal . . ." Nelson pressed.

Maris nodded. "I did and saw Sal's fancy car sitting nose down in a gully about twenty yards off the road. He'd crawled out of the car and was walking around, though I can't say for certain what shape that car is in. When I got to Rapid City and parked at the college, I called a wrecker for him. Anonymously."

Yancy stood and refilled all their cups as he stomped his feet to keep circulation in them. "I still don't understand why he'd follow you—"

"Because Bruno and his goons are being shut out of information, and Bruno desperately needs to know what Gino mailed to the School of Mines if he's ever going to find Gino's killer," Nelson said. "Lazy Stefano's murder . . . I got the impression Bruno could care less about that except for his ego—one of *his* men getting killed is an affront to him." He reached over and grabbed a slip of paper with his notes on it. "When I talked with the sheriff in Washoe County in Reno and explained the situation here, he suggested I speak with the director of the Reno Basin Lab about the package Gino sent them after I emphasized that whatever Gino sent was to be revealed to *no one*.

"The sheriff called me back within the hour and gave me the name of the administrative director of the lab, so I called him. He said some slick-talking feller smelling like a private detective had already stopped by the lab and tried to find out what Gino sent for testing."

"What *did* he send?" Yancy said. "You're getting as bad as Maris about giving up information."

Nelson dug his reading glasses out of his shirt pocket and tapped the paper. "Gino sent in nine soil samples. The director I talked with—Frank Doss—said Gene . . . Gino . . . often sent samples to the lab when he worked at the silver mine in Tonopah."

"The samples from Lucky's place showed silver?" Maris asked.

"They didn't show a thing, except dry Wyoming dirt. There were trace metals in the samples, like there are trace metals in all kinds of soil. Gino never asked him to test for anything specific, as he didn't want to taint the results. Frank doesn't know *what* Gino thought the samples contained, because he was murdered before Frank could get back to him and question him." Nelson stood and stretched his back. "The only thing we managed to do is keep information from Bruno that he *thinks* will lead him to Gino's murderer."

"At least one of us found out something," Maris said. She took off one cowboy boot and grabbed a cardboard box, and then scissors. She began cutting cardboard to stuff into her boots, which were pockmarked with holes in the soles. "What Gino sent to the college was nothing more nefarious than money. Exactly one hundred and two dollars."

"About the amount Gino won in that card game with Natty," Nelson said. "But why give it to the college?"

"Student loans from when Gino studied for his postgraduate degree in geology." Maris nodded to Yancy. "Something you'll never have."

"Hey, I went to college—the college of practicality. I can do a lot of things those fancy educated boys can't." Yancy looked at Nelson. "No offense."

Nelson waved the remark away. "But why the secrecy?"

"Brother Bruno," Maris said. "The admin clerk knew all about Gino being little brother to a gangster ever since said gangster-brother called when Gino was in school and offered to pay off his student debt. When Gino was called in with the good news his student loans were to be forgiven, he blew up. Said he wanted nothing to do with Bruno's blood money and told the admin clerk he intended paying off his college loans himself if it took the rest of his life. And ever since, Gino's been sending a few bucks here, a few bucks there, all to pay off what he owes the school."

"Keep that to yourself," Nelson said. "Let Bruno think we found out something significant."

"Tonight"—Maris winked at Yancy—"Sal will grill me in his own *special* way, and I'll tell him I found out nothing."

"He probably won't believe you," Nelson said.

"I'm counting on it," Maris said. "With any luck his . . . interrogation will last hours."

Chapter 28

"You don't think Andy will figure we're pards, with you having free rein of the ranch?" Yancy asked Nelson. He had spent the first night in his new place. He'd taken one room of the old ranch house and swept dirt and chicken bones and peanut hulls off the floor. Afterward, he rigged himself up a sleeping area, padding his old cot with extra horse blankets he always carried in his truck. He reinforced the only door to the house with extra bales of hay and some warped wood that had fallen off the barn that Lucky had failed to repair. Yancy had selected the area well, Nelson saw, and he had a clear view of anyone coming down his drive toward the house. "I bet Andy thinks we're in cahoots."

"Not if you remember to stick to our story—I wanted to search your property for Lucky, and, as the new owner, *you* welcome cooperation with the law."

"I got it." Yancy threw on his heavy coat and headed for his truck. "But what exactly am I looking for?"

Nelson scanned the area. Was someone watching, or was he just paranoid? Or scared? When he talked with Captain Koats about the Bonelli crime syndicate, Koats had said Bruno never got his hands dirty since muscling his way into being the sole operator of garbage trucks along the East Coast. But he *would* order his men to do literally anything. "If you let your guard down even for a second," Captain Koats warned, "one of Bruno's men—or several—will climb your frame. Bruno may seem like he has an interest in law enforcement, with his annual police picnic every year and donations to the Police Benevolent Fund. Just know that more than one policeman or trooper in the New Jersey and New York area never made it back to shift change after they rousted a Bonelli-protected truck."

"See something, Nels?" Yancy asked.

Nelson shook his head to clear it. "No, just feeling *itchy* right about now. I have the feeling we're being watched by one of Bruno's men."

"Bruno's thugs?" Yancy asked, looking about.

Nelson shrugged. "Them spying on us, hoping we'll lead them to Gino's killer. Or maybe Andy Olssen's the one watching. I can't imagine him just giving up the land without some shenanigans."

"I'll remember that as long as you tell me just what am I supposed to be looking for while you take a pleasure ride across the ranch?"

Nelson laughed and motioned to Lucky's horse—which now belonged to Yancy, along with everything else on the ranch. "If you think riding that old sorrel mare is a pleasure, *you* throw a leg over her."

"DeMyron has a standing offer to let you use his bay gelding."

Nelson dug a carrot out of his coat pocket. "I don't mind the ol' mare, not really. She doesn't have a lot of spunk at her age, but then, neither do I. Besides," he said as he headed to the barn for the saddle and bridle, "she actually loves to get out of that tiny corral and stretch her legs."

Nelson stopped to let the mare rest while he took off his gloves and dug in his pocket for a smoke. "Just what the hell was so important that you ran Maris off the property?" Nelson asked, as if Lucky were there to answer. The horse's only reply was a snort before pawing at the snow for the grama grass underneath. “And why the hell did Andy hire a mining engineer?” he asked the horse. “I bet you could tell me why that blowhard was so enraged when he didn’t get the ranch on the quick sale.”

Lucky’s mare had no answers for any of it, yet Gino Bonelli had lost his life for something he had found, and someone didn’t want Bruno’s man on the property. Did Lazy’s killer know what Gino thought was beneath the worthless ranch land?

“Only way we’re going to find out is if we keep looking, old girl.” Nelson nudged the sorrel through snow that came up to her knees. She didn’t complain as she plodded along slowly, crisscrossing the property. She accepted another carrot while Nelson studied the land as they followed a deep ravine Marley had mentioned. The canyon got progressively deeper the closer to Rick Jones’s ranch he rode, and Nelson looked down now and again in case Lucky had fallen into it.

When they arrived at the fence separating Rick Jones’s ranch from Lucky’s, Nelson began riding the fence line. How many times had he ridden fence as a youngster at his father’s ranch, fence nippers in hand, hopping down every time he saw a break in the wire? Even though his father owned the Walking Horse, he expected everyone to start at the bottom. And nothing said *starting at the bottom* like riding fence line at twenty below zero.

Something caught his eye twenty yards farther along the fence, and he rode closer. A tiny torn piece of red flannel seemed to wave for attention with each gust of wind. He dismounted and walked toward the slip of cloth. It had caught on the top rung of barbed wire, just where a break in the fence had been spliced and repaired. Almost invisible. Someone had fixed the fence, the cut wire barely rusted. Recent. Toby? Nelson saw him riding fence a few days ago, but he didn’t think the boy could splice wire so expertly. Mac? Nothing in the man’s actions showed he was ambitious enough to actually earn his keep working for Rick Jones. But Lucky—being a rancher all his life, even a poor rancher—would be capable of it.

Nelson dropped the reins. The mare stayed and pawed at the grass under the snow once again while he walked the fence line. A few yards farther on, he saw another splice, just as expertly made. And the width of the break *might* accommodate a wagon if it could navigate in this deep snow.

"You been thisaway before?" Nelson asked the mare.

He dropped to the ground and brushed snow away, but it was too deep to show any tracks. If Lucky had driven his wagon this way, it was before the last heavy snowfall.

He walked back to the sorrel, dug into the saddlebags, and came away with his fence pliers. He returned to the splice, cut all four strands of wire, and peeled them back for a makeshift gate. "Here we go, girl," he said as he swung up into the cracked and weathered saddle. "Don't tell Rick we're trespassing on his land."

He crossed into Rick's pasture where a dozen head of cattle grazed, and he temporarily pulled the fence closed so the cows couldn't get out before he continued following the ravine. Now and again, Nelson stopped long enough to look down, expecting to see a body lying there. *Lucky's body.* At one point, a glint of sunlight off something in the canyon caught his eye. "What's down there, girl?"

He dismounted and dug into the saddlebags for his binoculars. He stood staring at *something* metal that lay in a heap at the bottom of the canyon for long moments before . . . "Shit! That's what's left of a still. And it hasn't been there very long. Shit," he said again. "I'd bet that's what Lucky hitched you up to his wagon for. That's *just* why he didn't want Maris to evict him then. He didn't want to get caught making moonshine." Sheriff Jarvis and DeMyron had been hell on wheels ferreting out stills in their county, yet Lucky had successfully hidden his.

Until he was evicted—then the gig would be up.

Nelson walked a few yards farther, glassing the still that was scattered in pieces fifty yards down the ravine. Lucky had pulled up alongside the canyon and heaved his still into it. "But why Rick's place?" Nelson asked the horse, then answered his own question. "In case anyone found it, they'd figure Rick was the one running moonshine. Not Lucky. He might have been lazy and a crappy rancher, but he wasn't stupid." *Did I just think of Lucky in the past tense?*

Nelson started walking back to the mare, still grazing up the hill, when a bullet clipped the brim of his Stetson. He dropped to the ground and rolled behind two discarded fence posts, just as another round whizzed by where he'd stood a moment before.

He looked at his rifle in the scabbard hanging off the saddle, calculating whether or not he could reach it before getting ventilated, when another shot echoed off the canyon walls. The round struck the fence posts, wood peppering Nelson's cheek. *The shooter had the range,* and Nelson knew he couldn't reach his rifle ten yards away.

Where the hell was the shooter? Nelson scanned the hills overlooking where he lay, any one of which could conceal a killer. His only hope was to make the shooter fire again and miss, the smoke from the shot revealing his position.

He gathered his legs and stood abruptly, dropping a heartbeat later as gunfire cracked once more. From a hill to his left a hundred yards distant rose a faint puff of smoke, the bullet kicking up snow inches from Nelson's head.

Nelson saw a smudge mark in the snow north of where the puff of smoke came as he drew his .45. He would use that as an aiming point. During the Great War when his unit faced off against the Germans at Belleau Wood, the Marines had taken pot shots across the lines, often at impossible ranges with their Springfield rifles, hoping one or more rounds would find their mark. Just for fun, they had taken out their pistols and winged rounds towards the Germans as well. Nelson never knew if his bullets hit any enemy or not, but he liked to think some spanked the Germans.

He looked once again at the mare grazing, seemingly oblivious to bullets hitting mere yards away, the rifle in the saddle scabbard. He couldn't get to it without being shot. And the only weapon he had was his Colt automatic.

He dropped his hat on the fence posts and rested his gun hand on it, his other hand gripping to steady the weapon as he slipped the safety off.

He took a deep breath.

Let it out.

Tickled the trigger ever so gently . . . The gun fired, kicking up snow twenty yards in front of the smudge in the earth uphill.

He raised the muzzle slightly and fired again. The bullet hit only a few feet from his aiming point, and he raised the muzzle once again and fired. Three. Four. Five more rounds in quick succession.

He dropped his empty magazine, clawed in his coat pocket for another, and inserted it. *I might not have hit the shooter, but for damn sure I threw dirt and snow in his face.* He fired again.

And again.

And when the slide on his pistol locked back—empty—he snatched another magazine and reloaded.

He lay still, barely peeking around the fence posts. Waiting for another rifle round to come whizzing his way. After what seemed like an hour with no more shooting, he stood and pocketed his empty magazines as he eyed the hill where the shooter had lain. He walked to where the old mare still stood grazing through all the commotion, grabbed his rifle, and swung into the saddle. He held the Springfield loosely across the saddle bow as he coaxed the sorrel up the hill.

Hoping for blood in the snow.

He saw none, but he spotted where the shooter had hidden behind snow he'd gathered around him to conceal himself. *Smart way to ambush a man,* Nelson thought. *I'd have done the same. Just like DeMyron said he would have done, camouflaged himself in the snow if he were to watch Lucky's ranch.*

The shooter's tracks led straight for the road, where it would be impossible to follow them with the vehicle traffic smothering the footprints. Nelson dismounted and squatted beside the tracks. He had seen that footprint before: the deep yet indistinct impressions. As if the shooter wore something over his boots to mask any identifying marks that could give him away once caught. Sure, Nelson had seen that track.

It was the footprint DeMyron had so proudly cast of the Pearl's Drug burglar.

"Congratulations, whoever the hell you are," Nelson said aloud. "You've graduated to ambushing a U.S.marshal."

Chapter 29

After Nelson dug the soft lead slug out of the fence post that had saved his life, he rode back up the hill and began following the tracks. As he feared, the footprints disappeared among the car and truck traffic on the county road.

As he turned the mare towards Rick Jones's ranch house, a horn pierced the quiet. A truck sped toward Nelson, and he unsheathed the rifle once again. The truck slid to a stop in front of Nelson, kicking snow up, and Nelson shielded his eyes until the snow blew away. Rick Jones jumped out of his truck and fell on the icy road. He grabbed onto the bumper and stood. "My God, Nelson, was that you shooting?"

Nelson explained that he had cut the fence on the notion that Lucky had done so a week earlier, only to be ambushed. "I was fortunate enough that the shooter hightailed it," he said. "I'll head on back and fix your fence."

"Don't worry about that, Marshal. I'll send Toby to do it when he gets back." Rick nodded to the sorrel. "He went over to feed her until the new owner can move in."

"He already has. Yancy Stands Close slept his first night there."

"Toby'll be upset he wasted a walk in the snow." Rick took off his hat and wiped his face with his bandana. "I'm just glad you're not hurt."

"Me, too."

"Where you headed now?" Rick nodded to the mare. "Hope

not very far. I think that old girl's get up and go has got up and went years ago."

Nelson patted the sorrel's neck and dug into his pocket for another carrot. "She did just fine today."

"All right, then," Rick said. "If you don't need me to hang around—"

"I'll be okay." Nelson patted the horse's neck again. "We'll take it easy riding back to Lucky's—Yancy's—ranch."

Nelson rode the mare slowly on the county road, nudging her into the barrow ditch whenever a car passed, yet the old horse never faltered, never spooked, and Nelson was almost sorry the ride was over when he rode into Yancy's yard and dismounted. Nelson looked around for him but could not spot Yancy until he yelled, "Up here, Nels. In the loft."

Nelson shielded his eyes from the sun glare off the snow and finally spied Yancy lying on the second-floor loft of the barn, hay gathered around him, just the tip of his rifle muzzle sticking out. "You gotta come on down *here,*" Nelson called out, " 'cause I'm too damn old to be skinning up ladders."

He stripped the saddle off the mare, slipped the bridle over her head, and turned her out into the corral, giving her the last two carrots he had in his pocket. She'd earned them.

Yancy walked toward him, rifle cradled in the crook of his arm. He looked at Nelson's dirty jeans and coat. "You been playing in the snow again?"

Nelson explained what had happened, from spotting the piece of cloth to finding Lucky's still scattered all down the ravine moments before Nelson was ambushed.

"Damn, Nels, you are a shit magnet. Crap always happens to you. Me, I was damn lucky *nothing* happened. That kid who lives in the next ranch over—"

"Toby," Nelson said. "His name is Toby."

"Yeah, him. He came around and was gonna feed the mare and break up the ice on the water tank. I told him you were out pleasure riding—had to tell him something. But when I told him I was the new owner of the ranch—and the horse—and that I'd take care of the old girl until she passed, he grew a mite sad. Got all slack jawed he did, like feeding the horse gave him a purpose."

"Slack jawed is Toby's usual look," Nelson said, "but you're probably right. I'm sure he got attached to the ol' girl, seeing her every day. Talking to her. I know I get attached to my mule, bonehead that he is. Maybe coming here every other day and talking with the horse gives him an excuse to take a break." Nelson closed the corral gate. "I think Mac rides the kid pretty hard. You ask me, Toby's the working member of that family." He stepped closer to Yancy. "You seem a little nervous, as if *you* were the one who got shot at."

Yancy looked all around, to the pasture north towards Rick's place, and to the south where the ranch butted up against public land. "I can't shake this feeling that I've been watched today." He chin-pointed to the barn. "That's why I was up there—someplace no would expect me to be."

"Have you seen anyone besides Toby?"

Yancy shook his head. "Just some cars and a few trucks going on by, but no one pulled in or stopped. It's just a feelin'—"

"Feel this." Nelson handed Yancy the slug he'd dug out of the fence post.

Yancy hefted it and shucked a round from his rifle to compare. "Little deformed 'cause it's so soft, but I'd say it must be from *some* .32 caliber rifle. Maybe a .30 but not from a gun like mine."

"Positive?"

" 'Course I'm positive. Look here." He laid the bullet from the fence post in his outstretched palm alongside one of his own cartridges. "See—something this soft is bound to get hung up on the feed ramp. These Remingtons take a hard bullet."

"That's what I thought, but it's good to know I wasn't nuts when I thought about it." Nelson tapped Yancy's rifle. "Gino carried a Model 8 just like yours."

Yancy ran his hand lovingly across the walnut stock he'd polished to a high luster. Brass tacks driven into the stock added personality to the weapon. "Lots of folks carry Remingtons like mine. I scrimped and saved for a goodly while before I could afford it."

"Shoots pretty quick, does it?"

"As quick as I pull the trigger," Yancy answered. "This going somewhere?"

Nelson looked at the deformed bullet and scratched the side of the lead with his fingernail. "The shooter today fired three *slow* rounds but stopped before he started shooting again. Between that and this"—he tossed the bullet up and caught it—"I'd say that narrows it down to a lever gun. Winchester. Savage. Marlin perhaps."

"Then we practically have the shooter in shackles," Yancy said. "Now all's we gotta' do is go through the thousand or more men in these parts who pack a lever rifle."

Chapter 30

By the time Nelson returned to Gillette, it was dark, and all he wanted was to clean up and hit the rack. This wasn't the first time he'd been shot at and nearly killed, but it still sent shivers down his spine recalling how close the bullets had come. Recalling the blood running down his cheeks in tiny rivulets from the splintered fence post.

As he drove to his rented cabin, he passed Saint Matthew's Catholic Church, the sound of the hourly bells filtering through the closed window of the panel truck. The vehicle used to belong to a funeral home, but Nelson dismissed the symbolism. He had come a hair's breadth from being shot today only because the shooter had given his position away and Nelson was able to scare him off. It unnerved him not knowing who his attacker was. He swiveled his head, looking about, scanning every car and truck he passed, eyeing every shadowed space between buildings wide enough to conceal a shooter.

As he turned onto Gillette Avenue and drove past the courthouse, he wondered if someone had left the light on in the sheriff's office or was working this late. He figured it wasn't Maris—she intended grilling Salvatore in her own way, and he had left Yancy guarding his new ranch, so it wasn't him. Had Sheriff Jarvis returned from his Phoenix trip? Nelson hoped so. As enthusiastic as DeMyron was in solving the two homicides in Campbell County, he lacked the experience—and good sense—to go about it properly. Systematically.

Nelson backtracked to the courthouse lot, doused his headlights before pulling in, and unsnapped his holster. "Guess I'm just getting too old and paranoid," he said to himself. *Especially after this afternoon's little shootout.*

The courthouse appeared empty, no sound anywhere . . . Nelson paused just inside the door and cupped his hand to his good ear. He heard faint noises from upstairs.

Cursing. Coming from the sheriff's office.

He climbed the staircase a step at a time, inching along the wall, careful not to put weight on the center where the old boards would creak and give him away. Careful not to scrape and make noise with his sheepskin jacket. He arrived outside the sheriff's office and rested his hand on the doorknob.

The cursing continued, indistinct.

Two voices.

He slowly turned the knob.

Unlocked.

He flung the door wide. Leading with his .45 as he burst into the room, running past Bonnie's empty desk into Jarvis's office.

Maris stood over DeMyron as he sat in a chair looking up at her. "Close that damn pneumonia hole," she said. "We should have locked it after what happened to DeMyron."

Nelson holstered his pistol and hung his hat on the rack. He grabbed his reading glasses for a closer look before turning to the deputy.

Maris stood bent over DeMyron, a needle and thread in her hand. She looked intently at the sliced skin above his upper eye lid. She pierced the skin with the needle tugged on the thread, closing the gash that wept blood onto his jeans. She tied a knot, cut the sinew, and started another stitch. "It'll be eight stitches by the time I'm finished," she said. "If DeMyron does nothing else, he manages to get a world class ass-beatin'." She looked at Nelson. "Looks like you didn't fare too well either at Lucky's today. Horse throw you?"

Nelson gave a shortened version of the ambush, being more concerned with what happened to DeMyron. He noted that Maris had already thrown three stitches in one of the deputy's ears and that one cheek was swollen and raw. "Who did this to you?"

DeMyron grunted. "Who did it or who do I *think* did it?"

"Either way," Nelson said, "who beat the hell outta you?"

DeMyron held up his hand for Maris to take a breather. "Nels, I've been bucked off saddle broncs more times than I care to admit and missed my steer when bulldogging once. I spent time on the mend after getting gored by a steer at branding time." He chuckled, then winced in pain as his hand went to his split lip. "I got tangled up on the flank strap of an old Brahma bull one rodeo, and he about beat the living daylights outta me 'til I got shuck of him. But this"—he winced again when he motioned to his face—"was the work of a real professional. Gavin Corrigan."

Nelson felt his anger build, and his hand shifted instinctively to his gun butt. "I'll wake the judge and get an assault warrant drawn up—"

"Don't bother," DeMyron said. "I couldn't swear it was Gavin anyhow."

"You just said he worked you over?"

"I said I *thought* he was the one."

"Hold still, dammit," Maris said and resumed stitching.

DeMyron jerked back. "It hurts. I'm no prolapsed heifer that you need to sew on."

"You want me to patch you up, or do you have extra money to pay Doc Sayles to do it?"

"Go on and finish the job," DeMyron said and looked at Nelson. "What makes me mad is that I just spent two bits this afternoon getting my hair cut at Bennick's Barber Shop and now *this.*"

"You'll still be pretty," Maris said. "After your hair grows back where I shaved it. Now stay still!"

Nelson backed up to the register. "I'm still waiting for an explanation."

"I'd just driven past Natty's Feed Store," DeMyron began, "when I looked in my rearview mirror and caught Sal DeLuca and Angel Gallo pulling up to the front door. They bailed out of their car and ran inside with bad intentions on their faces, so I went around the block and hid under the overhang of an evergreen to watch the place." He held up his hand again, and Maris stopped long enough for DeMyron to spit blood and a piece of a tooth into a water basin beside his chair.

"How long were they inside?"

"That's the thing," DeMyron answered. "After about fifteen minutes I figured something serious was happening, and I'd started motoring towards Natty's when they ran out, jumped in their car, and sped away. That's when I went inside. It wasn't pretty, and neither was Natty. I called his woman to take him to the sawbones. He was pretty busted up. Could hardly talk. He said Sal and Angel talked among themselves and figured Natty was lying about knowing more about Gino's interest in Lucky's ranch. He said they sounded desperate, like Bruno ordered them to find out about Gino *tonight.* They told Natty he had to know who killed Gino."

Maris finished her sewing and wrung out a rag in the bowl of water. She began dabbing at DeMyron's wounds. "You'll be sore for a few days—"

"I'll be *pissed* for a few days," the deputy blurted out. "Soon's I find that bastard, I'm going to break his neck—"

"You're in no shape to break anyone's neck," Nelson said.

"Just relax and tell me why you figure it was Gavin if you didn't see him."

Maris set the basin and rag aside and ladled water into a cup before handing it to DeMyron. He sipped it and said, "Like I said, I rushed into the feed store. Beat bad, Natty was. Scared to death I'd go arrest those two. Said they promised to return tomorrow and see if Natty had a change of heart, even though he knew nothing of why Gino was interested in Lucky's ranch. I called his missus, and she came down to take Natty to the doctor—"

"Where you should have gone," Maris said. "I've sewn prolapsed cows and a dog that'd gotten caught in a coyote trap once, but this is my first man."

"And *this* happened at the feed store?" Nelson asked, gesturing toward DeMyron's battered face.

DeMyron sipped his water again and flinched. "Not there. I intended doing what Natty was afeard of me doing—arresting Sal and Angel. I figured they'd be headed back to the Cottonwood Inn, so I drove over there. Their Lincoln wasn't around, but another one was parked in front of the common room." He chuckled, and his hand went to his split lip. "Guess that car Sal wrecked, compliments of Maris, must not be drivable."

"So you're at the Cottonwood . . ." Nelson pressed.

"Cottonwood. Sure." DeMyron set the cup on the desk. "I put the sneak on the motel, but Angel and Sal was nowhere to be seen."

"Maybe they took a drive out by Rick Jones's place and ambushed one U.S. marshal," Maris said.

"Timing would be right," Nelson said. "Go on."

"I waited. And waited. By this time, it was getting dark. Then I seen through that big window Gavin Corrigan and Bruno come into that common room and sit around the fireplace. Just like that"—he snapped his fingers—"Andy Olssen and Darby

Branigan came waltzing in. Plopped right down by Bruno like they were old pards and began chatting.

"When Gavin got up and left, I didn't think a thing of it until *pow!* Something hit me on the base of the neck." DeMyron rubbed the area where he'd gotten hit. "That first blow disoriented me like I ain't never been, Nels. I dropped to the ground and tried grabbing onto the side of the building to stand when two fists—quick as lightning—hit me a heartbeat before someone put the boots to me. I started passing out, but not before Gavin—I'm all but certain—wrapped his hand around my shirt and hit me flush in the face a couple times. Somewhere between the Cottonwood and Maris finding me, I lost two teeth because of that bastard."

"And you're sure you can't identify him?"

"After that first blow to the neck . . ." He shook his head. "That man is a professional at this if you ask me."

Nelson thought back to what Captain Koats had said about Gavin and what Bruno reinforced—*the man is pure poison.* "Gavin turned pro at only seventeen," Koats had told Nelson during that last phone call warning him about Bruno's bodyguard. "Had a pretty good record, too, until the boxing commission found out he was mob connected and stripped him of his boxing license. You be cautious around that thug. His fists are his weapon of choice, and he's killed more than a few men in New Jersey and New York. *Suspected,* that is."

DeMyron was lucky to be alive.

Maris lit two cigarettes and handed DeMyron one. "Why would Andy be socializing with the likes of Bruno?"

"My guess is that he wasn't socializing," Nelson said. "They were discussing business." He grabbed a lump of coal from a bucket beside the stove and tossed it into the fire, feeling the warmth before closing the stove door. "They have to be teaming up." Nelson explained his theory that both Andy and Bruno needed to know what Lucky knew about Gino's interest in the ranch. "They both win if they learn that. Bruno will have a solid suspect in Gino's death he can avenge, while Andy will find out just what's under that worthless piece of ground and proceed accordingly. Probably appeal the sale. Offer Yancy twice what he paid."

"But Natty doesn't know why Gino took all those samples that day he drove him around." DeMyron sipped water with one side of his mouth. "I've hunted and worked these parts all my life, and I never ran across anything worth prospecting for."

"Darby," Maris answered. "I see what you're saying, Nels. If Bruno's thugs can get access to Lucky's ranch—now Yancy's—Darby will have free rein to test the soil himself."

Nelson nodded. "And that will bring Bruno a step closer to finding Gino's killer—"

The telephone rang, and Nelson jumped, startled. He picked it up and listened and felt the color drain from his face.

"What is it?" Maris said as he hung up the phone. "You look like you seen a ghost."

"He's not a ghost yet." Nelson grabbed his hat and coat. "Yancy's been shot, but he's still hanging on."

CHAPTER 31

The nurse left Yancy's room and motioned to Nelson and Maris waiting in the hallway. "You want to know how he's doing?" The nurse tucked a gray lock of hair under her white cap. "I have no good news other than he's hanging on. The bullet clipped his spleen, and he's lost a lot of blood."

"Is he conscious?" Nelson asked.

"He comes in and out of it," the nurse said.

"I need to talk with him."

"I can't allow that—"

"Just for a moment," Nelson said. "Might be the *only* time I'll be able to talk with him. If he dies . . ." Nelson looked away, tears welling up in his eyes. Maris draped her arm around his shoulders. "If he dies, I want the son of a bitch who did this to him."

The nurse backed away. "No call for that language—"

"For God's sake!" Nelson said. "Yancy might die with no one ever knowing his killer."

The nurse backed away farther and finally said, "I'll give you just a moment, then I'm calling Doctor Schunk. He's the one who ordered Yancy be left alone."

"A moment is all I'll need." Nelson stepped around the nurse and entered Yancy's room. In all the years Nelson had known him, he'd never seen Yancy without a shirt and trousers on, both neatly pressed. Yet here he was in a sanitary hospital bed, an IV dripping into his arm, looking as pale as any white man.

Which in itself would—*will*—piss Yancy off. *When he recovers,* Nelson kept telling himself.

He pulled up a chair and scooted it beside the bed before he took Yancy's hand. "I don't know if you can hear me—"

"I can," Yancy uttered, his voice barely a whisper. He cracked an eye, red and bloodshot and swollen.

Nelson cocked his good ear when Yancy said, ". . . can feel you. Holding my hand. We engaged . . ." He trailed off, and his eyes closed.

"Yancy," Nelson said. "You need to pull through. There's a trout stream begging to be fished, and I can't drown my lures alone." But his friend didn't move, his breathing shallow. His chest rising and falling ever so slightly, Nelson had a hard time seeing it.

The nurse poked her head inside the room. "You have to leave now; the doctor is making his rounds."

"Okay," Nelson said. "Just another moment." He waited for her to leave before he told Yancy, "Fight it. I need you around for a few more years—"

"Boots," Yancy breathed, barely audible.

Nelson bent his good ear close to Yancy's mouth. "What's that?"

After another long moment, Yancy opened an eye and muttered, "Boots. Find the boots . . . you find my shooter . . ." and he drifted off once again.

Nelson left the room and motioned for Maris to join him in the waiting area. "The nurse said Mac McKeen brought Yancy in. Where the hell did *he* go? We need to find him—"

"I'm back," Mac said, walking quickly down the hallway toward Nelson. "I had to grab a quick bowl of stew at the R&R." He threw up his hands. "Don't look at me like that. I was hungry. Besides, not much I could do after bringing him to the hospital."

"Let's talk in here." Nelson led him to a small waiting room. A pot of water heated on the stove, likely set there by some nurse, and loose tea sat in an elaborately decorated container. A flowing green fern as high as the ceiling drooped its heavy branches toward the floor. Nelson motioned to chairs beside the foliage. "How did you find out Yancy was shot?"

"Me and Toby split riding the fence line this afternoon," Mac explained as he sat. "After some prodding, that is—the kid's been pretty jittery since Lucky went missing. He took the west pasture where you cut through yesterday, and I rode the area closest to Lucky's ranch . . . sorry, I still think of it as Lucky's."

Nelson waved it off. "Go on."

"I was riding for about an hour . . . terribly cold and windy out there, and colder'n hell still when the sun was setting. I stopped long enough to stomp my feet and get my circulation back. I hadn't resumed riding the fence line for more than a half hour when I heard shots. Two of them. Coming from Yancy's place. It took me another twenty minutes to ride over there, and that's when I saw Yancy. Lying in the snow right in front of the barn, seeping blood all over. I feared he was a goner."

"The nurse said that might be the only thing that saved Yancy," Maris said, "the damnable cold and snow that sealed off his wounds."

Mac nodded. "I'm here telling you, Marshal, I was plumb scared, worrying if the shooter was still there. But he weren't."

"Did Yancy manage to say anything to you?" Nelson asked. "Any idea who the shooter was?"

"He was about gone when I came on to him. No, he was plumb out of it. I carried him inside his house and rode hell bent for election back to my place for my truck and brought Yancy straight here."

"Did you pass any cars or trucks on the county road?"

Mac shook his head and accepted the cigarette Nelson offered him. "Mine was the only outfit on the road, and, believe me, I was on the lookout. I didn't even have a gun with me if I *did* run into the shooter." He looked toward Yancy's room as if he could see him through the wall, lying there, fighting for his life. "Nobody wants to see Yancy pull through more than me, him being a new neighbor and all."

Andy Olssen rapped on the door to the sheriff's office and entered. He sported a tweed suit jacket that reeked of money and privilege as he held a thick cigar between his fingers, unlit. "Let me be the first to offer my condolences on your friend being mortally shot."

"He's not dead yet," Nelson said, "and who said he's my friend?"

Andy sat in a chair and looked down at the cigar as he massaged it between his fingers. "One of the advantages of having . . . a little extra money is to be able to afford luxuries. Like a fine private investigator out of Boise who happened to turn up the fact that you and the Indian have known each other—and been *close* friends—for years." He wagged his finger. "That little game you played with Lucky's ranch was specifically meant to keep it out of my hands."

"Perhaps it's nothing more nefarious than Yancy Stands Close wanting to invest in land he can run some cows on."

Nelson poured a cup of coffee. Andy waved off the offer of some and said, "I won't be here long enough to drink it."

"Then why *are* you here?" Nelson asked. "To flaunt the fact that you never earned the right to be president of your bank? That your daddy left you with the bank right before he jumped off the top floor?"

"You've done your homework, too, Marshal. I like that in an adversary."

"Are we adversaries?"

Andy stood and walked to the window, pulling the drapes aside to look out at the snow blowing gently across the courthouse parking area. "I'm being magnanimous, Marshal, by not filing a formal complaint against you and this Yancy Stands Close for rigging the sale." He turned around, a wide smile on his face. "I'll have Lucky's ranch yet."

"Why do you want it so badly?" Nelson asked. "Is there something you *think* is underground that Gino Bonelli was so interested in, 'cause you sure don't want it for properties of the land."

"Tell me what Gino found out about it when he was poking around with Natty Barnes," Andy asked.

"What makes you think I know?"

"Marshal"—Andy massaged the cigar in his hand again—"Gino Bonelli sent two packages right before his death. One to a testing lab in Reno, and the other somewhere the postmaster failed to . . . remember. An engineer like Gino doesn't take interest in the land and send off soil samples if there isn't something there."

"Where did you learn that . . . oh, that's right—you've been talking with your new bestest friend, Bruno Bonelli. What were you two discussing yesterday when Gavin Corrigan jumped De-Myron Duggar and nearly blinded him?"

"Enough of this!" Andy jumped to his feet. "I only came here as a courtesy to let you know there is a clause in the sale you conducted. It says"—he took out a paper from his inside jacket pocket—"that upon the death of the purchaser, the seller—that's my bank—will have first right of refusal to the land."

"Let's see that."

Andy handed Nelson the paper. "It is a copy, in case you thought about confiscating it."

Nelson donned his readers and scanned it closely. Andy was right: if Yancy died, Stockman's Bank of Billings would have first chance to buy the ranch back.

Nelson read past the first page and flipped to the second, where he spotted another clause that took precedence over allowing Andy to buy it back. "See here." Nelson put his thumb on the last clause. "It says you will have right of first buyback—"

"That's what I said—"

"Unless the original buyer has willed the property to someone."

Andy's smile faded as Nelson folded the paper and stuffed it into Andy's coat pocket behind his green silk handkerchief. "But the Indian didn't have time to file a will—"

"How do you know?" Nelson said, enjoying the sight of Andy's face drooping as if he'd just lost a sizeable bet. "I'm here to tell you that the first thing Yancy did was make out a will deeding me the property."

"That can't be—"

"You said yourself, Yancy and I have been friends for years. He made out the will the day of the land sale," Nelson lied.

"This is . . . is just bullshit . . . let's see the will."

"Sorry, my friend," Nelson said, his turn to show off a wide smile. "It's in the hands of a competent local attorney, should anything happen. If Yancy dies, you still won't get the land. It'll be mine under the terms of his will."

"Unless you meet . . . an untimely death. Then it will revert back to the bank's option to buy it."

"I have no intention of croaking anytime soon," Nelson said.

"Let me see that will of his," Andy repeated.

"You have no legal standing to see it. Remember, the original purchaser is still alive, even though he's hanging on by a thread. *If* Yancy doesn't make it, *then* you'll have standing and will be free to file motions to your black heart's content."

"That could take months," Andy said, his tone almost pleading.

Nelson grinned. "Or tied up in the courts for years. Now you have to leave. Your cigar is stinking up the office."

"It's not even lit."

"Then, Andy, it must be *you* stinking the place up. Scat!"

Chapter 32

The following morning Maris entered the sheriff's office unusually early. She kept her left side hidden from Nelson as she hung up her coat. "Turn thisaway," he said.

When she did, he noticed a bruise below her eye and a puffed-up cheek. She'd covered it with face powder, nearly thick enough to crack, but it didn't quite do the job. "You have a run-in with a door?"

"Actually, I did run into a door."

Nelson bent for a closer look. "You never were much for lying. That's what I always admired about you—your honesty. So, with that major compliment as a foundation—what the hell happened to you?"

Maris lit a smoke and settled back into a chair in front of the desk. "Sal . . . got a little rough last night."

Nelson groaned. "Tell me you're not getting into that kinky stuff like you hear about in those confession magazines?"

"I'm afraid so."

"There goes that honesty thing again," Nelson said, noting that Maris could not look at him. "What *really* happened with Sal?"

Maris sighed. "Okay. Here's the skinny. Sal . . . he came on strong last night, and not in a sexual way either. As soon as he got into my room, he demanded to know what I was doing in the Black Hills. When I denied being there, he slapped me. Admitted to following me and was pissed that he ran his car into a ditch and lost me in Spearfish Canyon.

"I was there on official business, I told him, and he slapped me again before asking how our investigation into Gino's murder was coming along. I told him it had reached a point where I couldn't talk about it, but that we were very close to making an arrest."

"So much for your innate honesty," Nelson said.

"I had to lie. Damned if I was going to tell him we were no closer than we were the day Rick Jones found Gino draped across his fence."

"I bet Sal didn't believe you."

"He didn't," Maris said, flicking her ashes into a spittoon by the stove. "He shook the hell outta me, but I wouldn't tell him squat. That's when he reared back and hit me. For no bigger than Sal is, he sure packs a mean right cross." She gingerly felt her cheek. "You remember that." She stubbed her smoke out and stood, then started pacing the room. "After he hit me again, I actually think he was sorry. He picked me up and held me and kissed my cheek. The only way I figured I could get out of that room in one piece was . . . go along with his romance for the night."

"Do you want to press charges, because I'll hunt the bastard up right now and make sure he falls down the steps several times getting into a cell."

"The jail doesn't have stairs."

Nelson waved a hand in the air. "Just a formality."

Maris faced Nelson. "It would be his word against mine. He'd get arrested for simple assault at the most, and the judge would set bail that Bruno would post no matter how high. Besides, I might still be able to exploit Sal for information, especially if he thinks I'm angry with him. A damn Italian will always want to kiss and make up."

"You're not fixin' to be alone with him again?"

"Might be our best chance to find out what those thugs are up to. If Sal feels some remorse for roughing me up, it might loosen his tongue."

"I don't know," Nelson said. "I don't like the thought of you alone with him again after *that,*" he motioned to her bruise.

"You don't think I can take care of myself?"

Nelson knew she could. He had first met her while she was a deputy sheriff in El Reno, Oklahoma, when he travelled down there to apprehend a murder suspect from the Wind River Reservation. More than a few times Nelson had been impressed by the way she used her wits to deal with danger . . . and the times she used her pistol when her wits fell short. "I know you can take care of yourself. Just be damn careful. But why did Sal go off now?"

"I think Bruno and his thugs are getting desperate," Maris said. "I'm certain they expected to blow into town and locate Gino's murderer right off after twisting some arms like they do at home. They figured to be gone from Gillette in a few days with the killer's head in a bag. Since they've been here, all they managed to do was rough some people up and get one of their own killed. And they still don't have Gino's murderer."

"Maybe they managed to shoot Yancy," Nelson said.

"Speaking of which, did you ever understand what Yancy meant when he whispered 'boots' in his hospital room?"

Nelson had racked his brain after Yancy told him that. If Yancy knew he had the strength to tell Nelson one thing about his attacker before passing out, boots *had* to be significant. "I believe Yancy could identify his shooter by their boots."

"Fancy boots, like those silver-tipped dandy boots Bruno and his gangsters wear?"

"I don't know," Nelson said. "I just don't know. Could be. All the more reason to use caution." He put his coat on. "I'm going to see how Natty is doing and make sure he's still of this world. If they're getting desperate enough that Sal starts hitting you, I can see them coming after Natty."

"When do you want me to spell DeMyron? He's been watching Yancy's room since yesterday."

"I stopped up there a couple hours ago—DeMyron's still hurting from that beating he took. Wouldn't like to see him moving around any more than he has to. I think we better leave him just where he is for now."

Nelson had argued—and argued—with DeMyron, trying to convince the young deputy that he was in no shape to go after *anybody,* let alone any of Bruno's men. And especially Gavin Corrigan, after the beating the Irishman had given him. "Andy knows if Yancy dies, he gets first right of buyback on the ranch," Nelson had told DeMyron. "So it's important in more ways than one that Yancy pulls through without those goons coming around the hospital."

"I thought you conned Andy into thinking Yancy had drawn up a will leaving you the place if anything happened to him," DeMyron said.

Nelson nodded.

"Then that puts a target square on your back if Yancy doesn't make it."

"That's where you come in," Nelson had told him. "I want you to take your shotgun and a couple boxes of ammunition for that and your Colt and camp out at the foot of Yancy's bed. I had him moved to a room with no windows, so the only way anyone can get to him and finish the job is through the door. And through you."

In the end, DeMyron did as Nelson asked and promised he'd stay in Yancy's room until relieved.

On the way to the feed store, Nelson thought about Angel and Sal . . . thugs and gangsters, and both assuredly guilty of murders in the course of working for Bruno. One skill Nelson was certain they had acquired in their careers of beating confessions out of people was that—like good police interrogators—they must be skillful in cutting through the lies and deceptions of their victims. If they thought Natty was lying to them—if they'd promised to return for another session with a flat sap and bar of soap in a sock—they must believe he knew something about Gino's samples and why Lucky's ranch was so appealing.

Nelson pulled around back of the feed store, got out of his truck, and silently closed the driver's door. He eased open the back door to Natty's place and stood just inside the dim room lined with feed sacks, a single overhead window admitting light, the wind that cut through the corrugated tin building causing the light to sway and cast eerie shadows.

Once his eyes adjusted to the darkness, Nelson started walking cautiously around the inside of the store, working his way toward Natty's darkened office. He put his ear to the wall but heard nothing, except cottonwood sap crackling and popping in Natty's stove.

Nelson turned the knob and tried opening the door, but something blocked it. He managed to open it an inch and peeked in. Natty's desk had been shoved against the door. Nelson said, "Natty, let me in."

Silence except for heavy panting.

"Natty, it's Marshal Lane. I know you're in there. Move your desk aside. If you're trying to keep Bruno's goons out, this desk will slow those two bruisers down for about fifteen seconds. Now let me in."

Silence. He wasn't sure if Natty intended moving his desk and had drawn breath to try again when it scraped across the floor. "I figured maybe you were Mac and Toby again," Natty said as he opened the door. His voice sounded oddly thick and nasal. "The kid dropped two coyote pelts off for the fur buyer before they headed back to Rick's ranch. And believe me, when they saw how I was beat yesterday and that Bruno's goons might return for a rematch, they hightailed it home."

"And you think this little desk will slow down those two even for a minute?"

"I had to do something," Natty said. "They promised to hunt me up for another ass-whoopin'. Or worse. I figured they'd look for me at the house first, so I sent the missus to her sister's place in Sundance. Figured to hole up here."

As Nelson's eyes adjusted to the dark of the office, he drew in a breath. DeMyron had been right—Sal and Angel had done a number on Natty. He looked at Nelson out of one eye, the other completely swollen shut. And Nelson saw why he spoke oddly—tape had been plastered across his broken nose. One corner of his mouth had been turned to mush, and blood still matted his beard.

He grabbed Nelson's lapels and said, "Marshal, you gotta protect me. I kept telling them I don't know why Gino wanted me to stop so many times that day we drove around Lucky's ranch, but they didn't believe me. 'Think it over,' Angel told me. 'We'll be back tomorrow and youse better sing the song I want to hear.' Marshal, they think I'm lying—"

"So do I," Nelson said. "I think you know just what Gino expected to find when he took those samples in Lucky's pasture."

"I don't know a thing."

"Then I can't give you protection." Nelson turned to leave.

Natty grabbed his arm. "Don't leave me here. Those thugs are going to come back—"

"You'd be safe if I locked you up in the jail."

"I would," Natty said. "I would. That's it—you escort me to the jail and—"

"As soon as you tell me all about Gino."

Natty said nothing. Nelson shrugged. "Suit yourself. If I walk out of here, you might be the next customer in Mount Pisgah."

"Okay, Marshal." Natty hung his head. "I'll tell you. Once I'm safely behind bars, I'll tell you everything."

"Let me get this straight—you know why Gino was testing the soil at Lucky's?"

"I do."

"Was he expecting to find a new coal seam? Maybe bentonite or trona?"

"I ain't saying nothin' yet."

"At least tell me if what Gino was hoping to find worth killing for?"

"Men have been killed over a pack of cigarettes," Natty said. "I'll let you be the judge. Just get me to the jail in one piece, and I'll tell you everything."

"All right. Grab your coat and follow me. I'm parked out back."

When they arrived at the back door, Nelson opened it a few inches. He saw no one, no other vehicles parked in the back lot. He stepped outside and held the door for Natty. Backing towards his panel truck, Nelson said, "Hop in and scoot down in the seat—"

A loud *smack* echoed in his head, reverberating through his ears. His vision blurred, and he felt sick like he had on the ship over to France.

His legs buckled.

He turned to face his attacker. Struck again and dropped to the ground. Natty's form increasingly fuzzy, indistinct.

Just before he lost consciousness, Nelson saw Natty running across the lot. Following *someone*.

Chapter 33

"I can't leave you alone for even a minute." Maris looked down at Nelson lying in a hospital bed. "The doctor threw a couple stitches in your noggin, and you'll have a nasty bump for a while, but you can function."

"What the hell happened?"

"Obviously someone hit you from behind—"

"How long was I out . . . in back of Natty's?"

"Who knows," Maris said. "Oliver Hight was making his milk rounds when his horse balked as he drove in back of the feed store. That's who found you. He said he about got a hernia lifting you into his milk wagon."

"What did Natty say?"

"I haven't found him yet."

Nelson tried sitting up in the bed, but Maris eased him back down.

"After the doctor called and said Oliver found you unconscious behind the feed store, I figured Natty had been grabbed by Sal and Angel. I drove over to the motel, but Natty was nowhere to be seen. I suspect the worst."

"They'll get the information out of Natty for sure this time," Nelson said and started to sit up.

Maris eased him back down. "You need to rest up for a bit—"

"Like you said, I can still function. And right now, I need to find Natty if they haven't already beat him to death. Hand me my trousers and step outside while I dress."

"You need to stay here—"

"That's an order!"

Maris grudgingly left the room. It took Nelson longer than usual to dress, his head still serving up blurred vision and his equilibrium off by enough that he had to steady himself against the bed rail. Finally dressed, he strapped his belt and gun on and stepped into the hallway, using the wall to steady himself.

"You sure you want to get up just yet?" Maris asked. "You're still a little wobbly."

"Then stay close while we pay Yancy and DeMyron a visit. Just in case I look like I'm going to take a dive."

They walked down the hallway of the small hospital until they arrived at Yancy's room. Nelson rapped three quick times, then paused and knocked again—his signal to DeMyron that it was Nelson and not Bruno's men come calling.

Nelson slowly opened the door. DeMyron sat in a chair with his back against the wall, his shotgun pointed towards the doorway. He lowered the gun when he saw Nelson and Maris. "No change, if that's what you're wondering . . . What the devil happened to you?"

"Bruno's men," Nelson answered, "but I'll live." He motioned to Yancy's bed. "He hasn't come out of it even for a moment?"

DeMyron shook his head. "Yancy's not in a coma, but he hasn't so much as moved an inch."

Nelson laid his hand on Yancy's arm with the IV stuck into it. "Get well, my friend."

"You figure Bruno's thugs?" DeMyron asked as he nodded toward Yancy.

Nelson's balance faltered, and he leaned against Maris for support. "Who else? They're at the top of my suspect list."

DeMyron suddenly cocked his head as he looked at Nelson and Maris and forced a laugh. "Look at all of us—we've either been shot, or we've had the hell beat outta every one of us."

"We're still ahead of Bruno's boys," Nelson said. "At least we're on this side of the grass." He lit two smokes and handed DeMyron one. "Which is what Natty is likely to be if we don't find him fast."

"I'll find out where they took him," Maris said. "Tonight. When Sal comes to my motel room."

Nelson brushed her bruised cheek with his hand. "I don't think that's a good idea. He got physical last time and may be getting even more desperate—"

"Especially since he's wanting a drink awfully bad," DeMyron said. "I don't have proof that he's the one who broke into Pearl's and stole all the medicinal alcohol, but he fits the profile of an alkie needing a drink: irritable. Snaps at the slightest things. Like Maris." He glanced at her. "I think he's getting worse from what you tell me."

"DeMyron's right," Nelson said. "Sal getting violent with you is a bad sign. I don't want you alone with him tonight or any night again—"

"My private life is my own business," Maris said. "That was our agreement when you hired me, 'member."

"This goes beyond private life," Nelson said. "Sal DeLuca is a suspect in more than a dozen murders back on the East Coast. And the Pearl's break-in. And now Natty's disappearance and possible death. If that isn't enough to tell you it isn't safe—"

"How dangerous can it be"—Maris winked—"with you living just a couple cabins over if I need help?"

A sharp *crack* woke Nelson, and for a second he thought it was the throbbing wound on his head acting up again. *A shot?* He sat upright, straining his ears, knowing that—unless a follow-up report pierced the night—he might not find out where this one came from.

It *had* been a shot—he was certain of that.

And it had been close.

He swung his legs over the edge of the lumpy mattress and hastily slipped his trousers on. "Where the hell did the shot come from?" he muttered, his own voice startling him.

He started to flick on the lamp beside the bed, then stopped himself. His night vision upon waking in a darkened room was complete. Intense. Turning a light on and then venturing into the darkness outside meant his good eye would take many minutes to adjust again, so he left the light off. He groped for his socks and boots, stopping now and then. Straining to hear anything.

Silence.

He threw his coat on and hitched his holster higher on his hip before opening the door and peering out. The sole street-light a block away cast odd shadows as it highlighted the swaying of the trees with the whim of the wind, snow filtering down from the branches.

He cupped his hand to his good ear and cursed his inability to hear better, when . . . riding that same wind, a noise drifted past. A woman's faint wailing. Coming from . . . Maris's cabin.

Nelson drew his .45 and walked as fast as he dared until he reached her cabin down from his. He crouched under windows until he reached her door and pressed his ear to it.

Sobbing.

Nelson gently tried the knob. Unlocked.

He cracked the door. The faint odor of gunpowder reached him, and he had started inside when . . .

The sobbing stopped and in the same instant . . .

. . . the distinct click of a gun cocking sounded loud in the darkness.

He moved to one side of the door. "Maris. Maris. It's Nelson. Are you all right?"

"Oh, Nels." She flung the door open and threw her arms

around him. Sticky, fresh blood ran from her cheek and smeared his coat front as he pulled away.

"You're cut," he said, trying to see the extent of it in the faint gleam from that solitary streetlight. "You're cut . . . what the hell? Are you all right?"

She pulled away, back into the cabin, and grabbed her pillowcase from the bed to dab at her cheek. "I am. But . . . but I'm in better shape than Sal." She flicked on the dim lamp on the bedstead and stepped aside. Salvatore DeLuca, ladies' man extraordinaire, lay face up on the floor on the bed's far side, eyes open, staring at things Nelson could never see in *this* life.

He brushed past Maris and dropped beside Sal. "Man's got no pulse."

"Didn't figure he would," she said. "Hard to miss his heart from a foot away."

Nelson ripped Sal's shirt apart. He had, indeed, been shot center chest, his death instantaneous. Little blood had pumped out except the spot on his silken shirt.

Blood from Maris's sliced cheek dripped onto the floor. She had bent down to clean it up when Nelson caught gentle hold of her and eased her into a chair. "We'll have time for that later. You better sit down before you fall down." He took her revolver, decocked it, and stuck it into his waistband. She wouldn't need it anymore tonight.

Maris slumped in the occasional chair while Nelson squatted beside her. He turned her face to the light so he could see the damage. "That cheek's ripped open pretty bad. It'll require a few stitches," he said over his shoulder before standing and walking to the bathroom sink. "I'll clean up best I can while you tell me what happened. Then we'll visit the sawbones."

She grabbed her pack of Luckys from the bedstead and shook one out. Two more dropped onto the floor from her trembling hand. Nelson lit a kitchen match and grabbed onto her hand holding the cigarette to steady it. "He wanted to know . . . no, Sal *demanded* to know . . . where Natty was. I lied and said I didn't know Natty was missing. He said he and Angel drove to the feed store. They were fixin' to pull in when they saw your panel truck stop out back, so they drove on. Figured they'd come by when you weren't around." Maris stood and paced, walking off her adrenaline rush, chancing a glance at Sal's lifeless body.

"They came back later," she said, "but your panel truck was still parked out back. Sal said you'd been there for hours, probably protecting Natty, when all that time you were in the hospital getting patched up. Of course, they couldn't have known that. After a while, Sal said they took a chance and sneaked into the store, but Natty wasn't there. Nels"—she looked at Sal's corpse again—"he *didn't* know where Natty was, and he thought for sure that I did. He slapped me so hard I thought my eye teeth were going to get knocked out, but he still didn't believe me. 'Baby,' he says, 'you've been good company, but this is strictly business,' and he drew his stiletto. *Flicked* it out"—she snapped her fingers—"just that quick and did *this* to my cheek."

Maris's face turned red in the glow of the cigarette as she tipped ash onto Sal's corpse. " 'I'm going to have to carve a little piece of flesh every time my little friend here snakes out toward your face, baby, unless you tell me where the Marshal hid Natty Barnes.' That's what the bastard said."

She began to tremble violently, and Nelson led her back to the chair to sit. "Take your time."

Maris put her head between her legs and breathed deeply to collect herself. "When I didn't have an answer for him," she resumed, "he grinned and stepped toward me, slicing the air with his blade. I kicked him hard in the *cajones,* but I missed and caught him inside his thigh. His legs buckled just long enough for me to leap for my gun. He was not a foot away when I turned and shot him." She looked down at Sal. "What are we going to do—Bruno's not going to take this lightly, another of his men killed. Especially by a woman."

Nelson pondered that as he sat inches away from the body and lit one of Maris's Lucky Strikes. He watched the smoke rise and said, "Tell me—if you had the choice tonight—what would you have done instead of shooting him?"

"If I could have disarmed him, I suppose I'd have arrested him."

Nelson threw up his hands. "Good decision—we'll arrest Sal."

Maris stopped with her cigarette barely touching her lips. "You're going to arrest a dead man?"

Nelson nodded. "I vote we arrest one Salvatore DeLuca for aggravated assault on a deputy U.S. marshal and transport him directly to jail. Cover him up where he can keep real comfy until his trial—"

"What trial?"

"The trial for him as soon as this business with Natty is completed. We'll restrict access for any visitors—that being Bruno and company—and I'll talk to the judge and make sure no bail is set for Sal."

Maris wiped her tears and grinned for the first time. "Think it'll work?"

"It has to work," Nelson answered. "Besides, it'll pad our arrest stats. Bobby Witherspoon's gotta love that."

Chapter 34

Nelson stopped in at the hospital to check on Yancy's progress. There was no improvement, but he wasn't any worse, either. DeMyron tried talking Nelson into asking Maris to relieve him so he could look for Natty, but the deputy was in no shape to run around the county. He could barely focus on Nelson with the eye that hadn't closed completely, and he wheezed from his broken ribs every time he breathed. All he needed was one more beating from Gavin Corrigan and DeMyron's law enforcement career might be over. His life might be over.

Nelson picked Maris up from the doctor's office and headed to the R&R. He figured the least he could do was spring for a decent breakfast after what she went through last night. "Have you thought about what Yancy mumbled before going under again?" Nelson asked as they took a corner booth. "Find the boots, you find his shooter?"

Maris's hand went to her cheek, and she jerked it away from the dressing the doctor had taped on. Afterwards, Nelson and Maris had *arrested* Sal DeLuca's body and secreted him away in the city jail. "Yancy must remember something distinctive about his shooter's boots. A color. A style, perhaps. Pull-ons or lace-up ropers, who knows. Maybe they were fancy enough, or crappy enough, that it stuck in Yancy's mind." She shrugged. "Perhaps an unusual style for this part of the country."

"I've had no luck either, especially when Yancy mentioned DeMyron's name." This morning when Nelson visited Yancy and gave DeMyron a chance to go to the kitchen for a bite of breakfast, Yancy had come to just long enough to whisper the deputy's name before losing consciousness again.

Maris looked at Nelson. "Have you looked at DeMyron's boots? Hate to say it, but Yancy wouldn't have expended his energy saying DeMyron's name if there wasn't something there."

Marley started over to their booth. A couple of feet away, she stopped and stared at Maris's wound. "Did you win that cat fight you got into?"

"Barely," Maris said, omitting that Sal's stiletto gash had taken four stitches to close.

"Well," Marley said as she poured their coffee, "you still look beautiful."

Maris forced a laugh. "Thanks for lying so well."

"By the way," Marley said to Nelson, "Mac McKeen was in earlier and wanted to know if you've been in lately. He said he'll stop by the courthouse before dropping by Natty's Feed Store. Toby shot a couple foxes that he wants to sell to the fur buyer. Asked you to stop there if he misses you at the sheriff's office."

Marley left the table to make her rounds with the coffee pot, and Nelson said, "Mac doesn't know that Natty's gone missing, apparently."

"I wonder what Mac wants that's so important?" Maris said, aware that two railroaders sitting at a table opposite them were staring at her face.

Nelson picked up on it. "You're bound to get those looks until your cheek's healed. I've gotten plenty of stares after getting patched up." His hand went to his head, but he resisted the urge to rub the stitches.

Maris nodded at his head. "It's different for a woman."

Nelson laid his hand on hers. "Like Marley said, you're still beautiful."

Maris lowered her voice. "Funny, I don't feel beautiful after what I done last night."

"Would you rather be in Sal's shoes?"

"Good point," she said as Marley returned with their flapjacks and deer sausage.

Nelson waited until the waitress was out of earshot before asking, "You honestly believe Sal didn't know where Natty was?"

"He didn't, and over this last week I've gotten to spot when he was bullshitting me and when he was sincere."

"If Sal didn't know, that means Bruno and the rest of his owlhoots don't know either. Where the hell could Natty have gone, and who hit me over the head?"

Maris drizzled blueberry syrup over her flapjacks. "Somebody who wanted to know what Natty knew about Gino's interest in Lucky's ranch is the only answer I can think of."

"About the only other ones who even want to know that are Darby and Andy Olssen."

"Makes sense," Maris said. "All our other suspects are getting themselves killed."

When Nelson didn't see Mac's Model T at the courthouse, he drove to Natty's Feed Store, where the dilapidated truck sat in front. Nelson walked inside, half expecting Natty to be sitting around his pot-bellied stove, warming himself with one hand wrapped around a hot cup of bitter cocoa. But he wasn't, and Mac spotted Nelson as he shut the door. "Been looking for you, Marshal. Been looking for Natty, too. Heard you took a couple big hits to the head and was knocked out when you were coming out of the back of the feed store with him. I'm worried about Natty and hoped you knew where he was."

"I would ask you the same thing. Any ideas?"

"I called over to Sundance, but Natty's wife ain't heard from him."

"I would have checked with his friends if I knew who they

were," Nelson said.

"Tell you a secret, Marshal—even though Natty seems personable enough, I'm about his only real friend, and I sure the hell don't know. Do you think"—he lowered his voice as if Bruno's men were within earshot—"those gangsters could have taken him?"

Nelson quickly changed the subject, not wanting Mac to know anything more than necessary as he motioned to a coyote pelt and two fox hides. "You always have the run of the place when Natty's not around?"

Mac sat on blocks of mineral cake and wiped sweat from his forehead. "Natty gave me a key to the place. Whenever he's gone on business or visiting his in-laws, me and Toby help him out, especially when the truck comes in."

"What truck?"

"Truck delivering feed, but it don't come today." Mac spied an empty cardboard box and began cutting pieces with his pocketknife to fit his boots. "When I heard you got waylaid and folks said Natty went missing, I thought I'd make a run into town to look for him my ownself, and I carted Toby's hides along. The fur buyer stops in most mornings, and the kid needs some candy money." Mac held his boots up and shoved the cardboard in, the soles worn smooth with little tread. He noticed Nelson staring at the procedure. "I'll bet you don't have to insulate *your* holey boots."

Nelson shook his head. "The government—God bless the legislature's soul—allots me money to buy a new pair every year."

"Oh," Mac said. "What do you do with your old ones . . . maybe you can toss them my direction?"

Nelson smiled. "I will if you can wear a size thirteen."

"If they're free," Mac said, "I'll wear *any* size."

Nelson made a last, quick check of Natty's office before he

left, but it appeared just like when Nelson had last been here. Before he was knocked out and before Natty ran off with *someone.*

"You will let me know if you find him, won't you?" Mac called after Nelson as he was leaving.

"You'll be at the top of the list," Nelson said and headed for the hospital to check on Yancy. Again.

Nelson told DeMyron to take a break and go ask the kitchen staff to round him up a sandwich and coffee. After the deputy left Nelson on guard duty, he scooted a chair close to the bed and once again took Yancy's hand. Had his color grown even paler since Nelson's last visit?

"What the hell did you mean, find the boots? And why even mention DeMyron?" Nelson asked, expecting no answer. Receiving no answer.

Nelson had talked with the doctor upon entering the hospital this morning, but there was no change. "Yancy hasn't come out of it since that time he said something to you," Doctor Schunk said. "But I'm optimistic that his spleen is healing, if I trust the blood test results we run every night. As to when—if ever—he fights his way back to consciousness . . . it's in God's hands." Schunk draped his hand over Nelson's shoulder. "Were I you, I would contact his next of kin and ask that they come to Gillette. In case my optimism is unwarranted."

Yancy's next of kin. Who *were* Yancy's next of kin? As long as Nelson had known him, he couldn't say if Yancy had *any* next of kin, and he thought back to what he did know. The Northern Arapaho on the hospital bed—forty but looking more like thirty with his boyish good looks and black braids he often wore dangling down his chest—had been a tribal policeman on and off for ten years. Nelson did not know where Yancy's family lived, or if he even had any family on the Wind River Reservation. Nelson knew more about the numerous women Yancy had wooed, many married around the rez, than he did about the man's life. He knew Yancy wasn't a religious man, in the Christian sense. But he did believe in the traditional ways of the Arapaho. Nelson wondered if he should contact the tribe and ask that an Arapaho sacred man drive over to Gillette to give Yancy their version of last rites. "Pull out of this, my friend, and you and me are going to have a lengthy conversation. It's long overdue that I know more about you."

DeMyron rapped on the door with their signal knock, and Nelson laid Yancy's hand on the bed before telling DeMyron to come in. The deputy carried a mug of coffee and a sack bulging with food from the kitchen. "They loaded me up," DeMyron said. "Thought with my bumps and bruises, I needed extra nourishment." He nodded to the bed. "No change though, I 'spect?"

Nelson shook his head. "None. But if you get a chance to talk with him, do so. The doctor tells me Yancy probably hears what we say, he just can't respond." He put his hat and coat back on. "You stay with him even when they give him his sponge bath?"

"Always," DeMyron said, then added, "Could you drop by my room on Eighth Street and grab me a clean change of clothes and . . . you're not going to send Maris to my place, are you?"

"I could if you want—"

"I don't want," DeMyron blurted out, " 'cause I need a pair of clean skivvies, and I sure don't want her rummaging through my undie drawer."

"I'm sure she's seen the likes of what you're wearing, but I'll go myself."

Before Nelson left, DeMyron handed him the key to his room on the second floor of the Goings Hotel. "I'll let you know if there's even a small change in Yancy's condition," DeMyron called after him, but Nelson had left the room before the deputy could see the tears in his eyes.

Bruno burst into the sheriff's office as Nelson was hanging up the phone. Gavin Corrigan followed his boss and melted into one corner of the office. "Why the hell can't I see Sal—"

Nelson pointed to Gavin. "I'll talk, but I don't want that son of a bitch in this office when we do."

Gavin came off the wall he was leaning on, instant crimson that nearly matched the color of his hair slowly spreading from his neck to his face.

"Gavin stays," Bruno said.

"Then get the hell out of here. I got nothing to say to you."

Gavin stepped toward the desk. Nelson laid his pistol on it, muzzle pointing loosely at Gavin's gut. The Irishman stopped and eyed the gun.

"If I had time, I'd put a boot into your sorry ass—" Nelson said.

"What you got against Gavin all of a sudden?" Bruno asked.

"There's a young deputy nearly got his eye put out by *that,*" he pointed to the Irishman. "Lost some teeth and has cracked ribs because of *him.*"

"Gavin," Bruno said, "did you hurt that young deputy sheriff . . . what's his name?"

"DeMyron Duggar," Nelson said.

"Well, did you?"

"I mind me own business, you knows that, boss," Gavin answered, a slight smile crossing his face. "I had me share of trouble with the *gardai* before, and I didn't need any more."

"That's back in Gavin's younger days when he'd get absolutely ossified. Knee walking drunk and people would pick a fight with him until the police came and carted him away for thc night."

"And does he still get that way? Does he crave a drink so badly he goes off the deep end?" *Or it drives him to break into Pearl's to steal the medicinal booze.*

Bruno smiled. "All Gavin drinks now is fresh-squeezed juice. He hasn't touched a drop in—"

"In donkey years," Gavin said.

"Just the same," Nelson said, "either he leaves or you both do."

Bruno's jaw muscles worked overtime, and his fists knotted at his sides. He wasn't used to being told what to do. "Step outside," he told Gavin at last. "I'll be all right."

As Gavin left the office, Nelson looked at his boots. Or rather, shoes. New and shiny and pointed as if they were made for kicking deputies in the face, and he just wished to God he knew what Yancy meant by finding his attacker's *boots.* "Now what do you want?"

"I told you," Bruno said. "I demand to see Sal."

"He's in jail."

"I know he's in jail, dammit. On what charge?"

"Have you seen my lady deputy's face recently?"

"Can't say that I have."

"That . . . man of yours in the jail cell cut her. Badly." Now it was Nelson's turn to get angry, his neck flushed with the warmth of his rage. He took deep breaths to calm himself. "That . . . animal would rot in that cell, were it up to me."

"But it's not up to you," Bruno said. He exaggerated taking a silver cigarette case from his jacket and selecting a cigarette. "Sal has his rights. He is entitled to an attorney—"

"We do things a mite different here in the wild West," Nelson said, relishing telling Bruno no as many times as Nelson could. "There is a circuit judge who actually hears all felony cases—"

"What felony? Cutting your deputy a little bit?"

"Aggravated assault," Nelson lied. "Not like that chicken-shit simple assault Lazy was charged with earlier that you so easily made bond for. Sal will have his arraignment"—Nelson glanced at the Currier and Ives hanging on the wall—"a week from Tuesday."

Bruno slammed his fist on the table, and Gavin burst through the door.

"Do you want a dead bodyguard?" Nelson said and leveled his .45 at Gavin.

Bruno waved the Irishman out of the room. "Better stay out before this crazy bastard shoots you." When Gavin ducked out again and shut the door behind him, Bruno said, "I have attorneys that will eat your prosecutor alive—"

"*When* Sal gets his day in court you can see him."

Nelson smiled as warmly as he could muster. "A week from Tuesday."

Chapter 35

"How secure is the jail?" Nelson asked. He had sent Maris to the jail, letting carpenters from Saunder's Lumber in to reinforce the outside cell door. Just in case Bruno decided to break his dead man out of the hoosegow.

"I don't think I could tear down that jail door if I hitched a team of drays to it," she said. "Bruno's not going to get in there unless we let him in." She sat in the chair and gingerly touched the bandage over the stitches on her face. "But I'm not sure how long we can keep Bruno out *legally.* His attorneys might be able to get an injunction—"

"We only have to keep Sal's body on ice until I can think of *something.*"

"Good," Maris said, "because I have other problems—Angelo's been tailing me."

"Since when?"

Maris shrugged. "The first time I picked up his car in my rearview was right after I pulled out of the lumber yard to escort them to the jail. With everything going on, especially with Sal, you'd think I'd be more cautious."

"You'd better be damned cautious," Nelson warned. "Bruno's getting desperate. He about blew his top when he found out Sal was on ice and he couldn't see him." Nelson laughed, recalling Gavin's rage that he'd barely kept in check in the sheriff's office. "And I pissed off that mad dog of Bruno's who hangs on his elbow. Another minute and Gavin would have come at me."

"I'll be more cautious," she said, just as the phone rang. Maris picked up and listened briefly, then put her hand over the receiver. "An anonymous caller wants to talk with you. It's Rick Jones."

Nelson smiled as he took the receiver from her and held it to his ear. "Rick, what can I do for you?"

"I didn't give my name."

"You didn't have to," Nelson said. "Maris has ears like a coyote. A dozen times better than mine. What is it?"

"Ain't nobody gonna find out I called—"

"Just spit it out, and don't worry about me telling them."

"All right. All right. There are people at Lucky's ranch. Driving around—"

"How do you know this?"

"Toby went to feed Lucky's—Yancy's—mare, and he saw Andy Olssen and that skunk of an engineer traipsing around like they took possession of the place."

"Who else is there?"

"Toby said just those two, and he's been on the lookout for those thugs from the East Coast. He don't want to get beat any more than the rest of us."

"Tell Toby to stay away from Yancy's place. I'll be out there as soon as I can."

Nelson hung up and explained to Maris that he had to confront Andy and Darby Branigan snooping around the ranch. When she stood to grab her coat, he stopped her. "I need you here in Gillette—"

"You're just afraid I can't handle myself if things go to hell out there."

"Sal's present condition tells me otherwise." Nelson buttoned his coat. "Bruno's down to him, Gavin, and Angelo. I don't want them to follow me out to Yancy's ranch, so you'll have to be the decoy." Nelson told Maris they were to go to their separate trucks together, but that Nelson would drive away slowly while she raced away as if she had new information she was following up on. "They're surely watching the courthouse. If they see you leaving hell bent for election, they're bound to figure you're headed somewhere urgent. To something that'll affect the case. Or they'll figure you've found Natty Barnes."

"Like you said, I *can* handle myself, but I'm not sure against the three of them when they finally stop me."

"I don't want you to go into the county to draw them away. All you have to do is motor around town like you're going someplace important, then pull into . . . Daly's General Store. There's usually a lot of cowboys hanging around there, so Bruno's men won't dare start anything. They're sure to stake out the place, and by the time they figure out you sped away for nothing more than a few sundry items, I'll be long on my way to Yancy's ranch."

They left the courthouse at the same time, Maris running for her truck while Nelson ambled to his. As Maris jumped into her truck and spun snow backing away from her parking place, Nelson nonchalantly looked about, finally spotting a Lincoln partially hidden by the overhanging bough of an evergreen half a block away. Movement caught his eye as he watched Maris swing out and drive down the street, and he spotted the other car pull away from in front of Taft's Bakery and follow her. By the time she'd disappeared around the next block, both Lincolns and Maris were out of sight. A few minutes later, Nelson easily motored out of Gillette. Alone.

He turned onto the county road, driving as fast as he dared on the snow-packed gravel. Another vehicle sped toward him. The driver stuck his arm out the window and waved for Nelson to stop.

"I'm damned glad you're here," Vilas Hall said. "It ain't right, a postman getting . . . harassed."

"Take a breath," Nelson said. "What happened?"

"One of those gangsters," Vilas said, his hand animated like he was trying to bleed off some energy. Or anger. "When I pulled up to put Lucky's mail in his box, one of those fancy new cars blocked the drive. You saw how Lucky set his mailbox and post back a few yards off the road? Did it 'cause the post was getting clipped by cars—"

"The problem?" Nelson said. "Don't mean to rush you, but I need to get to Lucky's—Yancy's, quick."

"Well then, you can chew that damned gangster out. Like I said, he was blocking the road, and I had to show him I was an honest-to-God postal carrier before he let me on the drive." He spit tobacco juice onto the snowy road. "Maybe those goons have been stealing the mail."

"Lucky's mail?"

Vilas nodded. "All Lucky ever gets is bills and notices from the bank . . . not that I peek or anything."

"Never crossed my mind," Nelson lied, as Vilas had just now. "I will have a heart-to-heart with whoever's blocking Lucky's drive."

Nelson motored down the road, frantic now to get to the ranch to catch Darby and Andy before they took off. When he rounded the curve right before the cattle guard, he saw one of Bruno's new touring cars blocking Lucky's drive, just as the postman had said. He nosed up to the front of the Lincoln and stopped.

Angel Gallo's hand went under his jacket, and Nelson grabbed his rifle. "You thinking of skinning that gun?"

"I don't know what you're talking about, Marshal," Angel said. He brought his hand slowly away from his jacket and gripped the steering wheel where Nelson could see.

"Next you're going to tell me you're not blocking Yancy's drive?"

"I'm breaking no laws sitting here on the county road," Angel said. "I'm far enough off that traffic can get by." He smirked. "So, there's really nothing you can roust me about."

"You're blocking Yancy's driveway so folks can't get in."

"They're not supposed to get in there," Angel said. "It's private property, didn't you say?"

Nelson grabbed his binoculars. "You are so right. If there's anyone on the property, they're trespassing, so I am here officially." He stepped onto the running board and glassed the ranch yard and the house when he spotted Andy emerge from the barn. Andy carried a box over to his Packard and set it in the trunk. But where was Darby? "What the hell you doing here, anyway?"

Angel said nothing.

"Maybe waiting to see if Lucky Graber stops by?"

Angel shrugged. "Andy Olssen said it was okay to sit here—"

"Andy doesn't own this driveway."

"Yet, he don't," Angel said.

"Move this car so I can get through. Leave. And if you interfere with whatever goes down there in the ranch yard, I will toss you into the pokey along with Sal. Now scat!"

Angel started the car, the twelve cylinders purring, unlike Nelson's panel truck hitting on seven of the eight cylinders. Nelson waited until the Lincoln was out of sight before he mashed gears and sped along the drive. He skidded to a stop in back of Andy's car to block him from leaving the ranch.

Nelson bailed out of his truck and walked hurriedly to the Packard. He jerked the door open and said, "Climb out of there."

"Okay, Marshal. No need to lose your temper." Andy stepped out of the car. He leaned against a fender and produced his cigarette case from his inside jacket pocket. "What's the problem now?"

"Same problem as before—you're trespassing."

"This place," Andy waved his hand around, "*will* be mine, my attorneys assure me."

"You've been driving across Yancy's pastures. Did it have something to do with that box you put in the trunk?"

Andy shrugged.

"Open the trunk."

"Come on now, Marshal, isn't this a little . . . theatrical?"

"Open it or I'll grab a pry bar in my panel truck that opens most things. Including the trunks of fancy cars."

Andy hesitated a moment before reaching into his pocket and grabbing the keys. He walked to the back of the Packard and opened the trunk, which was little more than a giant suitcase strapped to the big touring car's back end. "There," he said as he stepped aside. "Just pieces of dirt in a box."

Nelson bent for a closer look. Cylindrical-shaped cores had been taken from the ground and arranged neatly in a row. Each one had a piece of paper with a location scribbled on it and pinned to the sample.

"You're under arrest."

"Oh, this ought to look good in court—getting arrested for stealing . . . dirt."

"I'm not arresting you for that," Nelson said. "I'm arresting you for trespassing."

"You can't make that stick," Andy said. "The owner's in no condition to press charges."

"I don't have to make it stick. All I need to do is park your ass in jail for the night. And if you come here the next day after you're released, I'll arrest you again. And again. Now turn around and we'll see just how these shackles fit those fat wrists of yours."

"I don't think so!"

Darby Branigan had approached Nelson's blind side. He stood with his Army Colt dangling low alongside his leg, ready to bring the muzzle up at a moment's notice. "Let Andy go."

Nelson nodded at Darby's pistol. "You intend shooting me if I don't?"

Darby smiled. "You *are* smarter than most lawmen. Let him go!"

Nelson released Andy, and he stepped out of the line of fire. "You know I have to arrest you if you put that gun on me."

"I suspect there'll be no arrest to it," Darby said. He grinned as he chewed a piece of straw out the side of his mouth.

"How do you expect to prevent that?"

Darby brought the gun up and aimed the muzzle at Nelson's chest. "You know, marshals in the old days most often didn't get the luxury of their man just surrendering peaceable-like. More often, they had to go one-on-one with their . . . desperados. Sometimes they prevailed and killed their man. Sometimes they were killed." He slowly lowered the muzzle and eased his pistol into its holster. "That's what we're going to have us here—an old-fashioned gunfight to see who walks away."

"You're shitting me," Nelson said.

"Not hardly." Darby stepped backwards, creating distance between him and Nelson.

Nelson didn't take his eyes off Darby as he said to Andy, "You condone this?"

"What can I say—Darby's his own man. I can't make decisions for him."

"Are you getting nervous, Marshal?"

"Are you?" Nelson said, slowly taking off his coat and dropping it onto the ground. The action covered his hand as he unsnapped the restraining strap on his holster.

Darby smiled at Nelson. "You ever been in a gunfight?"

"Not like this." Nelson stepped back, creating as much distance between them as possible. When was the last time he'd had to fast draw his .45? He couldn't recall he *ever* had and wondered what his odds were.

"Well, I've been in several gunfights, Marshal. Killed a couple *banditos* down Sonora way."

Nelson continued backing up. "Then with your vast experience at the fast draw—and wearing that cut-down holster of yours—you ought to give me a handicap. Certainly, more than you gave Yancy before you gunned him down."

"Who's Yancy?" Darby said.

Nelson kept his eyes on Darby's as he called to Andy, "You can stop this."

"Don't look to him to save you," Darby said. "Sorry, Marshal, but this is the hand you were dealt today. Andy!"

Andy had backed away toward the ranch house, well out of the line of fire. "Yes?"

"Give the word."

"I don't want anything to do with—"

"You wanted him out of the way," Darby yelled back. "Count it down from three. Now!"

"Sorry, Marshal," Andy said. He began slowly counting. "Three . . ." Nelson's arm brushed his pistol in the holster. "Two . . ." Andy's eyes darted between them. "One!"

The world—as Nelson often experienced it in battle, in other gunfights he'd been in—slowed. His callused hand went for his pistol, wrapped around the grip. Drawing. Snapping off the safety when . . . Darby's Colt, already cleared of the holster as his thumb came up. Pointing at Nelson's chest. Cocking the hammer . . .

Nelson drew as he threw himself to the ground.

A Colt .45 bullet. Loud. Deadly. Whizzed by the spot where Nelson's head had been a moment before, just as he touched off his own round. The big automatic bucked in his hand, a red splotch appearing high on Darby's chest a heartbeat before Nelson fired again. Disbelief etched on Darby's face as he collapsed facedown in the snow.

Nelson rolled over and aimed his weapon at Andy, who was cowering behind a pillar on the porch. Slowly, Nelson stood and replaced his magazine with a fresh one before holstering.

"You beat him," Andy said, staring wild-eyed at Darby's corpse. "How . . ."

"Distance," Nelson said. "Most men have never shot a hand cannon at objects more than a few yards away. I created as much distance as I could before he drew. And"—Nelson went on as he walked toward Andy—"I didn't play fair. The damn fool expected me to stand up and take it like a man, like the old-time gunfighters are portrayed." Nelson spit at the corpse, adrenaline still working overtime.

He reached Andy, wrapped his hand around Andy's silk ascot, and tightened it as he drew the banker toward the corpse. He threw him down atop Darby, blood smearing Andy's fine tweed coat, his white ascot dappled with red as he tried crawling away. But Nelson wouldn't let him. "What did that piece of garbage think was under this ranch?" Nelson yelled.

"I don't—"

Nelson kicked Andy hard on the thigh, and he winced in pain. "I'll beat the information out of you!" Nelson cocked his leg for another kick.

"All right! All right, Marshal." Andy held up his hands as if in surrender. "Coal. At least that's why Darby thought Gino was so interested in Lucky's place."

"There's coal all over the eastern part of the county. Why here?"

"If the concentration of the coal seam was great enough . . . there have been dozens of coal mines come and shut down when they ran out. You know that. Darby was certain Gino had figured out there was enough coal under Lucky's ranch that it'd make the man who owned the land a fortune."

Nelson processed that. The WyoDak mine east of Gillette had been going for years, and numerous smaller ones were in operation selling small amounts of coal to heat homes and businesses. If Lucky's coal seam was equal to WyoDak's on the east side of Gillette, he would indeed become wealthy.

"What are you going to do now, Marshal?" Andy asked when Nelson finally allowed him to stand.

Nelson thought about that. As bad as he wanted to arrest Andy, the man would have to share cells with one Salvatore DeLuca, recently of the living, who would be starting to smell a mite rank covered up in the jail cell like he was. "I'm going to file accessory charges against you. You knew Darby intended killing me. You could have prevented it. That bull about him being his own man is pure horseshit. I heard him—you wanted me out of the way. To me, that sounds like conspiracy to commit murder. I'm certain our mutual good friend Bobby Witherspoon will see it the same way. I'm certain convicting a prominent Billings banker of conspiracy will be a feather in the cap he's wearing on his climb to the top."

"I can't go through a trial like that," Andy said. "My family can't be dragged through a trial like that."

Nelson took Andy's face in his hands and squeezed hard. "Remember what your father did when the stock market crashed and he decided to leave a failing business to you?"

"He shot himself," Andy breathed. "You know he couldn't face his family . . . the shame . . . what are you suggesting?"

"It will take me only a matter of days before I have your arrest warrant for conspiracy to commit murder for this little stunt." Nelson motioned to Darby's Colt lying beside the body. "Be a man. Make it easy on your family."

"You mean use a gun on myself?"

Nelson shrugged.

"I don't even know how to use one."

"I can give you a crash course in it. All you have to do is use it *once*."

Chapter 36

Most U.S. marshals—police too, for that matter—loathed paperwork. But not Nelson. He had gotten used to writing essays and opinion pieces when he "attended" college while recuperating at Portsmouth Naval Hospital after the Great War. It gave him time to sort through things, to systematically go over each moment that led up to an incident. To slow down what happened in the blink of an eye and expand on it so that he, and others, knew just what had occurred.

And right now, he needed to get it right as to why Andy and Darby thought the possibility of coal under Lucky's ranch was worth killing a U.S. marshal. In Nelson's world it would take a lot more than that to risk hanging from a piece of hemp or sizzling in the electric chair. Would Andy do what Nelson suggested—kill himself rather than go through the humiliation of being arrested and tried for conspiracy to kill a marshal? Nelson doubted it. Men like Andy Olssen rarely thought they would be found guilty. A trial was just one more inconvenience for them. But if Nelson was cautious in how he worded his report, explaining in detail what led him to kill Darby, Bobby Witherspoon would have no choice but to issue a federal arrest warrant for Andy.

Footsteps approaching the sheriff's office startled Nelson. His hand went to his .45 resting on the table when Maris came in and shut the door. She carried a flour sack stuffed with clothes and set it on the floor beside the desk. "This ought to be enough to last DeMyron for a couple more days."

"Thanks," Nelson said. "I would have fetched his clothes my ownself, but something came up."

"Something came up? You had to kill Darby Branigan and 'something came up'? Kind of—"

"Cold?"

"Yeah. Cold," Maris said. "I like that in a man."

Nelson took off his reading glasses and laid them atop the completed report as he rubbed his eyes. "What can I say—the man's dead. No use for me to lose any sleep over it. Like I always said, some men just need killin'. But just so you don't think I'm heartless, I wish he hadn't pressed the gunfight."

He smiled as he leaned over and grabbed the flour sack Maris had brought. "For the record if he asks, *I* went into DeMyron's room and grabbed some clothes for him. He'd have a fit if he knew you were . . . rummaging through his skivvies."

"Then don't tell him I said he needed new ones. All his underwear has more holes than a cheese grater." She lit a Lucky Strike and settled back in a chair. "While I was there, I got a chance to look in his closet for boots. He has one pair of cowboy boots with a riding heel that are like new, and that's it. But we still don't know what Yancy meant by finding the boots and we'll find his shooter. And why he mentioned DeMyron in the same breath."

Nelson stood and handed her the sack. "Get over to the hospital before Rick Jones stops here. After I capped Darby Branigan, I stopped by Rick's and told him to meet me at the sheriff's office to sign a statement as to when he saw Andy and Darby at Yancy's place. The way Rick was shaking, he'd be too scared to give a statement if there was a witness to him being here."

"He's still afraid of Bruno's men?"

"Aren't you?"

Maris's hand went instinctively to her cheek. "I suppose I am, even though Sal's dead and *resting* comfortably in his jail cell. You figure out what you're going to do about him?"

"Still thinking about it," Nelson answered. "Now get to the hospital."

A few minutes after Maris left the office, Rick Jones came through the door. He glanced down the hallway before locking the door behind him. "Sorry if I'm a mite skittish."

"Not to worry," Nelson said. "After the last few days, I'm wary myself."

He handed Rick a pencil and sheet of paper. "All I need from you is that you saw Andy and Darby on Yancy's ranch and that you called me. I'm just tying up loose ends, and your call will establish my legal presence there."

When Rick had finished with his statement, Nelson dipped a pen in ink and signed as a witness. Rick stood to leave when Nelson stopped him. "Why would Lucky dump his liquor still on *your* land?"

Rick shrugged. "Me and Lucky weren't exactly friendly neighbors. He was always kinda . . . drifty. Never seemed up to ranching, though he was on that place with his folks long before I bought my spread. He probably figured if some revenuer came snooping around, I'd get the blame for the still down in that ravine."

"When did you know he was cooking moonshine?"

"I didn't, Marshal—"

"Rick, you don't lie worth a damn. Now *when* did you know he was cooking mash?"

Rick took off his hat and ran his fingers through what little hair he had left. "Okay. I've known for a while. I went over there myself now and again for a . . . short nip. I even caught Toby coming back from there with a jar of 'shine in his hand, and I gave him hell. Sure, I knew. I took Toby's booze and poured it out, then went over and had words with Lucky. Told him if I ever caught him selling moonshine to Toby or another *kid,* I'd kill him."

"Did you?" Nelson asked. "Did you kill Lucky, 'cause no one's seen him for . . . pushing two weeks?"

"Naw," Rick answered. "I'm no killer. I just lost my temper when I saw him giving Toby hooch, but that was the only time I went off on him."

"Do you think Lucky's still alive?"

Rick paused, seeming to ponder that before he said, "I don't know. I just don't know." He walked to the window and looked out onto a parking lot quickly covering with fresh snow. "My gut tells me he's still alive." He laughed. "Hell, Lucky has lived as long as he has being a ne'er-do-well of sorts. I'd bet that he's still on this side of the grass."

"But where? And where's Natty?"

"Haven't the slightest idea," Rick answered. "I know you're hunting him hard. I heard down at the R&R that someone cold-cocked you a couple days ago when you were coming out of his feed store and that he ran off for some reason." Rick approached Nelson. "And I'd also wager he didn't run off because he was in any trouble."

"He wasn't in any trouble. He just had . . . information that would tell me why Gino—and Andy Olssen, it seemed—wanted Lucky's land."

"I still don't know why," Rick said. "The only thing his place was ever good for was running a few sheep. Like that far west pasture of mine when I ran two hundred head of mutton there . . . musta been twenty years ago. But it never made me enough money for all the hassle, so I abandoned it along with that old cabin my sheepherder lived in."

"I don't recall seeing a sheepherder's cabin on your place," Nelson said, suddenly interested in Rick's ranch.

Rick waved a hand. "Probably 'cause it's way at the north edge of my west pasture. I never get that far—no reason to. The sagebrush has long ago choked out the grass, so the land's not good enough to run any cows. I just never turn them out in that pasture anymore."

"Have you seen anyone around it recently?"

"I haven't seen the *cabin* recently. Last time I was there was when I had to tell my hired hand I was selling off all the sheep, and he'd have to move on. Like I said, been more 'n twenty years ago.

"Would Natty know about it?" Nelson asked.

Rick shrugged. "Possibly. Mac or Lucky might have mentioned it during one of their Monday morning coffee and cards."

"Can a feller get to it by horseback?"

"In the summer," Rick said. "Hard to now. With the snow being so deep, the only way to get there is by a two-track that skirts that deep ravine where you found Lucky's still. The edge of the ravine almost forms a snow break along that dirt trail."

"Could I get to it with my truck?"

"You can if you chain it up, but why would you want to?"

"Call it a little sightseeing adventure. Can you draw me a map?"

Rick tore off a piece of a paper tablet and drew a map for Nelson. "Just don't call me if you slide off into that canyon. That trail will be as slick as snot on a billiard ball."

If Natty knew about Rick's abandoned shack, it would be a remote place for him to hide out, which looked to Nelson where he might be. That Bruno's men didn't know Natty's whereabouts was a certainty now. But it wouldn't take them long to find out.

Nelson studied the map Rick drew, seeking the nearest place where he could park his panel truck without it being spotted from the cabin. From there, Nelson would have to hike the pasture to approach it unseen. He grabbed his gloves drying on the register and his wool Sherpa hat from his bag. He'd need both if he were to hump Rick's west pasture very far.

He turned down the steam register and had just buttoned up his coat when Maris returned. "Where're you headed?"

He explained that Rick had an abandoned shack in a remote part of his property. "I'm headed there now to check it. *If* Natty knew about it, he might go there. I would wager he's more frightened of Bruno's thugs than he is of me."

"Then who do you think hit you over the head that day?"

"I only wish I knew, but I have my suspicions."

"Let's hear it."

"I don't want to say anything until I'm positive," he said and started for the door.

Maris stopped him. "How positive are you that Natty or Lucky might be at that sheepherder's cabin?"

"Not very," Nelson said. "It's little more than a long shot. Why?"

"Then if it's no emergency, take a little detour to Pearl's Drug Store. Someone broke in and tried stealing the medicinal booze again."

"You'll have to take the report—"

"Not me," Maris said, grinning. "For once it's nice to be just a *peon.* In case you forgot, Sheriff Jarvis never swore *me* in as a special deputy. And DeMyron's still guarding Yancy." She exaggerated a wide grin while she ladled water into the coffee pot. "Let me know what old man Pearl says while I keep warm right here."

"Don't get too comfortable," Nelson said. "I want you out looking for Bruno and his men. I want to know just where they are before I take a drive out to that old line shack of Rick's. Last thing I need is them following me."

Chapter 37

When Nelson walked into the drugstore, five men and a lady surrounded Walter Pearl as they listened to his exploits of chasing off the burglar. Beside him a gray grizzle-haired wolfhound quietly lay half asleep, his eyelids closing, looking like Natty Barnes's old weather-forecasting mongrel. Pearl gestured wildly with his hands and raised his voice like a fine theater actor as he related what happened. Probably for the umpteenth time, Nelson imagined. "And just about the time that feller crawled through the window," Pearl said, "ol' Fred here sprang into action."

"I ain't never seen Fred spring for anything," one man said, and the others laughed. "Except maybe for a piece of meat."

Pearl raised his hand to calm the crowd down. "I'll admit Fred does his share of lying around and taking it easy. Saving up his energy for when he senses danger—"

"If that old hound ever sensed danger," another man said, "he'd be apt to run the other way. Unless there's a meal involved. What did the burglar have, a steak in his hand?" and the crowd laughed again.

"Go on, all of you," Pearl said. "I have work to do."

The crowd chuckled as folks dispersed, some shopping the aisles, others leaving with their goods already bought and bagged.

Walter Pearl spotted Nelson and walked his way. Or did he stagger in Nelson's direction? "You're here to find my thief?"

"I am," Nelson said. The odor of alcohol on Pearl's breath was overpowering. Medicinal alcohol? Nelson's thoughts turned immediately to his own drinking days when he awoke every morning smelling just like Walter Pearl. "Tell me about your break-in."

"My break-in would have happened had it not been for Fred here." The wolfhound struggled to stand, his great head reaching Pearl's waist. Upright now, Fred sauntered away, no doubt looking for a quieter place to nap. "I didn't hear anybody come through the window—I have a studio apartment upstairs that I nap in now and again when me and the missus are on the outs."

"Understood," Nelson said. "Go on."

"Anyhow, first thing I knew, Fred there started growling, and he don't muster up enough energy to growl very often. Pretty soon he walked to the back room. I got to tell you, Marshal, the burglar made a terrible holler when he saw my Fred, and he scurried right back through the window."

"So, he never made it to your medicinal booze like last time?"

Pearl hiccupped and said, "He got into some. I have customers that genuinely need theirs. But before you ask, I didn't get a look at him neither. All I heard was him busting his ass getting back through that window before Fred tore into him."

Nelson looked at the hound snoring peaceably under the counter. "Think he would have taken a chunk out of the guy?"

"Fred? He sure would have about ten years ago when he had a full set of choppers." Pearl motioned to Nelson to follow him. "The burglar might have left a glove behind. Show you."

He led Nelson to a large box on the floor beside the counter with *Lost and Found* scribbled on the side. He bent and pushed aside a child's sweater and a bag of railroad nails, a floppy hat and a fishing lure, before coming out of the box with a glove that he handed to Nelson. "I don't recognize this, but it was on the floor in that back room the burglar came through. Might or might not belong to him." He nodded to the box. "But everything I find lying around, I toss in there in case a customer lost something."

Nelson turned the glove over in his hand. Light tan and worn leather, there were no markings on it, nothing to distinguish or identify it. Even the size did Nelson little good as he couldn't get it on his big paw. "Mind if I keep it?"

"Help yourself," Pearl said. "I hope it helps to catch the rascal that took some of that . . . medicine I was saving for some folks. *Hiccup.*"

Nelson buttoned his coat and walked outside to the window through which the burglar had entered. He knelt on the hard-packed, snow-covered dirt and looked at the footprints, indistinct. His first thought was that the burglar wore moccasins, but he doubted it in this cold.

He bent to a track and ran his hand around the impression, faint around the edges as if someone had slipped something over their boot to disguise it. Just like the print DeMyron had cast the first time Walter Pearl had been broken into. *Damn smart crook.*

Nelson stood and brushed the snow and dirt off his trousers as he studied the tracks. He began following them, but before long they washed out, the faintness of the indentations fading altogether.

With the glove as his only piece of evidence, he left the store just as more people had gathered around Walter Pearl to listen to his tale of Samson running off the thief. By the time Nelson got back to the sheriff's office, it was midmorning, and he'd wasted enough time. He needed to head out to Rick's west pasture before the sun set. He entered the sheriff's office just as Maris was putting a pot of water for coffee on top of the Franklin stove. She nodded at a sack with donuts from Taft Bakery. "We're free of Bruno Bonelli and his gangsters," she announced.

"They checked out of the Cottonwood Inn this morning. They—and their damned fancy cars—are nowhere to be found."

Nelson grabbed a coffee cup and blew dust out of it. "You mean they're not around town?"

"I mean they're *gone.* And believe me, I drove all over Gillette for the better part of an hour and saw neither hide nor hair of them, and neither has anyone else."

"I don't like it."

"What's not to like—we're rid of the bastards."

"*If* we are," Nelson said. "I can't see Bruno giving up finding his brother's killer. Not after losing a man and with another stuck in jail. Dead though he might be."

"I can, if you take Sal into consideration. The clerk at the Cottonwood said Bruno was pissed that Sal lit out on him. Know what he was talking about?"

Nelson grinned. After he had made a secret deal with Prost Funeral Home to quietly bury Sal in Mount Pisgah, Nelson had stopped by Bruno's motel and told him he'd dropped assault charges on Sal for the time being, but that he intended charging Sal for felony assault in state court. He explained all this to Maris. " 'Last I saw your man,' I told Bruno, 'he was hopping a bus riding east before he had to face the court.' "

"There you have it," Maris said. "That explains why Bruno left. My guess is, he figured it was just a little too difficult dealing with lawmen here in the West. I can see Bruno saying, 'Hey boys, we got us a whole easier way of life back in Jersey where we got the cops in our hip pockets' and taking off."

"I just don't think Bruno would give up so easily, even though I did my best to persuade him to leave."

She shook out a cigarette and lit it. "All's I know is that he and his bunch are not in the area." She offered Nelson a smoke, which he accepted. "You still heading out to Rick's to look for that cabin?"

Nelson ran his fingers through what was left of his hair. "I don't know what else to do. Natty told me he definitely knows why Gino wanted those soil samples that day. Thought there was a coal seam underground. And now Natty's gone, either into hiding or someone whisked him away. Just hope we don't find him at the bottom of a water well somewhere." Nelson sat down and lit the cigarette, which tasted as sour as his mood. "I'm thinking it would be a waste of time driving all the way out there. I'm thinking I'll just sit here by the fire and warm myself. Wait for Yancy to pull through. Wait for that arrest warrant to come down for Andy Olssen."

"That doesn't sound like the Marshal Lane I know," Maris said. "The one who hired me up from Oklahoma because there's more to being a lawman than kicking ranchers off their property. 'Now and again, we get into some shit that's more challenging than evictions,' you told me over the phone that day in El Reno."

Nelson just shrugged.

"You need to snap out of it," Maris said. "Think—do you figure there could be two different killers? One who did Gino in and another who killed Lazarro Stefano?"

"Possible."

"So, which one shot Yancy—Gino's killer or Lazy's murderer?"

Which one did shoot Yancy? Or were they killed by the same man? The question had kept Nelson awake ever since someone shot Yancy at the ranch. Nelson thought it might have been Darby Branigan who gunned Yancy down, perhaps when he confronted Darby trespassing at the ranch. The day Nelson killed Darby in the gunfight, he had accused the engineer of doing just that. Darby had acted as if he didn't know what Nelson was talking about. If Darby thought he'd soon kill Nelson, there'd be no reason not to admit he'd shot Yancy.

"Did you ever get anything back from the Bureau of

Identification on those fingerprints you lifted off Gino's Cadillac?"

"I called them yesterday," Maris said, "and was told it might take months before they could be matched with anyone. And that was *if* a suspect's prints were even on file."

"What the hell's the good of going through all that work, then?"

"Someday, fingerprints will be *the* way to identify people and help solve crimes."

"Doubt it." This was one of those times Nelson craved a drink, and the only thing that would cure the urge was finding bad actors. "Why was Gino's car abandoned in Buffalo?" He hit the side of the desk. "Dammit, there has to be a reason the killer drove it all the way over there."

"Maybe no more reason than the pleasure of driving a fancy Cadillac," Maris said. "When I went to this last evidence school in Denver, they had a rash of what they referred to as *joyriders.* People who stole a car and just drove it off only to ditch it later. Usually when it ran out of gas."

Nelson felt a headache coming on, and he massaged his forehead. "You might have something there." He turned in his chair. "As much as I replayed that staged crime scene where someone tried to make it look like Gino had a hunting accident, I'm still at odds with that. It *had* to be someone who doesn't know much about rifles and ammunition to drop that Remington case by Gino only to have a soft lead bullet recovered from the body—"

"What is it?" Maris asked when Nelson stopped mid-sentence.

"The bullet," Nelson breathed. "Lucky dumping his still on Rick's land. Lucky's absence from his ranch. His empty mailbox. A burglar stealing Walter Pearl's medicinal alcohol." His mind raced. *People get jittery, desperate for a drink just like I used to get desperate for hooch. Faint tracks outside Pearl's window. The druggist's lost and found box* . . . He hefted the bullet again. "Maris, go to the hospital and check on Yancy's condition. Tell DeMyron I *am* going to Rick's old sheepherder's shack."

"I'm going with you."

"You can't," Nelson said and held up his hand when Maris objected. "Bruno and Angel and Gavin Corrigan didn't leave town. They're still here. Somewhere. Find them. I don't care who you gotta ask, but three gangsters from New Jersey in fancy Lincoln touring cars can't hide forever."

"What do I do when I find them?" Maris asked.

"Throw them off my trail. I can't risk them finding out where I'm going."

Nelson got up, snatched his coat and hat from the rack, and ran to the door as the phone rang. Maris answered it, and a smile broke across her face. "Yancy's coming out of it. He said a few words to DeMyron—"

"That is great news," Nelson said. "When you get to the hospital, and if he's able to talk, ask Yancy what he knows about the boots, and if he remembers his attacker, since we know it's not DeMyron."

"I feel a little ashamed even suspecting him," Maris said as she put her own coat on.

"Forget about it. Get to the hospital and talk with Yancy. Then find Bruno and his thugs."

"When will you be back to town?"

"I don't think it'll take me long to find that cabin—just long enough to check on some things I *just* realized."

CHAPTER 38

On the west pasture of Rick's ranch, a trail cut hard to the north. Windblown due to the deep ravine rimmed with cottonwood trees acting as a snow break, Nelson found the going surprisingly easy, the heavy truck threatening to slip off the trail only once when he crested a hill and stopped to glass the area twenty minutes ago. He had picked his way among the cactus and sage, driving the better part of an hour when . . . a hundred yards down a slope, a shack stood in contrast to the snow that had blown around it. A thin tendril of smoke rose from the chimney, and Nelson backed the truck up before grabbing his binoculars and stepping out.

He walked to the top of the hill and squatted down while he glassed the cabin. Except for the chimney smoke, there was no movement, nothing to indicate anyone was inside. But Nelson knew someone wouldn't come all the way out here just to build a fire in a rundown sheepherder's shack.

How did anyone get this far out without a car, or a horse, unless someone brought them? That Natty was inside Nelson had no doubt. But the unknown worried him. Who had driven Natty this far, and where was Natty's benefactor?

There was no easy way to approach the cabin, and Nelson climbed back into his truck. He cut the engine and coasted down, silently approaching save for the crunch of ice under tires. He unsnapped the strap on his holster and pulled his coat aside before moving his rifle where he could grab it easier. He feared little from Natty. But whoever had hit Nelson on the back of the head that day behind the feed store would not hesitate to shoot a U.S.marshal. Was it the same person who had shot at Nelson the day he searched for Lucky? He cursed himself that he'd told Rick Jones he intended checking the cabin. Right now, Nelson suspected most everyone.

He stopped fifty yards from the shack, grabbed his rifle, and got out, shutting his truck door ever so gently. He flicked the safety off and started toward the cabin, putting down each foot deliberately, testing the snow, the ice, making sure his weight came down on nothing that would give him away as he approached.

Nelson strained to hear a voice coming from inside the cabin when another voice sounded. One he'd heard several times this since being in Gillette.

And the boot prints leading away from the cabin in the fresh snow.

Boot prints he also recognized, having seen them many times, and not just in the plaster that DeMyron cast. Boot prints made by Gino's killer, and probably Lazy Stefano's, as well as the burglar of Pearl's Drug Store, whose tracks he had looked at this morning.

Nelson leaned his rifle against a stack of firewood beside the cabin and drew his slab-sided pistol. He rested his hand on the doorknob. Broken, it turned freely.

He breathed deep, calming breaths, not knowing who was inside, though he suspected. He shoved hard on the door. It moved inward an inch. Stopped.

Something butted against it.

The voices inside yelled. Nelson threw his shoulder against the door, and it broke free. He stumbled and caught himself on the doorjamb as he scrambled to keep his footing.

"Don't shoot, Marshal!" Natty yelled. "Me and Lucky ain't armed."

Lucky Graber stood against the far wall of the small shack. His beard had grown even more scraggly since Nelson had seen him last. Food stains had dripped down from his mouth onto his beard, his tattered flannel shirt.

And Lucky's eyes. They had the frightened look Nelson had seen in other men who'd been on the lam and finally caught. "At least shut the door," Lucky said. "And prop that there broom handle agin' it so it stays shut. This stove cain't hardly keep up with the cold."

Nelson looked around the one room shack. He saw no weapons, but he recalled Lucky had trained a rifle on Maris when she tried serving him a foreclosure notice. "Where's that rifle of yours?"

"My rifle . . ." Lucky forced a laugh. "That old thing hasn't seen a round through it since I broke the firing pin and I couldn't afford to fix it . . . two years ago, it's been."

Nelson holstered his gun and motioned for Natty and Lucky to sit on chairs made from slabs of cottonwood.

Natty said, "I can explain you getting cold cocked the other day—"

"Shut up," Nelson told him. "I'll get to you in a minute."

He motioned to an empty can of peaches jutting out of an overfilled paper bag, and to rabbit bones picked clean that stuck out of the top of the can. "No, you didn't need your rifle to hunt when you had someone bringing food for you. Poaching deer and killing rabbits for you."

Lucky eyed Nelson suspiciously. "Who do you think's been doing that?"

"The same guy that's been bringing your mail most every day when he drops off food so you can avoid me. The same one who killed Gino, though I don't have a clue why—"

"Because I thought he was a revenuer." Toby stepped through the door, his lever rifle centered on Nelson's chest. "Get his gun, Pa."

"I don't know about this." Mac McKeen followed Toby in and stood beside his son. "We's dealing with a U.S. marshal—"

"Get the gun!" Toby yelled.

"Sorry, Marshal," Mac said and snatched Nelson's gun from the holster.

"Now sit," Toby ordered.

Nelson took the last stump-seat across from Lucky and Natty. He glanced around the tiny shack, looking for anything he could use as a weapon.

"You really never figured out it was me what killed Gene Bone now, did you?" Toby said.

Nelson spotted the broom handle on the floor. It would fit his hand perfectly. If he got a chance to use it. "I've known it was you for some time," he lied. "And my deputy marshal and DeMyron know it as well."

"How could you?" Toby said, the muzzle of his rifle never leaving Nelson's chest. "I didn't do anything to give myself away."

Nelson almost felt dumb telling Toby the many things that pointed to the kid. *Things I should have realized even before I thought about it at the sheriff's office today.* "That rifle of yours, for one . . . you staged that hunting accident with Gino and you . . . what? You fired off a round from his Remington so you'd have a shell casing to drop beside him. Am I getting close?" If Nelson could keep Toby talking, it might buy time to formulate a hasty plan.

"I grabbed Gene's rifle out of his car after I shot him," Toby said. "I thought he was fixin' to arrest Lucky for running 'shine. I thought he was a federal man poking around, looking for Lucky's still. I thought about taking his rifle—it was a dandy—

but I was too smart for that."

"And after you broke into Pearl's Drug Store that second time, I finally realized it was you who broke into Pearl's *both* times."

"How could you know that?"

"One of your fishing lures." Nelson recognized Toby's craftsmanship this morning when he took the burglary report but assumed the kid had just lost it in the drug store. "Walter Pearl found it on the floor and tossed it into his lost and found box after that first break-in. You dropped it the *first* time you broke in, but I never saw any lost and found box until Walter showed me it earlier today."

"So it was one of my lures," Toby sputtered. "Lot of people buy my lures. I make a lot of them—"

"Indeed you do," Nelson said, "but those tracks DeMyron cast and the ones I saw this morning were . . . like someone wearing moccasins made them, the impressions were so faint."

"I don't wear moccasins," Toby said.

"No, you don't," Nelson said. "But your boots are so worn down, there's hardly any tread left on them. Hike your foot up and let me see the bottom of what's left."

Toby remained silent until Nelson said, "I realized with all those wheel weights you smelt down, you must sell a bunch, like to folks up around Sheridan—like when you drove Gino's Caddy to Baggy's Diner last week?"

"I don't know what you're—"

"Of course you do," Nelson said, leaning closer to the broomstick. "But you couldn't use all those pounds of wheel weights you collected from tire shops, and it finally dawned on me what else you were doing with that much lead." Nelson nodded toward Toby's lever gun. "I would wager you mold all your own bullets for that .30-.30 of yours—really soft bullets. Like I dug out of the fence post that day you ambushed me.

Soft like the bullets the medical examiner dug out of Gino Bonelli and Lazarro Stefano. Bullets too soft to use in a Remington auto rifle or they would cause a jam."

Again, Nelson eyed the broomstick. "But what I don't understand is why you shot Yancy Stands Close. He was never a threat to you."

"Him . . . him I didn't really want to kill," Toby said. "But he came after me like he meant bad things that day I went to feed Lucky's mare. He didn't see me carrying my rifle under my coat until the last moment. I didn't want to kill him—"

"You didn't," Nelson said. "He's still alive and under guard. He identified you by your boots."

"You don't have to say anything," Mac said. "He can't make you."

"Shut up. I want to know what he knows and who he told," Toby said.

"I've told my deputy and DeMyron."

"What'd you tell 'em?" Toby asked, his hands trembling, finger white on the trigger of his rifle.

Kid's getting worried now, Nelson thought. *He thinks his game might be up. Thinks he'll be caught and pay the ultimate price for his crimes.* "I told them for certain you were the one who killed Lazarro. What I want to know is why?"

Toby forced a laugh. "I'd come to Lucky's ranch to grab the mail and feed the mare when that Lazy feller come out of the barn. He was holding a pistol on me until he seen me. 'Where's Lucky?' he asked. All I did was amble up to him easy like, him figuring I was too . . . slow to do anything, and he rested the gun agin' his leg like he had no worry. I got close enough to grab him, and that gun of his came up, but he was too slow. I grabbed it and nearly broke his hand before I laid him out and finished him off."

"That's just what I told my deputy and DeMyron," Nelson

lied again. "Even if you kill me here, my deputy and Deputy Duggar know that you killed Gino and stole his car. Ran it out of gas over by Buffalo when you left it and hoofed it back to Gillette."

The muzzle of the rifle wobbled slightly, Toby's eyes darting to Nelson. To the door. To his father. Darting like the eyes of a cornered animal looking for an escape.

"My deputy processed the car and found your prints on the broke door handle. Guess doing all that ranch work has made you so bull-strong."

Mac scowled. "Don't say no more—"

"Shut up, Pa. I need to know what the Marshal knows." Toby brought the rifle up again. "Just because the handle of that car broke don't mean I did it."

"No?" Nelson said. "You shot a nice, big wolf from that pack that hangs around Buffalo. Game warden was surprised you shot it along the Powder River, and I was, too. Same place you said you'd done some hunting. Been years since a wolf's been spotted there. Fur buyer didn't give you much—those soft cast bullets you use in that rifle of yours made a hell of an exit hole."

"Damn old wolf was heavy carrying it back home, even after I skinned it."

"Mac, are you going to be a part of this?" Nelson asked, knowing that Toby would not, *could* not, allow Nelson to walk free with what he knew.

"I told Toby he'd get caught," Mac said.

"But you covered for him whenever you could. Like when we talked in the feed store and you acted like you didn't know about Natty's disappearance—"

"I didn't."

"Bullshit!" Nelson said, the broom handle mere feet away now. "You knew damn well it was Toby who coldcocked me as I was sneaking Natty out the back of his store."

Mac shook his head. "I told Toby to run far away. That he'd get caught if he didn't."

"Did you also tell him to keep buying moonshine from Lucky?"

"You knew about that?" Mac said.

"I just now confirmed it, smelling it on Toby's breath."

"You do not—"

"You reek of it," Nelson said. "Did you get the jitters when Lucky destroyed his still and you had to steal the medicinal alcohol from Pearl's Drug Store? And—the way you smell now—I bet you found some cologne with a high alcohol content to take the edge off."

"Old man Pearl wouldn't give me a prescription for booze," Mac said. "He thought I was too poor to pay his high prices—"

"We are, Pa," Toby said and turned to Lucky. "I still can't figure out why you broke up your still."

"I told you a dozen times—"

"I don't remember."

Lucky hitched up his denims that threatened to fall down his meatless hips and explained. "I knew that lady deputy marshal would be kicking me off the place, and I damn sure didn't want her finding my still to add to my problems."

"You must have carted your still off to Rick's pasture just about the time Toby killed Gino," said Nelson.

Lucky nodded and hung his head. "Later, talking with Toby, I learned we nearly passed ourselves as I was hauling the still to Rick's ravine." He looked at Toby with sad eyes. "I should never have given you that first drink when you were younger. I should have been stronger. Refused you."

"But you didn't," Nelson said. "And Toby was hooked on hooch. Had to have it. Got damned anxious when he didn't have it." His gaze fell on Toby. "Like when you jumped Lazy

Stefano and choked hell out of him . . . you were just so edgy you went off at the slightest provocation." *Just like I often did back in my drinking days.*

The muzzle of Toby's rifle drooped again as he looked at Lucky. Nelson drew his legs beneath him. Eyeing the broomstick. If he could lunge for it before Toby reacted . . .

"You didn't turn me away 'cause we're friends, Lucky," Toby said. "That's the reason I had to shoot Gene Bone—I couldn't imagine him arresting you."

"But you heard the marshal," Lucky said. "Gene wasn't a revenuer. He was just some mining engineer who wanted to take soil samples." He shrugged. "So, I let him and Natty on my pasture. Not like he could do any harm driving on *that* land."

"Did you figure there might be a major coal seam under your pasture to bail you out of your troubles?" Nelson asked.

"I thought there must be *something* when Gene approached me wanting to take samples," Lucky said. "I thought maybe there'd be something underground that would dig me out of the financial hole I was in."

"But it wasn't coal Gene thought was underground," Nelson said and turned to Natty. "Was it? That day you chauffeured Gino around, he thought there might be some mineral besides coal under Lucky's land, didn't he?"

"You knew?" Natty asked.

"I only know what Gino asked the lab in Nevada to test for," Nelson said. "I only found out after they finally got back to me."

Natty stood and walked around the cabin, not getting between Nelson and the muzzle of Toby's rifle. "Gene figured there might just be oil on Lucky's ranch. There's that wildcat rig they drilled over by Rozet that showed promise, and he thought the same might rest under Lucky's land." He stopped and clamped his hands together to stop their shaking. "Gene claimed he'd perfected a new method of preparing the soil samples for testing that might show if oil was present."

"And if you knew," Nelson said to Natty, "Andy Olssen knew, too, didn't he?"

"You figured that out?"

"Just now I did," Nelson answered. "I remember you were just a little too friendly with Andy, him being a man of means and you—"

"And me owing him money. A lot. He owns the note on my feed store, and I got in over my head. When Andy said to let him know if there was any place in Campbell County that he could turn a profit with and he'd give me an extension on the note, I figured it wouldn't do no harm."

"That's when you told him Gene's theory about potential oil?"

"You son of a bitch!" Lucky said. "If that old gun of mine actually shot, I'd ventilate you right this moment. Oil on my place would solve all my financial problems, but you didn't even tell me?"

"Enough!" Toby said. "We know Lucky's got oil on his land, and we can *all* make some money. Right, Pa?"

"We could have," Mac said, "until the marshal came into the picture. Son, you're bound to go away for a long time—"

"The marshal won't be in the picture soon's I march him outside."

"You can't just kill him," Lucky said. "He's a human being."

"He's right." Natty stepped between Toby and Nelson.

Nelson's eyes darted between the muzzle of Toby's rifle and the broomstick a few feet away that might save his life.

"Then what am I supposed to do?" Toby asked, his voice pleading. Uncertain. "He knows I killed Gene and Lazy, Pa. Knows I broke into the drugstore. Knows I shot that Indian.

Knows about Gene's car. He knows all these things. What other choice do I have than to kill him?"

"I ought to let you do that—Marshal's been a pain in my behind since I come here." Bruno's thick accent filled the cabin. "Angel."

Angelo Gallo shoved Mac and Toby aside. As Toby turned toward them with his rifle, Gavin Corrigan slapped him hard on the back of the head. The Irishman snatched the rifle before it dropped to the floor.

"All of you get your asses over by the marshal." Bruno grabbed Toby by the back of the collar and pulled him off balance. "Not you." He spun Toby around and slapped him hard across the face. When Toby's legs buckled, Bruno caught him and held him upright. "That's one of many for Gino."

Gavin cocked his fist, but Toby caught the motion and grabbed Bruno by the throat. He lifted the gangster nearly off the ground, shoving him against the wall of the cabin just as Gavin's hand shot out and punched Toby flush in the kidneys.

Toby's legs folded. He dropped Bruno. Before Toby fell to the floor of the shack, Gavin hit him twice in the face.

Toby landed on the dirt floor, blood spurting from his splayed nose. "Pick him up," Bruno ordered.

Gavin wrapped his hand around Toby's mop of hair and hauled him to his feet, jerking his head back, then shoved him toward Angel. "Keep the kid calm," Bruno said. "We'll have fun with him in a little while. For now, we have us a problem."

Bruno took out his cigarette case and plucked one from it, then handed the case to Nelson. "You ought to have one mild French cigarette before you die."

Nelson took a cigarette and handed the case back. He leaned over to the stove and opened the door, the broken broomstick still in his mind as he grabbed a piece of kindling from the stove and lit up. He inhaled deeply, lighting Bruno's cigarette before shutting the stove door. "I don't figure I'm old enough to die just yet," Nelson told Bruno. "Unless someone has plans to change that."

Bruno threw up his hands. "What else can I do, Marshal? Here I have my brother's killer . . . but in case you're wondering, I feel as bad about sneaking in here and listening to the kid's conversation as I did hiding in that old barn down the road, waiting for you to come by."

"If you feel so bad, give me my gun and let me take Toby to jail."

"He murdered my brother!"

"I can get a conviction. Toby will probably get the chair when he's found guilty—"

"That is not the way we do things in New Jersey," Bruno said. "We handle our own problems. Which you and these"—he waved his hand at Natty and Lucky—"fools are part of."

"So, you intend killing us all outright?"

"Marshal Lane," Bruno said slowly, deliberately, "I intend slowly killing this piece of human garbage." He backhanded Toby, who fell against Angel. "And when I do, you would have enough against me and my men that you will get a conviction against *us* for killing him. As you can see, I have a bit of a problem." Bruno dropped his cigarette butt on the floor and stubbed it out with the toe of his shoe. "Besides, you put the run on Sal, and I have hurt feelings over that. It's just not the way we do things in New Jersey, running out on your boss."

"But we do things a little different here in Wyoming, too." The voice was DeMyron's, a heartbeat before he touched off a shotgun round into the ceiling of the shack.

Dirt and rotten wood filtered down. Angel pushed Toby aside, swinging his pistol wildly around . . .

Nelson lunged for the broomstick. Angel saw the movement, but he was too slow. Nelson's fingers closed around the slender wooden shaft as he sprang erect, cocking the wood. He crashed it down hard on Angel's hand. The thug's pistol fell to the floor.

Toby leapt for it, but Nelson's boot swept his legs. The kid tripped and sprawled flat a moment before Bruno grabbed the gun.

"Those scatterguns were great in the trenches of France," Nelson said. "I bet if you don't drop that gun by the time I finish talking, Deputy Duggar will cut you in two."

"I will," DeMyron said, wheezing, turning so he could see with the eye that wasn't swollen shut from the beating Gavin gave him.

Bruno slowly eased the gun onto the floor and held up his hands in surrender. "I'd do the same, boys," he said, and Gavin and Angel held their hands high as well.

Nelson slid his hand inside Bruno's coat, skinned his revolver from his shoulder holster, and jammed it in his own waistband. "Now step back. And you," he said to Gavin, "ugly bastard . . . you're quick. Get on the floor and keep your hands out at your sides while I cuff you."

"Thank God you got the upper hand," Mac said. "I'm glad you're on our side."

Nelson grinned. "I'm *not* on your side. When we finally get all this sorted out, you might be lucky enough to get tossed into the same prison cell as your boy here."

He motioned to DeMyron. "Cover them while I move some things around in the back of my panel truck. If I jam everyone in there, I think I can take them all to the jail in one trip."

Chapter 39

"I'm just damn glad you came to and remembered about Toby and his boots," Nelson said to Yancy, who was propped up in his hospital bed being lorded over by Maris.

"It was about *all* I remembered until I came to for that brief moment," Yancy said. "After I was ambushed and lying in the dirt at Lucky's . . . my ranch, I recalled those worn-out boots of Toby's not a foot from me as the kid stood over me. Boots worn so paper thin there wasn't an ounce of tread on them."

"I finally realized it was Toby's footprints when I looked in back of Pearl's yesterday morning," Nelson said. "Funny how a man remembers some things when his life is in the balance, but I'm glad you did recall it. It'll make the case that much easier to prove."

"His boots were about the last thing I saw while he was standing beside my head, holding the rifle like he was going to shoot me again. When I passed out, I'm sure he figured I was dead for sure, so he left. But you can thank DeMyron for rushing out to Rick's old sheepherder's shack yesterday."

"Two seasons ago, Rick let me hunt deer along that canyon of his," DeMyron said. "When Maris said you were headed thataway in the unlikely event Natty was holed up there, I *knew* Toby would know about it, too. But what I wasn't counting on was Bruno and his thugs. About the time I turned that *S* curve right before you come abreast of Rick's south pasture, I spotted Bruno's Lincoln pulling out of that old barn on that other abandoned place, so I followed them a long ways back."

"Ah, that's where they were," Nelson said. "I was careful to watch my back trail, but they must have been waiting there—"

"Probably since the time they checked out of the Cottonwood Inn," Maris said.

She stood and patted her pocket when Nelson handed her a French cigarette in a silver case. "Bruno's?"

Nelson shrugged. "Abandoned on the floor of that sheepherder's cabin after the scuffle. If this were Pearl's Drug Store, it would be in the lost and found."

"Where you recognized Toby's lure in that box?" Yancy asked.

"I *suspected* it was Toby's by the looks of it, painted like it was."

"Tell me what kind of a case we'll have against him and his old man," Yancy said. He reached for a glass of water, and DeMyron handed it to him.

Nelson laid his hand on DeMyron's shoulder. "I think the *deputy* here will have a case against both of them. After all, it's his jurisdiction."

"I've got airtight cases against Toby," DeMyron said, "and one for Mac as well for being an accessory after the fact. He knew Toby killed Gino, but he figured his kid was worth more than some thug, so he let it pass. And he strongly suspected Toby killed Lazy Stefano and again figured Toby was worth more to him than seeing justice for a gangster. Mac even knew Toby shot Yancy. With Rick's cooperation, I'll have good cases worked up on both McKeens."

Nelson had gone over DeMyron's affidavit for the arrest warrant after the deputy had completed it. Though there were spelling and language errors—DeMyron was no college man like Nelson—and he'd gladly corrected the affidavit and his report so it would pass the scrutiny even of Clarence Darrow.

"That only leaves Andy Olssen," Maris said.

"Andy's going to have a *federal* charge of conspiring to kill a U.S. marshal," DeMyron said, slapping his palms together. "So that one is out of my hands."

"It's out of mine, too," Nelson said, finally tossing the nasty French cigarette into the spittoon. "Sheriff in Big Horn County, Montana, called and wanted to let me know that Andy had *been a man* and killed himself yesterday."

Yancy forced a sick laugh. "I guess all he had to know is how to use it *once*." He sipped water. "By the way, did Lucky get *lucky* and skate any charges?"

Nelson grabbed the coffee carafe the kitchen had dropped off in Yancy's room and refilled his cup. "Lucky didn't know anything about any of the killings. He just fled to that old line shack of Rick Jones's to hide out from me at the sheepherder's cabin. Toby didn't tell him a thing when he came every other day or so with the mail and some food."

"Don't tell me I'm stuck with that worthless ranch?" Yancy asked.

Nelson smiled. "Now you're the one who got lucky. Natty agreed to repay you the cost of the land sale, and Lucky will pay him when he gets back on his feet."

"Thank the Creator," Yancy said as he squirmed in his bed.

Maris fluffed Yancy's pillow and said to DeMyron, "How's the case against Bruno and Angel and Gavin?"

"Borderline," DeMyron said. "The judge figured Bruno's threats were on the periphery of the law, and that Angel never *actually* intended shooting anyone. So, he set their bail low, and they bonded out this morning."

"They'll never come back for trial," Yancy said.

" 'Spect not," Nelson said. "I doubt they'll be back for anything, including ever visiting Gino's gravesite."

"And what's the skinny with Gavin Corrigan?" Maris asked. "With the judge dismissing all state charges against him."

"He's the one out of the bunch who kept quiet and never implicated himself with anything."

"I'd have loved to implicate him in that attack on me," DeMyron said, "but I just couldn't identify him as the one who beat me."

"Speaking of which," Nelson said, digging his Waltham watch out of his pocket, "it's time to release Mr. Corrigan."

"Want me to come with?" Maris asked. "As a witness in case he pulls something?"

Nelson shook his head. "Naw. This is one time I don't want a witness."

The noonday sun had melted much of the snow in the back of the courthouse as Nelson watched people come and go on their various jobs. This part of the country hadn't been hit as hard as the cities, and folks still busied themselves during the day.

Which Nelson was thankful for as he walked the two blocks up Gillette Avenue to the city jail where the county housed their prisoners as well.

"Hey, Marshal, that you?" Gavin called out when Nelson shut the door.

Nelson said nothing as he grabbed the keys from the desk drawer.

"Guess you kept me here just long enough that Mr. Bonelli and Angelo left me to make me own way 'ome," Gavin said. "But it'll be worth it just to see your sorry face when you have to let me out."

Nelson felt his temper flare, the temper that often rose in his drinking days until it exploded, and then folks got hurt. Badly. Today, he did nothing to calm that rage as he slowly and deliberately turned the tumblers and swung the door open.

"Pisses you off, don't it, old man, to have to let me walk?"

Gavin said. "Just give me my things, and I'll catch a train back 'ome."

"You want your things?" Nelson asked. "Follow me." The rage was building, and he breathed deep to control it for just a few more moments. Until the time was right.

He grabbed a sack with Gavin's personal belongings and opened the outside door. Gavin shielded his eyes against the bright sun. Nelson shoved him hard, and he fell onto the pavement.

Gavin got to his feet. "What the 'ell—"

"Pisses you off, does it now?" Nelson said and shoved him again.

Gavin backed up, his hands in front of his chest as if to ward off Nelson. "If you're trying to goad me into swing on a federal marshal so's you can arrest me . . ."

Nelson took off his coat, slid his pistol through the belt, and set both on the ground. He exaggerated taking off his badge and laying it atop the gun. "See—no badge. No gun. All unofficial."

Gavin grinned. "So, old timer, you give me one last present before I leave jolly Gillette." He began circling Nelson. "I am sure you've learned that I was a professional fighter."

"I have," Nelson said, feeling the heat radiate all the way from the base of his neck to his face, the rage ready to erupt. "While I only fought amateur in the Marines," he'd just gotten out as Gavin stepped in. The man jabbed twice faster than Nelson could see and followed up with a right cross that rattled Nelson's teeth. Nelson stumbled back, struggling to remain on his feet.

"Pisses you off that you can't knock me down, doesn't it, *little* man," Nelson said, his lip split and bleeding a heartbeat before he let his fury go. He stepped in toward Gavin, who hit him twice on the cheek and then drove a fist into his belly that should have dropped him.

Instead, Nelson put all two hundred forty pounds behind a left hook that caught Gavin's cheekbone, the crunch satisfying.

Gavin staggered back. As he started to go down, Nelson grabbed ahold of Gavin's shirtfront and drove an elbow into his face, feeling the Irishman's nose flatten.

Nelson let Gavin go, and he dropped to the ground. Nelson stood over him with his hands on his hips as he cocked his leg. "I guess elbows and boots are not . . . sportsmanlike," he said and swung. Even through the toe of his boot, Nelson could feel Gavin's ribs break, the air whooshing out of him. He curled up holding his side, a groan of intense pain coming from his bloody lips.

Nelson turned, grabbed the sack with Gavin's belongings, and dropped them on the ground. He picked up Gavin's brass knuckles and tapped them hard on the Irishman's forehead.

Gavin spit out a tooth while blood ran down his chin. He blinked, focusing on his tormenter. "I'll see you spend time in prison for this—"

"No, you won't," Nelson said, looking around. "Because there's no witnesses. Just like there were no witnesses that day you beat the hell out of that young deputy." He grabbed Gavin by the front of his coat and stood him up. The Irishman's scream of pain echoed off the wall in back of the jail.

Nelson took hold of Gavin's arm. He bent over in pain, but Nelson jerked him erect and pointed him north. "You go right down to Second Avenue and head east. Don't stop. Don't talk to a living soul. Walk about half a mile, where you'll find the bus depot. Take the first bus east. Don't wait for the train. Because if I see you here—or anywhere, anytime—I will use these brass knuckles of yours and beat the lumps on your ugly face until it's smooth."

Nelson watched Gavin stagger north down the street, people

in passing cars and trucks giving him only cursory glances as they went about their daily jobs. After a few moments, Nelson hefted the brass knuckles and shoved them into his pocket. "I almost wish you *would* come back for a rematch," he said.

Epilogue

The high noon sun beat hot overhead when Nelson drove past the jail where he and Gavin Corrigan had danced that first week in November. Nelson had received a fresh batch of foreclosure notices at his office in Buffalo last week and was about to order Maris to Gillette to serve them when he thought twice—he had one piece of unfinished business from six months ago that he needed to follow up on anyway in Campbell County.

He drove by the courthouse, amazed that he still had a job after the election last year. After Roosevelt had won the presidency by a landslide, a rumor floated around that Nelson was to be replaced as U.S. marshal for the State of Wyoming. Except no one wanted to move to the wild West, so he'd kept his job. Which was more than he could say for that guttersnipe lawyer Bobby Witherspoon, who had lost his U.S. attorney position and was back taking *pro bono* cases at a defense firm in Chicago when Roosevelt picked another man to be attorney general.

Nelson pulled into the courthouse lot and stopped beside two sheriff's trucks parked in front of signs marked *Reserved for Sheriff* and *Reserved for Undersheriff.* He killed the engine, got out of his truck, and entered the courthouse.

He mounted the stairs and slowly walked down the hallway—nothing having changed since last winter—and entered the sheriff's office. "The sheriff's expecting you," Bonnie said and went back to reading her *Underground Confessions.*

Sheriff Jarvis sat behind his desk, half-glasses perched over his nose and a pencil in hand as DeMyron bent over his shoulder, studying a map. They looked up and smiled when Nelson shut the door. "Am I interrupting something?"

"Heard about a couple o' stills been operating down south end of the county towards the Thunder Basin Grasslands," Jarvis said. "We're going over our plan of attack."

"But Prohibition's been repealed."

Jarvis set his glasses on the desk. "It has, but these stills have been manufacturing *rotgut.* Real coffin varnish. Killed two people that we know of who can't afford to buy the legit stuff." He turned to DeMyron. "Don't just stand there like you've just seen a living legend walk through the door. Get Nels some coffee."

"Yeah, *Undersheriff* Duggar—get me some coffee," Nelson said.

"Like my new title, do you?" DeMyron asked.

"If your sheriff likes it—"

"With the job he did getting Toby McKeen and his father prosecuted and sentenced, DeMyron needed an appropriate title. But now," Jarvis said as he scowled at DeMyron, "you have civil papers to serve after you pour him coffee. Get to it!"

Nelson winked at DeMyron when the younger man handed him the coffee. "Catch up before you leave town?" DeMyron said.

"Wouldn't have it any other way," Nelson answered and watched DeMyron leave the office.

"The kid's turned into a mighty fine deputy," Jarvis said. "Thanks to you."

"I take little credit for it. It was DeMyron's own ambition that showed what kind of a lawman he could be."

"Don't sell yourself short," Jarvis said. "DeMyron told me how you took control of the situation this winter—"

Nelson held up a hand to stop him. "Let's just agree that you came away with a lot better deputy than when you left for Phoenix."

"Agreed." Jarvis held up his cup to click it against Nelson's, then nodded to the folder tucked under Nelson's arm. "More foreclosures?"

" 'Fraid so," Nelson answered. "The mood of the country is that we had this damned Depression long enough, and it was time for a change at the top. Except my job"—he held up the folder—"never changes."

"Speaking of foreclosures, DeMyron told me you had eviction papers for Lucky Graber last fall."

"I did," Nelson said. After sorting through the nightmare that had happened in Gillette and Campbell County last autumn, Nelson was just glad that Lucky was back on his own ranch, and Yancy was back on Wind River where he could be coaxed out for the occasional fishing trip. "How is ol' Lucky doing? Must be paying Natty Barnes on time. And I haven't gotten a single foreclosure paper from the Billings Stockman's Bank since last November on any rancher hereabouts. These," he held up the folder, "are from a lander in Denver."

"I talked to the sheriff in Billings," Jarvis said. "The bank still hasn't appointed a new CEO after Andy killed himself. But word is the bank wouldn't have wanted Lucky's land very badly anyhow." Jarvis refilled their cups. "To answer your question, Lucky's doing . . . better. Him and Rick Jones are getting along . . . better. Rick sold Lucky ten head of bred heifers and gave him some tips for raising a decent crop of hay. Lucky is actually trying to make a go of it now that he realizes there was no oil under his place."

"Just what that Reno lab told me."

Jarvis lowered his voice as if there were others in the room. "And a plus—whenever Lucky comes into town, he's *clean*—he don't stink anymore."

"Thank God for that," Nelson said and finished his coffee.

"You off to kick some poor rancher off his land?"

"Later," Nelson said. "Right now, I have to pay respects to someone in Mount Pisgah."

"You know someone up there?"

"In a way," Nelson said, "I do. I'll visit him again, just as soon as I stop at Gretch Loftin's flower shop for a nice bouquet of carnations."

Nelson checked his watch, and, right on time, Montgomery Mortuary Company showed up with a truck and two stout boys. He watched them as they took hold of the headstone, the bruisers directed by a grizzled old man telling them where to set it. Bruno Bonelli had bought and paid for his brother's marker the day after the funeral, but Nelson had lucked out and caught the stone company before they could fetch the piece of granite, telling Montgomery Mortuary to change the headstone. Nelson had been certain that—with an outstanding warrant for failure to appear on DeMyron's charges—Bruno would never return to Gillette *or* to visit his brother's gravesite to know the difference.

But Nelson would. At least this once to make sure the monument company got it exactly as Nelson had ordered it changed.

"Didn't think I'd ever see you in this part of the state again."

Jamie Romano had approached from Nelson's blind side, and he cursed himself. He'd gotten so wrapped up in watching the monument team set the stone that he had let his guard down. "This the one *big* story your editor assigned you to?" he asked, nodding at the notebook in her hand.

She wet the tip of a pencil stub with her tongue and spoke as she wrote, "U.S. Marshal Lane returns for Gino Bonelli's grave marker ceremony." She looked up at him. "How's that for an opening of my last story here."

"Last story? Have you decided to get into a more honest line of work, like bank robbery or car theft?"

Jamie smiled at him. "No. I interviewed for a reporter position at the *Denver Post,* and they called last Friday. I handed my editor here my notice and will be headed south tomorrow with all my worldly possessions."

"That's good," Nelson said. "I'm glad to hear you finally landed a newspaper that will appreciate your abilities." He motioned to the notebook still in her hand. "You might leave out Gino's name."

"Why?"

"Look at the headstone."

Jamie stepped closer and said, "Why in the world did Bruno want his brother's *assumed* name on the marker?"

"He didn't," Nelson said. "I did."

"Why—"

"If Bruno ever gets the urge to sneak back here to visit his brother's grave, he won't find it anywhere in Mount Pisgah."

"But that wouldn't be much of a story without a name," Jamie said.

"Can't argue there," Nelson said.

Jamie closed her notebook and slipped the pencil behind her ear. "Perhaps the article I wrote *yesterday* will be my last one with this newspaper."

"Good choice." Nelson turned back to watching the monument team go about setting the stone.

The two bruisers set the marker on another flat piece of granite while the old man grabbed tools, a square, and a level, before staking it to the ground. When they finished, all three stone workers stood and wiped their sweaty faces with their bandanas. The old man glanced at Nelson for approval before leaving the cemetery.

When they had left and Nelson was alone amongst all the

other quiet graves, he took off his Stetson and walked to the gravesite while Jamie stood silently, reverently watching. On the gray granite were the birth and death dates of one *Gene Bone*. Just like he would have wanted, Nelson was certain.

"Even if your brother does show up one day, he still won't find you," Nelson said to the headstone and left to serve his eviction notices.

ABOUT THE AUTHOR

C. M. Wendelboe is a prolific author of murder mysteries with a Western flair, as well as traditional Westerns. He entered the law enforcement profession when he was discharged from the Marines as the Vietnam War was winding down. During his thirty-eight-year career in law enforcement, he served in various roles for several agencies. Yet he always felt most proud of "working the street." He was a patrol supervisor in Gillette, Wyoming, when he retired as a sheriff's deputy to pursue his true vocation as a fiction writer. *Marshal and the Fatal Foreclosure* is the latest volume in his *Nelson Lane Frontier Mystery* series (Five Star). Other published works include the *Spirit Road Mystery* series (Berkley Prime Crime; Encircle Publications), the *Bitter Wind Mystery* series (Midnight Ink; Encircle Publications), and the *Tucker Ashley Western Adventure* series (Five Star), plus standalone novels *The Man Who Hated Hickok* (Five Star) and *An Extralegal Affair* (Speaking Volumes).

C. M. Wendelboe currently lives in Cheyenne, Wyoming. He can be reached at cmwendelboe.com.

The employees of Five Star Publishing hope you have enjoyed this book.

Our Five Star novels explore little-known chapters from America's history, stories told from unique perspectives that will entertain a broad range of readers.

Other Five Star books are available at your local library, bookstore, all major book distributors, and directly from Five Star/Gale.

Connect with Five Star Publishing

Website:
gale.com/five-star

Facebook:
facebook.com/FiveStarCengage

Twitter:
twitter.com/FiveStarCengage

Email:
FiveStar@cengage.com

For information about titles and placing orders:
(800) 223-1244
gale.orders@cengage.com

To share your comments, write to us:
Five Star Publishing
Attn: Publisher
10 Water St., Suite 310
Waterville, ME 04901